WAR CAN BE WAGED W

D0253995

continued . . .

DEBT OF HONOR

*It begins with the murder of an American woman
in the back streets of Tokyo. It ends in war . . .*

"A SHOCKER." —*Entertainment Weekly*

THE HUNT FOR RED OCTOBER

*The smash bestseller that launched Clancy's career—
the incredible search for a Soviet defector
and the nuclear submarine he commands . . .*

"BREATHLESSLY EXCITING." —*The Washington Post*

RED STORM RISING

*The ultimate scenario for World War III—
the final battle for global control . . .*

"THE ULTIMATE WAR GAME . . . BRILLIANT."
—*Newsweek*

PATRIOT GAMES

*CIA analyst Jack Ryan stops an assassination—
and incurs the wrath of Irish terrorists . . .*

"A HIGH PITCH OF EXCITEMENT."
—*The Wall Street Journal*

Tom Clancy's

SPLINTER CELL®

CHECKMATE

WRITTEN BY

DAVID MICHAELS

BERKLEY BOOKS, NEW YORK

THE BERKLEY PUBLISHING GROUP
Published by the Penguin Group
Penguin Group (USA) Inc.
375 Hudson Street, New York, New York 10014, USA
Penguin Group (Canada), 90 Eglinton Avenue East, Suite 700, Toronto, Ontario M4P 2Y3, Canada
(a division of Pearson Penguin Canada Inc.)
Penguin Books Ltd., 80 Strand, London WC2R 0RL, England
Penguin Group Ireland, 25 St. Stephen's Green, Dublin 2, Ireland (a division of Penguin Books Ltd.)
Penguin Group (Australia), 250 Camberwell Road, Camberwell, Victoria 3124, Australia
(a division of Pearson Australia Group Pty. Ltd.)
Penguin Books India Pvt. Ltd., 11 Community Centre, Panchsheel Park, New Delhi—110 017, India
Penguin Group (NZ), Cnr. Airborne and Rosedale Roads, Albany, Auckland 1310, New Zealand
(a division of Pearson New Zealand Ltd.)
Penguin Books (South Africa) (Pty.) Ltd., 24 Sturdee Avenue, Rosebank, Johannesburg 2196,
South Africa

Penguin Books Ltd., Registered Offices: 80 Strand, London WC2R 0RL, England

This is a work of fiction. Names, characters, places, and incidents either are the product of the author's imagination or are used fictitiously, and any resemblance to actual persons, living or dead, business establishments, events, or locales is entirely coincidental. The publisher does not have any control over and does not assume any responsibility for author or third-party websites or their content.

TOM CLANCY'S SPLINTER CELL®: CHECKMATE

A Berkley Book / published by arrangement with Rubicon, Inc.

PRINTING HISTORY
Berkley edition / November 2006

Copyright © 2006 by Rubicon, Inc.
Splinter Cell, Sam Fisher, Ubisoft, and the Ubisoft logo are trademarks of Ubisoft in the U.S. and other
countries. Tom Clancy's Splinter Cell © 2004 by Ubisoft Entertainment S.A.
Cover illustration by axb group / Greg Horn.
Stepback art by Greg Horn.
Cover design by Rita Frangie.
Interior text design by Kristin del Rosario.

ISBN: 0-425-21278-5

BERKLEY®
Berkley Books are published by The Berkley Publishing Group,
a division of Penguin Group (USA) Inc.,
375 Hudson Street, New York, New York 10014.
BERKLEY is a registered trademark of Penguin Group (USA) Inc.
The "B" design is a trademark belonging to Penguin Group (USA) Inc.

PRINTED IN THE UNITED STATES OF AMERICA

10 9 8 7 6 5 4 3 2 1

ACKNOWLEDGMENTS

The name on a book's cover rarely tells the whole story of its birth. Many thanks to the following for their energy and input. Couldn't have done it without you . . .

Julie, who was with me every step of the way. As always.

The steadfast Tom Colgan and all of the good folks at Penguin Group (USA) Inc.

Vanessa, for her dedication and creativity.

Michael, for the vision and the opportunity.

──── *PROLOGUE* ────

IN retrospect, he would find it an astonishing way to start a war.

But then again, he didn't start this war.

The meeting, and the information it had subsequently revealed, came to him purely by chance. Synchronicity, the Swiss psychiatrist Carl Jung had called it. A confluence of seemingly unrelated events that have meaning—albeit hidden to all but the most discerning. It was a sophisticated concept, especially for a Western mind, Kuan-Yin Zhao thought.

Of course, there were corollaries in his own life. Xiangqi, one of his passions, was an exercise in manipulated synchronicity. At its heart, the mastery of Xiangqi, and its lesser cousin, chess, was nothing more than recognizing the patterns your opponent was trying to hide, and creating patterns your opponent will fail to see until too late. Great Xiangqi players never move a single piece. On the board, it may be a *pao* moving five squares, but in the mind of a master, it is the *pao*'s move, combined with the myriad moves available to his opponent, combined with a countermove, and so on until victory or defeat.

Though pleased that Xiangqi might inspire a solution to his dilemma, he was also unsurprised. All he'd needed was the hint of an opening move, and now he had it. From there his mind would expand across the board—or in this case, across nations.

IF not for an underling's father who had left China thirty years earlier to find greener pastures, he would have never found the linchpin of his plan. Like the rest of the world, he'd believed the public stories, but of course public stories were usually generated by governments, and governments weren't known for their forthrightness—especially the Russians, whose natural gift for deception was second only to that of Beijing's politicians.

A coal mine in Evenki collapses, killing hundreds, and the world knows nothing about it; a Russian submarine sinks to the bottom of the Kara Sea with all hands, and it simply ceases to exist; a Russian death squad sneaks onto Chinese soil, breaks into a man's home, and murders him in front of his children and it's called war.

Why would this secret be any different? *All the better,* Zhao thought.

What better way to begin the greatest game of his life than with a move no one would ever see?

IT'S there, I tell you," the old man said.

"You're sure of this? You've seen it with your own eyes?"

The old man nodded. "I was there, with a shovel like all the rest." The old man took a gulp of tea and timidly held out his cup for a refill. "It's a cursed place, I can tell you that."

"Why do you say that?"

"It's haunted. I saw things . . . strange things."

Zhao tried not to suppress a smile. The old man was addled. Even so, his background had checked out; he was who and what he said he was. "How easy is it to find?"

"As easy to find as your own toes. It might take a little work getting to it, but it's there."

"Tell me this: You did this for how long?"

The old man scratched his scalp. "I lived there for twenty years. When I got sick, I wanted to come home, to be buried in Chinese soil—not that garbage over there."

"Why did you remember this one detail? Out of everything you'd been through, why this one?"

"Because I watched them do it and I thought how stupid they must be. I'm a simple man—not a smart man—and even I couldn't believe what they were doing."

"Who else knows about this?"

The old man pursed his lips, thinking. "Many, I imagine, but many are dead as well. Those that remember probably do their best to forget. Besides, who would want it?"

Who indeed? Zhao thought.

"Who have you told?"

"No one!" the old man said, stiffening in his chair. "My son, no one else."

"That's not quite true, is it, old man? You've told me."

"That's different. It's my granddaughter, you see—"

"Yes, yes . . . very sick—you told me that, too."

"She's all I have. I convinced her to join me there. I wanted her to go to school, make something of herself. Instead . . . They've done things to her. Drugs. Men. She can't get away from them."

Of course she can't, he thought. The teenage prostitution market had always been profitable, and in the right country a petite Chinese girl would bring thousands. Drugged or sober, the clientele didn't care. In fact, drugs made them easier to handle.

"I heard you were a decent man," the old man said. "I don't believe the stories. They're all liars. You're a decent man. You can help her."

He refilled the old man's cup. "And I will. You'll have your granddaughter back before another month passes. But first, you're going to draw me a map, aren't you?"

The old man nodded vigorously.

1

SIXTY miles and thirty thousand feet above Washington, D.C., the MC-130H Combat Talon began its second hour of circling in the dark night sky. Designed to covertly insert special operators into sensitive areas, the Talon could fly in rain, snow, high winds, pitch darkness, and radar-saturated environments.

The lone man in the black Nomex bodysuit sitting in the cargo bay was worried about none of these things. He'd ridden, jumped from, and in some cases flown, the Talon dozens of times into dozens of hot spots, and it had always delivered him safely. Of course, "delivery" usually meant being dropped into a denied area full of heavily armed bad guys only too happy to kill him. It came with the job.

Tonight what Sam Fisher was worried most about was death by boredom.

He shifted his body on the bench seat, trying to find a position that didn't put either his legs or butt to sleep, and wondered if the Talon's designers had gone out of their way to find the most uncomfortable seats they could find. Either way, they'd succeeded.

The glamour of special ops, he thought, extending his foot and stretching his calf.

Between missions and looking to keep his skills honed, he'd volunteered to test one of DARPA's newest gadgets, in this case an extended-range radar-absorbent HAHO (High-Altitude, High-Opening) parafoil code-named Goshawk. Not only was the Defense Advanced Research Projects Agency the Pentagon's ultrasecret think tank for all things military, but it also supplied Third Echelon with much of the gadgetry and weapons that made Fisher's job easier—and survivable. If nothing else, when the Goshawk finally went into service, he'd be assured of its reliability. Providing it didn't kill him, of course.

The two-hour wait was courtesy of a malfunctioning radar station on Rhode Island that NORAD had set up to track—or hopefully fail to track—Fisher's descent on the Goshawk. If the stations failed to detect him, the Goshawk would go operational as the first stealth parachute, capable of dropping soldiers 150 miles outside a target area and allowing them glide in, invisible to radar.

And Third Echelon would probably get the first working model.

As a subdivision of the National Security Agency,

Third Echelon was tasked with handling covert missions either too sensitive or too risky for traditional entities, such as the CIA or standard special forces. Like all of Third Echelon's operatives, Fisher was known as a Splinter Cell—a self-contained and lone operator. How many other Splinter Cells existed Fisher had no idea, nor did he wish to know. Third Echelon was about invisibility. Deniability. Zero footprint. Only a handful of people knew where Splinter Cells went and what they did.

A voice crackled to life in Fisher's subdermal: "Incoming traffic for you, Major."

As far as the Talon's crew knew, Fisher was a major in the 3rd Battalion, 75th Ranger Regiment out of Fort Benning, Georgia. Not that they cared; given the nature of their work, Talon crews knew how to not ask questions.

"Patch it through."

"Roger. On your button five."

Fisher's communications system was a far cry from the traditional headset he'd worn in his pre–Third Echelon days. The two-part system was comprised of a nickel-sized subdermal receiver implanted beneath the skin behind Fisher's ear. The subdermal bypassed the route normally traveled by sound waves—through the outer ear to the tympanic membrane—and sent vibrations directly into the set of tiny bones within the ear (known as the ossicles), or the hammer, anvil, and stirrup, which then transmitted the signal to the brain for decoding.

For speaking, Fisher wore a butterfly-shaped adhesive patch known as a SVT, or Sub-Vocal Transceiver, across his throat just above his Adam's apple. Learning to use the SVT had required a skill Fisher likened to a cross between whispering and ventriloquism.

Together, they allowed him a virtually silent communications system.

Fisher tapped his subdermal to switch channels, then said, "Up on button five."

"Standby for Xerxes," a tinny voice said in Fisher's ear, followed by a few seconds of clicks and buzzes as the encryption scrubbers engaged. Xerxes was Fisher's boss and longtime friend, Colonel Irving Lambert, Third Echelon's Director of Operations. Lambert's voice came on: "Change of plans, Sam."

"Let me guess," Fisher said. "We're going to fly around until the wings come off."

"As of now, you're on-mission."

As if on cue, Fisher felt the Talon bank sharply to starboard. The drone of the engines increased in pitch, going to full throttle.

"Your OPSAT's being updated now."

Fisher pulled back the cuff of his jumpsuit and pressed his thumb to the OPSAT, or Operational Satellite Uplink, screen, which glowed to life:

// . . . BIOMETRIC SCAN ENGAGED . . .
. . . SCANNING FINGERPRINT . . .
. . . IDENTITY CONFIRMED . . . //

There was a flash of static, and then the screen resolved into a gray-green satellite image. The biometric scan feature was an upgrade to the OPSAT, designed not only to prevent prying eyes from using it, but to keep an inadvertent bump of the touch screen from changing modes. During his last mission, Fisher, on the run, had found himself suddenly staring at a map of downtown Kyoto, rather than the schematic of the Nampo shipyard he was trying to escape.

"What am I looking at?" he asked.

Anna Grimsdottir, Lambert's chief technical guru, replied, "Real-time feed from an advanced KH-12 Crystal. You're looking at the Atlantic Ocean, about six miles east of Cape Hatteras, North Carolina. See the highlighted blip?" A tiny football shape in the top right corner pulsed once.

"I see it. Cargo freighter. So what?"

"Here's the infrared side."

The OPSAT screen shimmered, then resolved. The freighter had turned into a bloom of red and orange. "That's hot," Fisher said. "Somebody forget to change the antifreeze in the engines?"

Lambert said, "We wish. The radiometric signature makes the source nuclear. We're trying to nail it down right now, but something on that ship is radioactive. And it's headed toward our coast."

"Radio contact?"

"She's ignored all hails. At current speed and course, she'll run aground in twenty-two minutes."

WITH a minimal load-out for the training jump that didn't include weapons, Fisher had to improvise. He made his way to the cockpit, where he found the crew had already gotten Lambert's order. The pilot handed Fisher his personal sidearm, a Beretta model 92F 9mm, along with an extra magazine.

"How far?" Fisher asked him. Two minutes had passed since Lambert's message.

"We're thirty miles out; I'll drop you at five."

"Cutting it close."

Lambert was listening in. "Close calls are what you're good at, Sam."

"You always say the nicest things."

"We've got two Coast Guard cutters and a Navy destroyer en route, but you'll still get there first. A pair of F-16s are lifting off from Homestead, should be overhead about the time you hit the deck."

Providing I hit the deck, Fisher thought. Dropping by parachute onto a pitching deck in the black of night was dicey—and deadly if you missed the target. "Who's making the calls on this?" he asked.

"SecDef. If you can't stop the ship, he's going to order the F-16s to sink her."

"If she's full of what we think she is—"

"Then we'll have an ecological nightmare on our hands. Good luck."

"Thanks so much. I'll be in touch."

The pilot said, "Two minutes to drop, Major."

And then what? Fisher thought. What would he find once aboard that ship?

2

ARMS braced on either side of the open cargo door, legs spread apart and coiled, Fisher stared at the red bulb above his head and waited for the green go signal. Wind tore through the door, whipping cargo webbing and rattling tie-down buckles. The C-130's engines—before a dull drone—were now a deafening roar he felt in the pit of his stomach. Cold, metallic-tasting oxygen hissed through his face mask. Beyond the door he saw only blackness, punctuated every few seconds by the flash of the plane's navigation strobes.

As it always did before a mission, the image of his daughter Sarah's face flashed through his mind. He squeezed his eyes shut, forced himself back to reality.

Concentrate on what's in front of you, he commanded himself.

Above his head, the red bulb flashed once, turned yellow, went dark, then flashed green.

He jumped.

The slipstream caught him immediately and almost before his brain could register it, the plane's fuselage zipped past his field of vision and was gone. He counted, *One . . . two . . . three . . .* Then he reached across his chest and pulled the release toggle. With a *whoosh-whump* the parafoil sprang open. Sam felt himself jerked upward. His stomach lurched into his throat.

Silence. Floating. Surrounded by blackness and with no points of reference, he felt strangely motionless. Suspended in space. Aside from the initial leap out the door, this transition was always the most unnerving for airborne soldiers. To suddenly go from hurricane winds tearing at your body to floating in virtual dead silence was a jarring sensation.

He glanced up to check the parafoil. It was cleanly deployed, a wedge-shaped shadow against an even darker sky. Had the chute failed to deploy, a visual check wouldn't have been necessary. His uncontrolled tumbling toward the ocean at 150 mph would have been his first clue he was in trouble.

He lifted his wrist to his faceplate and studied the OPSAT's screen, which had changed to a ringed radar picture superimposed on a faint grid. In the southwest corner of the screen, some thirty thousand feet below, the freighter was a slowly pulsing red dot. Numbers along each side of the screen told him his airspeed, altitude, rate-of-descent, angle-of-descent, and time-to-target.

He shifted his body weight ever so slightly, which his motion-sensitive harness translated into steering for the Goshawk. He banked slightly to the west until his course was aligned with that of the freighter's.

He heard a squelch in his earpiece, then Lambert's voice. "Sam, you there?"

"I'm here."

"I take it the Goshawk's working as designed."

"Like I said, I'm here."

Grimsdottir's voice: "Sam, check your OPSAT; we've got info on the freighter."

Sam punched up the screen. A model of the ship appeared, complete with exploded deck schematics and the ship's details:

VESSEL NAME/DESIGNATION: TREGO/DRY
BULK TRAMPER
LENGTH/BEAM: 481/62
CREW MANIFEST: 10
REGISTRATION: LIBERIA
DESTINATION: BALTIMORE

"Right past Washington," Fisher said. "How convenient."

"Thank God for small miracles," Lambert said.

Everything's relative, Fisher thought. If the *Trego* ran

aground, anyone exposed to her cargo wouldn't call the experience miraculous. Fisher had seen radiation poisoning up close; the memories were haunting.

Grimsdottir said, "Projected impact point is False Cape Landing, just south of Virginia Beach. You've got fourteen minutes."

"Any sign of life aboard?"

"None. The infrared signature is so hot we can't tell if there are warm bodies aboard."

Lambert said, "Best to assume so, Sam. What's your time-to-target?"

"Nine minutes."

"Not much time. The F-16s are authorized to shoot four minutes after you land."

"Then I guess I better show up early," Fisher said, and signed off.

He flipped his trident goggles down over his eyes and switched to night vision, then rotated his body, head down, legs straight out and up. The Goshawk responded instantly and dove toward the ocean.

He kept his eyes fixed on the OPSAT's altimeter as the numbers wound down:

2000 feet . . . 1500 . . . 1000 . . . 500 . . .
300.

He arched his back and swung his knees to his chest. The Goshawk shuddered. In the gray-green of Fisher's NV goggles, the ocean's surface loomed, a black wall filling his field of vision. *Come on.* . . . The Goshawk flared out and went level. The horizon appeared in the goggles.

Call that the Goshawk's extreme field test, Fisher thought, giving the parafoil a silent thanks.

He checked the OPSAT. The freighter was two miles ahead and slightly to the east. He banked that way and descended to one hundred feet.

He tapped **APPROACH** on the OPSAT's screen and the view changed to a wire-frame 3D model of the *Trego* bracketed by a pair of flashing diagonal lines. He switched his goggles to binocular view and zoomed in until he could see the faint outline of the ship's superstructure silhouetted against the sky. He saw no movement on deck. Astern, the ship's wake showed as a churned white fan. Aside from the port and starboard running lights, everything was dark.

Sam zoomed again. Two miles beyond the freighter's bow he could see the dark smudge of the coast; beyond that, the twinkling lights of Virginia Beach.

And half a million people, he thought.

He matched his angle-of-descent with the OPSAT's readout until he was one hundred feet off the *Trego*'s stern, then arched his back, lifting the Goshawk's nose. As he flared out and the aft rail passed beneath his feet, a gust of wind caught the Goshawk. Fisher was pushed sideways, back over the water. He twisted his body. The Goshawk veered right. He bent his knees to take the impact.

With a surprisingly gentle thump, he touched down.

In one fluid movement, he reached up, pulled the Goshawk's "crumple bar" to collapse the parafoil, disengaged his harness, then dragged it to a nearby tie-down cleat in the deck and locked it down using the D ring.

Suddenly, to his right he heard a roar. He glanced up in time to see the underbelly of an F-16 swoop past, wing strobes flashing in the darkness. Then it was gone, climbing up and away.

Giving me fair warning? Sam wondered. *Or wishing me good luck?*

He looked around to get his bearings, tapped his earpiece, said, "I'm on deck," then drew his Beretta and sprinted toward the nearest ladder.

3

WHEN he reached the top of the ladder, he dropped into a crouch and ducked behind a nearby crate. He went still, listened. Aside from the rhythmic chug of the *Trego*'s engines and the snapping of tarps in the wind, all was quiet.

He called up the ship's blueprint on the OPSAT. He was on the main deck; the bridge was near the bow, some four hundred feet away. To get there, he could either duck belowdecks and make a stealthy approach, or make a straight sprint in the open. His preference would have been the former, but time was not on his side.

He keyed his subdermal: "Tell me something, Grimsdottir: Exactly how hot is this ship?"

"You mean how long can you stay aboard before you start glowing?"

"Yeah."

"Hard to say, but I wouldn't linger more than fifteen minutes."

"Good to know. Out."

Fisher took a breath and started running.

IN the murky display of his NV goggles the deck was a flat moonscape broken only by the occasional stack of crates. He felt naked, exposed. However necessary, this dash in the open went against his every instinct. *Don't think,* he commanded himself. *Run.*

Halfway to the bridge, he glanced up and saw a shadowed figure standing on the port bridge wing. The figure turned and darted through the bridge hatch.

"I've got company," Fisher told Lambert. "Somebody's on the bridge."

"Where there's one, there's more."

Maybe, Fisher thought. *Maybe not.* One possibility was that the ship was automated. If so, the man he just saw could be the fail-safe.

"How much time, Grim?" Fisher asked.

"Four minutes. The F-16s have gone weapons-free, waiting for the order to fire."

HE reached the superstructure, flattened himself against the bulkhead, and slid forward to the foot of the ladder.

He glanced up through the slats, looking for movement. There was nothing. On flat feet, he started upward, taking steps two at a time until he was near the top, where he dropped to his belly, slithered up the final three steps, and peeked his head up.

Through the open bridge hatch he saw the man hunched over the helm console, his face bathed in milky white glow of a laptop screen. He looked Middle Eastern. Suddenly the man slapped his palm against the laptop and cursed. Over the whistling of the wind, Fisher couldn't make out the words.

The man cursed again, then stepped to the ship's wheel—a wagon-wheel style with spoked grips—and leaned over it, grunting with the strain.

Fisher rose up, leveled his Beretta, and stepped through the hatch.

"**STOP** right there, Admiral." Fisher called.

The man whipped his head around. His eyes went wide.

"Not even a twitch, or you're dead where you stand."

The main straightened up and turned to face him.

Fisher said, "Step away from the—"

The man spun toward the laptop.

Fisher fired once. The bullet went where he wanted it, in this case squarely into the man's right hip. The impact spun him like a top. As he fell, his outstretch arm caught the laptop, sending it crashing to the deck. Groaning, the man rolled onto his side and reached for the laptop.

What's he—

Then Fisher saw it. Jutting from the side of the laptop was a wireless network card. He was linked to something, controlling something.

"Don't move!" Fisher ordered.

The man's hand stretched toward the keyboard.

Fisher fired. As with his first round, this one struck true, drilling into the the man's right shoulder blade. He groaned and slumped forward, still.

Except for his right hand.

The man's finger gave a spasmodic jerk and struck the ENTER key.

INSTANTLY, the pitch of the *Trego*'s engines changed. The deck shivered beneath his feet.

Grimsdottir's voice came on the line: "Fisher, the ship's just—"

"Picked up speed, I know."

He made a snap decision. The man's frustration with the helm console was proof enough the wheel was locked down. That left only one other option.

He started running.

"Grim, I'm headed down the aft interior ladder. I need a countdown and I need on-the-fly directions to the engine room."

"Go down three decks, turn right to port passage, and keep heading aft."

The *Trego*'s passageways were dark, save for the red glow of emergency lights. Pipes and conduits flashed in

Fisher's peripheral vision as he ran. He leapt through a hatch and called, "Passing the mess hall," and kept going.

Grimsdottir said, "Two more hatches, then you'll reach an intersection. Go left. The engine room is at midships, aft side of the passage."

"Time?"

"One minute, twenty seconds."

He reached the passageway outside the engine room and skidded to a stop. He had a plan, but whether it would work he didn't know. As with all ships, engine spaces are the most vulnerable to fire, so Fisher had little trouble finding a hose-reel locker. He jerked open the cabinet and punched the quick-release lever. The hose fell in a coil on the deck.

Lambert's voice: "One minute, Fisher. The F-16s will be targeting the engine rooms."

Of course they will, Fisher thought. Wrong place, wrong time, but there was no other way.

Each Falcon would be shooting a pair of AGM-65 Maverick missiles. Deadly accurate and fast, each Maverick carried a three-hundred-pound high-explosive warhead. One way or another, crippled or sunk, the *Trego* would be stopped. On the upside, Fisher consoled himself, he would never feel a thing.

He drew his knife, pulled the hose taut, and sliced it off at the bulkhead. With one hand wrapped around the nozzle, Fisher used the other to undog the engine room hatch. He kicked it open and rushed through.

The thunder of the engines and the heat washed over

him like a wave. He squinted, put his head down, and stumbled forward. Steam swirled around him. The space was a tangle of railing, catwalks, and pipes.

"Forty-five seconds, Fisher."

"Working on it," he replied through gritted teeth.

Luckily, the layout of the *Trego*'s engine room varied little from that of most ships. He made his way to the center of the space, looked for the largest structure, in this case a pair of car-sized shapes astride the main catwalk. The engines. Eyes fixed on the catwalk beneath his feet, he sprinted between the engines until he glimpsed a flash of spinning metal. *There*. He dropped to his knees.

"Thirty seconds . . ."

He pried back the catwalk grating to reveal the reduction gear—essentially, the ship's driveshaft that transferred power from the engines to the screws beneath the stern. Spinning at full speed, the reduction gear was nothing but a blur of cogs.

If this worked, Fisher knew, the effect would be instantaneous. And if not . . .

He gathered the hose around his knees, then shoved it through the grate.

4

THE National Security Agency lies five miles outside the town of Laurel, Maryland, within the confines of an Army post named after the Civil War Union general George Gordon Meade. Once home to a boot camp and a WWII prisoner-of-war camp, Fort Meade has since the 1950s become best known as the headquarters of the most advanced, most secretive intelligence organization on earth.

Primarily tasked with the conduct of SIGINT (Signals Intelligence) in all its forms, the NSA can, and has at times, intercept and analyze every form of communication known to man, from cell phone signals and e-mail messages, to microwave emissions, and ELF (Extremely Low Frequency) burst transmissions from submarines thousands of feet beneath the surface of the ocean.

Hoping to bridge the chasm between simply gathering actionable intelligence and acting on that intelligence, the NSA had years earlier been directed by special Presidential charter to form Third Echelon, its own in-house covert operations unit.

Third Echelon operatives, known individually as Splinter Cells, were recruited from the special forces communities of the Navy, Army, Marine Corps, and Air Force, then shaped into the ultimate lone operators, men and women capable of not only working alone in hostile environments, but of doing so without leaving a trace.

FISHER'S sudden introduction of the fire hose to the *Trego*'s reduction gear had had an immediate effect. With a sound that was a cross between a massive zipper and a bullwhip, all fifty feet of the hose disappeared into the catwalk in the blink of an eye. Fisher threw himself backward and curled into a ball.

The engines gave a screech of metal on metal. The catwalk trembled. Black smoke burst through the grating, followed by thirty seconds of rapid-fire pings and clunks as the reduction gear tore itself apart. Shrapnel zinged around the engine room, bouncing off bulkheads and railings and punching holes in conduits. Alarms began blaring.

And then suddenly it was over. Through the slowly clearing smoke he could see the smoldering remnants of the fire hose wrapped around the mangled shaft. He became aware of the faint voice in his subdermal. It was Lambert. ". . . Fisher . . . Fisher, are you—"

"I'm here."

"Whatever you did, it worked. The *Trego*'s slowing, coming to a stop."

"I sure as hell hope so. Now tell the pilots to break off before I get a missile down my throat."

NOW, four hours later, sitting under dimmed track lighting at the polished teak conference table in Third Echelon's Situation Room, Fisher shifted in his chair, trying to avoid the dozen or so bruises he'd gathered aboard the *Trego*. It was nothing a liberal dose of ibuprofen wouldn't cure. Besides, he told himself, given the alternatives, he'd take bruises over shrapnel or flaming chunks of fire hose any day. Getting old was hell, but getting dead was worse.

Per Lambert's orders, his first stop after leaving the *Trego* had been at the Army's Chemical Casualty Care Division, located at Aberdeen Proving Ground in Maryland. A division of the Army's Medical Research Institute, the CCCD specializes in the decontamination and treatment of biological, chemical, and radiological exposure. Fisher was sent through a series of decon showers and then poked and prodded by space-suited doctors before being declared "contaminant free."

"Where are they taking the *Trego*?" he asked Lambert.

"She's being towed to Norfolk's secure shipyard."

Lambert aimed a remote control at one of the half-dozen plasma screens that lined the Situation Room's walls. A satellite image of Norfolk harbor faded into view.

The *Trego* was easy to spot. Flanked by three Navy frigates and an Arleigh Burke–class destroyer, the freighter was under tow by a harbor tug.

"They're prepping a dry dock for the NEST team as we speak." Lambert said, referring to a Nuclear Emergency Search Team from the Department of Energy.

Before FBI investigators could board the *Trego*, the NEST would have to determine the source and level of the ship's radioactivity. Luckily, so far it appeared nothing hot had leaked from the hull—something that certainly would have happened had she run aground.

"And our prisoner and his laptop?" Before boarding the Blackhawk helicopter Lambert had dispatched for him, Fisher had grabbed the laptop and then hoisted the *Trego*'s lone crewman onto his shoulder. In some cases, prisoners were better than corpses.

"Grim is working the laptop. Whatever key he pressed did more than set the engines to flank. It scrambled the hard drive, too."

"Yeah, he seemed a tad determined. He's in medical?"

Lambert nodded. "He'll make it."

"Good," Fisher said, taking a sip of coffee. He screwed up his face and frowned at the mug. "Who made this?"

"I did, thank you very much," a voice said. William Redding, Fisher's advance man and field handler, walked through the door. With his horn-rimmed glasses, sweater vest, and pocket protector, Redding was a bookworm of the highest caliber with an almost fanatical focus on planning and details. As annoying as his intensity could be,

Fisher couldn't imagine going into the field without Redding guarding his flanks.

"And by the way," Redding said, "the nerds from DARPA called. They want to know what you did with their Goshawk."

Fisher said, "Let me get this straight: You're calling the DARPA people nerds?"

Lambert chuckled under his breath. Redding wasn't known for his sense of humor.

"I'm a geek, Sam. They're nerds. There's a profound difference."

"My apologies."

"The Goshawk?"

"Safe in the equipment room."

"And its condition?"

"Hard to say, given how little there was left of it."

Redding's eyes narrowed. "Pardon me?"

"There was fire—"

"*Pardon me?*"

"A joke. Relax, it's as good as new."

Redding was already heading for the door. He stopped at the threshold, hesitated a moment, then turned back. "Sam?"

"Yeah?"

"Glad you're in one piece."

GRIMSDOTTIR walked in twenty minutes later. Born in Iceland, Anna was tall and statuesque, with a model's cheekbones and short, brown-auburn hair—a choice

Fisher suspected had more to do with function than it did with fashion. Above all else, Anna was practical. Worry about whether she was having a "hair day"—good or bad—wasn't on her list of priorities.

"Welcome back, Sam. I don't see anything glowing."

"The day is young."

"I talked to the docs at Aberdeen. They confirmed that whatever's aboard the *Trego*, you didn't receive enough of a dose to worry about." She walked over to a nearby computer workstation and tapped a few keys. A frisbee-shaped 3D model of what Fisher assumed was the hard drive from *Trego* laptop appeared on the screen. The disk was broken into irregularly sized geometric chunks outlined in either red, green, or yellow.

Grimsdottir said, "Okay, what do you want first, the good news or the bad news?"

Lambert said, "Bad news."

"All the red data sectors you see were wiped clean by the self-destruct program. They're gone, period. No coming back."

"That's a lot of red," Fisher said.

"About eighty percent. Green is probably recoverable; yellow is iffy."

"And the good news?" Lambert said.

"I may be able to tell who wrote the self-destruct program."

"How?"

"Most programmers have a signature—the way they block code, handle syntax, write background comments. . . . Those kinds of things. Sometimes it's as distinctive as handwriting. And I can tell you this: Whoever wrote this program is sophisticated; his signature is unique. It may take me a few—"

Suddenly a muted alarm came over the loudspeakers. In unison, all the computer monitors began flashing, their screens overlaid by a large red exclamation mark.

"Oh, God," Grimsdottir murmured, staring at the screen.

"What?" Lambert said. "What's going on?"

"A virus just got past our firewall. It's attacking the mainframe!"

5

SILENCE those alarms, Anna," Lambert ordered.

The room went quiet.

"How's this possible?" Lambert asked. "This is the NSA, for God's sake, not eBay. How could something get past our firewalls?"

"The laptop," Fisher murmured.

Grimsdottir nodded, eyes fixed on the screen. "You got it. Colonel, there was a virus buried in one of the hard drive's sectors. A worm, designed to come alive as soon as it detected a connection with any of the laptop's ports. As soon as I hooked it up to run diagnostics—"

"Can you stop it?"

"Working on it. It's moving fast, spreading through the mainframe. I'm trying to get ahead of it . . . set up a firebreak. If I can divert it into a unused server, I can trap it. Damn, it's moving fast!"

For the next fifteen minutes Fisher and Lambert watched in silence as she worked. Blocks of green-on-black computer code streamed across the monitor. Grimsdottir's hands became a blur on the keyboard. Slowly the code seemed to lose momentum, coming in erratic bursts, until finally she leaned back and exhaled. Her face glistened with sweat. Her hands were shaking.

"I got it," she said. "It's trapped on an empty archive server."

"How much damage did it do?" Lambert asked.

"A lot, but it didn't reach the backup systems, so we'll be able to rebuild most of the mainframe."

"And the laptop?" Fisher asked.

"Gone. Well and truly dead. One piece of good news, though: There's only a few people in the world with the voodoo it takes to write that kind of virus. Give me a day, and I'll have a name."

"Go," Lambert ordered.

ONCE she was gone, Fisher turned to Lambert. "I have an idea about the *Trego*."

"I'm listening."

"I don't buy the Liberia registration."

"Me neither."

"You can disguise a ship in a lot of ways, but there's one thing you can't hide: the engine serial numbers. They're stamped everywhere. Here's the rub, though:

The FBI will eventually find the numbers and eventually the info will trickle down to us—"

Lambert grinned. "I hate the word eventually."

In this case, "eventually" could mean weeks of bureaucratic wrangling. Fisher returned Lambert's smile. "Me too."

Fisher had known Lambert for nearly twenty years, having first worked with him in the Army's Delta Force, then again as they were both tapped for an experimental program that took special ops soldiers from each branch of the military and transferred them to counterpart units. Rangers went to Delta; Delta went to Marine Force Recon; and in Fisher and Lambert's case, Delta went to the U.S. Navy's Special Warfare Sea-Air-Land unit—the SEALs. The idea was to create operators of the highest caliber, trained to be the elite of the military's special forces community.

Lambert said, "As luck would have it, I've already had this discussion with the President. The FBI's taking the lead on the case, but we've been cleared to conduct our own parallel investigation—separate from the FBI."

Fisher understood the order. While he loathed politics in general and did his best to stay out of it, he knew what was driving the President's caution: the war in Iraq. Someone had just launched an attack on the U.S. that could have killed thousands of people and rendered a section of the Virginia shoreline radioactive for decades, perhaps centuries. So far, the only suspect was a lone man of Middle Eastern descent aboard the *Trego*. If America was headed toward another war in the Middle

East, the President didn't want another intelligence fiasco. America had just started rebuilding the credibility it had lost over Iraq. It would be Third Echelon's job to make doubly sure all t's were crossed and i's were dotted.

"Restrictions?" Fisher asked.

"None," Lambert replied. "We do it our way; gloves off."

"The only way to fly."

"Amen. Now, go get some sleep. Tomorrow night, you're breaking into a U.S. naval base."

FISHER lived outside Germantown, Maryland, about thirty minutes northwest of Washington, in a small farmhouse surrounded by two acres of red maple and pine. He'd tried living a normal bachelor life: a townhouse, socializing with neighbors, sitting around the pool. . . . But he'd quickly admitted what he already knew in the back of his mind: He wasn't much of a people person. Not that he disliked people per se, but he had a limited tolerance for most of them.

It was a hazard that came with the job. Dealing with the worst of men in the worst of situations tended to change you. Living in the condo, Fisher had found himself mentally dissecting both his neighbors and his surroundings: threat or no threat; likely ambush sites; clear lines of fire. . . . Living on the razor's edge, while often exciting, was also all-consuming. You didn't survive long in special operations without fully immersing yourself in that world. Not having a home where he could let down his guard and decompress had gotten very old, very quickly.

At the farmhouse, his closest neighbor was half a mile away. He could sit on his porch at night and hear nothing but the hum of the cicadas and the croaking of frogs. Surprisingly, he'd found the land itself therapeutic. He'd bought the property at a deep discount from an owner who'd allowed it to fall into disrepair, so he spent much of his time working at taming the landscaping or restoring the farmhouse, which needed new everything, from windows to shingles to plumbing. Fisher took comfort in the work—in the ordinariness of it all. Even the briefest of layovers at the farmhouse between missions helped recharge his batteries.

By the time he got home it was near dawn. He threw in a load of laundry, took a shower, checked his e-mail, and stretched out on the couch. He found the remote and turned on the TV. The channel was set to CNN.

". . . what few initial eyewitness reports we've come across talk of dozens of people collapsing where they were standing or slumping over at the dining table. . . ."

Fisher sat bolt upright. He turned up the volume.

"The spokesperson for the governor's office issued a statement stating that investigators were en route to the small town of Slipstone and that the governor himself would be holding a press conference later this morning. Meanwhile, speculation abounds as to what may be behind the sudden and mysterious deaths in the remote town of Slipstone, New Mexico."

Fisher felt the hair on the back of his neck stand up. His cell phone started ringing.

HE was back at Situation Room forty minutes later. Lambert stood at the conference table watching an MSNBC report. Grimsdottir and Redding were seated at workstations on either side of him. In the background Fisher heard the static hiss of radio punctuated by a female voice:

"Slipstone Nine-one-one, please hold . . . Slipstone Nine-one-one, please hold . . . Slipstone Nine-one-one, please hold. . . ."

Lambert looked over his shoulder at Fisher. "Two hundred emergency calls and counting. As far as we can decipher, there are hundreds dead. They're laying in the streets, in homes, dead at their steering wheels. . . ."

"Good God," Fisher murmured.

Grimsdottir called, "I've got it, Colonel."

"Put it up."

The main monitor resolved into a thermal satellite image of what Fisher assumed was Slipstone.

"Give me the overlay, Anna."

Grimsdottir tapped the keyboard and the image changed to a maze of yellow and orange lines punctuated by circular blooms of red. To Fisher the colors looked eerily familiar. Already guessing the answer, he asked, "What are we seeing, Colonel?"

"Slipstone's water system."

"There're only a few ways that many people can die that quickly: waterborne or airborne."

His eyes still fixed on the monitor, Lambert nodded grimly. "How long, Anna?"

"Almost there, Colonel." A few moments later: "Confirmed: it's the same signature as the *Trego*."

Fisher felt like he'd been punched in the stomach. He turned away from the screen and took a deep breath. The *Trego* had just been the opening salvo. This was the real event.

Someone had just poisoned an entire American town.

6

FISHER angled downward until his depth gauge read thirty feet, then leveled off and checked his OPSAT. He was on track, almost dead center in the middle of the Elizabeth River. A quarter mile to go. His rebreather unit hissed softly in his ears. As it always did, the sound reminded Fisher of a mellower version of Darth Vader.

Displayed across his facemask was a HUD, or Heads-Up Display. Like the display projected onto the windscreen of a modern jet fighter, the faint green overlay on his face mask told him virtually everything he needed to know about his environment, including a map of the river and the shipyard, his current position, the river's depth and temperature, and distance and bearing to his next waypoint, which showed as a yellow arrow near the upper edge of his mask that changed position and length according to his position. *Follow the yellow brick arrow*.

Deciding best how to penetrate the shipyard's Southgate Annex, one of the most secure yards on the Eastern Seaboard, had been the easiest part of his mission. Given the high level of base security, an approach by land was a nonstarter, which had left only one other option: water. This suited Fisher's preference. His SEAL days had taught him to trust the water. Water was safety; water was camouflage; water was anonymity.

Norfolk Naval Shipyard is one of the busiest in the country, servicing on any given day as much as fifteen percent of the U.S. Navy's fleet. With seven thousand employees, five hundred acres, and sixty-nine production buildings, the shipyard was an impressive site—more so since it was located eight miles south of the Norfolk Naval Station proper, in the southern branch of the relatively quiet Elizabeth River.

An hour earlier Fisher had parked his car in a wooded parking lot overlooking the eastern bank of the river, and waited until a teenage couple in a steamed-up Ford Escort finished their business and drove off. He'd then retrieved his duffel and walked a few hundred yards through the woods to the shoreline, where he changed into his wet suit, rebreather harness, mask, and fins, then slipped into the water.

Now Fisher craned his head back, checking the surface for boats. It was two A.M. He'd seen virtually no traffic, save for the occasional civilian motor cruiser returning home late after a day of fishing in the Chesapeake. He finned upward and broke the surface, careful to allow only the upper half of his mask to show. To his right, upriver, he could see car headlights crossing the Jordan Bridge, which linked the western and eastern shores.

Directly in front of him, a quarter mile across the water, the shipyard's Southgate Annex was brightly lit by sodium-vapor lights. Fisher counted ten ships of various sizes, from frigates to refrigerator ships, moored at the piers, and here and there he could see the sparkle of welding torches. A loudspeaker crackled to life and a voice made an annoucement, too distorted for Fisher to hear. As long as the message wasn't "Intruder in the water," he didn't care.

South of the main line of piers was a row of five man-made inlets, each covered by a hangarlike structure fronted by a massive rolling door wide enough to accommodate warships as large as cruisers. These were the annex's secure docks, or sheds, numbered one through five. The *Trego* had been towed into Secure Shed Four, Five being the last in the line.

To reach her, Fisher would have to first have to get past the annex's sea fence, which stretched some three hundred yards across the entrance to the annex and was marked by a line of blue-lighted buoys, each linked to the next by floating aluminum pipes.

Of course, it wasn't the fence itself that concerned Fisher, but rather the spotlight-equipped Navy speedboat that constantly patrolled its length.

He picked out a few landmarks he'd chosen from his map before the mission, confirmed their position on his HUD display, then flipped over and dove.

* * *

TEN minutes later, he stopped swimming and coasted to a stop. He adjusted the compensator on his vest until he was neutrally buoyant, hovering motionless in the water. Aside from the glow of his HUD, he was surrounded by absolute blackness. Night diving could be an exercise in mind control, Fisher knew. Without any external reference points, a vertigo-like confusion can quickly take over. Fisher had seen the bravest of men, divers with hundreds of hours of bottom time, panic while simply floating motionless in dark water. Even he could feel it nipping at the edges of his mind: a primal urge to rush to the surface. He quashed the feeling and focused on his face mask; the soft green glow was reassuring. If his navigation was accurate, the sea fence lay directly ahead.

To his right he heard a the muffled chugging of a marine engine. Fifty yards away the gray, teardrop-shaped hull of the patrol boat was cutting across the surface, parallel to the fence. The boat's wake fanned out behind it, spreading outward until it met the fence, where it curled back on itself and slowly dissolved. A spotlight clicked on and pierced the surface, turning the water around it turquoise.

Fisher waited until the boat crossed his front, then swam ahead. He had two minutes until the patrol boat returned. The sea fence appeared out of the gloom, a steel-cable net that stretched from its anchor bolts in the seabed to the linked buoys on the surface. Looking at the net, Fisher said a silent thanks to EPA, which had years earlier urged the Navy's secure facilities to change the gap width of its sea fences so the indigenous fish population could come and go freely. In this case, the gaps were a foot square, which made Fisher's job much easier.

He checked the time display in the upper-right-hand corner of his mask. Even as he did so he heard the chug of the patrol boat to his left. He flipped over and dove straight down, hand trailing over the fence until he reached the bottom. The boat passed overhead, spotlight arcing through the water and playing over the fence. Once it was gone, he ascended ten feet and went to work.

From his harness he pulled a "burn tie," an eight-inch length of magnesium primacord. Ignited, magnesium burned hot and fast at five thousand degrees Fahrenheit, cutting through virtually anything it touched like a scalpel through jello.

He curled the tie around the cable before him, then jammed his thumbnail into the chemical detonator at the end and backed away. There was a half-second flash of blinding white light; the fence disappeared in a cloud of bubbles. When they cleared, Fisher swam ahead. The cable had been sheared neatly in two, turning the foot-wide gap into a two-foot-wide gap. He took off his rebreather harness, pushed it through the hole, then swam on.

TEN minutes later he drew to a stop in front of shed's steel door, a wall of corrugated metal painted battleship gray. He flipped himself upside down and finned downward. He switched on his task light.

The muddy seabed appeared before his faceplate. He turned horizontal and banked right. He passed the right edge of the door and then, abruptly, there it was: a circular scuttle set into the wall. He reached out and tried the hand wheel. Predictably, it was locked and, according to Grimsdottir, alarmed. If he tampered with it, he'd find himself surrounded by patrol boats before he got a hundred yards away.

"Anyone home?" Fisher radioed.

"I'm here, Sam," Grimsdottir replied.

"I'm at the hatch."

"Okay," Grimsdottir replied. "Give me thirty seconds. I'm hacked into the Shed's control room, but they've got the locks on an eight-digit public key encryption—"

"That's nice, Anna, but maybe we save the technobabble for another day?"

"Yeah, sorry, hang on." She was back a minute later: "Okay, locks and alarms are disengaged."

"Going in," Fisher replied.

The hand wheel was well oiled and it turned smoothly under his grip. He spun it until he heard the soft clank of metal on metal, then gently pulled. The scuttle swung open. Arms extended before him, he swam through.

His fins had barely cleared the opening when suddenly he heard the muffled shriek of alarm klaxons. In the distance, a water-muffled voice came over the loudspeaker: "Intruder alert . . . intruder alert. Security Alert Team to armory. This is not a drill! I say again: This is not a drill. . . ."

7

GRIMSDOTTIR'S panicked voice was immediately in his ear: "Sam, I—"

Fisher reached up and hit his transmit switch twice, then once, telling Lambert and Grimsdottir, *Radio silence; wait for contact.*

In or out, he commanded himself. If he got out now, they'd lock the dock down and his chance would be lost. If he stayed on mission, he'd be facing a security force on high alert, hunting for an intruder. It was an easy decision. This is what he did.

He quickly shut the scuttle, then pushed off the wall and finned downward, hands outstretched. When he touched the rough concrete of the dock's bed, he rolled to the right and kept swimming. He had one chance and one chance only. The shed was divided by a main water-course bracketed on both sides by working piers. If he could find a hiding place deep within the pier's pilings, he might be able wait out the security sweep.

Above him, the water went suddenly from dark green to turquoise as the dock's security lights came on, bathing the interior in bright light. He heard the muffled pounding of boots on the dock and voices shouting back and forth to one another.

His fingertips touched wood: a piling. He hooked his arm around it and pulled himself under the pier. The water went dark again. He switched on his task lights and was engulfed in hazy red light. He kept swimming, weaving his way through the pilings. Covered in mottled gray barnacles, they reminded him of elephant legs.

Somewhere behind him he heard multiple splashes. *Divers in the water.* The dock's security team was well trained and moving fast. *Keep going.*

The inner wall of the dock appeared before his faceplate. He looked up. Above his head he could just make out the understructure of the pier, a warren of crisscrossing girders and conduits.

Fisher finned around the piling nearest the wall, then switched off his lights and broke the surface. He shed his fins and clipped them to his harness. *Now the hard part,* he thought. Here was where all the hours of grueling exercise to keep his forty-something body in shape would pay off. He hoped.

Arms and feet braced against the wall and the piling, he began inching himself upward, using only the tensing of his muscles as leverage. Known in the mountaineering world as a chimneying, the manuever took supreme concentration. Fisher felt sweat running down his back inside the wet suit. His set his jaw and kept climbing.

Out in the watercourse he heard more splashing. To his left he saw a black wet-suit-covered head break the surface. A flashlight beam played over the pilings. Fisher froze. The beam passed over him, paused for a beat, then two, then three, then moved on. The diver turned and kept swimming.

Fisher pushed himself up the wall a few more feet and looked up. The understructure was within reach. He reached up, grabbed a water pipe, and let his legs swing free.

Somewhere nearby, a radio squelched: "Dock Boss, this is Diver Two-One. Approaching north wall, section nine. I'm going into the pilings. Thought I saw something."

"Roger, Two-One."

The diver had turned back. Hanging perfectly still, Fisher scanned his eyes left. The diver was there, head just above the surface, flashlight playing over the water as he made his way through the pilings toward him.

Quick and quiet, Sam. Go.

He tensed his abdominal muscles, drew his knees up to his chest, then hooked his ankles over the pipe and began inching his body along it until he was tucked tight against it. He looked down. The diver was almost directly beneath him.

With one palm pressed against a neighboring pipe for leverage, Fisher rolled his body until he was balanced lengthwise atop the conduit. He went still again. The diver's flashlight appeared again, closer yet, casting slivers of light and broken shadows through the understructure.

Fisher closed his eyes and willed himself invisible.

Nothing here but us pipes, pal, Fisher thought. *Swim along now.*

After what seemed like minutes, but was likely less than twenty seconds, the diver clicked off his flashlight and finned away. Fisher let himself exhale.

WITH nothing to do until the security sweep was completed and the stand-down order given, he had to choose between sitting still and waiting it out, or doing a little exploring. He decided on the latter.

A quick check of his OPSAT confirmed what he'd predicted: The pier's understructure wasn't included in the dock's blueprints. He scrolled through the schematics to be sure. There was nothing.

He set out.

He crawled along the maze of conduits until he intersected a grated maintenance catwalk. All around him he heard the gurgling of water through pipes, the hissing of steam, and the low hum of electricity. The ceiling, a mere four feet above the catwalk, dripped with condensation and was covered with tiny stalagtites of mineral deposits. In the distance he could hear the crackle of acetylene cutting torches.

He keyed his subdermal: "I'm back."

Grimsdottir said, "Thank God. I was worried."

"Didn't know you cared."

"Dummy. Sam, I don't know what went wrong. I was sure I'd covered the alarm redundancies."

"The curse of modern technology. No harm done."

Lambert said, "Are you in or out? Scratch that; dumb question. What's your status?"

"Doing a little spelunking while they finish their security sweep."

"Okay, stay—"

A voice came over the dock's PA system. Fisher told Lambert, "Wait," then listened: "All hands, security alert stand down. Security Alert Team report to control for debriefing."

Lambert said, "I heard. Stay safe and stay in touch."

Fisher signed off.

Hunched over, occasionally ducking under valve junctions or cloverleafs of piping, he began picking his way down the catwalk. He paused every few seconds to switch his trident goggles to infrared for a quick scan of the area ahead; with the swirling steam, he found the NV unreliable. Aside from the red and yellow heat signatures of the conduits, he saw nothing.

With a screech, a parrot-sized rat scurried across his path and darted down the catwalk. Fisher realized he'd drawn his SC; he holstered it. Constant training made for good reflexes and a lot of almost-dead rats.

After another fifty feet he came to a T-intersection. He switched to IR. Clear. Ahead, the catwalk continued to who knows where; to his right, a ladder rose from the catwalk and disappeared.

Thank God for maintenance hatches.

The ladder was but a few rungs tall and ended at a manholelike opening. He took out his flexi-cam, plugged the AV cable into his OPSAT, waited for the image to resolve on the screen, then snaked the camera through one of the cover's holes.

It took him a moment to realize what he was seeing. A boot; a black leather boot. He froze. Standard Navy-issue Chukka, size 12. He knew the model only too well. He'd worn out three pair during BUD/S, the Navy's six-month SEAL boot camp.

Ever so slowly he eased the flexi-cam back through the hole.

Above him, the sailor's boot was joined by a second. Fisher could smell the tang of cigarette smoke. "They find anything?" the first sailor asked.

"Nah. You know how it is: They always say, 'This is not a drill,' but it almost always is."

"Yeah. So what's the deal with this ship? What's with all the guys in space suits?"

"That's biohazard gear, idiot. The Master Chief says its an exercise, but I don't buy it. I think there's something—"

A grizzled voice interrupted. "You two! Got nothing to do, I see. Follow me. I'll find you something."

"Come on, Chief, we're just taking a break."

"Break's over, ladies. Back to work."

Fisher waited for the count of thirty, then slipped the

flexi-cam back through the hole. The boots were gone. He switched to IR and did a 360 scan. There was nothing. No bodies, no movement.

Using his fingertips, he gently lifted the manhole cover, slid it aside, and crawled out.

8

HE slid the cover back into place, crab-walked four steps to his right, and ducked behind a pallet of crates. Now that the security sweep was over, the dock had returned to normal work lighting. Sodium-vapor lamps hung from cross-girders high in the vaulted ceiling, casting the dock in gray light. Farther down the dock, amid the loading derricks, a group of sailors moved crates around on a hand truck. Here and there he could see the sparkle of welding torches, could smell the sulfer stench of acetylene.

To his right was a familiar sight: the *Trego*. She was moored bow-first toward the dock door. Her deck hatches, portholes, and windows were covered with yellow plastic sheeting and sealed with red duct tape. At the midships hatch a tentlike structure had been erected—the decontamination entry and exit, he assumed. As he watched, a pair of NEST people in white biohazard suits stepped out of the tent. They were met by a trio of similarly dressed figures who began hosing them down with a foamy liquid.

Fisher felt a flutter in his stomach. Grimsdottir had assured him the radiation levels aboard the *Trego* were well below a risky dose, but watching the decontamination procedure made him wary. His harness was fitted with a pen-sized quartz-fiber dosimeter linked to both his subdermal and his OPSAT, so he would get plenty of advance warning if he were taking on a radioactive load. Or so the theory went.

This is why you're paid the big money, Sam, he told himself.

He scanned the dock and the *Trego* in both infrared and night-vision modes until satisfied he knew the positions and movments of all the NEST people, then chose his best route.

Sticking to the shadows, he moved down the dock, heading toward the *Trego*'s stern. Once he drew even with it, he crept to the edge of the dock, grasped the aft mooring line in both hands, and began shimmying his way over the water. Twice he had to pause as biohazard-suited figures shuffled across the deck and through the decon tent, but at last he reached the railing, swung his legs over, and dropped to the deck in a crouch.

He took two quick steps, mounted a ladder on the superstructure, and started climbing.

* * *

HE'D gotten only ten rungs when he heard the scrape of a boot.

He froze, looked down.

Below him, a NEST person was standing at the rail. The man pulled back his hood and titled his head backward, gulping fresh air. A tinny voice called, "Len, where're you at?"

The man pulled a portable radio off his belt and replied, "Main deck. Taking a breather."

"When you're done, come over to starboard midships. I've got a team rotating out. They need a wash down."

"On my way."

The man pulled his hood back in place and walked off. Fisher kept climbing.

ONCE on the superstructure, it took but two minutes for him to find the deck scuttle he was looking for. While a main deck hatch would have provided him a more direct route to the engine room, his penetration of any of the quarantine barriers would not only raise immediate suspicion but also prompt another security sweep.

The scuttle he'd chosen was similarly sealed, but the duct tape separated from the deck's nonstick coating easily. He turned the wheel and lifted. Inside, a ladder dropped into darkness. He did a quick IR/NV scan, saw nothing, then slipped his legs through the opening and started down. He paused to close the scuttle behind him, then dropped to the deck.

"I'm inside," Fisher radioed.

Lambert replied, "According the radio transmissions we've been monitoring, most of the NEST personnel are in the forward part of the ship. Whatever the radioactive material is, it looks like it's somewhere in the bow ballast tank. Grim's updated your OPSAT; the waypoint markers will take you to the engine room."

"Been there before."

Grimsdottir said, "I've analyzed the paths the dock workers have been taking. My route will skirt those areas."

Fisher checked his OPSAT. The *Trego*'s blueprint, shown in a rotatable 3D view, was overlayed with a dotted amber line, starting with his position—shown as a blue square—and ending at the *Trego*'s engine room—shown as a pink square.

"Got it," Fisher replied. "Grim, just so we're clear—"

"You have my word, Sam. The inspectors have to wear those suits. Government regs. Hell, you know better than anyone how persnickety government is. I've done the calculations backward and forward. As long as you're out of there in an hour, you're fine."

And at sixty-one minutes? he thought.

Over the years he'd faced every nightmare an operator can imagine, but like most people, radiation held a special, dark place in his mind and heart. Invisible and virtually inescapable, radiation mutated the human body at the core level, destroying and twisting cells in monstrous ways. He'd seen it up close and in person. It was a horrific way to die.

His mind immediately went to Slipstone. If in fact the town's water supply had been poisoned with some type of radiation, he hated to imagine what the surviving residents were going through: nausea, vomiting, skin burns, hair loss, lungs filling with fluid, accelerated tumor growth. . . .

Eyes on the job, Sam. Deal with what's in front of you.

The bottom line was he trusted Grimsdottir and Lambert with his life and had done so dozens of times before. He would do so again now. "Okay," he said. "I'm moving."

TO avoid interfering with the NEST team's equipment, the *Trego*'s generators had been powered down and switched over to the dock's power grid, so the passageway was darkened, lit only by red emergency lanterns affixed to the bulkhead at ten-foot intervals.

With one eye fixed on the OPSAT and one eye scanning for movement, Fisher padded down the passagway to a T-turn. Right led further aft; left, forward to the bow. He went left. The engine room was eighty feet forward of his position and down three decks. To get there he'd have to navigate five ladders and two deck scuttles.

As he reached the next intersection and started down a ladder, the OPSAT's screen flickered. The *Trego*'s blueprint began to pixelize before his eyes. He pressed himself against the bulkhead and got on the radio: "Who forgot to pay the cable bill? My OPSAT's losing signal."

"Grim was afraid of that," Lambert replied. "The NEST people are degaussing."

Degaussing was a fancy term for demagnetization. Over time, steel-hulled ships pick up a magnetic charge that can interfere with radio and navigation systems. In this case, the charge was making it hard for the NEST inspectors to nail down the signature of whatever material was hidden in the *Trego*'s ballast tanks, so they were using degaussing emitters.

"Switch to internal," Grimsdottir said. "You'll still have the blueprint, but no overlay."

"No problem," Fisher said. "I'll improvise."

HE returned to the head of the ladder and drew his SC-20 from its back holster.

Compact and lightweight, the SC-20 was equipped with a flash/sound suppressor and it fired a standard NATO 5.56mm Bullpup round. That, however, was where similarities to other weapons ended. The SC-20's modular under-barrel attachment gave Fisher an unprecedented array of options, including a gas/frag/chaff grenade launcher; LTL (Less-Than-Lethal) weapons such as ring airfoil projectiles (RAFs) and sticky shockers; an EM (Electro-Magnetic) pod with a laser-based directional microphone, a signal jammer, and a laser port sniffer for at-a-distance data transfers with IR computer ports; SPs (Surveillance Projectiles) such as a self-adhesive remote camera nicknamed, predictably, a "sticky cam," and finally a gadget Fisher had dubbed the ASE, or All-Seeing-Eye, a micro-camera embedded in a tiny parachute made from a substance called aero-gel.

Consisting of ninety percent air, aero-gel could hold four thousand times its own weight and had a surface area that boggled the mind: Spread flat, each cubic inch of aero-gel—roughly the size of four nickels stacked atop one another—could cover a football field from end zone to end zone. In the case of the ASE, its palm-sized, self-deploying aero-gel chute could keep the camera aloft for as long as ninety seconds, giving Fisher a high-resolution bird's-eye view of nearly a square mile.

Unfortunately, tonight, he wasn't likely to need the ASE; he was hoping he wouldn't need the SC-20 at all, but then again, ring airfoils and sticky shockers could turn out to be his best tools should he encounter trouble aboard the *Trego*.

He flipped his NV goggles into place and heard the faint electronic whistle in his earpiece as the they powered up. He scanned the darkened deck below. He saw nothing.

"Proceeding belowdecks," Fisher radioed.

9

WITH the SC-20 held at ready-low, Fisher crept down to the next deck, turned the corner, and headed aft. He was halfway down the passageway when he froze. With exaggerated slowness, he crouched down, crab-stepped to the left, and pressed himself against the bulkhead.

Thirty feet down the passageway he'd seen a pencil-eraser-sized red spot on the bulkhead.

Sensor, he thought. But what type? Infrared, motion . . .

The spot moved. *Not a sensor.* It was the tip of a cigarette. Whether it was a security guard or a NEST person, he couldn't be sure, but someone was leaning against the bulkhead behind a stanchion, taking an illicit smoke break.

Moving on flat feet, Fisher started easing himself backward.

The figure moved, stepping from behind the stanchion. Fisher raised the SC-20 and pressed his eye to the scope.

The man was in a white bioharzard suit, the hood tilted back onto his forehead. On his hip was a model-1911 Colt .45 automatic—standard issue for armed Navy watch personnel.

Other way, sailor. Turn the other way. . . .

The man turned toward Fisher. He went still. His body tensed. He cocked his head, obviously seeing something in the dim light, but not sure what. His hand drifted toward the hip holster.

Fisher fired. The SC-20 coughed, a barely perceptible *thwump*.

The RAF struck high on the man's sternum. He crumpled, unconscious before he hit the deck. Fisher trotted forward and knelt down beside the man. He felt for a pulse; it was strong and steady. While classified as an LTL weapon, a ring airfoil projectile had a punch to it, and Fisher had seen it kill men, usually from a lung clot.

He unholstered the guard's Colt, ejected the magazine, and hid it inside a pipe bundle near the ceiling, then reholstered the gun. If things went to hell, this would be one less gun shooting at him.

He found a dark corner for the guard's body, covered it with a few scraps of discarded cardboard he found nearby, then pulled the man's hood back in place and fired a dart into the man's thigh for good measure.

He doubted he'd need more than the two hours the tranqulizer would buy him, but as with the Colt, if things went to hell, this would be one less guard to deal with.

HE reached the passageway outside the engine room and crouched before the hatch. He switched his goggles to IR, then rose up until he could see through the porthole. Having been powered down for the past eighteen hours, the engine room was a field of dark blue structures broken only by still-warm yellow pipes and the lighter blue outlines of the engines. He saw no one moving about.

He checked his dosimeter reading on the OPSAT: All green. What was the rule with these things? Fisher thought. *Green, good; red, dead.*

He undogged the hatch and slipped inside.

HE found the section of catwalk between the engines just as he'd left it: pried back and tossed to one side. The fire hose he'd used to stop the *Trego* was also still there, a charred and tangled mass wrapped around the reduction gear. Aside from the ticking of cooling pipes and the occasional hiss of steam, the space was quiet.

He heard the metallic *thunk* of a hatch opening. He switched his goggles to NV and turned around. A pair of figures in bio-hazard suits were stepping through the hatch.

". . . I told you: I don't know why," said one of the men. His voice was muffled inside the hood. "The boss wants another reading, so we're getting another reading." He held up a Geiger counter and panned it through the air; it gave off a steady but slow chirping.

"Yeah, well, this place gives me the creeps."

"Join the club. Come on, let's get it done."

They started down the catwalk, circling the space's outer bulkhead. Fisher waited until they were out of sight, then reached up, grabbed a pipe, and lifted his legs off the deck and hooked them over the pipe. He reached again, this time snagging the edge of a ceiling I-beam with his fingertips. He rolled himself onto his belly with his thighs and chest resting across the conduits.

Below, he heard the clunk of the men's footsteps on the catwalk.

The chirp of the Geiger counter grew louder.

Fisher drew his pistol. He thumbed the safety off and switched the selector to DART.

In his peripheral vision, through a tangle of pipes, Fisher caught a glimpse of a biohazard suit coming closer. The men appeared at the head of the catwalk and walked beneath Fisher. They stopped at the open grating. "You have any idea what this is all about?" one man asked.

"Just the rumors. Somebody was in a hurry to stop the ship."

"Well, hell, I'd say they got the job done. No way they're going to be able to cut that outa there. That gear is fried, but good."

"Not our problem." The man passed the Geiger first over the engines and then the grating, then knelt down and checked the fire hose. The chirping remained steady. "I got nothing. Control, this is Peterson."

"Go ahead, Pete."

"Second engine room sweep is done. All clear."

"Good. Come topside. Time for you to rotate out."

ONCE they were gone, Fisher lowered himself back to the deck and slipped feetfirst through the grating. Using the loops in the fire hose as handholds, he lowered himself to the deck, which was ankle-deep in a frothy mix of bilgewater and firefighting foam. The latter had been pumped aboard by the first rescue ship on scene, a Navy destroyer, in hopes of pre-smothering any fires before they had a chance to start. Fire is a ship's worst enemy, and it was deadlier still aboard a ship carrying hazardous materials.

True to the blueprints, he found the *Trego*'s twin-diesel engines mounted atop massive dampening springs. Each spring was the size of a fire hydrant and was secured to the deck by bolts as big around as his wrist and as long as his forearm.

As he'd feared, the tightly packed springs made it impossible to wiggle under the engines, so he pulled out his flexi-cam, affixed the telescoping extension, then snaked the lens underneath. He flipped on the cam's light. The rough metal exterior of the engine casing appeared on the OPSAT's screen. He started scanning, moving inch by inch.

It took three minutes, but finally the serial number plate came into focus. Fisher steadied the cam and hit the shutter button. He withdrew the cam and tucked it away. He keyed his subdermal, but got only a squelch in return. He looked up. *Too much steel overhead*.

He climbed back to the catwalk and retraced his steps to the hatch and into the passageway. He keyed his subdermal again. "I'm out. Got the numbers."

"Good work," Lambert said. "Change of plans. Go to Extraction Point Bravo."

Extraction Point Bravo was the designated emergency pickup.

"What's happened?" Fisher asked.

"We think we know what happened to the rest of the *Trego*'s crew."

10

THE satellite feed had been siphoned from a commerical LANDSAT by an NSA picket station, so the angle was heavily oblique and the colors faded, but there was no mistaking the single ship in the middle of the plasma screen.

"The *Trego*, I presume?" Fisher said.

"The one and only," Lambert replied. "Two hundred miles off the coast of Virginia the morning before your encounter with her. Okay, go ahead, Grim."

Sitting at the other end of the conference table, Grimsdottir tapped a few keys on her laptop and the image changed. A second ship, clearly smaller than the *Trego,* appeared in the upper left-hand corner of the screen. "Now we move ahead thirty minutes. Note the *Trego*'s wake has disappeared. She's sitting dead in the water." She tapped the keyboard again. "Ahead forty-two minutes."

The *Trego* and the second ship were sitting next to one another.

"Ahead twelve minutes. Zooming in."

The image flickered, then zoomed in until the two ships filled the screen. In the water between them Fisher could make out what looked like a Zodiac raft.

"The whole operation took twenty-two minutes," Lambert said. "The Zodiac goes over to the *Trego* with one man aboard. Nineteen minutes it comes back with nine more men."

"The *Trego*'s crew minus one," Fisher said.

"Right. We're guessing the intervening time was used to set up the automation system."

"And to draw straws to see who stays behind. Speaking of which, anything from our prisoner?"

"Still not talking," Lambert said.

Shortly after the man had woken up handcuffed to a bed in Third Echelon's medical bay, Redding had begun questioning him. It was another tidbit Fisher didn't know about Redding: He was in fact a Marine Corps–trained interrogator.

"We're turning him over to the FBI; let them take a crack at him. Okay, back to the *Trego*. Here's what we know: Ten minutes after the *Trego*'s crew boards the mystery ship, they both get under way and part company, the *Trego* heading west toward the Atlantic Seaboard, the other ship heading south."

"Please tell me we know more than that."

Grimsdottir tapped some more keys. Another satellite image appeared. "Welcome to the harbor at Freeport City, Bahamas. Check the center-right of screen. Behold our mystery ship: the oceangoing yacht *Duroc*. She's been anchored there since yesterday. I'm working on the registration."

Fisher stared at the yacht for a few seconds, then turned to Lambert. "When do I leave?"

THIRD Echelon maintained a private airstrip outside Hanover, eight miles northeast of NSA headquarters. It was just past one in the morning when Fisher pulled his car onto to the tarmac beside a Boeing V-22 Osprey.

The Osprey was Third Echelon's workhorse, used for insertion and extraction missions. Billed as a half-helicopter, half-turboprop aircraft, the Osprey had twin engines, each one mounted on a rotatable nacelle, combining the maneuverability and vertical takeoff capability of a helicopter and the high speed and altitude limits of a standard airplane.

The Osprey's rotors were already spinning at idle. Through the lighted cockpit window Fisher could see the pilot, Bird, and his copilot, Sandy, going through the preflight. Bird was a typical Southern boy, with an aw-shucks drawl and a carefree personality to match. Sandy, on the other hand, was all business, one of the first women to break into the typically male-dominated special operations community.

Fisher gathered his duffel bag from the trunk and walked to the rear ramp. He was surprised to see Redding standing at the bottom.

"Didn't know I was going to have company," Fisher said.

"I wasn't getting anywhere with our prisoner, so I thought I'd come keep you out of trouble."

"Will, getting into trouble is what I do for a living."

"How nice for you. I've got some new gear for you. Come on, we've got some air to cover."

ONCE they were airborne and heading south, Redding pulled a black duffel bag from the overhead bin and dropped it on the floor between their seats. Fisher's standard equipment load-out was maintained in several places, the Osprey one of them. Fisher assumed that whatever was in this duffel was brand-new.

Redding unzipped it and pulled out a familiar item: Fisher's tactical suit, a one-piece black coverall fitted with the various pouches, pockets, and harness attachments needed to carry all his equipment. Fisher could see immediately this tac-suit was different.

"First and most important," Redding said, "you're familiar with Dragon Skin?"

Fisher was. Originally developed by Pinnacle Armor, Dragon Skin was the world's first "move when you move" body armor. Lightweight and flexible, Dragon Skin could stop bullets as heavy as an AK-47's 7.62mm. For years DARPA had been working with Dragon Skin–like composites for special operators, but hadn't been able to decrease the weight enough to make it feasible.

"DARPA's figured it out," Fisher said.

Redding nodded. "Meet the Mark V Tactical Operations Suit, code-named RhinoPlate. Weight, four pounds unloaded; thickness, eight millimeters—about a quarter inch. Outer shell is Kevlar; core material RhinoPlate; inner layer is seventh-generation Gore-tex."

"Stats?"

"Good against shrapnel at twelve feet; rifle rounds at fifteen; pistol and shotgun at eight feet. The Gore-Tex is tested to maintain core body temperatures down to fifteen degrees Fahrenheit with the hood up, and as high as one hundred ten. You could go from Alaska to the Sahara and stay relatively comfortable."

"The color's different."

"Good eye. New camouflage. The outer layer of the Kevlar is treated with a polymer fiber similar to the coating on stealth aircraft: matte-black, slightly rough to the touch for maximum light absorption. I won't bore you with the physics, but the micro-roughened exterior partially defuses light. Basically, about thirty percent of whatever photons strike the surface gets trapped—if for only a split second—but enough to diffuse them. Bottom line: You stand still in a shadow, you're virtually part of the shadow."

"And the pouches and harness points? Everything's moved. It looks . . . lumpy."

"Disruptive patterning. We've resized and rearranged them to break up your form."

Mother Nature abhors straight lines. In low-light conditions the human eye tends to seek out movement, color difference, and geometric form. Of the three, movement was the easiest to address: stand still. Color difference was also easy: Black gives the eye little to draw from the background. Form, however, was problematic. The human body is a unique collection of angles and lines easily discernible to the human eye. By rearranging the pouches to various spots on the suit, the familiar outline of the body becomes fuzzy.

Fisher took the suit from Redding and examined it. He nodded. "I like it. One question."

"What?"

"Where do I put my car keys?"

"**OKAY**, one more item," Redding said. "An add-on to the SC-20. Again, I'll spare you the technical stuff. We've nicknamed it Cottonball." He handed Fisher two items: what looked like a standard shotgun shell, and a spiked soft rubber ball roughly the size of marble. "The basic firing mechanism is the same as the sticky shocker and ring airfoil, but with a big difference. Once it's out of the barrel, the sabot breakes away, leaving only the Cottonball. When it strikes a hard object, an inner pod of aerosol tranquilizer is released. The cloud radius is three feet. Anyone inside that will be unconscious in three or four seconds."

"Impressive. Duration?"

"For a hundred-eighty-pound man, a waist-up strike will give you about twenty minutes."

"Accuracy?"

"Plus or minus six inches over fifty feet."

Bird's voice came over the intercom: "Hey, boys, incoming transmission for you."

Fisher tapped his subdermal. "Go ahead," Fisher said.

Lambert's voice: "Your target's gone mobile, Fisher. The *Duroc* just lifted anchor; she's steaming northeast out of Freeport City harbor."

"Destination?"

"Working on it, but we've confirmed she took on provisions the day before, including fuel."

"Probably not a day trip, then. So we either wait for her to put in somewhere, or intercept her under way."

On headphones, Redding said, "Uh, Colonel, we've got a full load-out onboard. I was thinking . . ."

"Skipjack?"

"Skipjack."

Fisher groaned. "Ah, man, I hate the Skipjack."

—11—

"**SEVEN** minutes to target," Fisher heard Bird say in his subdermal. "Descending to five thousand."

"Roger. Give me the ramp, Bird."

"Ramp descending."

With a mechanical groan, a gap appeared along the curved upper lip of the ramp, revealing a slice of dark night sky. Fisher felt a slight vacuum sensation as the pressure equalized. After a few seconds, the ramp was down level with the deck. Through the opening Fisher could see nothing but a carpet of black water and the distant twinkling lights of the Bahamian mainland.

"Ramp down and locked," Bird called.

At the bulkhead control panel, Redding checked the gauges and nodded confirmation.

"Surface conditions?" Fisher asked.

"Sea state one, low chop. Winds five to seven knots from the northeast."

"Give me a two-minute warning."

"Will do."

Redding's voice came over his earpiece: "So, tell me again, Sam: Why do you hate this thing?"

The "thing" in question was a covert insertion vehicle known as a Skipjack. Essentially a one-man IKS (Inflatable Kayak, Small) equipped with a silent electric motor, the Skipjack was enclosed in a bullet-shaped shell of reinforced fiberglass designed to make the IKS aerodynamic, allowing it to be launched from aircraft and skip along the surface at sixty knots before the shell peeled away from the IKS and sank to the bottom.

Insertion is often the diciest part of any mission, especially an airdrop of any kind. Most enemy radar stations, while immediately suspicious of low-flying unidentified aircraft, don't push the panic button until the target dramatically slows down and/or drops from radar for thirty seconds or more, which could, for example, indicate troops fast-roping from a helicopter.

The Osprey, traveling at 125 knots, could drop off radar without reducing speed, eject the Skipjack, and climb back to altitude within twenty seconds. To radar operators that appeared as nothing more than an inexperienced Cessna pilot who'd lost some altitude before correcting.

There were few things Fisher feared, and none of them involved work. His problem with the Skipjack was the seemingly endless twenty or thirty seconds after it was disgorged from the plane. Being strapped like a piece of luggage inside the IKS and unable to control his fate went against his every instinct.

"I don't hate it," Fisher replied. "It's just not my favorite ride."

"Sam, can you hear me?" Lambert's voice.

"Go ahead."

"The FBI's on to the *Duroc*. They've got a team landing in Freeport City in twenty minutes. The Bahamian Navy's got a boat waiting for them."

"How much time do I have?"

"They'll probably intercept within seventy minutes. You need to get aboard, get some answers, and get out before then. Remember, you don't exist—"

"—and we're not doing this. I know. I'll be in touch."

Fisher climbed into the Skipjack, which was locked to the deck by four ratchet straps, and strapped himself in.

Bird called, "Descending through five hundred feet. Target on radar. One minute to drop."

Fisher felt the Osprey bank again as Bird bled off altitude. The drone of the engines changed pitch. Strapped into the IKS with the Skipjack's shell around him, Fisher could only see the outside world through a small Plexiglas view port.

"Where's my target?" he asked.

"We're coming in astern and close to shore. When you hit the water, they'll be a mile off your port bow. Current heading, three-two-zero; speed, eight knots. We're passing through two hundred feet. Hold tight. Go on green."

"Roger, go on green," Fisher replied.

Redding knelt beside the Skipjack, patted Fisher once on the shoulder, then sealed Skipjack's roof over his head. The Osprey's engines went to half volume.

"Eighty feet," Bird called. "Ten seconds."

The Osprey began trembling as its own prop wash reacted with the ocean's surface. Through the port Fisher could see mist swirling around the end of the ramp.

"Five seconds."

Above Fisher's head, the bulb turned yellow.

Then green.

In his peripheral vision he saw Redding pull the master release toggle. Fisher felt himself sliding forward.

HITTING the water was like being rear-ended at a stoplight. He knew it was coming, was braced for it, but still the impact took his breath away. He was thrown forward against the harness as the Skipjack's airspeed went from 125 knots to 80 knots in the space of two seconds. A wave crashed into the view port; then he felt the nose rise a few feet as the Skipjack's aerodyamics took over.

He glanced down. Beside his knee, a rudimentary gauge built into the shell gave him a LED speed readout: 60 knots . . . 55 . . . 48 . . . 42 . . . He peered through the view port. True to Bird's call, a half mile off his port bow he could see the *Duroc*'s white mast light.

37 . . . 33 . . . 25 . . .

Fisher reached forward and grasped the shell-release

lever. He gave it a hard jerk, a full twist, then tucked his head between his knees. The sound of of the shell separation was dinstinct: like a massive piece of sheet metal being rattled as the wind tore away the two halves.

The truth was, he'd lied to Redding. He did hate the Skipjack, and for a very good reason. As with the Goshawk, the Skipjack had started out as a DARPA project. A friend of Fisher's from his Navy days, Jon Goodin, had volunteered to test-drive the prototype. On the first run, the Skipjack's shell had failed to separate properly and one of its edges caught Goodin in the head. He survived, but the impact neatly scalped him, from his forehead to the base of his skull. To this day, Goodin looked as though someone had taken a cheese grater to his forehead.

Fisher waited for the IKS's speed to drop below ten knots, then reached behind him and flipped a switch. With a hum, the electric motor engaged. He adjusted the tiller and turned the nose toward the *Duroc*.

"**DOWN** and safe," Fisher radiod.

"Scalp still in one piece?" Lambert asked.

"Very funny." Fisher had once made the mistake of sharing his misgivings about the Skipjack with Lambert; since then the gibes had never stopped. "Where's the FBI?"

"Just leaving Freeport harbor aboard a Bahamian fast-patrol boat. They'll catch up to you in about fifty minutes."

"By the way, what's my ROE?" Fisher asked, referring to Rules of Engagement.

"Weapons free." No restrictions; lethal force authorized. "But a witness would come in handy."

"I'll do my best."

TWO hundred yards off the *Duroc*'s stern, Fisher pulled
out his binoculars and scanned the decks. Aside from the
mast and navigation beacons, the only visible light came
from the yacht's main salon: A yellow glow peeked from
between the curtains covering the sliding glass doors. As
he watched, a man-shaped figure passed before the curtains, then moved out of view.

Something on the starboard side caught Fisher's eye.
He panned and zoomed in.

A man walked onto the afterdeck, shining a flashlight
as he went. Fisher could clearly see the outline of a gun in
his other hand. *KSC/Ingram MAC-11 submachine gun,* he
thought, recalling the stats. *Firing rate, twenty rounds per
second; standard magazine holds forty-eight*. The MAC-11
was not the most accurate of weapons, but what it lacked
in precision was balanced by sheer firepower.

Fisher keyed his subdermal. "Lambert, better get word
to the FBI: The *Duroc*'s crew is armed."

THOUGH his time was rapidly dwindling, he forced
himself to wait and watch until certain the guard was
alone and on a fixed schedule. Hollywood movies aside,
covert work was as much about patience and preparation
as it was about skulking in the shadows with a knife in

your teeth. Among the dozens of axioms special operators lived by, the Six P's were arguably the most important: Prior Planning Prevents Piss-Poor Performance.

Dying on paper before a mission was preferable to dying in the real world, and attention to detail could save your life. Of course, this didn't fit the romanticized version of covert work most civilians held, but it was reality.

He waited until the guard finished his second round of the decks, then cranked the IKS's throttle to full and sprinted ahead until he was under the *Duroc*'s stern rail. Having rehearsed his movements in his head, Fisher went into action. He tapped a series of buttons on the OP-SAT, engaging the smart-chip in the IKS's engine that would keep the kayak loitering a few hundred yards off the *Duroc*'s stern, then stood up, grabbed the lowermost railing, then started climbing.

AS soon as his foot touched the deck, he heard the salon door sliding open. A shaft of yellow light poured out. A silhouetted figure appeared in the doorway.

Fisher lowered himself onto his belly and eased to his right behind a coil of mooring line. It wouldn't be enough to hide him, he knew, but it would break up his form.

"Hey, Chon, where you at?" the figure called

The language was English, but the accent was not. *Americanized Chinese,* Fisher thought.

The MAC-11-armed guard walked down the side deck. "I'm here. Stop yelling."

"Boss needs a cigarette."

That told Fisher something: The guard probably didn't have a radio, which in turn meant he probably wasn't required to check in with anyone. Good news. If it became necessary, the man's disapperance wouldn't immediately raise an alarm.

The guard fished around in his shirt pocket and handed over a cigarette. "Anything on the police scanner?" he asked.

The first man shook his head. "Nothing on the fire band either. They haven't found it yet."

It? Fisher wondered. He assumed they were talking about Bahamian radio bands. Were they listening for signs of pursuit, or was it something else?

"They will," the other man replied with a chuckle. "Believe me, they will."

Not pursuit, Fisher decided. *Something else.*

The men chatted for a few more seconds, then parted company. The first man went back into the salon and closed the door. The guard turned to the railing and lingered there, staring over the side.

Come on, pal, where're you going?

Fisher drew his pistol and thumbed off the safety.

Five seconds passed. Ten.

The guard drew his flashlight, clicked it on, and started walking toward Fisher.

12

FISHER didn't hesitate. He lifted the pistol and fired. The SC gave a muted cough. The bullet struck squarely in the center of the man's forehead and he crumpled.

Fisher remained motionless, waiting to see if the shot had attracted attention. After thirty seconds, he holstered the pistol and crab-walked to the body. The 5.72mm bullet had left a neat, nearly bloodless hole between the man's eyes. Only a trickle of blood had leaked onto the deck.

Contrary to movie portrayals, this type of nearly bloodless wound was as much the rule as the exception when it came to handguns. In this case, however, Fisher had an edge: His pistol was loaded with low-velocity Glaser Safety Slugs. Prefragmented and loaded with dozens of pellets, each the size of a pencil tip, a Glaser goes in cleanly and then shatters, spreading shrapnel inside the wound.

He quickly frisked the body, found a wallet, a pack of cigarettes, a lighter, and an electronic card key. He kept the wallet and key and tossed the rest overboard. He used the sleeve of the man's jacket to wipe up the trickle of blood on the deck, then manhandled the body to the aft railing and slipped it into the water.

He keyed his subdermal and whispered two words: "Sleeper; clean."

Even with the operational autonomy Fisher enjoyed, Third Echelon was still part of the bureaucratic machine known as Washington, D.C., and Lambert was still required to file after-action reports, including details of how and why lethal force was used.

"Sleeper; clean" translated as "lethal casualty; no complications." "Napper; clean" stood for "nonlethal casualty, no complications." Similarly, the word "mess" meant Fisher's use of force had drawn attention or was likely to. "Wildfire" meant he was engaged in an open gun battle. "Breakline" meant he'd been compromised and the mission was in jeopardy. "Skyfall" meant he was now operating in E&E (Escape and Evasion) mode.

And the list went on. Of course, having been an operator himself, Lambert wasn't a stickler for details, especially when things got hot. "Mind yourself and the mission first," he was fond of saying. "If the paper-pushers want details, they can make some up."

Still, Fisher saw some value in real-time reporting.

Over the years he'd seen a lot of operators die because they'd reacted too fast, had failed to think a step ahead. In this case, even before the guard had turned toward him, Fisher had already decided lethal force was his best choice and there was a low chance it would jeopardize the mission. Even when it came to quick decisions, the Six P's applied.

"Roger," Lambert replied.

"Going to the bridge."

Fisher checked his watch: forty minutes until the FBI arrived.

HE headed down the port-side deck. Over the railing he could hear the hiss of water skimming along the *Duroc*'s hull. He paused, pressed himself against the bulkhead, and lowered into a crouch. He needed a moment to think.

The puzzle of who was behind the *Trego* and Slipstone attacks was rapidly becoming complicated: The *Trego*, true registry and owner unknown, had been manned by a single Middle Eastern man who'd set the ship on a collision course with the Virginia coastline. The conclusion was easy to jump to and, in this case, seemingly correct. But now this, the puzzle piece that didn't fit. So far, the *Duroc*'s crew appeared uniformly Asian—Chinese American, judging by their accents. If the satellite images were correct and the *Duroc* had in fact taken the remainder of the *Trego*'s crew to Freeport City, where did this Chinese crew fit in? And why the Bahamas? And why were they monitoring the fire bands—

Then it struck him: *loose ends*. He should have seen this immediately. He keyed his subdermal. "Lambert, put Grim to work: Unless I miss my guess, the *Trego*'s crew is dead. Executed and buried in a burned-out or burning building somewhere on the island."

"How do you figure?"

"Just adding two and two together. I'll explain later. Just have her monitoring the fire radio bands."

"Will do."

Fisher stood up and crept forward until he could see through the bridge hatch porthole.

Inside, the bridge was dimly lit by bulkhead sconces and a single white light filtering up from what Fisher assumed was the rear interior ladder. A lone man sat in an elevated chair at the helm console. Fisher craned his neck until he could see all of the rear bulkhead, which he scanned until he spotted what he was looking for: an electrical panel.

He drew the SC-20 from his back holster and thumbed the selector to STICKY SHOCKER: LOW. The charge would be enough to paralyze the helmsman for thirty seconds to a minute. He needed the man alive and able to talk.

He reached up and tested the doorknob—slowly turning it until certain it wasn't locked. The helmsman would be instantly alerted when the door opened, and Fisher had to assume he was well trained and ready to sound the alarm. He took a deep breath, then pushed open the door.

Surprisingly, the man didn't turn, but instead laughed. "Man . . . It took you long enough."

What . . . ?

"Where'd you go for the coffee? Peru?"

Now the man turned.

Fisher didn't give him a chance to react. He fired.

The sticky shocker struck the man in the neck, just below the right ear. Fisher heard a faint sizzle. The man stiffened, then slumped over, his torso hanging toward the deck. The man's limbs, still stimulated by the shocker, continued to twitch. His hand thumped rhythmically against the chair leg.

Fisher shut the door, crouched down. He holstered the SC-20 and drew his pistol. *Expecting coffee* . . . As if on cue, he heard the clang of footsteps on the rear ladder. A head rose from the ladder well, followed by a torso. "Hey, Tommy, here's your . . . What the hell are you doing? What's wrong with you?"

The man turned his head. Fisher fired. The man's head snapped to the left and he toppled over. The coffee mug clattered to the deck and rolled away.

Wrong place, wrong time, friend.

Fisher holstered the pistol, hurried forward, grabbed the dead man's collar, dragged him under the nearby chart table, then turned his attention to the helmsman.

He pulled Tommy the helsman from the chair and bound his hands using a flexi-cuff. Tommy groaned, slowly regaining consciousness. Fisher dragged him to the rear bulkhead and propped him up. Tommy's eyes fluttered open. "What's going—"

"If you want to live, stay quiet," Fisher whispered. "Nod if you understand."

"What? What's going—"

Sam slapped him across the face. "Quiet. Nod if you understand."

He nodded groggily.

"Do I have your attention?"

Another nod.

"Let's make sure."

From his calf sheath, Fisher drew his only sentimental weapon, a genuine Sykes Fairbairn commando dagger.

Given to him by an old family friend, one of the original combat instructors at STS 103 — also known as the legendary WWII Camp X commando training school — the Sykes was more than an artifact. Finely balanced and razor sharp, it was arguably the finest special ops knife ever made. And at seven inches, the dagger's double-edge blade and needle-sharp point was the ultimate attention-getter.

Fisher inserted the tip of the Sykes inside Tommy's left nostril and stretched it outward. Tommy's eyes went wide.

"I've got a few questions for you, and one job," Fisher said. "Do you understand?"

Tommy nodded.

"There's a man in charge on this boat. What's his name and where is he? Lie to me and I'll give you a pig snout."

Fisher considered pressing him for more information, but it was unlikely someone at Tommy's level would have the details he needed. Besides, in about thirty minutes, the FBI would be here to squeeze every last bit information from the crew.

"His . . . his name is Lei. He's in the captain's cabin. Down one deck, then forward through the main salon and down the ladder. Last cabin at the end of the passage."

"How many men on board?"

"Six."

Make that three now, Fisher thought. "Can the power to the boat be restored anywhere else but here?"

"Yes, in engine room, but I'm the engineer. It would take a while for anyone else to do it."

"Good. In about a minute I'm going to cut the power. When I do, someone will call up here to ask about it, yes?" The man nodded. "You're going to tell them a circuit blew and that you'll have it back on in a few minutes. Do you understand?"

Tommy nodded.

"If you say anything else, it'll go badly for you." To reinforce his point, Fisher lifted the tip of the Sykes, stretching the man's nostril even more. "Are we clear? You can answer."

"Yes, I understand."

He sheathed the Sykes, then rolled the man onto his belly, grabbed him by the flexi-cuffs, and stood him up. Fisher opened the electrical panel and threw the main breaker. The bridge went dark. He flipped his trident goggles into place and switched to NV.

On the intercom, a faint voice called, "Hey, Tommy, what's going on? We lost power."

Fisher pulled Tommy close and whispered, "Showtime. No mistakes."

The voice said, "Tommy, you up there? Answer, damnit!"

Fisher guided Tommy to the console and keyed the intercom's **TALK** button.

Tommy said, "Give me a minute! A circuit blew. I'll have it back in five minutes."

"Well, hurry it up. I'm sitting on the can in the dark."

Fisher flipped off the intercom. "Was that Lei?"

Tommy nodded. "What now?"

"Now, you get lucky," Fisher replied.

He reversed the Sykes and struck Tommy behind the ear with the haft. Fisher dragged his limp body to the chart table and shoved him under with the other man.

He keyed his subdermal. "Going belowdecks."

13

FISHER started down the ladder, then stopped and returned to the helm console. It took five seconds to find what he was looking for. He keyed his subdermal. "Grim, you there?"

"I'm here."

"I'm looking at a computerized helm console with both a USB and an IR port on the front."

"Excellent," she replied. He could hear the excitment in her voice. *Like a kid at Christmas*. Grim lived for this. "Sync up the OPSAT and I'll scan the system," she said. "Let's see where the *Duroc*'s been."

Fisher punched a few buttons on the OPSAT. The screen replied,

INFRARED PORT INITIATED. READY FOR SYN-
CHRONIZATION.

Fisher aimed the OPSAT at the console's IR port.

LINK ESTABLISHED . . . DATA FILES LOCATED . . .
DOWNLOAD? (Y/N)

Grimsdottir said, "I'm in. Downloading . . . Ah, that's
beautiful . . . look at that. Jackpot."

"Pictures of Brad Pitt?" Fisher asked.

Grim snorted. "God, no. I prefer my men a little
more . . . roughened. And mature."

Oh, really? Fisher thought.

"Okay, I've got it. You can disconnect. There's a lot of
data here, Sam. I'll get started on it."

"Time check?"

Lambert replied. "We're tracking the FBI's boat.
Twenty more minutes and you're out of there."

"Understood."

Fisher took the ladder down one deck. At the bottom
was a single door, which he assumed led into the salon.
To his right was a steel hatch. He pressed his ear to it and
heard the hum of engine noise.

He crouched down and snaked the flexi-cam beneath
the door. The salon was lit only by a few nightlights—
probably run by emergency backup power—but even in
the washed-out glow of NV, Fisher could see the salon
was well appointed: cream-colored Berber carpet, a leather

couch and matching club chairs, and teak wall paneling.

Someone had spent a lot of money on the *Duroc*. Who, though?

He played the flexi-cam around until he spotted a man sitting in the far right chair near the lamp. Feet up, head back, mouth open, newspaper splayed in his lap. Fisher smiled. He loved lazy guards. Made his job so easy. Perhaps this was the right time for a little experiment.

He retracted the flexi-cam, then drew the SC-20 and thumbed the selector to Cottonball. He turned the doorknob and eased it open. He stepped inside, shut the door. The man didn't stir. Fisher picked up a magazine off the coffee table and tossed it onto the man's chest. The man gave a grunt and sat up. Fisher fired.

He heard a soft thump, followed by a faint *pffft*.

The man shook his head as though he'd been slapped, said, "What the—" then slumped sideways in his chair.

I'll be damned, Fisher thought. He hadn't doubted Redding's word, but there was no substitute for real-world testing.

He dragged the man behind the couch, then smashed the two nearby nightlights and keyed his subdermal. "Napper; clean."

Only two left, Fisher thought. The boss—Lei—who was awake and presumably no longer occupied in the main cabin's bathroom, and the last crewman, location unknown. Fisher checked his watch: No time to go looking for him. *Keep moving.*

*   *   *

THERE were four cabins in the salon passage, two to port, one to starboard, and one at the end—the captain's cabin. Facing the door, he found himself grateful he'd frisked Chon the guard. The door's lock was card-key access. There was a downside, though. Like most card-key doors, this one would do two things when the card slid through the reader: flash a green light and give a solid *thunk* as the bolt was thrown back.

Fisher did a check with the flexi-cam. Unlike the salon, the cabin showed no emergency nightlights. In the glow of the NV he could see a figure lying on the queen-sized bed. This was Lei, he guessed. The man's eyes were closed, hands folded across his chest. The cabin was small, perhaps ten feet by twelve feet. If Fisher moved quickly enough, he could reach the bed in less than a second.

Fisher drew his pistol, then took a few seconds to mentally rehearse his entry. He slid the key through the reader and pushed in.

Lei was immediately awake, sitting up in bed, hand reaching toward the nightstand.

Fisher fired once. Lei yelped and jerked his hand back, his hand shattered by the 7.62 slug.

"Next one goes in your eye," Fisher said, shutting the door behind him. "Lay back down. Hands back on your chest."

His face twisted in pain, Lei complied. "Who are you, what do you want?"

"The boogeyman, here to kill you if you move again."

Fisher was impressed. Lei was the boss for good reason.

Most men, shot in the hand, facing a ghostlike apparition, would have been cowed. Not this one.

"You've made a mistake, friend," Lei said. "You don't know who you're dealing with."

"Funny you should say that. Tell me who I'm dealing with."

"No."

Fisher fired again. The bullet slammed into the pillow beside Lei's head.

Lei jerked to one side, but the scowl on his face never wavered.

Very tough. Plan B, then. Fisher had brought an extra flotation vest for this very contingency. They already had one prisoner; two was better. The interrogators could work on Lei's attitude.

"Sit up," he said. "You and I are going on a little trip. Move very slow—"

Fisher heard the thunk of the door latch being thrown. In that instant, as his eyes instinctively flicked toward the door, Lei had moved. His good hand was coming up and around. Fisher saw a blade flashing toward his face. He jerked his head backward, felt the blade slice the space where his neck had just been. The door opened. In his peripheral vision Fisher saw a figure standing at the threshold.

"Run!" Lei shouted. "Blow it! Blow it now!"

Fisher fired. Lei's head snapped back. As he fell backward, Fisher saw a black quarter-sized cavity where Lei's right eye once was.

"Warned you," Fisher muttered, then turned and rushed out the door.

14

BACK in the corridor, he turned and headed toward the ladder just in time to see the crewman's foot disappear from the top step. Fisher raised the pistol and fired, hoping for a lucky leg shot, but it was a half second too late. He started running.

Blow it, Fisher thought. Lei's command could mean only two things: One, destroy something aboard the *Duroc*; or two, destroy the *Duroc* itself. The sinking feeling in the pit of his stomach had him betting on the latter.

But why? And who commanded such respect and/or fear in these men that they would essentially commit suicide? Was it Lei, or someone bigger? Fisher shoved the questions aside.

As he reached the top of the ladder, he heard the forward door bang against the bulkhead. He stopped, pressed himself to the wall. Pistol extended, he slid forward until he could see the doorway. Clear. He sprinted forward, peeked into the corridor. To his left, the engine room hatch was open, revealing a ladder. A flashlight beam was playing across bulkhead below.

Fisher stepped to the hatch and peeked through. A figure was standing on the deck. The man raised his arm. Fisher jerked his head back. Two gunshots rang out. A pair of holes appeared in the corridor bulkhead.

"Give it up," Fisher called. "Whatever you're thinking, don't do it."

No response.

"We can work this out. Just drop your gun—"

Footsteps pounded, then faded away.

Fisher peeked around the corner again, saw nothing. He started down the ladder. At the bottom, to his right, around a stanchion, he saw the glow of the flashlight on the other side of the engine. He stepped to the stanchion, pressed himself to it.

Something clanged. Like sheet metal clattering to the deck. *Access cover,* Fisher thought. *Move, move now!*

Gun raised, he stepped out.

The last crewman was crouched beside the engine, hands fumbling inside an access hatch.

"Stop!" Fisher commanded.

The man turned his head, stared at him for a few seconds, then turned back and kept working.

Fisher fired twice. The man grunted and rolled onto his side. Fisher rushed forward. He kicked the man's gun away. It skittered across the deck. The man, barely conscious, let out a wet, bloody cough and grinned at him. "Too late," he croaked.

Inside the engine's access hatch, a blue LED readout blinked from 10 to 9, then to 8.

Fisher turned and ran.

WITH a countdown running in his head he was up the ladder in two seconds. He turned, charged up the bridge ladder, turned again, and headed for the door.

Five . . . four . . . three . . .

He threw open the hatch, rushed through, sprinted toward the railing, vaulted over it. Behind him, somewhere deep within the *Duroc,* there came a muffled *crump*. Fisher absently thought, *First charge; fuel tanks will follow*. . . .

It took him a split second to orient himself in the air. He looked down. The ocean surface rushed toward him. He curled into a ball, hoping to protect himself from the heat and shrapnel that was coming. Then he was underwater. All went silent.

Resisting the urge to kick to the surface, he flipped over and kicked hard, arms spread in a wide breaststroke. He heard a *whoomp* and felt himself shoved from behind as the shock wave hit him. The air was compressed from his lungs. He started rolling.

When he stopped, he righted himself in the water.

Above his head, the surface glowed orange for a few seconds, then faded. Lungs burning, his every instinct screaming for air, he forced himself to stay submerged. The danger now was pools of burning oil and fuel. If he surfaced into one of them, his lungs would be seared.

His heartbeat pounded behind his eyes and he felt a fuzziness creep into his brain as his body consumed the last molecules of oxygen left in his system.

Wait, he commanded himself. *Wait . . .*

He counted to five, then ten, and then seeing nothing above him, he kicked to the surface. He gulped air until his vision cleared, then looked to where the *Duroc* had been.

There was nothing. Chunks of fiberglass and tiny pockets of burning fuel dotted the surface, but the yacht was gone, sinking toward the seafloor.

To his left he saw a twinkle of light. In the distance, still a few miles away, a searchlight played over the water's surface. *The Bahamian Navy and the FBI to the rescue,* Fisher thought. It was time to leave.

He punched up the IKS's control menu on the OP-SAT and pressed buttons until the screen read, IKS: MODE: HOME TO SIGNAL. He keyed his subdermal. "Lambert, get Bird to the extraction point."

"Status?"

"Mission clean." *No footprints, no evidence, no nothing.*

"Very clean."

"Explain."

"Later. I'm on my way home."

He turned and started swimming.

SHANGHAI

KUAN-YIN Zhao heard a knock on his door, then feet softly padding toward his desk. He knew without looking who it was. *Xun*. His hesitant, mincing steps were unmistakable. Xun stopped before Zhao's desk and stood quietly, waiting.

Zhao's desk was covered in an array of newspapers from London, New York, Moscow, and Beijing. So far, the coverage was remarkably similar. No significant variations. The board was intact, all the pieces and players being taken at face value.

Zhao looked up. "Yes?"

"Message from Lei, sir. They've weighed anchor and are under way. The job is done."

Zhao sighed. Even Xun's voice was weak. The boy was smart enough, with degrees from Oxford and MIT, but he had no *Lān-hút*—no *stones*, as the Americans say. Xun was a distant nephew, one of the few with his family name left alive. *This,* he thought, *is what I am left with.* A boy who had a mind for this business, but no heart for the brutality it required to not only survive, but to rule. Given time, Xun might be a worthy successor to the empire; but time was a precious commodity. During war, time was a luxury you couldn't afford to squander.

"No complications?" Zhao asked.

"No, sir."

Zhao nodded. *Another pawn steps forward, joining the first two, shielding the king.*

"The emergency bands?"

"We're monitoring. The island is small; it shouldn't take long. May I ask, sir. . . ."

"Go ahead."

"What are we listening for?"

"We're listening for the faint scrape of our opponent's piece moving across the board."

"I don't understand."

"You will. Watch and learn."

Zhao waved Xun out. Alone again, Zhao closed his eyes and visualized the board. He imagined his opponent reaching out, fingers hesitating over one piece, before lifting it from the board.

Your move.

15

HAVING only been gone for fifteen hours, Fisher was stunned at what had changed during that time.

The town of Slipstone was lost.

Within minutes of local environmental officials determining that the source of the water supply's contamination was neither natural nor accidental, the small New Mexico town had became the focal point of a massive relief effort, starting with the President's order to activate the Radiological Emergency Response Plan, or RERP.

Assets from every branch of government, from the FBI to the Environmental Protection Agency, from the Department of Energy to Homeland Security, sprang into action, dispatching first-responder teams. Within six hours of the RERP's initiation, Slipstone was quarantined.

Every road, highway, and trail leading to and from the town was put under guard by state troopers. Those residents who had panicked upon hearing the news and hurried to leave the area were quickly rounded up and placed in the mobile quarantine and treatment camp that had been established by the Army's Chemical Casualty Care Division. Unfortunately, this camp was one of the first scenes captured by news cameras: families being unceremoniously marched by biohazard-suited soldiers into a sterile white tent in the middle of the desert. The image sent shock waves across the country as Americans realized their worst nightmare had finally become reality: Terrorists had attacked the U.S. with a radiological weapon.

Meanwhile, the first responders to enter the town, a NEST team, found a greater nightmare waiting for them. Slipstone was a ghost town. Investigation would later show the water supply had been poisoned sometime in the afternoon, shortly before residents finished work and started heading home. Consquently, the streets were mostly deserted, with only a handful of bodies found, most of them in their cars as they had tried to escape the town. The bulk of the corpses were found in their homes, asleep, in front of television sets, in their bathrooms, and, heartbreakingly, sprawled beside the beds of their children, dead where they had fallen trying to reach their children.

Those few residents found alive shuffled through the streets like zombies: glassy-eyed, hair falling out in clumps, blood streaming from their eyes as the radiological poison slowly killed them. Those with any strength left headed toward the edge of town and the quarantine barriers, where they were stopped by state troopers and National Guard soldiers. This, too, was broadcast across the country: ghostly-white Slipstone residents, begging to be allowed to leave, while stone-faced soldiers and police officers forced them back into the hell they knew was killing them.

IN the Situation Room, Fisher watched, stunned, as the images paraded across the monitors. Across the country every broadcast and cable television channel, from the Food Network to Home Shopping Central, had either switched to emergency programming or had surrendered their signals to cable and network news coverage.

Sitting on either side of Fisher at the conference table, Grimsdottir and Lambert also watched in silence. Anna stifled a sob, then stood up and walked away.

"Good God," Lambert muttered.

"How many?" Fisher asked. "Any idea?"

"Official figures won't be released for a couple days, but Grim's been monitoring the RERP's secure frequencies. So far they only found fourteen survivors."

"Out of how many?"

"According to the last census, five thousand plus."

It took a moment for Fisher to absorb this number. He exhaled and pinched the bridge of his nose. Unless the response teams were wrong and somewhere, somehow, there was a large group of survivors yet to be found in Slipstone, the death toll would far surpass that of 9/11.

"What's happening in Washington?" Fisher asked.

"Both the House and Senate are in emergency session. The vote will be unanimous, I'm sure."

"Declaration of war," Sam murmured.

Lambert nodded. "Against nations unknown. The President is scheduled to talk to the nation at noon, our time."

"What does this do to our mission?"

"Nothing. I spoke with the President while you were in the Bahamas. War is coming; there's no way around that. Against who is the only question. He wants no stone left unturned, and no doubt about who's responsible. Things are starting to snowball at the FBI and CIA now. Conclusions will be reached; recommendations made; targets chosen. Our job is to make sure—damn sure—we've got the right targets."

The television screens went dark. Standing behind Fisher, Grimsdottir laid the remote on the table and said, "I can't watch this anymore. I can't, I'm sorry."

"It's okay, Anna," Lambert said. "Tell us about the *Duroc*."

"Right . . ." She went to the table and paged through a folder, then selected a file. "Here. I haven't had any luck tracing an owner, but based on the data Sam downloaded from the helm console, I know where she came from: Port St. Lucie, Florida. Shouldn't take too long to narrow down a list."

A phone on the table trilled. Lambert picked it up, listened for a few minutes, then replaced the receiver. "Good call on the Bahamian fire bands, Sam. Twenty minutes ago the local police found nine bodies inside a burned-out coffee warehouse outside Freeport City. We should have preliminary autopsy results in a few hours."

"That explains what happened to the *Trego*'s crew, but not how the *Duroc* got involved. The one prisoner we've got is Middle Eastern and I'm betting those nine bodies will be, too."

"The question is," Grimsdottir asked, "why were they picked up, then executed by a yacht full of Chinese? What's the connection?" Nearby, her computer workstation chimed. She walked to it, sat down, and studied the screen for a few moments. "Gotchya," she muttered.

"Got what?" Lambert asked.

"Remember the virus from the *Trego* laptop? Well, I knew its code was unique—the work of a pro. It took a while, but our database found him: Marcus Greenhorn."

"Please tell me you know where he is," Lambert said.

"I'll do even better than that, Colonel. I'll give you his room number."

16

WHILE Sam had never heard of Marcus Greenhorn, both Grimsdottir and Lambert assured him Greenhorn was as dangerous as any terrorist—so much so he'd earned himself a spot on the FBI's Ten Most Wanted List.

A mathematical prodigy who graduated from high school at age seven, from Princeton at ten, and MIT at fourteen, Marcus Greenhorn, now twenty-two, had at the age of eighteen nearly handed a nuclear weapon over to Iranian-backed Hamas extremists, having used his cyber-wizardry to hack into the Air Force's security grid and steal access codes to the Kirtland Underground Munitions Storage Complex in New Mexico, home to a plethora of nuclear warheads, including the W56 Minuteman II and the W84 GLCM, or Ground Launched Cruise Missile.

Brilliant as he was, Greenhorn fell victim to a pedestrian flaw—greed. After collecting his half-million-dollar advance from Hamas, Greenhorn had turned around and tried to extort the U.S. government, promising to turn over details of Hamas's planned raid on Kirtland for two million dollars. While Greenhorn's skills were impressive, they weren't a match for the full and focused effort of the National Security Agency, which tracked the extortion demand back to Greenhorn, extracted the details of the Hamas raid from his computer, then proceeded to wipe clean the Swiss account he'd set up for his early retirement.

Broke, on the run, and hiding from his disgruntled Hamas customers, Greenhorn had gone underground and become a cyber-mercenary.

Since that incident, the authorities had kept Greenhorn's former friends and compatriots under electronic surveillance, but to no avail. Until now.

"This virus he wrote for the *Trego* laptop is pure Greenhorn," Grimsdottir said, "but with a twist—a bit of security code he's used once too often. I took the code and turned the mainframe loose on all the e-mails we've intercepted from Greenhorn's old friends. We got a hit."

"Explain," said Lambert.

"We ran the same encryption protocols in Greenhorn's virus through all the e-mail intercepts. It seems one of Greenhorn's ex-girlfriends has been getting love letters—all disguised as spam: mortgage offers, discount pharmacies . . . the usual stuff. Well, yesterday this woman got an e-mail from Greenhorn. Decrypted, it read, 'Ticket waiting for you at airport. Meet me, Burj al Arab. Champaign and caviar.'"

"Where's Burj al Arab?" Lambert asked.

Fisher answered. "Not where—what. The Burj al Arab is a hotel—probably the most luxurious resort on the planet. It's in Dubai."

Lambert squinted at him. "How do you know this?"

Fisher shrugged, offered a half smile. "Guy's got to vacation somewhere, doesn't he?"

"Well, consider yourself on vacation. Bring me back a souvenir."

DUBAI, UNITED ARAB EMIRATES

THE taxi pulled over and Fisher paid the driver and climbed out. Though in mission prep he'd read every piece of literature and memorized every drawing and schematic, seeing the Burj al Arab in person took his breath away, as did the heat, which, despite it not yet being noon, had risen to ninety degrees Fahrenheit.

Sitting on a palm-lined, artificial island a quarter mile offshore, the hotel was connected to the mainland by a raised two-lane bridge bordered by high guardrails and secured at each end by a gate manned by a pair of armed guards. At sixty stories and 1,053 feet, the curved, stark white Burj al Arab was not only the tallest hotel in the world, but also the most lavish, featuring a six-hundred-foot-tall atrium, a helipad, a rooftop tennis court, suites with more square footage than the average person's home, personal butlers, and chauffeur-driven Rolls-Royces.

Designed by its architects to resemble a giant, wind-filled sail, the hotel's impact was dramatic, both at a distance and up close. Taking it in, Fisher's eyes and brain were momentarily tricked into believing they were watching a clipper ship gliding into port.

And a security system second to none, Fisher thought, snapping off a photograph. He wasn't alone in his gawking. Dozens of tourists stood at the head of the bridge shooting pictures over the heads of the smiling, white-shirted guards. The Burj al Arab's reputation as a prime Middle Eastern tourist attraction made Fisher's surveillance much easier.

While he'd been in the air, Grimsdottir had been doing her own reconnaissance, albeit of the cyber variety. According to the Burj al Arab's mainframe intranet, Marcus Greenhorn was staying in the three-thousand-square-foot, six-thousand-dollar-per-night penthouse suite. And he wasn't alone. Aside from his girlfriend, who had arrived the previous day, Greenhorn was being attended by no less than five bodyguards supplied by the Emir himself and drawn from the ranks of UAE special forces troops known as Al-Mughaaweer, or "The Raiders."

This told Fisher two things: One, whoever Greenhorn was working for had unparalleled influence in the Middle East; and two, his own penetration of the Burj al Arab had just become an even tougher proposition.

He checked his watch. Three hours till nightfall.

* * *

THE lack of security boats patrolling the waters around the hotel spoke volumes about either the security staff's laziness, or its confidence in the internal security system. Fisher assumed the latter, and this was backed up by his final call to the Situation Room.

"I've download the hotel's blueprints and schematics to your OPSAT," Grimsdottir said. "I'm not going to lie to you, Sam, it's ugly."

"Define ugly."

"Redundancies upon redundancies. I'm hacked into their security grid, but in most cases I'll only be able to bypass alarms and sensors for twenty seconds before backup systems kick in. When I say 'move,' you'll have to move fast. When I say 'freeze,' you'll have to freeze."

"I'm at your command."

Lambert said, "Sam, I've confirmed your equipment drop. Just follow the GPS marker and dive straight down."

Given the nature of the target, he and Lambert had agreed a typical insertion method was a nonstarter. The hotel was kept under watch by a nearby Naval radar station, which meant any air approach would draw the attention of UAE fighter-interceptors. Even without that complication, Fisher wasn't confident about parachuting in. The winds around the hotel were volatile and the rooftop small. If he missed the target, he'd find himself in a one-thousand-foot free fall.

That left only one option: underwater. To that end, earlier that day the CIA's deputy station chief in the Dubai consulate had been sent on a fishing trip up the coast from the Burj al Arab, where he'd dropped a weighted duffel containing Fisher's equipment load-out.

"How far down?"

"Twenty-five feet, give or take. Nothing for you."

Years earlier Fisher had taken up open-ocean free-diving, in which divers hold their breath and plunge to depths ranging from one hundred to four hundred feet. Initially attracted to the sport by simple curiosity, Fisher had immediately found himself hooked by not only the physical challenges—which were substantial—but also the mental ones. Free-diving was the ultimate test of one's ability to focus the mind and control fear.

"It's never the dive, Colonel, it's the ascent."

Getting in was only half the battle; getting out, the other half.

17

AN hour after the sun dropped below the horizon, Fisher left his hotel and took a taxi to Dubai's nightclub district, where he got out and strolled around until certain he hadn't been followed. Then, following his mental map, he walked two blocks west to the shore. A quick check with his mini-NV monocular showed no one on the beach. He walked to the tide line.

To his left, a mile away, the Burj al Arab was ablaze, lit from within by amber light and from without by strategically placed green floodlights shining up against the snow-white exterior. As designed, it looked like the massive, glowing sail of a clipper ship resting on the ocean's surface. On the rooftop, Fisher could see ant-sized tennis players scurring back and forth under the glare of stadium lights. The sky was clear, but the stars were dulled by the pollution of nearby refineries and wells.

He checked his watch's built-in GPS readout: He was where he needed to be.

He took a final look around, then sprinted ahead, and dove into an oncoming wave.

FOLLOWING the GPS, he reached the correct spot after only a few minutes' swimming. He took a breath, flipped himself into a pike dive, and kicked to the bottom. The coordinates were dead on. As he neared the bottom, a pulsing red strobe emerged from the gloom. He reached out. His hand touched rubber.

He stipped off his civilian clothes, under which he was wearing his tac-suit, then, working from feel alone, he unzipped the duffel and found the rebreather's face mask. He placed it over his face and tightened the straps until he felt it seal on his skin, then pressed the bleed valve and blew out a lungful of air, clearing the mask. He sucked in a breath. He heard a hiss, which was quickly followed by a bitter taste on his tongue as the rebreather's chemical scrubber started working. He felt the flow of cool oxygen entering his mouth.

Next came the rebreather's harness, his fins, and weight belt. Finally, he strapped the OPSAT to his wrist, the pistol to his leg, and slid the SC-20 into its back-holster.

He clicked on his face mask's task light, and was surrounded by a bubble of soft red light. He clicked it off, then keyed his subdermal. "Comm check."

"Read you loud and clear, Sam," said Grimsdottir.

"Heading to insertion point."

AFTER twenty minutes, Fisher's first indication he was nearing his target was the sound—a distant roar and a low-frequency rumble in his belly. He checked the OPSAT's readout: four hundred yards to go.

Having ruled out an airdrop, Fisher had chosen what he felt was the Burj al Arab's most vulnerable point: its water supply. Rather than rely on the mainland for fresh water, the Burj al Arab's architects had equipped the hotel with its own desalinization and pump stations, which were supplied by massive, propeller-driven intake ducts, two of them embedded in the island's concrete foundation. According the schematics, each duct was as big around as a bus and driven by propellers worthy of a battleship. Working together, the intakes fed enough salt water into the desalinization/pump stations to supply the guests and staff with fresh drinking and bathing water while maintaining the fire-suppression systems at the same time.

There was a hitch to his plan, however: getting through one of the intake ducts without being chopped into chum. His first hurdle wouldn't be the propeller blades themselves, but rather the protective mesh screen on their outside. Still, that was little comfort. If he lost control and found himself trapped against the mesh, the force would pull him through like tomato sauce through a sieve.

"I'm a quarter mile out," he reported.

"Watch yourself," Lambert said. "Keep an eye on your current gauge. By the time you feel those pumps drawing you in, it'll be too late."

"Got it."

He swam on.

HE kept a steady pace and a steady watch on his OPSAT, checking his Distance-To-Target against Speed-Through-Water.

DTT: 310 METERS/STW: 2.8 MPH . . .
DTT: 260 METERS/STW: 2.8 MPH . . .
DTT: 190 METERS/STW: 2.8 MPH . . . STW: 2.9
MPH . . . STW: 3.0 MPH . . .

"My speed just increased," Fisher reported. Still six hundred feet away and the intakes were already creating their own riptide. Fisher felt the prickle of fear on his neck. With each foot he drew closer, the more he would pick up speed.

"Stop kicking," Grimsdottir ordered.

"Already have." In the few seconds they'd been talking, his speed had increased to 4.5 mph—on land, a slow jog; in water, a fast clip.

He clicked on his light and looked down. A few feet below his belly, the seabed was rushing by, a dizzying blur of white sand and rocks. At this rate, he'd hit the intake screen at twenty mph. He clicked off his light. *Don't think; just do.*

"Grim, anytime you want to shut them down is fine with me."

"Relax, I've run the simulations backwards and forewards."

Fisher checked his OPSAT: DTT: 90 METERS/STW: 10.2 MPH . . .

"Hold it . . . hold it . . ." Grimsdottir said. "Remember, Sam, I can loop a system casualty for at most seventy-five seconds before the backups kick in. Twenty seconds after that the intakes will be back up to full power."

"Got it."

DTT: 60 METERS/STW: 16.8 MPH . . .

"Hold it. . . . Now! Shutting down!"

Immediately, Fisher heard the roar of the intakes change pitch and begin to wind down. He felt the riptide loosen its grip on his body. The OPSAT readout scrolled down from fifty meters, to thirty, then twenty. His speed dropped past eight mph.

He reached up and switched on his task light.

Suddenly, the mesh screen was there, a massive grid-like wall emerging out of the darkness. Fisher kicked his legs out just in time for his fins to take the brunt of the impact. Still, the draw of the current was strong enough to plaster him face-first against the mesh. Through it, cast in the red glow of his light, the propeller was slowly winding down, each blade a massive scmimitar-shaped shadow.

Fisher let out the breath he'd been holding.

Grimsdottir's voice: "Sam, you there?"

"I'm here."

"The clock is ticking. Backups will start coming back on-line in fifty seconds."

From his waist pouch Fisher withdrew an eight-foot long cord. Nearly identical to the burn-ties he'd used during his penetration of the Newport News shipyard, this cord was coated with a water-resistant adhesive.

He mashed the cord against the mesh in a rough circle, then jammed his thumb into the chemical detonator and backed away. Two seconds passed. The oval-shaped flash of white light lasted eight seconds. When the bubbles cleared, Fisher finned ahead, hand outstretched, and grabbed the severed section of mesh. He gave it a quick jerk and it came free. He tossed it away.

"Time check," he said.

"Forty seconds."

He swam through.

18

ONCE through the gap, Fisher instantly realized they'd all misread the schematics for the ducts. Unlike a ship's propeller, where each blade was mounted alongside its neighbor on the shaft, here they were mounted one behind the next lengthwise along the shaft, like threads on a screw. Worse still, looking down the shaft, he counted eight blades rather than four. The setup made sense, he realized, given their purpose was to provide suction, not propulsion.

"Got a problem here," Fisher radioed. "How much time?"

"Thirty seconds."

He grabbed the edge of the first blade and pulled

himself beneath it, then finned ahead, weaving and ducking his way beneath and over blades two, three, four, five.

"Fifteen seconds, Sam."

Beside him, the barrel-sized shaft emitted an electronic buzz, then a series of steel-on-steel clanks as the propellers gears began to re-engage. He ducked under blade six, then veered right and arched his body, feeling the trailing edge of the blade seven scrape his thighs.

"Eight seconds . . . seven . . . six . . ."

He put all his strength into his legs and kicked. He felt rather than saw the propellers begin to move, as though he'd been shoved from behind by a crashing wave.

"Starting up . . . power's at twenty percent."

"I'm through."

"Don't slow down. The maintenance shaft is fifty feet down the tunnel. Should be a circular opening in the roof. It won't be marked; you'll have to feel your way. If you don't reach it in time—"

"I know, I remember." *Into the desalinization tank for boiling*.

"Power at fifty percent."

Already, the roar of the propellers was nearly deafening. Beyond his mask he saw only froth. He angled his body upward. His outstretched hand touched corrugated metal.

"Power at seventy-five percent," Grimsdottir called. "There should be a ladder jutting from the maintence shaft, Sam. Coming up quick now . . . Thirty feet . . . twenty-five . . ."

With his hand thumping over the ribbed steel of the roof, Fisher had sense of his speed. He switched on his light, hoping to catch a glimpse of the ladder as it approached, but the swirling bubbles had reduced visibility to zero. He switched off the light. He'd have to do it by feel and reflexes alone.

"Fifteen feet . . . You're dead on track, Sam. Almost there . . ."

For a split second the froth cleared and he caught a glimpse of something, a horizontal steel bar. He latched onto the rung with both hands and was jerked to a sudden halt. Pain shot through his wrists, up his arms, and exploded in his shoulder sockets. His legs, fully caught in the slipstream, felt impossibly heavy. One of his fins was ripped from his foot, then the next.

Climb, Sam, climb!

He reached up, hooked his hand on the next rung, and pulled. Then again, and again. The draw on his legs lessened. He kept climbing, one rung at a time, until suddenly, his head broke into a pocket of air. Just as abruptly, the drag on his legs disappeared.

He took in a few lungfuls of air until his heart rate settled; then he clicked on his task light and looked down. A few inches below his bottom foot, the water in the duct was rushing by as though driven by a fire hose—which, in essense, it was.

He keyed his subdermal: "I'm in the shaft, all limbs and digits accounted for."

"Good work, Sam," Lambert replied.

"Any alarms, change of routine?"

Grimsdottir said, "None. I'm tapped into the hotel's security and maintenence frequencies. They read the intake shutdown as a routine glitch. Check in when you reach your first waypoint. That's where the real fun begins."

"Roger."

It took some patience in the tight confines of the shaft to remove his rebreather harness and weight belt and get them hooked on the ladder, but after a few contortions he got it done. Though he didn't plan to exfiltrate the hotel the same way he'd come in, he knew better than to assume anything. Having his gear here would give him insurance against not only Murphy's Law—"If it can go wrong, it will go wrong"—but also what he'd come to think of as Fisher's Law: "The road of assumptions is lined with coffins."

HE climbed to the top of the ladder, then spun the locking wheel, and lifted the hatch just enough to slip the tip of the flexi-cam through. The lens revealed what he'd expected: the hotel's maintenance center. Dimly illuminated by fluorescent shop lights spaced down the length of the ceiling, the space was roughly one hundred feet long by fifty feet wide. The walls were lined with banks of monitoring consoles and framed blueprints. Down the center of the room stood row after row of floor-to-ceiling shelving for the odds and ends it took to keep the hotel running, from the smallest of screws to new showerheads to cleaning supplies and paint. Here and there were stacks of crates containing what he assumed were larger items like motors, pumps, electrical switch panels.

After the roar of the intake tunnels, the maintainence room seemed eerily quiet, with only the occasional crackle of radio static and a faint electrical hum to break the silence. He panned the flexi-cam around. At the far end he saw a forklift pass between a row of shelves and disappear. Aside from that, he saw no movement. He wasn't surprised. At this time of night the maintainence shift was likely run by a skeleton crew. Unfortunately, the same couldn't be said for the security staff. According to Grimsdottir, it was fully manned twenty-four hours a day.

He switched to EM, or Electro-Magnetic, view and looked for odd signatures that would indicate sensor grids or cameras. There was nothing. He withdrew the flexi-cam.

"Okay, Grim, I'm not reading any cameras or sensors."

"Confirmed," she answered. "There's nothing until you reach the outer corridor."

"Roger, I'm moving."

He lifted the hatch, climbed out, closed the hatch. He paused in a crouch, waiting and watching. The fluorescent lights, which were likely fully lit during the day, had been switched to half-power. The walls and shelving units were cast in shadow.

He sprinted to the nearest wall and flattened himself against it, then slid to his right, eyes scanning the room, hand resting on the butt of his pistol. His other hand touched steel. He knew without looking it what it was.

"I'm at the main door," he radioed.

"First camera is twenty feet down the corridor. It's on a ten-second span, no thermal, no NV."

"Waiting for your mark," Fisher whispered.

"Ready . . . ready . . . Go!"

He turned the knob, swung open the door, and slipped into the corridor.

19

BURJ AL ARAB

HE stepped into the corridor and pressed himself to the far wall. The first camera was twenty feet down the hall, high on the wall. Like the maintenance room, the corridor's lights were dimmed for the night shift. Small halogen bulbs cast pools of light along the seam between the wall and the ceiling.

He started sliding, eyes fixed on the camera as it finished its scan and began turning back toward him. There would be a blind spot directly beneath the mount. He kept moving: step, slide, step, slide. . . . The camera reached its midpoint. The lens caught a glimmer of halogen light and winked at him. He could hear the hum of the pivot motor.

He stepped beneath the camera mount and froze. "At camera one," he radioed.

There was an art to the proper use of surveillance cameras, and luckily for him most security personnel either didn't understand the nuances of it, or were too lazy to bother with it.

Cameras that provided overlapping coverage were usually calibrated one of three ways: synchronized, offset, and random offset. Synchronized was just that, cameras moving in unison; offset staggered camera movements to better cover gaps; random offset used computer algorithms to provide full-area coverage combined with unpredictable movement.

The most common and the easiest to defeat was synchronized, followed by offset. Random offset was a nightmare—and of course this was the method the Burj al Arab employed. Here, in the narrow confines of the hallway where the camera spans were restricted, the problem was negligible, but later, as he penetrated deeper into the hotel, it would require some finesse.

"Blueprint overlay on your OPSAT," Grimsdottir replied. "I've worked out the algorithim patterns. Just follow your traffic lights."

Sam checked his screen: His next waypoint was a supply closet between this camera and the next. He was tempted to watch the cameras, but he kept his eyes fixed on the OPSAT. On the blueprint, the hall cameras were depicted as solid yellow triangles; as each camera panned, the triangles changed colors—red for stop, green for go.

When the camera above and the next one down turned green, he trotted forward. As he drew even with the supply closet door, it opened and a guard stepped out. He saw Fisher and opened his mouth. Fisher thumb-punched him in the larynx and his mouth snapped shut with a gagging sound. Fisher shoved him back into the closet, followed, and slammed the door shut behind him.

Clutching at his throat, the guard backed into the wall and stood there gasping. Fisher drew his pistol and aimed it the man's chest. "The pain will pass. When it does, if you shout, I'll shoot you. Do you understand?"

The guard nodded and croaked out what sounded like a "yes."

Fisher let him recover, then said, "Turn around."

"Are you going to kill me?"

"Do you want me to kill you?"

"No, please . . ."

"Then turn around."

The guard did so. Fisher keyed his subdermal and said to Grim, "I've got a voice for you."

"I'm ready."

Fisher pressed the pistol against the nape of the guard's neck, then reached over his shoulder and held the OPSAT before his mouth. "Say something."

"What do you want me to say?"

In Fisher's subdermal, Grimsdottir said, "Got it." To the guard, Sam replied, "Just that. It's nap time, pal." Fisher thumbed the pistol's selector to DART and shot the guard in the back of the neck. The man let out a groan and toppled forward onto his face. "Napper; clean," Fisher reported.

What the guard had just given Grimsdottir was a voice print she could now match to the backlog of recordings she'd been collecting from her eavesdropping on the hotel. Though a painstaking process, having a mosaic voice print to play back to the security center would keep anyone from missing an incapacitated guard. For the remainder of the mission, this guard, though unconscious on the floor, would continue to report in as required.

Fisher frisked the guard, but found only pocket litter and a key-card ID badge, which was useless to him. The hotel's roving patrols were assigned sectors; if this guard's badge was used anywhere outside his sector, the alarm would be raised.

He rolled the guard's body into a corner and covered it with a pile of painter's tarps. He rechecked his OPSAT, then walked to the closet's opposite wall, felt around until he found what he was looking for, and pried back a hidden access panel, revealing a crawl space roughly two feet by two feet. He crouched down and stared down the length of it.

"Waypoint two," he radioed.

He crawled inside.

TRUE to the schematics, his NV and IR checks of the crawl space revealed neither cameras nor sensors, and after twenty feet the tunnel ended at a second access hatch. He worked the release pins, then carefully set aside the hatch, crawled through, and pressed himself against the wall. He replaced the hatch and glanced upward. Twelve feet above his head a camera hummed, slowly turning on its mount.

He was now at the lowermost level of one of the Burj al Arab's six elevators—one of only two that remained inside the structure during their ascent. The other four left their interior shafts at the lobby level and rose along the hotel's exterior, providing breathtaking views of Dubai, the Persian Gulf, and to the north, Iran.

He stared up the one-thousand-plus feet of the shaft. Lit only by maintenance lights spaced every ten feet, the shaft itself seemed like a skyscraper rising into the night sky. The optical illusion gave him a momentary wave of vertigo. He shook it off and keyed his subdermal. "Waypoint three. Calling the elevator."

"Roger," Grimsdottir replied. "Remember, Sam, you'll only have twenty seconds."

"Yep."

The dozens of cameras located throughout the shaft were equipped with NV, laser-based beam sensors, and infrared cameras. If something moved or gave off heat, it would be detected. Knowing his chances of successfully climbing one thousand feet of elevator shaft while playing cat-and-mouse with the sensors were nil, he'd turned to another rule from the special operators credo: KISS. Keep it Simple, Stupid.

In this case, the simple solution came from the secret vaults of DARPA. Like most DARPA inventions, this one had an official moniker that involved a lot of incomprehensible letters and numbers, and like most DARPA inventions it also had a nickname: Shroud.

Essentially a heat-dissipating and radar-reflective blanket, the Shroud could for short intervals defeat infrared cameras and sensors. There was a catch, however. The user had to remain perfectly still and the coverage lasted only sixty to seventy seconds before his body heat overwhelmed the Shroud's dissipaters.

Fisher scrolled through the OPSAT's menu until he reached a screen showing an overhead view of six squares surrounding a central, larger square—the hotel's six elevators and, at the center, the hotel itself. He tapped one of the squares.

//ELEVATOR: NORTHEAST TWO//
//STATUS: IDLE, LEVEL 14//
//CALL TO THIS LEVEL? Y/N

Sam punched "Yes," then entered his floor number.

Two hundred feet up the shaft he heard a distant buzz, followed by a metallic clank as the car's gears engaged. An electrical whirring filled the shaft.

//NORTHEAST TWO DESCENDING//

As the car dropped toward him, the maintenance lights blinked out one by one as the car passed each floor. Moments later, the car appeared out of the darkness, slid smoothly past his face, and stopped.

"Ready to ride," Sam radioed. "Work your magic, Grim."

"Stand by."

Seven thousand miles away, Grimsdottir would be at her computer, threading her way through the hotel's security intranet and loading her own algorithm and taking temporary control of the shaft's cameras.

This was the one and only drawback of security cameras running in random-offset mode. Guards in the security center had no point of reference, no way of knowing whether the cameras were moving as designed, or had been hijacked. It would only be after a camera failed to provide three circuits of complete coverage that the computer would detect the error and sound the alarm. He would need twenty seconds, no more, to get into position.

"Got 'em," Grimsdottir said.

Fisher stood with his back against the wall, then reached over his head, grabbed the edge of the car's roof, and chinned himself up. From one of his tac-suit pouches he withdrew the Shroud, unfolded it, then slipped his left hand and both feet into the hemmed pockets, drawing it taut across his back. He laid himself flat on the car's roof. With his free hand, he scrolled the OPSAT screen:

//ELEVATOR: NORTHEAST TWO//
//STATUS: IDLE, LEVEL SUB ONE//
//CALL TO THIS LEVEL? Y/N

Sam punched in "Yes," then "59." The Shroud wouldn't conceal his body heat long enough to reach the penthouse level; he'd have to do last floor the hard way.

"Ready, Grim," Fisher said.

"Releasing cameras to hotel control."

With a slight shudder, the car started upward.

20

AS the car rose, Fisher slowed his breathing and con-
centrated on remaining still. In his mind's eye, he imagined the guards in the hotel's security center watching a
split monitor showing both NV and thermal views. The
Shroud would give nothing back, a perfect square of
darkness on the car's roof.

Unless, Fisher thought. Unless his foot was sticking
out, or the Shroud had failed, or—

Stop, he commanded himself.

The world was full of "unlesses" and "what ifs." The
trick was to control what you could, try to influence what
you might, and let the rest go.

On the OPSAT's screen, he watched the floor numbers
scroll upward: 25 . . . 26 . . . 27. Next to these numbers

were the words "Seconds to Shroud Failure" followed by a clock scrolling down: 50 . . . 49 . . . 48 . . .

With one eye fixed on the readout, he rehearsed the next phase in his head. To get past the last floor would require timing, patience, and stamina. Fisher felt a smile play over his lips. Just the kind of challenge he liked. *Careful, Sam.*

Just as getting killed or captured was one of the hazards of his line of work, so too was adrenaline addiction. Living life balanced on the razor's edge was a powerful drug, and without constant self-discipline, the pursuit of that drug could ruin an operator. At his age and given his level of experience, Fisher had for the most part insulated his mind to the lure of adrenaline, but it was always there.

Especially now, especially given the stakes.

He had little doubt the United States was marching toward war. Only one question remained; against whom? The *Trego*'s aborted collision with the Atlantic Seaboard, combined with the rapidly rising death toll in Slipstone, would not go unavenged. So far, all signs of guilt pointed toward a Middle East player. Whether an extremist faction, a terrorist group, or a nation was responsible mattered little; in the coming weeks and months, many lives would be lost. It was Third Echelon's job to make sure the right blood was shed. Fisher felt the mental weight of it.

Questions over what he'd found on the now-destroyed *Duroc* plagued him. It seemed clear the yacht had picked up the *Trego*'s crew, transported them to Freeport City, and then executed them in an abandoned coffee warehouse. If so, why had the *Duroc* been manned by a Chinese crew? What was the disconnect? He wasn't sure, but perhaps the man he'd come to see, this wayward hacker named Marcus Greenhorn, would have the answer.

Fisher felt the car's acceleration slow, then glide to a halt.

"I'm stopped," he radioed.

"Hold position," said Grimsdottir. "When I give you the word, stand up and step to the ledge directly behind you. To your right will be a stanchion. Press yourself against that and hold position."

"Roger."

"Ready . . . move!"

Fisher stood up, flipped the Shroud off his back, and took a step back until he felt his foot touch the ledge. He flattened himself against the wall and slid right until his shoulder bumped the stanchion.

"Releasing the elevator," Grimsdottirsaid.

The car groaned, then dropped away into the darkness.

Fisher tapped buttons on his OPSAT until the overhead schematic of the shaft appeared. Surrounded by green lines that represented the walls, his own position was a pulsing blue square. To his right, on the other side the stanchion, was a red dot. A camera. Opposite him, on the other side of the matching stanchion, another red dot, another camera.

"You next move is a leap, Sam," Grimsdottir said. "Straight across the shaft to the other ledge."

It was an eight-foot jump onto a ten-inch ledge. He

was good, but not that good. He glanced down the shaft; it was a bottomless pit.

"I'll be hanging by my fingernails, Grim," he said. "How long?"

"Twenty-two seconds. After that, climb back onto the ledge, slip around the stanchion, and hang again. The cameras will pan right over your head. At my next mark, you'll stand up and reach above your head. There'll be a maintenance ladder. Climb five rungs, then freeze."

"Got it," he said.

His destination was a maintenance crawl space that ran over the length of the penthouse's ceiling. Once there, away from the ever-watchful cameras and sensors, he could access a hatch the led to the roof.

He switched his trident goggles to NV and scanned the route Grimsdottir had indicated. He'd be dancing between the blind spots of two cameras. No room for error; no room for hesitation.

"Ready," Grimsdottir radioed. "Hold . . . hold . . . Go!"

He jumped. He hung in midair for what seemed seconds with a thousand feet of nothingness yawning beneath him. His hands slapped the ledge. He clamped down and lifted his knees to minimize his swing, which lasted only a few seconds. He let his legs dangle.

"Almost there," Grimsdottir said. "Camera's coming around. . . . Okay, go."

Fisher chinned himself up, then hooked his heel on the ledge and levered his body up. Then, using his right hand, he grabbed the stanchion and pulled until he could twist himself into a sitting position. He slid up the wall to a standing position.

"In place," he called.

"Next move in four seconds. Three . . . two . . . Go."

Fisher turned to face the stanchion, grabbed it with both hands, and leaned out, letting his own body weight and momentum swing him to the other side. He backed up until he felt his heels slip over the edge, then took a breath and stepped backward into space. He dropped straight down. As the ledge swept past his face, he snagged it with both hands.

"Seventeen seconds," Grimsdottir reported. "Hang in there."

Fisher thought, *Very funny*.

"Sorry, poor choice of words," she said. "Okay, up the ladder and you're home free. Go in five . . . four . . . three . . ."

Fisher was tensing his arms and shoulders for the movement when alarms began blaring.

"Go, Sam, move!"

He chinned himself up onto the ledge, snagged the rung above his head, and started climbing.

21

HE pushed through the maintenance hatch and squeezed himself into the crawl space. He was surrounded by water pipes and electrical conduits. He contorted himself until he was turned around, facing the hatch again. "What the hell just happened?" he asked.

"Not sure. I'm checking." Ten seconds later she was back: "Okay, it looks like they had a power surge. It threw the camera algorithms off. They must have caught a glimpse of something moving—probably not enough to know what it is, but enough to raise the alarm. Hunker down and wait. Company's coming."

The words had barely entered his earpiece when he heard the squelch of a radio somewhere below him, followed by a ratcheting sound. It took him a moment to place the noise: The guards were forcing open the elevator doors.

Voices in Arabic echoed in the shaft. Light from below seeped around the edges of the hatch as the guards panned their flashlights around. Fisher's Arabic was good, but the guards were talking in rapid-fire, so he caught only snippets:

"Anything? Do you see anything?"

"No, there's nothing. What did they see?"

"Let me check."

A radio squelched again. There was another exchange, too muffled for Fisher to make out, then a voice: "They're not sure. Just movement."

"Well, there's nothing here. We're a thousand feet up. What could be moving around?"

Radio squelch. "Control, all clear. Nothing here."

A few seconds passed. Fisher heard the thud of the elevator doors closing, then silence.

"Moving again," he said, and started crawling.

FIVE minutes later, having found the hatch with no trouble, Fisher crouched at the edge of the roof, looking down at the penthouse balcony. Somewhere down there Marcus Greenhorn waited.

The speed with which the hotel guards had responded to the alarm told Fisher they were very close by—as were, he assumed, the Emir's Al-Mughaaweer special forces soldiers. Fisher neither needed nor wanted a firefight on his hands, so he'd have to step carefully and get

Greenhorn under quick control before he could call for help.

He flipped his NV goggles into place, then lay down on his belly and scooted forward. Slowly, inch by inch, he lowered his torso over the edge of the roof until he was hanging upside down, arms braced on the eaves.

The balcony stretched the length of the penthouse, some hundred feet, and had its own hot tub, fountain, and outdoor dining room. Through the windows he could see the interior was mostly dark, the only light coming from a two-hundred-gallon aquarium glowing a soft blue. He switched to IR, scanned again, and saw nothing. He did a final check for sensors and cameras using EM, and likewise saw nothing. However many Al-Mughaaweer guards there were, they were probably stationed in the hall outside.

In one fluid motion, he slid himself over he edge, did a slow-motion somersault through his arms, hung for a split second, then dropped noiselessly to the balcony. He turned to face the windows, pistol drawn. He waited, stock still, for thirty seconds until certain he was alone.

The penthouse was accessed through three sets of French doors set at regular intervals down the balcony. He chose the one to his left. It was unlocked. He slipped inside. After spending the last hour sweating, the sudden chill of the air-conditioning on his face took his breath away.

The suite was done in earth tones, with gilded-frame mahogany walls, lush carpeting, and enough tapestries and artwork to stock a small museum. The fish tank, filled with a rainbow assortment of tropical fish, gurgled softly and cast wavering shadows on the ceiling.

He punched up the penthouse schematic on his OPSAT to get his bearings, then moved on.

HE found Greenhorn snoring in the master bedroom. Splayed a few feet away on the double king-sized bed was a nude woman that Fisher assumed was the girlfriend to whom Greenhorn had sent the invitation. Greenhorn was dressed in white jockey shorts, a T-shirt that said EAT MY ONES AND ZEROS, and a white terry-cloth robe bearing the Burj al Arab's crest. Despite being not yet thirty years old, Greenhorn looked ten years older, with his potbelly, pasty complexion, and mostly receded hairline.

Fisher walked to the woman's side of the bed, and was about to dart her when he noticed a medic alert bracelet on her wrist. *Ah, hell,* he thought. If he were to dart or Cottonball her, there was no telling how the drugs would interact with whatever condition she suffered, and he wasn't inclined to kill her simply because she was stupid enough to get mixed up with an idiot like Greenhorn. Besides, he consoled himself, she was all of five feet tall and ninety pounds. If she woke up, he'd deal with her.

He walked back to Greenhorn's side. He removed a dart from the pistol, then bent over and scratched Greenhorn on the forearm. He stirred, then mumbled something, rubbed his arm, and started snoring again. The dose wasn't enough to render Greenhorn unconscious, but rather dazed and docile for a few minutes.

Fisher gave the drug ten seconds to work, then removed his goggles and knelt beside the bed, one hand resting on the hilt of the Sykes Fairbairn sheathed on his calf. He lightly shook Greenhorn by the shoulder. "Mr. Greenhorn," he whispered. "Mr. Greenhorn, you need to wake up."

Greehorn groaned, and his eyes fluttered open. He turned and stared at Fisher through half-lidded eyes. "Huh?"

Greenhorn's breath was a fowl mixture of peanut butter, gin, and halitosis.

"We have a phone call for you, Mr. Greenhorn. Come with me, please."

Fisher helped him sit up, then stand up, then walked him out of the master bedroom, expertly frisking him as they walked.

"Who . . . who're you again?" Greenhorn muttered.

"Abdul, Mr. Greenhorn, from security, remember?"

"Oh, yeah, okay."

Fisher walked him to the opposite end of the penthouse to a seating alcove near the aquarium, then sat Greenhorn facing the aquarium, himself on the chair opposite. The backlight would cast him in shadow. Greenhorn slumped back into the couch and started snoring again.

Sam waited five minutes for the drug to dissipate, then pulled his chair forward until he was knee-to-knee with Greenhorn. He reached out and pressed his knuckle into the base of Greenhorn's septum. The pain snapped Greenhorn awake.

"Hey . . . hey, what the, what the—"

Fisher gripped him by the chin, thumb pressed into the hollow of his throat. "Don't make a sound." He jammed this thumb a little deeper; Greenhorn gagged. "Do you understand?"

Greenhorn nodded.

"I'm going to take my hand away and we're going to have a chat. If you give me the answers I want, you'll live to see another day. If you raise your voice or move a muscle, I shoot you dead where you sit. Understand?"

"Yeah, yeah. Can I ask you a question?"

Fisher nodded.

"Did Big Joey send you? 'Cuz if he did, I've got the money, I just haven't had a chance to—"

"Big Joey did not send me."

"Then who?"

"Santa Claus. You've been a bad boy, Marcus. You've been playing in cyberspace again."

Now Greenhorn understood; his eyes bulged. "Oh, Jesus . . ."

"Another good guess, but wrong again. Question one: Who's paying for your vacation here?"

"I don't know, I just got an e-mail."

"From?"

"I don't know."

"That's your second 'I don't know.' Three strikes and you're dead. I'm going to start a story, Marcus, and you're going to finish it. Here goes: Once upon a time you were hired to code a virus for someone. Now your turn."

"Uh . . . uh . . . I was hired by e-mail, I swear. They'd

already set up a Swiss account for me. I got a hundred thousand to start and another hundred when I delivered. You've got to believe me, I never dealt with anyone face-to-face."

Fisher did believe him. "When was this?"

"Two months ago."

"When were you instructed to come here?"

"A week, maybe ten days ago."

About the time the Trego *would have been heading to the U.S.* But why, Fisher wondered, if Greenhorn's employers were so worried about him being a loose end, didn't they just kill him?

"No one's contacted you since?"

"No. When I was told to come here, they said to just wait until I hear from them."

"You're sure the same person that hired you arranged this?"

"Yes."

"Clever guy like you would keep details, wouldn't he? E-mails, bank information . . . A little insurance."

"Uh . . . come on, man, they'll kill me."

Sam drew his pistol and pointed it at Greenhorn's forehead. "They'll be late."

"Jesus, okay, okay. Yeah, I kept some stuff." Greenhorn reached into the pocket of his robe and handed over a thumb-sized USB flash drive. "It's all there."

Fisher plugged the drive into the OPSAT's USB port, waited for the OPSAT to download the contents, then stuffed it into his arm pouch.

From the corner of his eye, Fisher saw something

move. Gun still trained on Greenhorn, he slowly turned his head. Greenhorn's girlfriend, now clad in panties and nothing else, padded across the room, rubbing her eyes. She saw Greenhorn and stopped. Fisher, still in shadow, lowered the pistol, leaned deeper into the couch.

"Hey, Marcus," she said, voice raspy. "Whatchya doing just sitting here in the dark?"

"Uh . . . you know, just looking at the fish. Couldn't sleep."

She took a step toward him. "Want some company?"

"No, babe, that's fine. Go on back to bed."

"Okay . . ."

She turned back toward the master bedroom, then stopped. She turned back. She looked at Fisher, then blinked a few times and cocked her head.

Ah, damnit, he thought. He had no desire to kill some woman Greenhorn had dragged into his mess of a life. He thumbed the pistol's selector to **DART**.

Greenhorn said, "Sweetie, just go back to bed, I'll be there in a minute."

She continued to stare at Fisher, blinking, trying to decipher what her still-fuzzy brain was registering. Fisher was about to dart her when she opened her mouth and started screaming.

22

WHAT came out of her mouth wasn't as much a scream as it was a shriek so piercing that Fisher was momentarily taken aback. In that split second, the woman turned and ran, nimble as a jackrabbit, around the fish tank and toward the door. "Help, help!"

Fisher stood up, grabbed Greenhorn, spun him, and got his neck in an elbow lock. He pressed the pistol's barrel to the soft spot just below Greenhorn's ear and then began stepping to his left, toward the windows and the nearest balcony door.

The door to the suite burst open and four figures in black coveralls rushed inside. Their entrance left Fisher with no doubt he was dealing with professionals. They moved as one in a crescent formation, each man scanning his own sector of the room. One of them shouted something and they all turned toward Fisher, their weapons raised and steady as they stalked forward.

Fisher's idea of taking Greenhorn with him had just evaporated, as had his original exfiltration plan. "Don't make a move unless I do," he whispered to Greenhorn.

"Okay, whatever you—"

Fisher heard a single, muted *pop*. Greenhorn's head snapped back. He went limp in Fisher's arms. That was no mistake, he realized instantly. These men were too disciplined to risk such a shot, and too good to miss what they were aiming at. They were following orders. If captured, Greenhorn was not to leave the hotel alive.

Fisher switched his grip on Greenhorn's body, grabbing him by the collar, then took aim on the nearest Al-Mughaaweer and fired. Even as the man fell, Fisher adjusted aim, fired again, and dropped a second man. The other two scattered toward the nearest cover and opened fire.

Greenhorn's body began jerking as it took the bullet strikes. Fisher felt something pluck at his left arm, then his right side. He felt no pain, and assumed/hoped the Rhino-Plate was doing its job. Behind him he heard the glass cracking. With Greenhorn as a shield, he kept firing, backing toward the door until he felt his heel bump against it.

He holstered the pistol, plucked a flash-bang grenade off his harness, pulled the pin, and tossed it. Per Fisher's preference, the grenade ran on a quick two-second fuse. He closed his eyes. Through his lids he sensed a flash of white light and felt the concussion ripple through Greenhorn's body.

Fisher drew the pistol again and started firing, hoping to keep the gunmen's heads down. He reached back, turned the doorknob, opened the door. He dropped Greenhorn's body, turned, sprinted across the balcony, and dove over the railing.

HIS decision against penetrating the hotel via parachute was proven right the instant he cleared the rail. He was grabbed by the cyclonic winds whipping around the building and sent tumbling. A thousand feet tall and sitting offshore, the hotel faced both inland and seaward weather systems, which included wind shears that would terrify any pilot, let alone a lone man with a parafoil strapped to his back.

He'd added the compact parafoil to his pack at the last minute in response to that little voice in the back of his head. Getting into the hotel would be a challenge; getting out could be an even bigger one. Better to have a backup and not need it rather than vice versa.

Whether the Al-Mughaaweer were firing on him from the balcony worried Fisher not at all. Though only seconds had passed since his leap, he was by now lost in the darkness, hurtling away from the hotel and toward the ocean's surface at sixty miles per hour He had thirty seconds, no more.

He arched his body, arms and legs spread wide to catch

as much air as possible. He felt himself lift ever so slightly. He glanced to his right and saw the lights of the seafront shops and restaurants. He twisted that way.

He lifted the OPSAT to his face and punched a button, bringing up his altimeter: 710 FEET. He'd lost a third of the hotel's height in roughly ten seconds. Given the volatility of the winds, he needed to wait until the last possible moment to open his chute.

He checked his OPSAT: 490 FEET/90 MPH.

A few more seconds . . .

He reached across his chest and ripped free a Velcro patch, revealing the chute's D-ring release.

390 FEET.

Wait. . . .

340 FEET.

He jerked the toggle, heard the swoosh and flutter of the parafoil deploying. He was jerked upward, felt his stomach rising into his throat, shoulders wrenched backward. He reached up, found the riser toggles, and gently pulled to counter the parafoil's initial lift. At this height, in the crosscurrent winds, the parafoil would naturally nose up, trading airspeed for lift, a combination sure to create a stall.

He checked the OPSAT: 255 FEET/40 MPH. He switched views to radar mode. To his left up the coast, a red triangle blinked. This too had been the result of Fisher's last-minute equipment change. Earlier, as he waited for nightfall, he'd meandered up the coast a few miles and secreted a pathfinder transponder on a rock outcropping.

By now every available cop in Dubai would be responding to the reports of gunfire at the city's most luxurious hotel. Of course, no one had his description, but the sooner he left the area, the better. He confirmed the transponder's bearing on the OPSAT, then pulled on the left toggle and banked north.

SHANGHAI

EYES closed, hands behind his back, Kuan-Yin Zhao paced the perimeter of the room, his shoes echoing off the marble floor and the vaulted ceiling. He'd walked this room hundreds of times over the last two years, seeing the game in his mind, imagining his opponent's moves and countermoves until nothing had been left to chance. And now . . . now it was all coming to fruition.

He stopped and turned to face the center of the room. Under the glare of halogen spotlights, the marble was inlaid with black mosaic tiles in the shape of a massive Xiangqi board, measuring twenty feet per side. There were no pieces, only the squares, and each opponent's home areas—called the Red Palace and the Black Palace—and a strip of dark blue representing the center division, or River.

Zhao imagined the pieces moving, dancing around one another, his opponent unaware until—

"Sir . . ." a voice intruded. "Sir, I'm sorry to bother you. . . ."

Zhao snapped out of his reverie and slowly turned around to face Xun. "Yes, what is it?"

"They've been apprehended—in Texas."

Zhao gave a half smile. "Good."

"Why is that good?" Xun asked. "The authorities have them. If they talk—"

"They will."

Xun frowned. "But if—"

Zhao waved his hands to encompass the room. "Xun, what do you see here?"

"A Xiangqi board."

"Let me ask you: Suppose a pair of enemy *paos* are advancing on your king. What do you do?"

"Move my king."

"Or?"

"Attack the attacking pieces."

"Or."

"Move other pieces in defense."

"How do you know that's not what your enemy wanted?"

"I don't."

"What if your every move is not your own, but only a response to arranged circumstances?"

"Then I lose the game."

"Correct. Now: Send a message to Sarani. Tell him

they should start preparing. Events will begin to speed up now."

Xun nodded and hurried out.

Zhao turned back to the board and moved another piece in his mind.

23

WHEN he touched down, Fisher's plans to quickly exit the area were foiled, not by the authorities, but rather by Lambert in a curtly worded OPSAT message—**PROCEED GRID REF 102.398, AWAIT PICKUP FOR TRANSPORT TO CHARLIE-ALPHA ONE (1)**—followed by the details his contact would use to identify himself or herself.

Fisher was concerned. The grid reference Lambert had given was virtually on top of his pathfinder beacon, overlooking Jumeirah Road north of the Burj al Arab. Rendevous Point Charlie-Alpha One was a CIA safe house on Al Garhoud Road near the Dubai Creek Golf & Yacht Club.

Lambert's order was unprecedented, not only because it required Fisher to remain in an OPAR (Operational

Area) that had gone hot, but also because it went against everything Third Echelon stood for: invisibility. Presenting himself to what would likely turn out to be a CIA case officer at a CIA safe house left a big footprint indeed. Though his contact was unlikely to know anything about him and would be ordered to forget his face, that did little to comfort him.

Twenty minutes after he touched down on the beach and stuffed his parafoil in a crevice in the rocks, a red two-door Peugeot pulled off the road and coasted to a stop on the dirt shoulder. The driver got out and knelt beside his front tire. Fisher saw a flashlight wink against the hubcap: one short, two long, three short.

He rose from the underbrush and walked over. Though he'd stripped off his exterior gear and stuffed it into his pack, he was still wearing his tac-suit. Even so, the man gave him the barest of glances, then said, "Are you Willard?"

Fisher shook his head. "My name is Bartle," he replied, completing the recognition code.

The man opened the back door and said, "Best if you lay down on the floor."

Fisher got in and did as instructed.

TWENTY minutes later the Peugeot coasted to a stop. Fisher heard the sound of a garage door opening. The car moved ahead and the garage door closed.

"It's okay to get up," the driver said. "We're clear."

Fisher sat up and climbed out of the car to find himself,

predictably, in a nondescript two-car garage. He followed the man into the house, which was lit by several floor lamps and decorated in Spanish-villa style. They were standing in the kitchen.

"I'm going to make some coffee," the man said. "Conference room's down the hall, first door on the right. Your call's cued up; just press the green button. The room's a tank."

All U.S. embassies and consulates and some CIA safe houses were equipped with a "tank"—a windowless, sound-tight room impervious to listening devices.

Fisher followed the man's directions to the room. It was small, ten feet by ten feet, and empty save for a desk table arrayed before a thirty-two-inch flat-screen television monitor. Recessed ceiling lights cast pools on the carpet. He sat down and pressed the green button. The monitor went first to static, then black again as a series of word scrolled across the screen:

**SEEKING   SIGNAL . . . SIGNAL   ENGAGED . . .
ENCRYPTION ENGAGED . . . SYSTEM CHECK . . .
READY . . .**

Lambert appeared on the screen. He was standing in what Fisher immediately recognized as the White House Situation Room. In the background he could see a few people milling around the gleaming oak conference table, including the Secretary of Defense, the Chairman of the Joint Chiefs, the head of Homeland Security, the director of the FBI, and the NID or National Intelligence Director.

"Morning, Sam," Lambert said.

"I've had better, Colonel. Tell me why I'm still in Dubai."

"Apologies. A lot has happened since you left."

"So it seems."

"You're the tip of the spear, Sam. I asked that you be allowed to listen in; you need to know what's happening, and what's coming. You'll be able to see them, but they won't be able to see you. Listen, but don't speak."

"I'm a ghost."

"Tell me about the Burj al Arab."

"Things got dicey. We're not compromised, but Greenhorn's dead—by his own bodyguards."

"Accident?"

"No chance. They were too good for that. They knew what they were doing."

"The question is, what did he know that was so important and who gave the order?"

"There's got to more here than what we're seeing. Maybe this'll give us a clue." Fisher held up the USB drive Greenhorn had given him. "His insurance policy."

"Good. Get that to Grim."

On the monitor, Fisher saw the President's Chief of Staff walk into the room and take a seat at the head of the conference table. Lambert said, "Stick around afterward. Grim has a new mission briefing for you." Lambert disappeared from view, then came back into frame as he took his seat.

"Okay, ladies and gentlemen," said the Chief of Staff, "let's take our seats. I'll be updating the President following this, so let's get started. "First, General, I understand you have updated figures from Slipstone."

The Chairman of the JCS nodded. "Yes, sir. As of three hours ago, the total confirmed dead roughly three thousand, six hundred."

There were murmurs of shock around the table.

"Of the reported two thousand survivors, approximately forty percent of them won't survive another three days. We're looking at a death toll that may exceed five thousand."

The Chief of Staff was silent for a few moments, then asked, "Why Slipstone? Why did they choose Slipstone?"

The JCS chairman replied, "Just guessing, I'd say for impact. Slipstone's a small town, in the middle of the country—in the middle of nowhere. The message is, 'we can get you anywhere, at any time.' Small town, big city, it doesn't matter."

The Chief of Staff considered this, then said, "Moving on. Jim, if you would. . . ."

The director of the FBI opened a folder, shuffled his notes, then started:

"Seventeen hours ago, our Special Agent in Charge on the ground in Slipstone acquired surveillance tapes of the local water treatment plant. Subsequent study of these tapes led our team to put out a nationwide BOLO for a late-model white Chevy Malibu, which was seen parked near the plant. Two unidentified men were recorded exiting the car, after which they disappeared from view. Twenty minutes later, they reappeared and drove away.

"An anonymous tip led to the traffic stop of the white Malibu by the Texas Highway Patrol units outside El Paso, Texas. The two occupants of the car were of Middle Eastern origin. They were in possesion of false drivers' licenses, two semiautomatic pistols, and cash in the amount of three thousand dollars. The men were transported to the El Paso County Jail for questioning.

"After initially refusing to cooperate, one of the men let slip details that confirmed their presence at Slipstone's water treatment plant, as well as their plans to exit the country. Using flight and credit card information, we've determined their destination was a house in Guatemala City, Guatemala.

"A raid of the house by the Guatemalan National Police turned up a cache of documents, which was immediately turned over to our local Legat, or Legal Attaché. We're still in the process of sorting through the documents, but so far we've determined the two men were ultimately bound for Ashgabat, Turkmenistan. Ashgabat is fifteen miles from the Iranian border."

Even from seven thousand miles away, Fisher felt the tension in the room skyrocket at the mention of Iran. This was the first true evidence pointing to the perpetrator of the Slipstone poisoning—and possibly the *Trego* incident. Fisher saw the Chairman of the Joint Chiefs was taking copious notes. *He knows,* Fisher thought. Unless something changed, he'd soon be asked for military options for Iran.

The NID added, "The CIA sent its chief of station from Uzbekistan over to Ashgabat to beat the bushes.

Problem is, we haven't had a solid presence in Turkmenistan for decades. We're just now redeveloping a network."

The FBI director continued. "The Ashgabat lead has been partially confirmed by the lone crew member captured from the cargo ship *Trego,* who was transferred to our custody from another agency three days ago. This subject claims his name is in fact Behfar Nassiri and that he spent time in Ashgabat before leaving to board the *Trego* at sea, off the coast of Mauritania."

That didn't take long, Fisher thought. While in Third Echelon's custody, the man named Nassiri had met Redding's interrogations with stone-faced silence. However they'd done it, the FBI had apparently found Nassiri's "Talk" button.

The director of the CIA interjected: "According to our database, the family name of Nassiri originates in the Mazandaran region of Iran."

There were a few moments of silence, then the Chief of Staff said, "Son of a bitch."

"Nassiri further claims he had been instructed to guide the *Trego* into the Virginia coastline and then, if still alive, kill himself in 'a glorious blow against the Great Satan.'"

"Straight from the Pasdaran hymnal," said the Secretary of Defense.

Fisher had had his own dealings with the Pasdaran. Officially called the Pasdaran-e Enghelab-e Islami, or the Islamic Revolutionary Guard Corps, the Pasdaran were elite troops chosen for their dedication to Islam and to the religious leaders of Iran. The average Pasdaran soldier's zealotry made a Palestinian suicide bomber look meek.

"Good Christ, what are they thinking?" said the head of Homeland Security. "Didn't they realize what this would bring down on them?"

Of course they know, Fisher thought. The extremist leadership in Tehran would like nothing more to finally join battle with its prime enemy. For them, this was a divine mission.

"Anything else on the FBI side?" the Chief of Staff asked.

"I'll have more for the morning briefing, but we're still working on the remains from the Freeport City coffee warehouse—"

"How are certain are we that these are the bodies of the *Trego*'s crew?" asked the SecDef.

"Ninety-nine percent. Autopsies are under way right now, so we should have some answers soon. As for the *Duroc*—the yacht—we believe it picked up the *Trego*'s crew and transported them to Freeport City. She exploded at sea before we could intercept her. There were no survivors, no remains. We're working on nailing down the registry."

An aide entered the room, walked the the FBI director, handed him a note, then left.

"What is it, Jim?" asked the Chief of Staff.

"Another piece of the puzzle. The financial information we recovered from the house in Guatemala City was tracked back to a bank in Masqat, Oman. It's a coporate account under the name Saracen Enterprises."

The NID was taking notes. He said, "We're on it."

The FBI director closed his folder. "That's all I have for now."

The Chief of Staff turned to the NID. "Doug?"

The NID stood up and walked to a nearby monitor, which came to life showing a satellite view of Slipstone. The image was in shades of gray, save for a few spots of orange-red.

"These are radioactive hot spots around Slipstone. We've coordinated satellite coverage with the EPA to find the limits of the contamination and quarantine the water supply. So far, it looks like there is no leakage into the surrounding ground water or geological structures."

"What are we talking about here?" asked the Chief of Staff. "What's the contaminate?"

"Cesium 137. It's a common waste element produced when uranium and/or plutonium are bombarded by neutrons. In essense, it's radioactive waste from either a reactor or the remnants of bomb production. Unfortunately, in the world of nuclear physics, cesium is a dime a dozen. Finding precisely where it came from is doable, but it's going to take some time."

"How persistent is this stuff?" asked Homeland Security. "How long before the town is habitable again?"

"The half-life of cesium 137 particles is thirty years. In other words, Slipstone will be off-limits to all human life long after most of us are dead."

THE meeting was adjourned and Fisher sat in silence, watching the attendees file out.

He was stunned. He'd heard the initial death toll predictions, but hearing them recited in such clinical fashion chilled him. *Five thousand dead . . . Slipstone a ghost town, uninhabitable for a generation or more . . .*

Lambert appeared before the screen. Over his shoulder, the situation room was empty.

"So: You heard."

"I heard," Fisher replied.

"Here's how it's going to happen: By the close of business today, Congress will officially name the government of Iran as the perpetrator of the *Trego* and Slipstone attacks. In a unanimous vote they'll reaffirm the President's authority to use all available military force in response. By this time tomorrow, the Joint Chiefs will have an operational plan on the Secretary of Defense's desk. Forty-eight hours from now, a U.S. Navy battle group will begin moving toward the Gulf of Oman."

It would happen, of that Fisher was certain. Whether it would precisely match Lambert's scenario he didn't know, but what his boss had just described was a fair prediction of what was coming. The only evidence that contradicted the seemingly irrefutable Iranian angle was his report of a Chinese crew aboard the *Duroc,* now scattered along with its crew on the bottom of the Atlantic Ocean.

The question was, how and when would the President choose to respond to the attacks? Full-scale war with boots on the ground in Iran; precision air strikes; tactical nuclear weapons?

"Where does this leave us?" Fisher asked.

"Same place, just a tighter deadline. If there's something more to all this, we're running out ot time to find it. But wherever the evidence leads, we have to have all of it. Grim, are you on?"

"I'm here. Sam, two items of interest: One, the data you pulled from the *Duroc*'s helm console was heavily encrypted—another Marcus Greenhorn masterpiece, but so far it looks like other than the trip from its home port in Port St. Lucie to the Bahamas, it had been up and down the Atlantic Coast, following the deep-sea fishing lanes with a couple stops in Savannah, Hilton Head, Charleston—places like that.

"The stomping grounds of the yacht-owning rich and famous," Fisher said.

"You got it. I'm still working on an owner, but whoever the *Duroc* belongs to, they're wealthy. Item number two: We've traced the serial numbers you took from the *Trego*'s engines. According to Lloyd's of London, the engines were installed two years ago aboard a freighter named *Sogon* at Kolobane Shipyard in Dakar, Senegal."

"Nassiri claims he boarded the *Trego* off the coast of Mauritania," Fisher said. "Dakar's only a hundred miles from the border."

"And I'll give you ten to one the *Sogon* and *Trego* are one in the same," Lambert said.

"Either that, or it was a swap. Do we know where the *Sogon* is now?"

Grimsdottir said, "I'm looking. As for the shipyard: I've tried to hack into their computer system, but it's rudimentary at best—e-mail and little more. All records are likely kept as hard copies in the shipyard itself."

Fisher thought for a moment, then said, "Last time I was in Dakar was two years ago."

"Then I'd say you're long overdue for another visit," Lambert said. "Pack your bags."

24

FISHER pulled his Range Rover off the road onto a dirt tract bordered on each side by jungle, and then doused his headlights and coasted to a stop. He shut off the engine and sat in silence—or what passed for silence here. He was surrounded by a symphony of the jungle's night sounds: chirping frogs, cawing birds, and, high in the canopy, the shrieking and rustling of monkeys disturbed by his arrival.

Though he was officially within the city limits of Dakar, the jungle refused to be tamed as it tried to encircle and retake the urban areas. Since his arrival that morning, Fisher had seen hundreds of laborers along Senegal's roads, hacking at the foliage with machetes.

So much the better, he thought. Like water, for him the

jungle meant cover, a place for stealthy approach; escape; evasion; ambush. He slapped at a bug buzzing around his ear, and was instantly reminded of the one thing he didn't like about the jungle.

He'd been to Dakar twice, the first time during his SEAL days when he and a team had been dispatched to track and eliminate a French black market arms dealer who'd been arming both sides of a brush war between Mali and Mauritania. Thousands had died on both sides, many of them child-soldiers, and thousands more would die in the months to come if the Frenchman had his way. He didn't get his way; he'd never gotten out of jungles along the Senegal-Mali border.

Dakar had been founded as a French colonial outpost by residents of the nearby island of Goree, and had over the last century and a half grown into a major commercial hub on the West African coast, an exotic mixture of French culture and Islamic architeture.

Fisher got out, grabbed his duffel from the backseat, then walked a dozen meters into the jungle. He quickly traded his Bermuda shorts and T-shirt for his tac-suit, web harness, and guns, then tucked the duffel into some foliage and set off at a trot.

ONE mile and eight minutes later, he saw a clearing appear through the branches. He stopped and crept to the edge of the tree line and crouched down. Ahead of him lay a fifty-foot-wide tract of ground that had been burned clear of jungle; beyond that was Kolobane Shipyard's eastern fence: twelve feet tall and topped with razor-tipped concertina wire. On the other side of the fence was more open ground, an acre of weeds and grass that gave way to the shipyard's outer buildings, a double line of low storage huts separated by a dirt road. Over their roofs he could see several cranes. Here and there klieg lights mounted atop telephone poles cast circles of light on the roads below.

While Kolobane was the busiest shipyard on the African coast between Morrocco to the north and Angola to the south, the shipyard had only enough work to keep it busy during the day. At night it was staffed only by security and maintainence crews.

Fisher pulled out his binoculars and scanned the area, first in NV mode, then in IR. According to Grimsdottir's brief, the shipyard maintained a skeleton staff of roving patrols. Before he moved into the yard he wanted a feeling for their routes and schedules.

Ten minutes later, he had what he needed. The nearest guard was a teenager dressed in shorts, sandals, and a T-shirt, with an AK-47 slung over his shoulder. Fisher knew better than to discount the boy. In Africa, some of the best soldiers and worst killers wouldn't be old enough for a driver's permit in the U.S. Nevertheless, they would shoot you dead without a moment's hesitation, strip your body of clothes, shoes, jewelry—along with fingers, if necessary—then leave you to rot on the side of the road.

Fisher waited until the boy had disappeared around the storage sheds; then he sprinted to the fence and dropped to his belly. From one of his pouches he pulled a miniature spray bottle filled with a special cocktail of enzymatic acids. In this case it was overkill: The ship-yard's fence was ungalvanized, so years of humidity had turned it more rust than not. Fisher gave the fence a lib-eral misting.

Five minutes was all it took. He reached out and pressed his palm against the fence. With a dull twang, a two-foot-by-two-foot oval sprang free and dropped to the grass on the other side. He did a quick scan with the binoculars to locate the guard, then crawled through the hole.

HE covered the open ground in two minutes, alternately sprinting and pausing as the teenage guard made his cir-cuitous route around the storage huts, down the dirt road, then back around again. His pace and route didn't vary, so Fisher had little trouble timing his movments. He slipped between a pair of huts, then across the dirt road and behind the second line of huts.

Before him was a narrow grove of stout-trunked baobab trees. Through them Fisher could see the scaf-folding of a crane and the shipyard's pier. Moored to it was a rusting cargo freighter.

Set among the baobabs were a dozen or so picnic tables—a break area for workers. He heard faint laughter. He flipped his trident goggles into place and switched to NV. At the far edge of the grove, perhaps fifty feet away, a pair of men sat at a table smoking. Scattered on the ground around them were what looked like hairy soccer balls; these were the baobab's fruit pods, also known as monkey bread. Fisher was only too familiar with them. Tracking down the French arms dealer had taken weeks. After their MREs had run out, he and his team had subsisted on monkey bread and roasted snake.

He settled down to wait, but it took only minutes before the men stubbed out their cigarettes, got up, and started ambling toward the shipyard. Fisher waited until they turned the corner around the crane, then got up and sprinted forward.

He paused at the edge of the baobabs to check for guards, but saw nothing. He was about to continue when something caught his eye, a glimmer of light on glass. Warning bells went off in his head. So faint was the glimmer that it took him thirty seconds to find it again. To his left, high atop the control cab of a crane, was a man. Dressed in black, his face covered by a black balaclava, he lay on his belly with an NV-scoped sniper rifle pressed to his shoulder.

Ambush or increased security? Fisher wondered. He doubted it was the latter; Kolobane's business was the repair and refit of decrepit cargo freighters, not warships. *Ambush,* then. He guessed it was not meant specifically for him, but rather for anyone coming to investigate the *Sogon/Trego*. But how had they known he would be here? What were they trying to prevent him from finding, and who were "they"? Another assumption he had to make was that where there was one sniper, there were more.

He slowly backed deeper into the trees, then turned and sprinted across the picnic area to the second line of storage huts. Watchful for the roving guard, he picked his along the edge of the road until he had a better angle on the sniper's perch through the trees.

It was time to find out how many players were on the field. He drew the SC-20 from his back-holster, then rotated the selector to the ASE, or All-Seeing-Eye. He pointed the barrel skyward and pulled the trigger. With a muffled *fwump* the ASE arced upward and disappeared into the night sky.

Fisher switched the OPSAT to the ASE's camera and was immediately rewarded with a bird's-eye view of the shipyard. The image swayed ever so slightly as the ASE's aero-gel parachute rode the air currents.

He located the crane for a point of reference, then switched to infrared. The sniper, still prone atop the control cab, changed into a man-shaped blotch of red, yellow, and green. Fisher panned down the pier, looking for more figures at roof level or higher. He disregarded moving bodies, which were likely shipyard workers.

It took twenty seconds to spot the second sniper. The man had chosen his spot well, on the roof of Fisher's ultimate destination—the shipyard's administration building. Between them, each sniper had all the approaches covered. But again, what were they guarding? What didn't they want uncovered about the *Sogon* and/or *Trego*?

Fisher was about to shut down the ASE and transmit the self-destruct signal when the rooftop sniper shifted position. It took Fisher a moment to reorient himself; with a start, he realized the sniper's new field of fire was centered on him. He killed the camera, raised the binoculars, and focused on Sniper One. All he saw in the magnified field was a head-on view of a bulky NV scope and a hood-covered head resting against the rifle stock.

Fisher dropped flat.

He heard a *swish-pfft*. A puff of dirt erupted beside him. He rolled right. Another bullet slammed into the dirt. He pushed himself into a crouch and double-stepped to his right behind the trunk of a baobab.

Five seconds passed, then ten. They knew his general location but didn't have a clear shot. Both snipers had shifted their aim toward him in unison; that was beyond coincidence, which could mean one thing: He'd been tagged, either visually or electronically. He switched to NV and scanned his surroundings, looking for likely observation posts. There were none; he was shielded to the left and right by the baobab grove and behind by the storage huts.

So he'd been electronically tagged.

He was pinned down.

25

HOW and when he'd been tagged would have to wait for later. *Or would it?* he thought, a memory coming back to him. What had Grimsdottir called the encryption program she'd found on the data from the *Duroc*'s helm console? *Another Marcus Greenhorn masterpiece*.

Another Marcus Greenhorn masterpiece . . .

His eyes were drawn to the OPSAT strapped to his wrist. Could it be? He'd used the OPSAT to scan both the *Duroc*'s helm console and Greenhorn's USB drive, and so far every encryption or virus they'd come across had been created by Greenhorn to protect whoever had hired him.

Had a Trojan horse hidden inside the OPSAT been piggybacking a tracking beacon on top of his own comm channels? It was possible, he decided. There was one way to find out. The method was decidedly low-tech, but it would do the job.

He took the OPSAT off and laid it at the foot of the tree, then backed away, using the baobab's trunk as cover until he was at the edge of the grove. He turned and sprinted parallel to the grove until he was certain Sniper Two's view was blocked by intervening buildings, then turned again and darted into the shadows between a pair of storage huts.

He waited for the teenage guard to pass by, then stepped onto an empty crate and slowly raised his head up until only his eyes showed over the hut's roof. He raised his binoculars and checked Sniper One. The man hadn't moved. He was still focused on the baobab tree shielding the OPSAT.

Fisher keyed his subdermal. "Grim, Lambert . . . You there?"

"We're here," replied Lambert.

"Greenhorn's broken another one of your firewalls and worked his magic again. The OPSAT's infected."

"What?" she cried.

Fisher explained and said, "There's no doubt; they knew where I was headed, and when."

"I'm sorry, Sam, I'm dumbfounded. Greenhorn is—*was*—good. Too damned good."

"No harm done. I'll bring the OPSAT back, but we have to cook it. Give me ten minutes, then send the self-destruct signal."

"You'll be able to operate without it?"

Fisher chuckled. "Grim, I was doing this kind of stuff when phones still had cords. I'll manage. Lambert, here's the problem: If they knew I was coming, they probably knew why I was coming and what I was looking for."

"And did some housekeeping."

"Right. Best to check, though. You never know."

"What's your status?"

"Safe for now, but between them they've got the routes to the admin building covered."

As this mission's target was a civilian facility, Fisher's Rules of Engagment had forbidden the use of lethal force. "Gloves are off," Lambert said. "Weapons free on combatants."

Fisher signed off. He had to hurry. The snipers wouldn't watch the OPSAT's position for long before they recognized the ruse.

He picked his way back along the edge of the grove until he reached its far end, where he again slipped into the shadows between the storage huts. With the binoculars he checked his firing lines. From this spot he had both sniper perches in sight. Both men were still fixed on OPSAT's baobab.

Behind him he heard the crunch of sandals on gravel. AK-47 slung over his shoulder, the teenage guard strolled past the gap. Sam unsheathed the SC-20, switched the selector to Cottonball, then stepped out of the shadows.

"Psst!"

The boy turned. Fisher fired. The Cottonball struck

the boy's chest. He swayed on his feet for a few seconds, then tipped over. Fisher collected the body and the AK and tucked them both into the shadows, then returned to his position.

He curled himself into a seated firing position, SC-20 cradled in his arms, elbows resting on his knees. Individually, the shots didn't worry him, but each sniper probably had the other in his peripheral vision. As soon as one went down, the other would instantly know about it.

Fisher chose the one on the admin building's roof first; the one atop the crane had no easy cover, no quick escape. He zoomed the scope until the crosshair's reticle was centered on the man's forehead. He took a breath, held it a moment, then released it slowly. Gently he squeezed the trigger. The SC-20 bucked on his shoulder. In the scope, he saw the man's head snap back, haloed in a dark mist of blood.

He changed position, reoriented, zoomed in. Atop the crane, the first sniper had in fact seen his partner die and was already moving, rolling right toward the control cab's ladder. Fisher adjusted his aim, leading him just a hair, then fired. The man jerked once, then went still.

Fisher keyed his subdermal. "Sleepers; two; clean. Moving to the admin building."

HE knew his check of the admin office would likely turn up nothing. If someone had known he was coming, they'd also known why, which meant all traces of both the *Sogon* and the *Trego* had probably been removed from

Kolobane's records. Still, he had to be sure. And the truth was, he was also satisfying his stubborn streak. Someone had gone to a lot of trouble to kill him, and that grated on his professionalism. Or was it his ego? Either way, he was going to finish the job.

He crouched beside the outer wall of the admin building and inspected the door. Despite the peeling paint and dilapidated appearance, the lock was an industrial-grade drop bolt with a reinforced jamb. Tough but not invincible. More often than not a lock was a lock, and this one too surrendered to his picks in thirty seconds.

He opened the door a crack and did a quick NV/IR scan with the flexi-cam. Seeing nothing, he slipped inside and shut the door behind him. The building was long and narrow, two hundred feet by one hundred feet, with a vaulted ceiling and skylights through which a sliver of pale moon showed. The floor was dominated by wooden storage units that rose to the rafters and were filled with dry goods ranging from rice and cornmeal to beans and coffee. This was also the shipyard's grocery store, a place for passing ships to resupply.

Directly ahead at the far end of the warehouse was the glassed-in administrative office. It sat on stilts above the floor, accessible only by a set of steps running up the wall.

Lovely place for an ambush, Fisher thought.

He turned right, sticking to the shadows and following the course of the wall until finally he'd circumnavigated the entire warehouse and was beneath the office.

He switched his goggles to IR and studied the floor above. He saw no man-shaped hot spots. He switched to EM, or Electro-Magnetic. In the swirling blue-black image, two objects immediately caught his eye, each pulsing with its own EM signature. One was attached to the inside of the office door, the other opposite it, on a filing cabinet. There was no mistaking what he was seeing: a laser-beam trigger and some kind of shaped explosive charge. Open the door, the beam is severed, the charge detonates.

He considered his options. Defeating the wall mine was possible, but iffy. The windows were out as well. Anyone sophisticated enough to employ this type of booby trap would also have the windows covered.

But . . .

He looked up at the ceiling. *Maybe.*

He backtracked along the wall, then darted across the floor and mounted one of the ladders affixed to the side of the shelving. He climbed to the top and then sidestepped along the shelf until he could reach up and grab the ceiling joist. He let his legs swing out, then used the momentum to lever himself atop the joist.

He crept down the joist until he was directly over the office roof, then tied a line to the beam and rappelled down. He walked to the nearest skylight; it was locked by a simple hook latch, which slid free using the tip of his knife.

A *click-clack* echoed through the building.

Sam dropped flat, switched to IR.

Crouched outside the door was a man. Fisher switched back to NV in time to see the door slowly swing inward. *Move, Sam!* Feet-first, he slid through the skylight, dropped to the floor in a crouch. The office was narrow, with one wall dominated by shoulder-high filing cabinets and the other by three battered, gray steel desks.

He switched to EM. As he'd guessed, there was a second trigger beam across the windows. He then went back to NV and slowly peeked up to window level.

The man, dressed all in black, his face covered by a balaclava, was running hunched over toward the office stairs. Fisher crossed the room, ducked under the trigger beam, and flattened himself against the wall. He drew the Sykes.

Footsteps padded up the stairs, then stopped. There was a soft double beep. Fisher switched to EM; the trigger beam was gone. He switched back to NV. The door swung inward. With the lightest of touches, Fisher palmed the knob, stopping the door's swing.

For a long five seconds nothing moved; then the man appeared, stepping cautiously.

Fisher would never know what had prompted the move—peripheral vision, intuition, something else—but the man suddenly spun around and lunged toward him, a knife in his hand. Fisher caught the man's wrist with his left hand and twisted hard while sweeping the ankle with his foot. As the man fell, Fisher stepped behind him, grabbed the man's chin, and lashed out with the Sykes. The dagger plunged into the hollow beside the man's collarbone, instantly severing the carotid artery, the subclavian, and the jugular. The man gasped, jerked once, then went still. Fisher eased him to the floor and swung the door shut.

He frisked the body. Unsurprisingly, the man carried nothing on him.

"Sleeper; clean," Fisher radioed.

He pulled off the man's balaclava. He was black.

Local talent, Fisher thought. Hired by whom, though?

HIS search took only minutes. None of the filing cabinets contained anything regarding either the *Trego* or the *Sogon.*

He keyed his subdermal. "Lambert, there's nothing here."

"Not surprised. Come on home."

Fisher turned to leave. Then he stopped. Turned back.

Sitting on top of one of the cabinets was an ancient microfiche reader. Fisher chuckled to himself. Kolobane's record-keeping methods might be lagging behind those of the cyber world, but they weren't entirely backward.

He searched the cabinets again without luck, then turned his attention to the desks. In the bottom drawer of the first one he found an accordian folder filled with microfiche transparencies. *Bingo.*

"Lambert?"

"I'm here."

"Disregard my last. We just caught a break."

26

TWELVE hours after slipping out of Kolobane Shipyard and meeting the Osprey at the extraction point, Fisher was back home. He knew it would be short-lived. It wouldn't take Grimsdottir long to find what they were looking for on the microfiches. However, as was par for the course, whatever information she found would probably lead to another diversion, another facade—behind which waited . . . What? Iran, or someone else? In the end, it might not matter, Fisher realized. Events were beginning to snowball and the snowball was rolling straight for Tehran.

While he had been in Dakar, the autopsies on the charred bodies found in the coffee warehouse in Freeport City were completed. All were male, between the ages of nineteen and twenty-four; all had been shot once in the back of the head prior to being set aflame, en masse, with an accelerant, probably kerosene. Each man's fingertips had been severed post mortem and his teeth removed by blunt-force trauma.

Someone had gone to a lot of trouble to make the men unidentifiable—and they would've succeeded, if not for the diligence of the FBI's chief medical examiner.

Two bits of evidence had survived the fire: one, a partially digested meal in the stomach of one of the corpses that was identified and chemically matched to tomato paste found in the *Trego*'s food stores. Two, whoever had knocked out the men's teeth had missed a molar in one of the mouths, and in the molar was a filling. It took only hours for the FBI's labs at Quantico to identify the composition.

The filling was a blend of tin and silver amalgam found only in the Zagros Mountains of Iran.

TRUE to Lambert's prediction, the President had taken the first step toward war with Iran, ordering the *Ronald Reagan* Carrier Battle Group to steam at best possible speed to the Gulf of Oman and take up station just outside Iran's territorial waters. In Iraq and Kuwait, elements of the 101st and 82nd Airborne Divisions were put on ready alert, as was the 1st Battalion, 87th Infantry of the 10th Mountain Division.

Meanwhile, while Iran's United Nations ambassador categorically denied his government's involvment in the

Trego and Slipstone attacks during a special General Assembly Session, the Security Council voted unanimously but toothlessly that the perpetrator of the attack on the United States was "in violation of international law and will be held fully accountable."

In the Arab world, reactions to the attacks were predictably split between moderate Muslims—both secular and devout—and extremists; the former condemning the attacks and offering support and condolences to the American people, the latter celebrating the catastrophe with street rallies and flag-burning protests outside U.S. embassies from Turkey to Sudan to Indonesia.

FISHER did his best to enjoy his off time, but he found himself anxious to move, to keeping plucking at the threads of the mystery. Where it would end might be a foregone conclusion—death and ruin for Iran—but as far as he was concerned, as long as there were questions unanswered, he still had a job to do. If another war in the Middle East was inevitable, history would judge the U.S. on the righteousness of its cause, and the accuracy of its intelligence. There could be no doubts, no question marks.

It was late afternoon when he gave up and left the house. He drove into town, picked up a couple of steaks and baking potatoes, a tub of sour cream, and a six-pack of Heineken, then got on Highway 270 and drove north to Frederick, where he pulled into the parking lot of the Cedar Bend Assisted Living Community. Grocery bags in hand, he walked to Apartment 302 and knocked on the door. Thirty seconds later, it opened to reveal a wizened old man in a blue cardigan.

Sam held up the bags. "Feel like some company?"

"Sam-o! Good to see you, good to see you, come in. You shoulda called ahead. Might've had a woman with me," said Frank Bunch.

Sam grinned. "I'll remember that next time."

Frank Bunch was an old family friend and the original owner of Sam's Sykes Fairbairn commando dagger, which Frank had presented to him upon graduation from BUD/S along with a whispered piece of advice Sam had never forgotten: "Violence is easy; living with violence isn't. Choose carefully."

Bunch had been friends with Sam's grandfather since their first day together at the Special Operations Executive's Camp X on the shores of Lake Ontario in Canada. Their friendship had been cemented during the training, and lasted through dozens of WWII drops into German-occupied Europe.

"Whatchya got in the bag?" Frank asked.

Sam set the contents out on the counter. "All the things your doctor tells you not to eat."

"Atta boy! Come on, I'll get the grill fired up."

As usual, Frank grilled the steaks to perfection and roasted the potatos until the skin was golden brown and slightly crispy. He had chives for the sour cream and frosted mugs for the beer. It was the best meal Sam had eaten in a long time.

Comfortably stuffed, they sat on Frank's back porch

overlooking the courtyard garden. The sun was an hour away from setting and the garden was cast in hues of orange.

"So, tell me," Frank said. "What's new?"

"Same old thing," Sam replied. As far as Frank knew, Sam had left government service to take a job as a private security consultant. "You know: meetings, airline food, bad hotels . . ."

Frank sipped his beer and glanced at Fisher over his glasses. "Up for a game?"

Sam smiled. Retired or not, Frank hadn't lost a mental step. At eighty-four, he beat Sam at chess more often than he lost. "Sure. No money this time, though."

"What's the fun in that?"

"For you, none. For me, I get to eat next week."

Frank gathered the chess set from inside, pushed aside the dishes, and laid out the board. By coin toss, Sam took black. Frank stared at the table for ten seconds, then moved a pawn.

Sam thought immediately, *Queen's Gambit*. It was a favorite opening of Frank's, but Sam knew better than to accept it at face value. As a man, Frank was without pretense; as a chess player, he was a shrewd and calculating opponent who gave no quarter. Sam had fallen too many times for his feints and ambushes; his rogue pawn charges that diverted Sam's attention; his fake bishop attacks that shielded a flanking queen.

The game went on for forty minutes until finally Frank frowned and looked up. "I'd call that a draw."

Sam's eyes remained fixed on the board. His mind was

whirling. *Feints and false bishop attacks* . . . When the movement of every piece on the board screams Queen's Gambit, save for a lone pawn moving behind the scenes, do you ignore the Gambit and concentrate on the pawn? Of course not. The pawn is a mosquito—an aberation to be discounted. The queen, the deadliest piece on the board, is what you're watching. The queen's attack is what you try to counter. . . .

"Sam . . . Sam, are you here, son?"

Sam looked up. "What? Sorry?"

"I said, I think we're at a draw."

Sam chuckled. "Yeah, I guess we are. With you, I'll take that any day."

Frank moved to clear the pieces from the board, but Sam stopped him.

"Leave it for a little bit. I'm working on something."

27

THIRTY minutes after receiving Lambert's terse "Come in" call, Fisher swiped his card through the reader and pushed through the Situation Room's door. Waiting for him at the conference table were Lambert, Grimsdottir, Redding, and a surprise guest: the CIA's DDO, or Deputy Director of Operations, Tom Richards. Richards was in charge of one of the CIA's two main arms: Operations, which put agents and case officers on the ground to collect intelligence. Intelligence then analyzed the collected data.

Richards's presence wasn't a good sign. As DDO, he knew about Third Echelon, but for the sake of compartmentalization, the CIA and Third Echelon generally remained distant cousins. Something significant had happened, and Fisher had a good idea what it was.

"Take a seat," Lambert said. "Tom, this is my top field operative. For simplicity's sake, let's call him Fred."

"Good to meet you, Fred."

Fisher gave him a nod.

Lambert said to Fisher, "The other shoe has dropped. Tom has come over at the request of the President to brief us. For reasons that you'll understand shortly, we're going to be taking the lead on what comes next. Go ahead, Tom."

Richards opened a folder lying on the table before him. "As you know, the predominant isotope we found in Slipstone's water supply was cesium 137. It's a natural byproduct of nuclear fission—whether from the detonation of nuclear weapons, or from the use of uranium fuel rods in nuclear power plants.

"The problem is, cesium 137 is too common. It's everywhere: in the soil from nuclear weapon testing . . . in the air from power plant leaks. It's the vanilla ice cream of nuclear waste—almost. In some cases, the cesium contains imperfections. For example, from where the uranium was mined, or in the case of fuel rods, from the chemical makeup of the water used to cool them.

"Since the 1950s the CIA has kept a database on isotopes—where and when it was found; its likely source . . . those sorts of things.

"It took a while, but we've identified the source of the cesium found at Slipstone. First of all, the material found aboard the *Trego* and the traces we found at Slipstone are of identical makeup. No surprise there. In this case, the database came up with a hit from twenty-plus years ago."

"When?" asked Grimsdottir.

"April 26th, 1986."

Fisher knew the date. "Chernobyl."

RICHARDS nodded. "You got it. On that date, following a systems test that got out of control, Chernobyl's Reactor Number Four exploded and spewed tons of cesium 137 into the atmosphere."

"How sure are you about this?" Lambert asked.

"That it's Chernobyl cesium we found? Ninety percent."

"And I assume we're not talking about trace amounts here, are we?" asked Redding.

"No, it's pure Chernobyl cesium. In the *Trego's* forward ballast tank we found three hundred fifty pounds of debris that we've determined came from actual fuel rods."

"From Chernobyl?" Grimsdottir repeated, incredulous. "*The* Chernobyl?"

"Yes. We've estimated it took upwards of thirty pounds of material to produce the level of contamination we found in Slipstone's water supply, so we're talking about a total of almost four hundred pounds. There's only one place you can get that much."

"Ukraine or Russia can't be behind this," Lambert said.

"Not directly," Richards replied, "but that's where the Iranians got it. How we don't know. That's what we're hoping you can answer. We need someone to go into Ukraine—into Chernobyl—and get a sample."

Someone, Fisher thought. *Good old Fred*.

"And, if possible, do some sleuthing," Richards added.

"If this stuff is from Chernobyl, we need to know how and who. It had to leave there somehow. As far as we know, only about half of the undamaged fuel rods from Reactor Number Four are still inside the reactor core—in what the Russians call 'the Sarcophagus.' The other half were blown outward, into the surrounding countryside."

Sarcophagus was an apt term, Fisher thought. The morning after the explosion, hundreds of thousands of Russian soldiers and volunteers from all around the Soviet Union began converging on Pripyat, the town nearest the Chernobyl plant, which by then was in the middle of an evacuation that would eventually transport 135,000 residents from the area.

Working with no safety equipment except for goggles and paper masks, soldiers and civilians began shoveling debris back into the crater that had been Reactor Number Four. Radioactive dust and dirt swirled around the site, coating everything and everyone it touched with a layer of deadly cesium. Hastily formed construction brigades began mixing thousands of tons of concrete, which were then transported to the lip of the crater and dumped over the side and onto the shattered roof until finally the open maw was overflowing with concrete.

Richards said, "As best we can determine, debris blown outside the reactor was collected and buried in bunkers somewhere nearby."

"Have the Ukrainians reported any thefts? Any missing material?" Fisher asked.

"No, but that doesn't surprise us. Hell, for days after

the explosion the Soviet government continued to call it a 'minor incident.' Even if they knew about something fishy, we wouldn't expect them to tell anyone."

Fisher could see what was coming. Aware of the missing material or not, when this revelation became public, Ukraine—and by proxy, Russia—would be held complicit, a silent partner in Iran's attack on the United States and the deaths of what could be as many as five thousand people.

In his mind's eye Fisher imagined a chessboard. What part did this news play? Was this a distraction strategy, the white knight jumping its way toward the black king, or something more—that lone pawn no one is paying attention to? Or was it exactly what it seemed: Iran's Queen's Gambit?

"We have some leads?" Fisher asked. "Chernobyl's Exclusion Zone covers a lot of territory. I assume you're not asking me to wander around with a Geiger counter waiting to get lucky."

"No. We're working to identify the bunkers most likely to contain the debris we're interested in. We also have some human assets in Ukraine that might point us in the right direction."

"What's our timeline?"

"You'll leave in five days," Lambert replied.

Richards closed his folder and stood up. "I'll leave you to it. Fred, good luck."

"Thanks."

* * *

ONCE Richards was gone, Lambert said, "Sam, this is a volunteer mission. You can decline with no questions asked."

"I'll go. How often do you get a tour of Chernobyl? One question, though: How long can I walk around that place before my hair starts falling out?"

"Longer than you think," Grimsdottir said. "Don't worry, we've got you covered. I'll brief you once you're en route."

Lambert said, "While the CIA is putting the pieces into place, we've got another lead—or maybe a red herring—for you to chase down. Go ahead, Grim."

"The microfiche you found in Kolobane's office was a gold mine. There was nothing specific about either the *Trego* or the *Sogon*, but there was loads of information on the diesel engines installed aboard the *Trego*."

"Another finger pointing at Iran?" Fisher asked.

"Maybe, maybe not. The engines were purchased and transported to Kolobane by a company called Song Woo Limited out of Hong Kong."

"Another layer of the onion."

"Unfortunately, I've found no trace of the company in cyberspace."

"Which means a personal visit," Fisher said.

28

HONG KONG

"**SLOW** down," Fisher ordered the driver, whose grasp of English was weak but probably better than he let on. Some taxi drivers didn't want to be bothered with "touristy" questions, and nothing shuts up a tourist quicker than a Hong Kong driver's practiced "Eh?"— which is exactly what he gave Fisher now.

"Slow down," Fisher repeated in Cantonese.

The driver slowed the taxi and Fisher stared out the window at the line of darkened windows trolling by. The characters on the windows were Chinese, but Fisher had memorized the ones he was looking for. It appeared in the window of the fourth storefront: **SONG WOO LTD.**

"Stop," Fisher said in Cantonese.

The street was more alley than thoroughfare, dark and

narrow and bracketed on both ends by the bustling nightlife of Kowloon, most of which involved laborers coming from or going to work, and shop owners closing down for the day. It had been raining all afternoon and the pavement glistened under the illumination of a lone streetlight farther down the alley. In the distance, like a faint melody, he could hear the sing-song babble of voices speaking in Mandarin and Cantonese.

Following Grimsdottir's map, he'd taken a taxi from his hotel on Hong Kong Island and through the Cross Harbor Tunnel to this mostly commercial area of Kowloon—commercial only on its face, Fisher knew. Many of the businesses were owned and run by families who lived in apartments above the shops.

Song Woo Limited's storefront stood out for two reasons: One, it was situated between an herbalist and a dim sum kiosk; two, the space was vacant—a rarity in Hong Kong, one of the most densly populated cities on the planet.

"What's that sign say?" Fisher asked in English.

"Eh?"

Fisher handed a five-dollar bill—about forty HKD—over the seat.

"Say, 'For Lease,' then give phone number for agent." The driver recited the number.

The fact that the space was still unleased told Fisher Song Woo Ltd. had only recently been vacated.

Fisher handed over another bill. "You know this place?" The driver grabbed the dollar, but Fisher held on. "You know how long it's been here?"

"Maybe two month. Gone last week. Never see nobody."

"Okay, take me back."

The driver drove to the end of the alley and turned onto the main road. Fisher let him get three blocks away, then said, "Let me out here." He paid the fare and got out, then flipped open his satellite phone and speed-dialed. Grimsdottir answered: "Extension forty-two ninety."

"Hey, it's me. Aunt Judy isn't home, but she left a forwarding number." He recited the leasing agent's phone number. "Give her a call and let me know what you find out."

"Will do."

Fisher hung up and started walking. In the distance, over the stacked rooflines of Kowloon, he could see a rainbow of searchlights crisscrossing the sky. This was a nightly event in Hong Kong, a light show atop the skyscrapers that lined the shores of Victoria Harbor. In contrast, here he was just a few miles inland walking past a coop full of clucking chickens. This was the lure of Hong Kong: two worlds, the modern and the traditional, crowded into a chunk of land one third the size of Rhode Island.

He took a circuitous route through the streets and alleys until certain he wasn't being followed, then made his way back to the alley where Song Woo was located. He wasn't hopeful of finding anything in the deserted office, but it was an i he needed to dot.

He found the alley as he'd left it: dark and deserted. He felt slightly naked without his tac-suit, but his pants were black and after turning it inside out, his jacket was as well.

He clicked on his flashlight and gave the door a quick study. He clicked off the flashlight and pulled a pick set from his pocket and went to work. Twenty seconds later, he got a satisfying *snick* as the lock snapped back. He eased open the door, slipped through, and shut it behind him.

The office, no bigger than an average bedroom, was devoid of furniture and furnishings. Even the overhead fluorescent lights were missing from their fixtures. At the back was a closed door. Inside he found storage closet lined with empty shelves. Sitting in the corner on a table was a multifunction printer/fax/copier. On its back side he found a sticker with Chinese characters.

He pulled out his sat phone, took picture, and sent it to Grimsdottir with the caption "Translation?" Her answer came back sixty seconds later:

EXCELSIOR OFFICE RENTALS
15 CAMERON ROAD, STE 443
KOWLOON
CALL ME - GRIM

He dialed and she picked up. "What's this you sent me?" she asked.

He explained. "It looks like Song Woo was more than just a front; they did some business here. My thought is, if they rented a copier, did they rent computers?"

"And if so, might someone have forgotten to erase everything? Good thinking."

"Anything on the leasing agent?"

"Working on it, but my guess is we're going to find another front company. I do have their account number at Excelsior, though."

CAMERON Road was only a ten-minute taxi ride away, but rather than finding another comfortably dark alley, Fisher found himself standing on the sidewalk before a four-story modern office building. He lingered for only a moment, then walked across the street and stepped into a darkened doorway to watch.

Through the front windows he could see a security guard sitting at a kidney-shaped reception desk. A woman in a charcoal gray business suit got off the elevator and walked past the desk with a wave, then pushed out the door and started down the sidewalk.

Fisher's first instinct was to study the building for weaknesses, but then he checked himself. Here, patience was his best weapon. The front doors weren't locked, which left only lone guard in his way. The man was in his seventies, so incapacitating him would be simple, but if the pot of tea on the guard's desk was any indication, nature might do the work for Fisher.

Five minutes passed, then ten.

The guard stood up, stretched, then walked to the far end of the lobby and pushed through a door. *Here's to an aged bladder,* Fisher thought.

He walked across the street, into the lobby, and straight to the elevators. To the right was a door bearing a stairstep pictograph. He pushed through.

He found Excelsior Office Rentals on the fourth floor. The door's lock was more modern than the one he'd encountered at Song Woo, but it gave way with little more effort. Once inside, he found a bank of filing cabinets in a side room. He found Song Woo's file and scanned it.

He dialed Grimsdottir. "Song Woo leased two computers from Excelsior. I've got an address for their warehouse." He gave it to her.

"Sam, that's north of you—way north, in Lo Wu."

Bad news. Lo Wu sat just a half mile from the border with China. Ever since the Brits handed Hong Kong back to China in 1999, the rule for tourists was, the farther north you travel, the tighter the security. Regular PLA (People's Liberation Army) troops patrolled the streets alongside civilian cops; roadblocks were more frequent and detentions more common—especially of Westerners, who rarely ventured outside Hong Kong proper and, as far as Beijing was concerned, had little business doing so.

"I know where it is," Fisher said. "Load the map on my OPSAT. I'll be in and out of there before you can say, 'Life sentence in a Chinese labor camp.'"

29

LO WU

FISHER paid the driver, got out, and shut the door. The driver did a hasty U-turn, then sped back down the dirt road, taillights disappearing into the fog. Fisher would've preferred a less conspicuous infiltration method than a bright yellow taxi, but he was short on time and the next KCR train from Kowloon to Lo Wu wasn't scheduled until the following tomorrow. As it was, he'd had to hail three taxis before finding a driver willing to take him to Lo Wu.

Still, he wasn't overly concerned. Hong Kong's taxi drivers had an uncanny ability to immediately forget whatever their fares did or said or where they went. This wasn't so much a function of discretion as it was of self-preservation. Since the British handover, not much had changed on the surface of Hong Kong, but there was an undercurrent of tension on the streets, as if the people knew Beijing was watching.

And if the Chinese government was watching Hong Kong, they were certainly watching Lo Wu, a stone's throw from the border. If he was being watched right now, he saw no sign of it. The road was empty and devoid of streetlights. To the north, perhaps half a mile away, he could see the lights of Lo Wu; beyond those, five miles away, the brighter lights of Shenzhen, China's southernmost metropolitan area at five million people.

According to Grimsdottir's map, Excelsior's warehouse was on the southern outskirts of Lo Wu, between a slaughterhouse and a sewage treatment plant. It was also only a few blocks from the Border District's Police Headquarters. He pulled the OPSAT from his jacket pocket, called up the map, and memorized the landmarks.

He turned up the collar of the jacket and started walking.

ONLY three cars passed him and none of them slowed, which he took as a good sign. Still, with each step he felt the tingle of fear in his belly grow. He'd had his share of missions on the Chinese mainland and each of them had been unpleasant at best. Both the PLA and the Guoanbu—the Chinese secret police—were ruthlessly efficient and tended to arrest first and interrogate later.

When he reached Kong Nga Po Road, he turned right and walked a few blocks, then turned again, into a small industrial park. He found Excelsior's warehouse next to the sewage plant's hurricane fence. Fisher walked around back to the loading dock and walked up the ramp. He tried the door. It was locked. There was a buzzer. He pulled a baseball cap from his pocket and put it on, then pulled a sheaf of papers from his pocket and pressed the buzzer.

Thirty seconds passed. The door swung open. Fisher lowered his head. Under the brim of the cap he saw a pair shiny dress shoes. *Security guard,* he thought.

"*Shen-me?*" a man's voice said. *What?*

Fisher pushed the papers toward the guard, who instinctively reached for them. Fisher grabbed his wrist and jerked him off balance. As he lurched forward, Fisher wrapped his arm around the man's neck and squeezed, cutting off the blood flow. After a few seconds, the man went limp.

Fisher dragged him through the door, dropped him, and and caught the door with his fingertips to keep it from slamming shut. He froze and listened. If there were other night-shift workers, they might be coming to investigate. No one came.

The loading dock was dark save for a yellow exit sign above the door. The walls were stacked high with boxes and crates in various states of loading. On the far wall were a pair of swinging doors. He dragged the man into the nearest shadow and headed for the doors.

On the other side was the warehouse itself. Long and narrow with a low ceiling, the space was divided into four aisles, each of those divided into eight-by-eight-foot caged, floor-to-ceiling bins. Each bin seemed to contained a category of office equipment, from copiers, to desks, to generic artwork for bare walls. He found the bin he was looking for at the end of the second aisle. Through the cage he saw metal shelves crowded with computer CPUs. With a little coaxing from his picks, the padlock popped open in his hand.

He went to work, and twenty minutes later he'd checked each CPUs serial number with no luck. Then it occurred to him: Song Woo had only recently returned its equipment. What would Excelsior do with recent returns? Maintenance check, perhaps?

IN the last aisle he found two bins that had been merged into a work space. Sitting on the bench were a half-a-dozen CPUs and monitors. He picked the gate lock and started checking numbers. He got lucky almost immediately. He dialed Grimsdottir. "Got 'em," he said.

"Excellent. Plug me in."

Fisher connected the OPSAT's USB cord into the first CPU.

Grimsdottir said, "No go. The hard drive's been reformatted."

Fisher plugged into the second one.

"Bingo. That one's been wiped, too, but not very well. There's data still there. Can you pull it?"

"Consider it done."

Five minutes later, he was back at the loading dock. As his hand touched the doorknob, he heard the slamming of a car door, then footsteps coming up the ramp. He checked his watch: five minutes to midnight. Shift change?

The door buzzer went off.

Fisher hurried to the guard's body and traded his own jacket for the uniform jacket; his ballcap for the guard's brimmed one. The buzzer went off again.

"*Wei!*" a voice shouted. *Hey!*

A fist pounded on the door.

Fisher took a breath and opened it.

The security guard had his fist poised over the door, ready for another strike. Down the ramp was a two-door Hongqi, with a magnetic sign affixed to the door. The man regarded Fisher for a moment, then cocked his head and opened his mouth to speak.

Fisher hit him, a short jab to the point of his chin. The man stumbled backward, landed hard on his butt, then did a reverse somersault down the ramp. Fisher jogged after him and stopped his roll. He took the car keys from the man's jacket pocket, then carried him to the trunk, peeled off of the magnetic logo, tossed it into the backseat, and drove away.

30

AFTER ninety minutes of nearly silent travel, Fisher's escort, Elena, pulled the car to the side of the road and shut off her headlights. "I have to smoke," she said in slightly accented but letter-perfect English. She got out and lit up. Fisher got out and stretched. His feet crunched on the gravel.

As it had been for the last hour, the road was deserted and dark. Without the glow of the headlights, Fisher now realized just how dark it was. On either side of the road, marshland disappeared into the blackness. They were truly in the middle of nowhere.

His turnaround time between his foray into Hong Kong and his landing at Kiev's Borispol Airport had been a too-short six hours—just enough time to deliver the hard drive he'd stolen from the Lo Wu warehouse to Grimsdottir, go through a quick Chernobyl mission brief with Lambert, then find an empty office couch to curl up on for two hours.

From the ear-jarring bustle of Hong Kong to the silent, barren wastelands of Chernobyl, Fisher thought. He wasn't even sure what time zone his body clock was running on.

"You're nervous," he said to Elena.

"Wouldn't you be?" Elena puffed and paced. Twenty-seven, she was tall and slender, with auburn hair held in a loose ponytail. "What I've been doing for your country is about information. I give information and they take it. They've never sent anyone here. Why would they send anyone here?"

Elena Androtov was a biologist with PRIA, or the Pripyat Research Industrial Association, which managed the thirty-kilometer exclusion zone around the now-infamous Chernobyl Nuclear Power Plant. Worried that the Ukrainian and Russian governments weren't fully sharing what they knew about the ongoing effects of the Chernobyl disaster with the world, Elena had walked into a U.S. consulate while on vacation in Bulgaria and offered to be a window on what she and her colleages were really learning inside the Exclusion Zone.

Ideology, Fisher thought. It was one of the four MICE. The reasons why people offer or agree to spy for a foreign agency usually fall into one of four categories: Money, Ideology, Compromise, or Ego. Elena had never asked for money or recognition, nor was she under duress. While the CIA was grateful for her information, none of it was earth-shattering. Her handler had repeatedly reminded her she could quit at any time, no questions asked.

Fisher understood her apprehension at his sudden apperance. For the last six years her handlers had simply accepted her data with a simple "Thanks, make contact when you have more." And now, inexplicably, she was being asked to play tour guide to some mysterious secret agent.

"How long have you worked here?" he asked. He knew the answer, but talking helped.

"Six years. I came right after university. I wanted to help."

"Have you?"

"You tell me. How many people do you think died because of Chernobyl?"

"The official count was thirty-one."

Elena snorted. "Thirty-one! Twice that number of firefighters died within five minutes of reaching the scene, charred to a crisp by gamma radiation. Poof! Gone!"

"How many, then?"

"Over the last twenty years, just counting Ukraine and Belarus, I'd say two hundred thousand. So I ask you: How can I be helping when the whole world still believes thirty-one?"

"Why don't you get out?"

"I've got another year on my contract," she replied, then seemed to relax slightly. She took a drag on her cigarette. "Then maybe I'll leave. Leave Ukraine." She looked up at him. "Maybe I'll come to America."

It was more a question than statement.

Fisher said, "Maybe I can help you with that. But for now, you need to get me inside the Exclusion Zone. Get me in, and I'll do the rest."

"Oh, really? The Exclusion Zone. Okay, James Bond, what do you know of the Exclusion Zone?" Not waiting for an answer, Elena pointed up the road. "Just over that hill is the checkpoint. Chernobyl is another thirty kilometers beyond that! Thirty kilometers! That's . . . that's . . ."

"Eighteen miles," Fisher said.

"Eighteen miles. Another fifteen kilometers past that is Ghost Town."

"You mean Pripyat?" Before the disaster, Pripyat had been an idyllic city of fifty thousand where most of the Chernobyl workers and their families had lived. For the last two decades it had been deserted.

"Yes, Pripyat. That's what the disaster did. That's how bad it was—is. I'll take you there. You can feel the ghosts. They walk the streets." Elena laughed and muttered to herself, "Thirty-one people. Hah!"

"You're pretty passionate about this. Were you always?"

"Oh, no. Just like everyone else, I'd believed the official reports. Why would our government lie about something like that? They're here to protect us. I was naive. I came here and my eyes were opened. Yours will be, too—if you want to see, that is."

"I do."

"Good." She checked her watch. "Get back in. We need to go."

31

ELENA drove for another few minutes, then, as Fisher had asked, pulled over again. "The checkpoint is one kilometer," she said. "You remember where you're going?"

Fisher grabbed his rucksack from the backseat and got out. "I remember. I'll meet you there in fifteen minutes."

"Fifteen minutes."

He shut the door, patted the car's roof, and she drove away. Her headlights disappeared into the mist. He shouldered the rucksack and walked down the embankment into the marsh. He pulled out the OPSAT, double-checked his map, then settled his trident goggles into place, switched to NV, and started jogging.

* * *

HE and Elena would face two checkpoints. The first one, placed at the outer edge of the thirty-kilometer Exclusion Zone, was manned by guards drawn from the Ukrainian Army; every soldier was required to spend six weeks guarding the zone.

No car was allowed to enter the Zone, lest it be contaminated. Outsiders were required to park their clean vehicles in the checkpoint parking lot, then walk through, where they were logged in and assigned a "dirty" vehicle from the motor pool.

The Inner Ring, eleven kilometers from Reactor Number Four, was guarded by a second checkpoint, where visitors were again required to trade cars—dirty for even dirtier—and change clothes. Civilian clothes, which would be decontaminated, sealed in plastic bags, then returned to the first checkpoint to await the wearer's return, were exchanged for dark blue coveralls, plastic boots, gloves, and white surgical masks.

According to PRIA, the use of the zone cars was not hazardous to humans, but their introduction to the world outside the zone might have "unforeseen ecological consequences."

TEN minutes after setting out, Fisher came to a line of scrub pines and stopped. A gust of wind whistled through the trees, causing the branches to creak. He pulled his collar up against the chill.

Whether by chance or by choice Fisher didn't know, but at least at this entrance, the tree line represented the outer ring. Irrational as it was, he wondered if things would look and feel different inside the zone. Was the grass rougher, more brittle? Were the leaves on the trees withered, trapped in in some endless radioactive autumn? Did the water smell different? He knew better, but such was the nature of radiation—an invisible rain of poison that left nothing untouched. Including the imagination.

He forced his mind back on track.

A half mile to his west was the first checkpoint. He slowed his breathing and listened. In the marshes sound traveled well, and after a few seconds he heard the distant *chunk* of a car door slamming, then voices speaking in Ukrainian. *Another visitor coming or going,* Fisher thought. Probably the latter. By now, Elena would already be through the checkpoint and waiting at the motor pool.

He stood up and started picking his way through the pines.

After a few hundred yards, the trees began to thin and he could see gray light filtering through the branches. He reached the edge and stopped. Ahead lay a gravel parking lot filled with dozens of cars and trucks. A single sodium-vapor light sitting atop a pole in the middle of the lot was the only illumination. As Elena had predicted, the ever-flirtatious checkpoint guards had assigned her her favorite car: a bright red 1964 Opel Kadett. Fisher could see her silhouetted in the driver's seat.

From habit, he waited and watched for another ten minutes. He wasn't necessarily concerned about her trustworthiness, but she'd been spying for the CIA for six years—a lot of time in which suspicions can be raised and investigations started.

Staying within the tree line, he circled the parking lot until satisfied no one else was about. He walked to Elena's Opel and got in. She put the car in gear, backed out of the lot, and started driving.

"What took you so long?" she asked. "Is everything okay?"

"Everything's fine. I'm just not as fast on my feet as I used to be. Getting old."

"Old? Rubbish. You look fine to me," she said, concentrating on the windshield.

"Thanks."

"You're welcome." She tapped her finger on the steering wheel. "Are you married?"

"No. You?"

"No."

They drove in silence for five minutes, then Elena said, "Have you ever had *borshch*? Real Ukrainian *borshch*?"

"I don't think I have."

"I make wonderful *borshch*."

"I'm not even sure what's in it."

"You start with pork stock, add beans, beets, lemons, vegetables, sorrel leaves, vinegar, strained rhubarb juice, garlic. . . . It's delicious. I'll make it for you."

"Where do the vegetables come from?"

She smiled. "You mean do I grow them in the zone? No, they're from from the outside. Kiev."

"Okay."

"It's only a few hours befor sunrise. Do you want to

go to the inner zone? I assume you'd rather do your skulking at night."

Fisher had the documentation and cover story to explain his presence if apprehended, but he preferred to avoid all contact with the authorities. He'd allotted himself three days inside the Exclusion Zone. More than simply a safety concern, he needed to do the job and get out. With a U.S. Navy battle group on its way to the Gulf of Oman, events would begin moving quickly. Iran would send elements of its own Navy to meet the battle group. Tensions would mount; shots would be fired.

"How do you know I'm a skulker?" he asked her.

She glanced sideways at him. "You have the eyes of a skulker. Kind, though—kind eyes."

"To answer your question: Yes, night would be best."

"Good. We'll go now. You really should see Pripyat. I can show you things you won't see in pictures."

Sightseeing wasn't part of his mission, but he had the time—and the curiosity. "Drive on."

IT was only fifteen kilometers, or seven miles, but along the way they passed east of the village of Chernobyl on the banks of the Pripyat River, which at the time of the accident fed the plant's cooling pond.

Elena arced around Chernobyl to the east, passing through dozens of villages, all abandoned save for a few hundred die-hard farmers who'd returned despite the government's warnings. Elena translated the Cyrillic signs as they drove: Yampol, Malyy Cherevach, Zapol'ye—one by one they appeared and disappeared in the Opel's head-lights, wooden farmhouses and sheds and barns, many of them crumbling, overgrown with foliage and moss, fences so coiled in vines and underbrush they leaned at wild an-gles to the ground, structures so primitive Fisher had lit-tle trouble imagining himself transported back a hundred years.

"This is surreal," Fisher said.

"This is nothing. Just wait."

AS they drew closer to the city, farmhouses and barns gave way to smaller buildings, made mostly of gray con-crete and faded brown brick. The signs were all in Cyril-lic, but there was something universal about the structures: a gas station, a grocery store; a bank. . . . Soon the scrub pines and marshland gave way to vacant lots and paved intersections.

They approached Pripyat from the west, so Fisher's first glimpse of the city's skyline was backlit by the first hints of sunlight on the horizon. Great rectangular blocks of buildings, tall and narrow, short and squat, rose from the terrain. In twilight they were dark and dimensionless, as though painted on the skyline by a movie set designer.

As they entered the city limits and the horizon bright-ened, details began to stand out.

Pripyat was in many ways a typical Soviet-era city. The structures, from apartment high-rises to four-story schools and office buildings, were built in gray cinder block. Every-thing had an almost Lego-like atmosphere, as though geometric blocks were simply dropped into the empty spaces between the streets and then given designations: Apartment Block 17; People's Bank Number 84; General Office Complex 21. The only bits of color Fisher saw were faded murals painted on the sides of buildings, traditional Revolution-era scenes of Lenin or of iron-jawed, blond-haired men standing knee deep in golden fields of wheat, one hand clutching a sickle, the other shielding eyes that stared at some distant horizon.

What struck Fisher the most was the utter stillness of the place. If the outlying farms seemed trapped in the 1800s, Pripyat seemed frozen on that fateful day in April of 1986. Cars sat parked in the middle of intersections, their doors still open as though the occupants had simply gotten out and run away. Suitcases and footlockers and wheelbarrows piled high with clothes, pots and pans, and framed pictures lay strewn on the sidewalks.

Just like in Slipstone, Fisher reminded himself.

They passed an elementary school. The playground, once a clearing surrounded by trees, had been reclaimed by weeds and bushes. A jungle gym rose from the undergrowth, its steel frame choked with vines; a raised playhouse in the shape of an elephant with a slide for a trunk was a nothing more than a rusted hulk. The school's doors stood yawning—shoved open, Fisher imagined, by fleeing children and teachers. As the school disappeared in the car's side window, Fisher glimpsed a child's doll sitting perfectly upright on the rim of a sandbox.

This, he decided, is what nuclear Armageddon would look like.

"Is it all like this?" he asked.

"Yes. And it will be for the next three hundred years. It'll take that long for the contamination levels to fade. I come here sometimes, just to remind myself it's real. But never at night. I never come at night."

"I don't blame you."

Next they passed a six-story apartment building, another gray cube lined with balconies that ran the length of the structure. With only a few exceptions, each balcony door on the sixth floor stood open. It took Fisher a moment to understand why. These apartments faced southeast—toward the power plant. The upper floor would have offered an unobstructed view of the reactor's explosion and subsequent fire. He imagined women in housecoats and children in pajamas standing at the railing watching the spectacle, not yet realizing what had happened. Not knowing an invisible cloud of cesium was already falling on them. Below, many of the balconies a faded number had been painted in red or orange.

"What are those?" Fisher asked.

"It wasn't until the next morning, after many of the children had left for school, that the evacuation order was given. People were told to mark their balconies with the number of their evacuation bus so if loved ones returned home, they would know."

"My God," Fisher murmured.

"Have you seen enough?"

Fisher nodded, still staring out the window.

32

THEY drove south for ten minutes before Fisher saw the first sign they were approaching Chernobyl itself. In the distance an obelisk rose from the marshlands. It was the plant's smokestack, Elena explained. As they drew closer, Fisher could see the stack was painted in faded red and white horizontal bands. Beside it stood a crane that he guessed was being used for nearly constant rebuilding of the Sarcophagus, which had over the years begun to crack and crumble.

Twelve kilometers from the plant, Elena veered off the paved road and onto a gravel track that wound through a copse of stunted pine trees. After a few hundred yards, she turned into a driveway. She pulled to a stop before a ranch-style bungalow painted a washed-out yellow. Like the farmhouses Fisher had seen in the outlying villages, the bungalow was encased in a labyrinth of vines that snaked up the walls, along the eaves, and around the front porch's post, like snakes frozen in mid-slither.

"PRIA's headquarters is just inside the inner zone," Elena said, getting out. "Moscow built it about a year after the disaster. Of course, we all spend as little time there as possible."

"Who does this place belong to?"

"Me, now. Back then, a local party boss from Kiev. When the plant was first build, Moscow ordered bigwigs to take dachas here, to prove the reactor was safe. Officially, all the PRIA scientists are supposed to live in a block of renovated apartments south of Pripyat."

"I saw them." Fisher grabbed his rucksack from the backseat. "Not very cozy."

"Yes, lovely, aren't they? This place is better. The outside isn't much, but the roof doesn't leak and the insulation is good. Plus, it wasn't in the plume."

"I don't understand."

"The plume of radioactive dust. Most of it was blown west and then north, toward Belorus. We're on the east side of the plant. Come on in." She started walking. She realized Fisher wasn't following, and turned back and smiled. "Relax. You see that?" She pointed to what looked like a weather vane jutting from the roof. "It's a dosimeter; I check it twice a day. Trust me, this is one of the cleanest places in Chernobyl."

"Guess it pays to be a biologist," Fisher said, and started walking toward the porch.

"I'm very careful. I would like to have children some day."

SHE directed Fisher to the spare bedroom, where he dropped his rucksack, and then he joined her in the kitchen. She was crouched before the open door of a woodstove, shoving sticks into a growing flame. She shut the door and stood up. "Sit. Tea will be ready in a few minutes."

She got a loaf of black bread and a tin of blackberry jam from the cupboard and laid them on the table. She chose an apple from the windowsill, washed it, then sliced it into a bowl.

"The water comes from a new artesian well," she said before he had a chance to ask. "I test that every day, too."

Fisher said, "Sorry. This takes some getting used to."

"Don't apologize. I was the same way when I first came here. I didn't want to touch anything. I even found myself holding my breath without realizing it. It's a natural reaction."

They ate breakfast and then Fisher helped her clean up. "I've got to go into work for a few hours," she said, wiping her hands on a towel. "I'm running an experiment on a three-headed cattail."

Fisher squinted at her, wondering if she were pulling his leg.

"I'm serious," she said. "Almost all the cattails around the reactor's cooling pond are mutated. Believe me, those are some of the tamer changes we've seen. You should see some of the carp they pull out of the pond." She sucked her lips and crossed her eyes. "Ugly, like that."

Fisher laughed.

"I'll be home around noon. On the way I've got to check on something in the village—a rumor I heard once. It might interest you."

"What's that?"

"Let me check first. Go to sleep. If anyone knocks, don't answer."

FISHER tried to sleep, but his body wouldn't fully cooperate, so he dozed on and off for a few hours, then got up and wandered around the house. Elena had a good book collection she kept inside an old china cabinet in the living room. The titles ranged from Tolstoy and Balzac to Stephen Hawking and Danielle Steel. He also found a milk crate full of old records, mostly from the Big Band era. He put a Mancini tribute on the turntable and sat down with an English language version of *War and Peace* and read until Elena came home.

She was carrying a sack of groceries.

"Borshch?" Fisher asked.

"Of course. I promised you."

After the groceries were put away, they sat down and shared a lunch of cold cuts, cheese, and wine. "So," Fisher said, "this rumor?"

"Yes, I checked. I wasn't sure I'd remembered it right, but the rumor is about four months ago a pair of soldiers went missing in the middle of the night. They were never found. Everyone, including the local commander, assumed they'd deserted. The were last seen heading toward the bunkers you were asking about. I've got the name of the man who saw them last: Alexi. He's ninety-five years old, but still sharp. An old warhorse."

"He'll talk to us?"

Elena smiled. "Alexi loves to talk. He was a tank commander during the Great Patriotic War. He claims to have killed eighteen Panzers at Kursk before he got captured. He spent the rest of the war in a labor camp in Poland. We'll go tonight, after *borshch*. I see you found my book collection."

"I'm sorry, I didn't mean to—"

Elena waved her hand. "No, no, I meant to show it to you. Here, I'll clean up. You go back and read. Maybe you'll have better luck than I did."

"I thought *War and Peace* was required reading for all Russians."

"Very funny. I've tried to read it four times. It bores me to tears. Besides, I'm Ukrainian."

33

SHORTLY after nightfall, with his belly full of *borshch* so good he felt cheated for having lived so long without it, Fisher and Elena left her bungalow.

Throughout the afternoon, a low-pressure front had moved in, bringing with it dark clouds and icy drizzle. The Kadett's headlights cut twin swaths through the dark, illuminating ruts and potholes rimmed with ice. The heater, which worked only on the highest setting, made a sound that Elena described as a "carrot being shoved into a fan blade."

The change in weather was a mixed blessing for Fisher. The clouds and lack of starlight would provide better cover, but the sleet and dropping temperatures would leave the fields and marshes coated in ice, which would crackle with every footfall.

He wasn't sure what to make of the story of the missing soldiers. Desertion was common in the Ukrainian Army—especially, he imagined, among troops pulling Chernobyl duty. Many of the conscripts were young and poorly educated, and all they knew about Chernobyl was that it had happened long before their births or when they were too young to remember, and that it was a place of ghosts and poison and sickness. Still, the rumor was also a place to start.

They drove for twenty minutes, following the road south along the Pripyat River. Three miles from the power plant, she turned off the main road and crossed a rickety bridge to the east side of the river. Set back in a stand of birch trees was a cabin. In the headlights Fisher could see the structure's walls were made of rough birch planks sealed with what looked like a mixture of mud and straw. The roof was piled high with sod.

The Kadett coasted to a stop and Elena doused the headlights.

"He lives here year-round?" Fisher asked.

She nodded. "For the last eighteen years. It's actually very warm in the winter; warmer than my place, even. I visit him once a week, bring him some *borshch*."

"Lucky man."

"What, you thought you were the only man I made *borshch* for? Men."

Fisher started to open the door, but Elena stopped him. "Let Alexi come out and see that it's me first.

He's ornery with strangers and handy with a shotgun."

"And a tank," Fisher said.

"And that."

The cabin's door opened and a lantern appeared on the porch. In its glow Fisher could see a gaunt face and bushy salt-and-pepper beard. Elena rolled down her window and called something in Ukrainian. Alexi grumbled something back and waved for them to come in.

"He promised not to shoot you," Elena said. "I told him you brought *borshch*."

FISHER hadn't brought *borsch*, but Elena had, and they sat in silence while Alexi ate all of it, then licked the bowl clean. The interior of the cabin wasn't what Fisher expected. Except for the mud-filled gaps between the planks, the walls were painted a butter yellow. Off the kitchen there were two bedrooms and a living room with a large open-hearth fireplace.

As were most WWII Soviet tankers, Alexi was short and sinewy—the kind of muscle that comes from hard labor. His hands were so calloused they looked like leather.

Alexi set the bowl aside and grabbed a bottle of vodka from the shelf and poured three shots. They all drank. Alexi and Elena talked for a few minutes before she turned to Fisher.

"He'll talk to you. I told him you weren't with the government—he doesn't like the government—and that you're writing a book about Chernobyl since the accident."

"Have him tell us the story of that night—the night the soldiers disappeared."

Elena translated Fisher's words, then listened as Alexi began talking. She translated.

"He says it was past midnight and he was fishing in the cooling pond beside the plant. He saw an Army truck appear on the road on the other side of the pond and then circle around to the 'mounds'—the bunker area—but before it got there, the headlights went out and the engine went quiet. A few minutes later another truck appeared, this one from the opposite direction, and parked facing the Army truck.

"The men who got out of the second truck weren't in uniform, so he got curious. He snuck through the reeds until he could see better. There were the two soldiers from the Army truck and four civilian men from the second truck. They talked for a few minutes; then the four civilians disappeared behind the truck and then reappeared wearing 'cosmonaut gear.'"

"A biohazard suit," Fisher said.

"Yes, I think so."

Alexi kept talking.

"Two of the men were each carrying a big shiny footlocker. They all walked behind one of the mounds. The soldiers stayed behind, leaning against their truck, smoking.

"About twenty minutes passed, and then the four men reappeared from behind the mound carrying the boxes, two of them to each box. They loaded the boxes into the back of the second truck, then stripped off their suits and joined the soldiers at their truck.

"They talked for a few minutes, and then one of the civilians opened the door to the truck, took out a suitcase, and walked back. He handed the briefcase to one of the soldiers. And that's when . . . That's when it happened."

"What?" Fisher asked.

She held up her hand to silence him, then leaned closer to Alexi and put her hand on his forearm. They spoke for a while, then she leaned back and frowned. She turned to Fisher.

"He says after the civilian handed over the briefcase, his three partners drew pistols and started shooting. The first soldier went down, but the second was faster. As he fell, he got off two rounds from his rifle, killing one of the civilians. Then the leader—the one with the briefcase—walked over and shot each soldier a final time time in the head, then reloaded and emptied his pistol into the dead civilian's face. The three of them dragged the bodies behind the mounds, then climbed into the truck and drove away.

"He says he buried the two soldiers and the civilian in the woods beyond the bunkers."

"Did you know about this?" Fisher asked.

"All I knew was the rumor: that Alexi had seen the men the night they disappeared."

"Did he tell anyone about this?"

Elena asked him, then said, "He thinks he did, but he's not sure. He may be confused."

"Tell me."

"He says he told the area commander."

34

IT took only fifteen minutes to reach the site Alexi had described. Before they got there, Fisher told her to pull over. He reached up and switched off the dome light, then opened the door. "I'll meet you on the main road in two hours," he said.

"Let me go with you. I can help you."

"You can help me by going home and waiting. I just need to check a few things; I'll move faster alone. Pop the trunk."

She did so. Fisher walked back and retrieved the bag of gear Elena had put together for him—a pair of hooded biohazard coveralls, a respirator, goggles, boots, and a double set of gloves.

"You remember how to put it all on?" she asked.

"Yes."

"And the duct tape? On the wrists and ankles and neck? Make sure you get a good seal."

"I will."

Fisher closed the door and Elena drove away. He waited until the Kadett's taillights disappeared around the bend, then shouldered his duffel and walked into the woods.

FISHER didn't think Alexi was confused. He believed every word of the old tanker's story. Someone had bought their way into the Exclusion Zone and then bought access to one the bunkers, and you don't buy that kind of access from a pair of privates in the Ukrainian Army, but from staff officers—like an area commander. Whether the man knew his soldiers were going to be murdered, Fisher didn't know, but according to Elena the commander in question, a colonel, had retired two months earlier and moved to the resort city of Yalta, on the Black Sea.

Alexi claimed that upon hearing the story of the shooting, the colonel thanked him, promised there would be a full investigation, and then swore him to secrecy. Alexi didn't quite believe him, so he told the colonel the soldiers and the other man had been taken away in the civilians' truck.

"The civilian he didn't care much about," Elena had translated, "but he didn't think the colonel would do right by the dead soldiers. They were comrades; they deserved a soldier's burial."

Fisher could only speculate as to why the colonel left Alexi alive, but he suspected Alexi's renown in Chernobyl had something to do with it. If two young privates go missing, it's desertion. If Alexi goes missing, it's a mystery that locals want solved.

FOLLOWING his memory of the map Elena had drawn him, Fisher weaved his way through the darkened woods until he came to a stream, which he followed east until it widened into an inlet choked with reeds and cattails. He was now on the eastern side of the plant's cooling pond.

He pulled out his Geiger counter and passed it over the dirt and nearby foliage. The rapid *tick-tick-tick* in his earpiece made his skin crawl, but the numbers were within acceptable range. According to Grimsdottir, his exposure here would amount to three chest X-rays.

Over the tops of the cattails he could see the outline of the power plant. He was a quarter mile from the site of the worst nuclear disaster in history.

The morning after the explosion, rescue workers finally realized they were fighting a losing battle against the fires in the crater, which were being fed by not only by the molten slag of the remaining fuel rods but also by the highly flammable graphite that had sloughed off the casings of the rods. Helicopters were called in to dump neutron absorbants into the pit.

Over the next six days nearly two thousand sorties were flown through the radioactive plume gushing from the reactor. Five thousand tons—some ten million pounds—of lead, sand, clay, dolomite, sodium phosphate, and polymer liquids were dropped into the crater until finally, a week after the initial explosion, the fires died out. None of the pilots who flew over the pit survived the exposure.

Across the cooling pond, Fisher could see the bunker mounds. They were arranged in three-by-three squares, each square separated from its neighbor by a hundred yards. The mounds, which were nothing more than bus-sized shipping containers, had been covered by layers of earth and then topped off with a conrete lid. As with everything at Chernobyl, nature had reclaimed the bunkers, turning them into shrub-covered hillocks. If he hadn't known what they were, Fisher might have mistaken the mounds for natural terrain features.

He made his way through the reeds until he reached the opposite shore. He was about to cross the road when he heard the growl of an engine. He crouched down.

A pair of headlights appeared on the road. The vehicle, moving slowly, paused at the first set of bunkers. A searchlight came on and panned over the mounds, then went out. The vehicle pulled ahead and repeated the process at the next grouping. As it drew closer, Fisher could see the vehicle was a GAZ-67, a WWII-era Soviet jeep. Two soldiers were sitting in the front seat.

The jeep drew even with Fisher's hiding place, paused, scanned the mounds, then moved on. After a long ten mintes, the GAZ rounded the bend and disappeared from view. Every few seconds the searchlight would pop on, skim over over the next set of bunkers, then shut off.

Fisher dashed across the road, down the embankment, and through the tall grass to the clearing surrounding the bunkers. He pulled out his Geiger counter. The numbers showed a slight rise, but they were still within limits.

Alexi claimed the bunker the civilians had been interested in was Number 3, the farthest back from the road. He ran between the first two mounds, then veered right and stopped at the base of Number 3. He scanned again with the Geiger scan: still okay.

He followed the edge of the mound to the back, then flipped his goggles into place and switched to infrared. The image was stunning. The ground beneath his feet was a dark blue that slowly faded to a neon blue where the slope started. From there the change was abrupt, a line of orangish-yellow that began at the base of the mound and went to the top.

After twenty-plus years, the radioactive debris was still pushing heat through several feet of soil and a layer of concrete. Again Fisher felt the tingle of apprehension. *Don't think, Sam,* he commanded himself. *Do what you came to do and then get out.*

He opened his rucksack and rummaged around until he found the collapsible entrenching tool, which he quickly assembled. He walked the length of the mound, pausing every foot or so to jam the shovel into the slope. After ten feet, the tip of the blade plunged through into open air. He twisted the shovel, pulling out clumps of soil until he'd cleared a small hole. He clicked on his flashlight and shined it inside.

There was tunnel in the sod. At the end of it Fisher could see a patch of rusted steel.

35

HE laid the shovel aside and scanned the tunnel with the Geiger. The numbers had spiked up significantly. He grabbed his duffel and backed away, then chose an open spot in the earth and dug a hole two feet wide and two feet deep.

Next he donned the biohazard gear, starting with the coveralls and ending with the respirator and goggles. He took his time, making sure the fit was right and that all the zippers and flaps were closed, then sealed all the seams with the duct tape as Elena had instructed. Despite the protective gear, she had been adamant about his time inside the container: "No more than four minutes. Don't touch anything you don't have to touch. Don't bump or brush up against anything. Walk slowly—very slowly, like you're moving through water."

Fisher clicked on his headlamp and returned to the mound. He began widening the tunnel. The task was easy. Whoever had been here before him had done all the hard work. The mouth of the tunnel had simply been overlaid with a lattice of birch branches, then recovered with chunks of sod carefully cut from the face of the mound.

After five minutes work, the full tunnel was exposed. Four feet tall and two feet wide, it led directly to the container's rusted door, which was secured by a crossbar. A soil-encrusted padlock, its shackle cut in two, lay at the foot of the door.

He paused to catch his breath. The coveralls, gloves, and boots were all chemically treated to retard radio-isotope absorption, but they also trapped body heat. He could feel sweat running down the back of his neck and his sides. Inside the respirator mask, his breath hissed. His goggles were perpetually fogged but, nervous about touching anything with his potentially tainted gloves, he left them alone.

This was just a glimpse into what rescuers had endured after the explosion, Fisher realized. Short of manpower and time, hundreds of soldiers and civilians spent days inside protective suits working at the lip of the crater with shovels and buckets and in some cases their hands to push radioactive debris back into the pit.

He set aside the shovel, then ducked down. Following the beam of his headlamp, he stepped into the tunnel. Pebbles and dirt rained down on him. Roots hung from the overhead like skeletal fingers. He reached the container door and stopped. *Deep breath*.

He gripped the crossbar and lifted. Half expecting to hear the shrief of rusted metal, he was surprised how soundlessly the latch moved. Curious, he peered at the mechanism; it glistened with oil. He felt his heart rate increase. This is where it had all started. Months ago, four men had crept down this same tunnel, oiled this same latch, then gone inside, stolen the radioactive debris that had ended up aboard the *Trego,* and had poisoned an entire city.

He swung the door open. Its passage dislodged a small avalanche of dirt. He waited, frozen in place, until it passed, then opened the door the rest of the way and shined his flashlight inside. He was immediately confronted by what looked like a chest-high wall of gray-black ash and scrap metal—which in fact it was, the only difference being this was so radioactive that even now, after two decades, direct exposure would kill you within minutes.

Up until now, there'd been a small part of Fisher's mind that found this too surreal to believe. But here, within arm's reach, was the piece of proof that made it real.

A section of the debris wall was missing, scooped out, he assumed, by the two discarded grain shovels at his feet.

SLOWLY, carefully, he backed out of the container and into the tunnel. From the leg pocket of his coveralls he pulled a cylindrical sample tube roughly the size of a coffee mug. This was the last piece of gear Elena had given him. Made of lightweight titanium, the double-walled tube was lead-lined and topped with a finely threaded lid.

He unscrewed the lid. Inside was a second, identical tube, this one the size of his thumb and secured in place by three spring-loaded prongs. He pulled this tube free and unscrewed the lid. Inside was a quarter-teaspoon titanium scoop.

With the scoop in one hand and the tube in the other, Fisher went back inside the container. He was halfway to a kneeling position when he caught himself. *Don't bump or brush up against anything.* He spread his legs wide for balance, then lowered himself into a crouch. He gently eased the tip of the scoop into a mound of debris at his feet. In the glow of his headlamp he saw a puff of ash surround his scoop. He went still and waited for the ash to settle, then pulled the scoop free and dumped its contents into the tube. He repeated the process five more times until the tube was filled with ash, then laid the scoop aside. He backed out of the container and into the tunnel, where he slid the smaller tube back into its mother, then screwed both lids back on.

He hadn't realized he'd been holding his breath. He let it out. He closed the container door and secured the crossbar.

Per Elena's adamant instructions, he took off his outer gloves and laid them aside, then picked up the tube and walked to the mouth of the tunnel and set the tube outside. He walked back inside, removed his boots, and laid them beside the gloves, then stepped out of the tunnel.

The cool, night air enveloped him. He had to resist the impulse to tear off his gear. *Slow down, Sam. Almost there.* A few more steps and he was done.

He walked to the hole he'd dug, and slowly removed his protective gear and placed each piece inside, followed by his inner layer of clothing, a thin cotton union suit Elena had given him. Now nude, he pulled a gallon jug of water from his rucksack and rinsed himself off, from the top of his head to the soles of his feet, then used the last few ounces to wash off the exterior of the sample tube.

He wiped the excess water from his skin and hair, then donned his own clothes and sat down to catch his breath. He was drenched in sweat and his legs felt rubbery.

From the other side of the mound he heard the growl of the GAZ's engine. He snatched up his rucksack and hurried behind the mound and dropped flat. Seconds later, the searchlight skimmed over the ground and up the side of the mound, just missing the tunnel opening. The searchlight blinked out. The GAZ's engine faded down the road.

After covering the hole and collapsing the tunnel entrance, he shouldered his rucksack, then pulled out the OPSAT. Alexi's map to the graves had been detailed enough for Fisher to find corresponding landmarks on the OPSAT's map, so now he got his bearings and slipped into the woods, heading northeast.

Alex had buried the soldiers together, under a spruce tree with a small cross made of twigs; the civilian he'd simply dumped in a shallow grave deeper in the forest.

After fifteen minutes of walking, Fisher matched up the landmarks on the OPSAT and found the spot.

He had a final hunch that needed satisfaction.

Using the entrenching tool, he scraped around until he found the perimeter of the grave, then shoveled along the edges until the tip of the shovel touched something solid. He shoved his hand into the soil until his hand closed around the object. With a start, he realized it was a wrist. The flesh was the consistency of rotten pumpkin.

He lifted the wrist slowly until a forearm rose from the dirt, followed by a shoulder. The stench of decomposition filled his nostrils He squeezed his eyes against it and swallowed. Now with an anatomical landmark with which to work, he started scooping away dirt until the corpse was uncovered.

Alexi had laid the man faceup, arms crossed over his chest. Four months in the earth had rotted away most of the skin, revealing patches of muscle that had turned greenish-black with mold. In some places he could see patches of bone. He lifted each hand and examined them more closely. The fingertips on each were gone. Similarly, the face was obliterated, save for some skin and flesh around the cheekbones and eye sockets, but even these were shattered from what Fisher assumed were bullets.

He leaned forward until he was within inches of the corpse's face. There was no way to be sure—no way to prove it beyond a doubt—but Fisher swore the corpse's eyes had an outer epicanthal fold. An Asian epicanthal fold.

36

"WOULD you bet your life on it?" Lambert asked. "Would you bet a war on it?"

Fisher considered the question. His gut instinct said, "Yes," but Lambert's point was well made: Lives were at stake—many thousands of lives that would be lost in a war that would not only forever change the Middle East but also America's place in the world. Decisions of this gravity weren't made on instinct.

"My life—yes," Fisher replied. "A war . . . No."

Fisher was convinced there was a game being played here, and that all the pieces had yet to be uncovered. But who was the driving force? The case against Iran was seemingly solid: the FBI had three suspects in custody, all of whom were talking, laying a trail a evidence that pointed to Tehran. And what did he have to counter that? A now-destroyed yacht and a corpse with vaguely Asian features.

After taking a dozen digital pictures of the corpse and then covering the grave again, Fisher had retraced his way through the forest to the main road. As promised, Elena had been waiting.

Wordlessly, she drove him to within a few blocks of the Exclusion Zone checkpoint. Their good-bye was awkward. Something had clearly grown between them over the past two days, but Fisher knew the situation was impossible. He briefly considered trying to take her out with him—CIA be damned—but he quickly quashed it. If they were caught, she would be imprisoned and, at best, he would be detained for questioning. There was too much at stake and too little time. In the end, all he could do was promise to talk to the CIA on her behalf. She'd simply nodded.

"So why the hesitation?" Lambert asked now.

"You mean, why am I not playing the good soldier?" Fisher replied. "Why don't I just take my marching orders and march? You know me better than that, Lamb."

"I do. And I also know how much you hate politics."

"When this started, you told me the President wanted all the t's crossed and i's dotted before he pulled the trigger. Consider this an i without a dot."

Pushing through the Situation Room's door, Grimsdottir said, "Colonel, there might be something to that." She sat down at the conference table and slid a manila folder across to Lambert. "I managed to pull a good chunk of data from the hard drive Sam brought back from Hong Kong."

Lambert studied the folder's contents for a few moments. "Give it to me in English."

"First of all, I found traces of Marcus Greenhorn all over the hard drive. I think I'm starting to learn his tricks. There was no virus, but he'd written the code for the CPU's built-in firewall. Too bad he's dead; I wouldn't mind going up against him again."

A phone at Lambert's elbow trilled and he picked up. He listened for a moment, said, "Escort him up," then hung up. "Tom Richards."

When Fisher had touched down at Andrews Air Force Base, his sample from Chernobyl had been taken by special CIA courier to the Department of Energy's Oak Ridge National Laboratory for anaysis.

"Before he gets here," Fisher said, "I need a favor." He explained Elena's situation. "She's burnt out, Colonel. Sooner or later she's going to get caught."

Lambert nodded thoughtfully, but Fisher could see the doubt in his eyes. While of value, the information Elena had been feeding the CIA wasn't earth-shattering, and in terms of lives and resources, it probably wasn't worth the risk of extracting her.

"I'll look into it, Sam, but you know what they're likely to say."

"Pull some strings."

A chime sounded at the Situation Room's door. Lambert pushed a button on the table; with a buzz, the cypher lock disengaged. Tom Richards walked in and sat down.

"I'm short on time, so I'll get to it: The sample you brought back from Chernobyl is a perfect match with what we found aboard the *Trego* and at Slipstone. No question."

"Where does that leave us?" Lambert asked.

"The President is scheduled to speak to the nation tonight. An hour before that, he'll be meeting with the ambassadors for the Russian Federation and Ukraine. The message will be simple: Either by negligence or complicity, Moscow and Kiev are each equally responsible for failing to properly secure the material used in the attacks."

Richards's words were clearly based on the talking points the public would hear again and again in the coming weeks from senators, representatives, and White House and Pentagon officials. This shot across Russia's and Ukraine's bow was as much an accusation as it was a warning: Don't interfere in what's coming.

The question was: Was it too late to stop the machine before shots were fired?

"Those are pretty broad strokes, Tom," Lambert said.

"The evidence supports it. The material came from Chernobyl—probably sold by that now-retired Army area commander—and it ended aboard a ship set on a collision course with our shores and in the water supply of one of our towns. At last count, over four thousand people are dead in Slipstone. Someone's going to answer for that."

"You still haven't answered my original question," Lambert said. "Where does all this leave us? Until I hear otherwise, I'm going to assume the President's order still stands. We're still on-mission."

Richards shrugged. "That's above my pay grade, Colonel. I serve at the President's pleasure."

"As do we all. Now spare me party line, Tom. What's the feeling at Langley?"

Richards closed his briefing folder and leaned back. "The case is solid. Almost airtight. But there's a feeling on our side—on the Ops side—that we're missing something."

"Join the club," Fisher replied.

"Here's my problem. Taken together, the *Trego* and Slipstone operations were far more complex than what happened on 9/11. The level of operational sophistication and financial backing required for this was enormous. To me, that usually means state-sponsored. But I can't shake the feeling we caught these guys a little too easily—maybe not the guy aboard the *Trego,* but the Slipstone suspects for sure. They were sloppy. Slow. Didn't have a layered exfiltration plan in place. The disparity between the operation itself and the way these guys behaved afterward is disturbing."

Grimsdottir said, "Maybe Tehran wanted them caught. That leaves them the option to either deny involvement or claim credit, depending which way the wind is blowing."

"We've thought of that," Richards said. "In the end, though, all out speculation changes nothing. Countries have gone to war with less provocation and evidence. We've got the support of the Congress, the United Nations, and most of the world." Richards checked his watch, then gathered his folder and stood up.

Lambert said, "Thanks for coming by, Tom."

"My pleasure. Good work, all of you."

After Richards was gone, Lambert said, "You heard the man: The clock is ticking. After the President's address tonight, we're on the eve of war. Have we got anything to suggest that's the wrong course?"

Grimsdottir cleared her throat. "I might."

37

"**WE'RE** all ears," Lambert said.

"It's ironic, really," Grimsdottir said. "Whoever tried to erase the hard drive before it was returned to Excelsior did a decent job—or would have, if not for Greenhorn's firewall. It protected not only a chunk of the drive for itself, but a buffer zone, too. That's where I found this."

She held up a computer printout that looked to Fisher like nothing more than a series of random numbers separated by colons, periods, and semicolons. There was, however, a highlighted portion that looked generically familiar:

207.142.131.247

"It's an IP address," Fisher said.

An IP, or Internet Protocol, address is a unique identifier assigned to any network device—from routers to servers to desktops to fax machines.

"A gold star for Mr. Fisher," Grimsdottir said. "This is the best clue we could have gotten. This particular IP led me to a service provider in Hong Kong, which in turn led me to an e-mail account, which finally led me to a mother company called Shinzhan Network Solutions based in Shanghai. Shinzhan specializes in wireless satellite Internet service.

"According their records, this account beams a broadband five-megabyte signal to an island off the coast of China called Cezi Maji." At this, Grimsdottir paused and looked at each of them in turn. "Nothing? That name doesn't ring any bells?"

Fisher and Lambert both shook their heads.

"Cezi Maji is the island that Bai Kang Shek allegedly disappeared to fifteen years ago."

Fisher leaned forward. "Say again?"

"Bai Kang Shek. That's his island—or so the legend goes."

Fisher was as surprised to simply hear a Chinese name reappear in the puzzle as he was to hear that name in particular.

Bai Kang Shek had been called the Howard Hughes of China. In the late 1930s, Shek's father had owned a small fleet of tugboats in Shanghai. After World War II, as China tried to restart its devastated economy and infrastructure, Shek Senior had gone to the government with a proposal: Give me exclusive salvage rights on all shipping sunk during the war in the East and South China Seas. In return, Shek Senior would sell back to China the scrap metal it so desperately needed.

A bargain was struck and the Shek family went to work, including young Bai Kang, who served first as a deckhand aboard his father's tug, then as a mate, then finally as a captain at the age of sixteen.

By the time Shek Senior retired and handed over the reigns to Bai Kang in 1956, the empire had expanded from salvage work into transport, manufacturing, arms production, agriculture, and mining.

For the next forty years, Shek stood at the helm of Shek International as the business grew. In 1990 Shek's personal net worth was estimated at six billion dollars. Then, one year later, as if someone had flipped a switch, Bai Kang Shek changed.

His behavior became erratic. He was prone to outbursts; he decreed that board members must wear hats during meetings; he began moving from place to place, staying in one of his dozens of homes for precisely eleven days before moving on to the next; he was said to have given up solid food, taking his meals only in blended form. The list went on.

Several times the board tried to wrest control of the the business from him, but despite his growing eccentricities, he remained formidable and able. Though his personal behavior grew more bizarre by the day, his mind for business never faltered as Shek International continued to show record profits.

And then suddenly in 1991, Shek called a rare press

conference. Dressed in a long-tailed tuxedo and carrying a cane, Shek announced to the world that he was retiring to pursue "spiritual endeavors" and that he had sold his stake in Shek International to the board for what amounted to sixteen U.S. dollars. Then he clumsily turned his cane into a bouquet of flowers, bowed to the assemblage, and left. The last time he was seen or photographed was as he climbed into his limousine and was driven away.

For the past fifteen years the rumors and tales of conspiracies surrounding Bai Kang Shek had grown to mythic proportions, but through them all was a common thread: He was still alive, sequestered from the world in some private sanctuary.

"Don't get me wrong," Fisher said. "I'm glad we've finally got something that supports my hunch, but the idea that our best suspect is someone who used to wear gold-sequined swim goggles in public makes me a little nervous."

"Ditto," Lambert said.

Grimsdottir spread her hands. "All I can give you are the facts: The engines aboard the *Trego* were purchased by Song Woo International, which has an account with Shinzhan Network Solutions, and that same account is paying for satellite Internet access for the island of Cezi Maji in the East China Sea.

"Which in turn may or may not be home to a recluse, who may or may not be insane, and who may or may not be alive," Fisher said.

"That's about the size of it," Grimsdottir said. "Except one last detail." She clicked the remote at a nearby flat-screen; the image of a heavily jungled island appeared. "According to reliable reports, Cezi Maji has a security system worthy of a military base: patrol boats, sensors, armed guards, and fences. Whether that's Bai Kang Shek out there or not, I don't know, but somebody's pretty serious about their privacy."

Fisher stared at the image for a few seconds, then said, "Sounds like an invitation to me."

38

THREE hours and one midair refueling after leaving Kadena Air Force Base in Okinawa, the Pave Low's pilot slowed the craft to a hover. The vibration that had been been jarring Fisher's butt and back for the last six hundred miles diminished to a tremor. The pilot's voice came over Fisher's subdermal. "Sir, we're at the rendevous point."

"Radio contact?"

"None. We'll wait them out. You know how squids are; probably got lost."

"Play nice, Major." Fisher checked his watch. They were on time; the submarine was late. "How's your fuel?"

"We're good. Thanks to whatever mojo you're carrying, we've got a Comet all to ourselves."

"Comet" was short for Vomit Comet, the nickname for the KC-135 Stratotanker, which did double duty as an in-flight refueling aircraft and a zero-g simulator for astronauts—the latter achieved through rapid climbs and sudden dives that left the occupants weightless and often violently nauseous. Currently, a Stratotanker from Kadena was orbiting above them at 35,000 feet, waiting to top off the helo should it become necessary.

Seated across from him on the bench were the Pave Low's two gunners/specialists. As they had been for the last hour, they were engrossed in a game of gin. Accustomed to ferrying dangerous men into dangerous areas, Pave Low crew members took everything in stride and didn't ask questions. Aside from a nod as Fisher had climbed aboard, neither man had paid him any attention.

The MH-53J Pave Low was a special operator's dream. Designed to covertly insert soldiers into denied areas, and then extract them out again, it was fast, quiet, and equipped with an avionics package that left nothing to chance: FLIR (Forward-Looking Infrared Radar), inertial global positioning system (GPS), terrain-following and terrain-avoidance radar.

Fisher glanced out the window. The helo's navigation strobes were turned off, but thanks to a full moon he could see the ocean twenty feet below, its surface chopped into mist by the rotor wash. This was another Pave Low specialty—the hover coupler, which, in conjunction with the GPS, could keep the helo fixed precisely over a spot on the earth, give or take six inches.

Ten minutes later, the pilot was back in Fisher's subdermal: "We've got company, sir. Marlin is on station, ready for pickup."

"Roger," Fisher said. "Tell them five minutes."

"What's your pleasure?"

"Ten feet will do. Don't wait around."

"You're sure?"

"Yep, go home. Thanks for the ride."

He caught the attention of the two specialists, then pointed to himself and jerked a thumb downward. They went into action. The cabin lights were switched to red and life vests were donned. The first crewman motioned for Fisher to stand up and turn around for gear inspection, then patted him once on the shoulder.

The second crewman slid open the cabin door. Legs braced at the threshhold, one arm braced across the door, he motioned Fisher forward. Fisher felt the *whump-whump-whump* of the Pave Low's rotors in his belly. Cold mist blew through the door and he tasted salt on his lips.

At the door, the crewman cupped his subdermal against his ear, then said something into the microphone. He flashed five fingers at Fisher once, then again, then laid his palm flat: *Steady hover at ten feet.*

Fisher nodded.

The second crewman pulled a chem-light from his vest, broke it open, and shook it until started glowing green, then tossed it out the door. It hit the water and started bobbing in the chop. In the darkness, the glow would give Fisher a reference point for his jump. The crewman at the door stood aside and gave Fisher an "after you" flourish.

BODY vertical, arms crossed over his chest, he plunged into the dark water. The thumping of the Pave Low's rotors became muffled, and for a brief second Fisher allowed himself to enjoy the quiet before finning to the surface. He raised a thumb above his head. The red rectangle of light that was the Pave Low's side door went dark as the crewman closed it. The helo lifted up, banked left, and skimmed away into the darkness.

Somewhere to his right, Fisher heard a rush of bubbles followed by a hissing whoosh. Thirty seconds later, a dot of light appeared in the darkness; it blinked once, then twice more. Fisher swam toward it.

THE Los Angeles-class submarine USS *Houston,* SSN-713, call sign Marlin, was sitting low in the water, deck partially awash, its sail looming out of the darkness like a two-story-tall building. A seaman was crouched on the deck at the head of a rope ladder. Fisher climbed up. If the crewman was fazed by picking up a lone man in the middle of the East China Sea, he showed no sign of it.

"Captain's compliments, sir. If you'll follow me."

He led Fisher aft along the sub's deck, past the sail, to an open escape trunk. At the bottom of the ladder, another crewman was waiting with a towel and a set of blue coveralls emblazoned with the *Houston*'s "Semper Vigilans" crest on the breast pocket.

Once Fisher was dried off and changed, he was led past the radio room and into the Control Center. The *Houston*'s captain, in a blue baseball cap with gold oak leaves on the brim, was standing at the chart table. Fisher was momentarily taken aback; this was an old friend.

"Welcome aboard, stranger," Captain Max Collins said, walking over.

Fisher shook the extended hand and smiled. "Permission to come aboard."

"Granted."

"Good to see you, Max. Been a while."

"Yeah, and as I recall, last time we didn't have to pluck your sorry butt out of the water. You walked aboard like a regular human being."

"Didn't want you to think I'd gone soft," Fisher replied.

Houston was home-ported in Apra Harbor, Guam, which is where Fisher had last boarded the sub for a mission. Before that, they'd worked together half-a-dozen times while Fisher was still attached to Navy Special Warfare. Arguably, Collins was one of the best "shoehorns" in the fleet, having earned a reputation for not only slipping operators into hard-target denied areas, but also getting them out alive again.

In Fisher's case, Collins had once sailed the *Houston* twenty-two miles into North Korea's heavily guarded Nampo harbor, all the way to the mouth of the Taedong River, then waited, dead silent, keel resting on the seabed, for eighteen hours as Fisher finished his mission and returned.

Characteristically, Collins attributed his success to his crew and to the *Houston*'s extraordinary "aural footprint"—or lack thereof. Driven by nuclear-powered, turbine-driven electric motors, Los Angeles-class submarines were so quiet they were known colloquially as "moving holes in the water."

Collins grinned. "Going soft? Hell, Sam, I know better. How about a cup of coffee?"

THEY settled into Collins's cabin, a cramped space with a fold-down desk, a bunk, and a small sink and mirror. As submarines went, it was luxurious. A steward knocked on the door and handed Collins a tray with two mugs and a carafe of coffee. Collins poured Fisher and himself a cup each. Fisher could feel the thrum of the *Houston*'s engines through his feet.

"I just got updated surveillance shots for you," Collins said. "I see you're invading another island all by yourself. Shame on you, Sam."

Fisher sipped his coffee; it was hot and bitter and overcooked—the Navy way. He loved it. "Just being a good soldier, Max. So, how's it look?"

"Ugly. What's the story?" Collins caught himself and quickly said, "Never mind, I don't want to know. With luck, we'll have you there in fourteen hours. Get some sleep, then I'll show you what you're facing."

39

AS they always did, the sounds of a submerged submarine lulled Fisher into a deep sleep. The combination of the hum of the engines, the faint hiss of the water skimming along the outer hull, and the white noise of the air circulators acted as a tranquilizer.

He needed the sleep. He'd been going hard since the *Trego*, and as accustomed as he was to the lifestyle, he knew the stress and lack of sleep would eventually catch up to him, slowing his reactions and his thinking. Given where he was headed, he couldn't allow that.

Four hours after Collins left the cabin, he returned and gently shook Fisher awake, waved a mug of coffee under his nose, and said, "Had enough beauty sleep?"

Fisher groaned and sat up, planting his feet on the

deck. "You tell me." He took the mug and sipped. It was scalding hot and salty.

Collins said, "Briefing in the wardroom in ten minutes."

FISHER was there in five. Like the rest of the sub, the officers' wardroom was a cramped affair: three sets of vinyl bench seats, tables bolted to the deck, and a small kitchenette in a side alcove. Pictures of the *Houston*, from her keel-laying to the current crew photo, lined the walls.

Waiting with Collins was his executive officer, Marty Smith. Fisher had never met Smith, but knew of his reputation. Halfway through his career, Smith had had a change of heart, leaving behind Naval Intelligence for a fleet posting, where he'd worked his way up the ladder of submariner billets—Supply and Admin, Weapons, Sonar, Engineering, to finally XO. In another five years he'd have his own boat to drive.

Fisher sat down and Collins made the introductions. "I asked Marty to sit in because of his intel background. He'll have some insights on the material we've got for you."

Collins opened the briefing folder and spread a series of ten eight-by-ten photos across the table. Each showed Shek's island, Cezi Maji, from different altitudes, angles, resolutions, and formats, including infrared, EM, and night vision—all taken either by satellite or P-3 Orion flights while Sam had been en route to Kadena.

"A little background first," Smith began. "Cezi Mali is part of the Zhoushan Archipelago at the mouth of

Shanghai's Hangzhou Bay. It consists of fourteen hundred islands spread across seventy miles of ocean. Of those, only about a hundred are inhabited. Cezi Mali is roughly seven thousand acres, or nine square miles."

"Terrain?" Fisher asked.

"A good-sized cove and natural harbor on the north side of the island; on the south, east, and west sides, the place is a fortress: fifty-foot cliffs and narrow beaches. The interior is triple-canopy rain forest punctuated by exposed rock escarpments, peaks, and ridges."

"Peachy," Fisher said, taking a sip of coffee.

"Now, the fun part," Smith said, pushing a photo across the table at Fisher. It was from a P-3, Fisher could see, but it was color-enhanced. Using a pen, Smith traced a faint white line that seemed to follow the contours of the cliffs. "That's a road. A dirt path, really, but wide enough for these." Smith pointed again, this time to a rectangular object on the path.

"Jeep," Fisher said.

"Yep. Six of them patrol the cliffs day and night, rain or shine. Two armed guards per vehicle."

"Pattern?"

"That's the good news. They're on a schedule. Your people loaded the details onto your thingamajig. She said you'd know what that meant."

Fisher nodded. *OPSAT. Good ol' Grim*.

"Once past the cliff road, you'll have a three-mile slog through the rain forest. More good news. No patrols and no EM emissions anywhere, which means no cameras or sensors. The wildlife probably makes them useless. More bad news. No matter which route you choose, you'll have two escarpments and three gorges to deal with."

This fact, more than any other, had ruled out a parafoil insertion. Jumping into triple-canopy jungle was dicey enough, but given its thickness, there was no way to tell what lay under it. Dropping through the canopy to find yourself plunging into a gorge tended to put a damper on your day.

"Once through the jungle," Smith continued, "you'll come to what I've named the inner ring. Whoever owns this place is diligent about his security. For a one-mile radius around the estate—which I'll get to in a minute—they've cut the rain forest back to single-canopy. Mother Nature's on your side, though. Jungle is hard to control, so there should be some cover on the forest floor—providing you don't mind crawling."

"I love crawling," Fisher muttered. "The cutback means cameras and sensors, I assume?"

Smith nodded. "Lots of them, but they're plotted and loaded on your . . ."

"Thingamajig."

"Right. Now, guards. The inner ring is divided into zones—twelve of them, like a clock. One guard per zone, moving randomly. No patterns or consistent timing that we could see."

This was a mixed blessing for Fisher. Sentries on random patrol could turn up anywhere at any time, and usually, per Murphy's Law, at the most inconvenient of moments. On the upside, sentries were only human, and the human mind subconsciously gravitates toward order and pattern. With enough patience, Fisher might be able to find a gap in the coverage and slip through.

"Radio signals?"

"All guards have portable radios, but it looks like there's no scheduled check-in procedure."

"Probaby by camera," Fisher replied.

Each guard was likely required to regularly appear before a camera in his zone and give an "all clear" signal. A missed check-in would either trigger a visit from a security supervisor or raise an alarm.

"Once through the cutback area, you'll find yourself facing fifty yards of open, well-groomed lawn."

"You're kidding."

"Nope One of these pics even shows a groundskeeper on a riding mower. Across the lawn is twelve-foot-high hurricane fence topped with razor wire."

"Of course there is," Fisher said.

"It's not electrified, though. The island is on the outer edge of the archipelago, so it gets a fair number of storms, which means a lot of blowing debris. Hard to keep an electric fence running smoothly when it gets bombarded frequently. There are sensors, though, attached to the fence. There's no way to tell whether they're motion, touch, or beam.

"Now, the estate itself," Smith said, pushing another photo across the table. "There's a central building—this one here with the red tile roof. It's a six-story Chinese pagoda. It's surrounded by smaller buildings, probably staff quarters, storage, workshops, utility spaces, all of them inside the fence. Lots of guards here, about eight per shift. As for the pagoda itself, we've got nothing. No details of the interior. Guess you'll have to play it by ear."

At this Max Collins smiled. "As I recall, Sam, playing it by ear is what you do best."

Fisher went silent for ten seconds, absorbing the details. "How long to the insertion point, Max?"

"We've only got about sixty miles to go, but there are a couple Ninety-threes in the area."

Collins was referring to Chinese Type 093 nuclear hunter-killer subs. Almost as quiet as the LA class, 093s boasted a sophisticated sonar package, including bow, flank, and towed passive arrays. Worse still, rumors had been floating around that Moscow had provided Beijing with enough core technology to copy the Russian Skval torpedo, which was said to travel at 200 to 230 miles per hour.

"It may take a little time to pick our way around them," Collins said.

The growler phone on the bulkhead chirped and Collins picked it up. He listened for a moment, then hung up. "We've got ELF traffic."

ELF stood for Extremely Low Frequency, a band used to signal submerged submarines. Fisher followed Collins and Smith to the Control Center, where the OOD, or officer of the deck, handed Collins a sheaf of paper. "Surface for signal, sir."

Collins scanned the message, then handed it to Fisher. "Somebody wants to talk to you."

Not good news, Fisher thought.

"Officer of the Deck, let's poke the wire."

"Poke the wire, aye, sir."

The Control Center went into action as the crew brought the *Houston* up to antenna depth. It took six minutes. "Antenna depth, Captain."

"Very well." To Fisher: "This way."

Fisher followed Collins to the radio room, where a senior chief radioman was waiting. "Link established, encrytion running. Call sign Xerxes."

"Thanks, Chief. Give us the room."

The senior chief ushered the other radiomen outside and closed the door behind him. Fisher donned the headset and keyed the microphone. "Go ahead, Xerxes."

"Sam, we've got a problem. Two hours ago there was an incident with a BARCAP," Lambert said, referring to Barrier Combat Air Patrol. Whenever a U.S. Navy carrier was on patrol, it was guarded by a ring of fleet-defense fighters, either F-14 Tomcats or F/A-18 Hornets.

"The Iranians claim we were in their airspace. They sent up a flight of F-16s. There was furball, some missile lock-ons, and then a midair bump—one of their Falcons and one of our Hornets. Both pilots had to bail out."

"Good Christ," Fisher said. Back when the U.S. was on speaking terms with Iran, the Pentagon had sold the IAF hundreds of F-16 Falcons and Tomcats. "Escalation?"

"Nothing yet. Both pilots were recovered, which helps, but this is just the start. Next time it won't be a bump. Next time it'll be missiles."

And once that happens, we're effectively at war, Fisher thought.

"If there's anything on Shek's island that can point us in another direction, we need it."

40

WITH a gentle kick of his fins, Fisher eased forward until he felt his belly scrape the soft sand of the beach. He felt a wave wash over his back and his vision was momentarily obscured by froth. As the wave receded, he lifted his head until his face mask broke the surface. Ahead, he could see the line of white beach that followed the base of the cliff, itself a vertical wall of mottled gray rock.

He'd timed his approach to coincide with high tide for two reasons: One, the breakers would be easier to manage, allowing him to crawl into the shoals while remaining partially awash. And two, the higher the tide, the less beach he would have to cross to reach the base of the cliff, decreasing his chance of being spotted.

True to to his reputation, Collins had expertly guided

the *Houston* northward into the heart of the East China Sea, past the Chinese 093s, and finally to the mouth of Hangzhou Bay and the Zhoushan Archipelago. For a standard special ops insertion, the *Houston*'s forward deck would have been fitted with a clamshell dry dock shelter and an SDV, or Swimmer Delivery Vehicle, but the accelerated nature of Fisher's mission had made this impossible, so he'd simply exited the sub's forward escape trunk and swum the half mile to the island.

So far the weather was partially cooperating with his plan. The sky was clear, with an occasional scud of clouds passing before the moon. According to Collins's weather officer, a tropical storm was working its way up from the South China Sea, pushing a line of rain squalls before it.

Fisher reached back and plucked his binoculars off his harness. He scanned the top of the cliff, looking for movement or headlights. He saw nothing. He replaced the binoculars and moved his left arm forward until his could see the OPSAT's screen. He punched a button and a map of Cezi Maji appeared in the green glow.

Grimsdottir had done her usual thorough job, having divided the map into three views: standard topographical with geographical features, EM, and infrared, each of which was labeled according to Smith's brief: cliff road; outer rain forest; inner cutback zone; and the estate proper. A variety of multicolored symbols marked known locations of cameras, sensors, sentry zones, and fences.

Looking at the fortress that was Bai Kang Shek's island, Fisher felt a momentary tingle of apprehension, but he shook it off. *Break it down, Sam,* he commanded himself. *One step at a time. One camera, one sensor, one sentry.*

He lowered his face mask back into the water and started inching forward.

TEN minutes later, he was across the beach and hidden amid the rocks at the base of the cliff. Behind him, waves hissed over the sand and retreated, leaving a cream of froth. He picked his way along the cliff until he had a clear view of the top, then waited.

His wait was short. Eight minutes later, he saw a pair of headlights moving through the foliage. They stopped and went dark. A few seconds later, a flashlight blinked on. In the moonlight Fisher could see a figure standing at the edge of the cliff. The guard played the flashlight over the rock face, then down and over the sand.

The flashlight blinked out. The headlights glowed to life and started moving away.

Fisher tapped the button of the OPSAT's screen labeled **LOCK** and the red diamond symbol on the cliff road started flashing. **LOCK ENABLED**. With the jeep patrols on a predictable schedule, all Fisher had to do was lock in the appearance of one them to track the rest. One by one, the remaining five jeep patrols popped onto the screen at various points along the cliff road.

A set of scrolling numbers next to each diamond showed the time remaining until it reached Fisher's position. He had six minutes until the next. He punched up the OPSAT's comm screen and tapped out a message—**FEET**

DRY—and hit send. Given the inordinately high level of the island's security, he and Lambert had agreed to forgo normal check-in procedures and keep transmissions to a minimum.

He trotted back to the spot he'd chosen earlier and started climbing.

THE cliff was at once a climber's dream and nightmare, a mix of granite, with plenty of lateral cleaves that made for good handholds, and volcanic basalt that was in some places worn smooth by millennia of weather, but in others, jagged, frangible, and as abrasive as steel wool.

By switching between NV and standard view, he was able to slowly pick his way upward, zigzagging from one granite run to the other until he was halfway to the top. His OPSAT vibrated once on his wrist, then again. He locked his right hand into a crevice and lifted the OPSAT to his face.

On the screen one of the red diamonds was moving down the cliff road, nearing his postion. The time display wound down past sixty seconds . . . fifty-five. . . .

Hand over hand, he moved left, toward a nose-shaped hump in the cliff. When his shoulder bumped against it, he lowered himself until he could duck under the tip of the nose. He shoved his hand into a crack until his knuckles were jammed against the stone, then released his left hand and let it dangle.

Above him, he heard the growl of an engine. Brakes squealed. A car door slammed. Then footfalls on gravel and the rustle of foliage. A flashlight beam skimmed horizontally along the cliff face toward him, then up and over the nose and out of sight. Fisher glanced down in time to see the beam track along the beach for a few seconds, then blink out.

He waited until the jeep's engines had faded, then glanced at the OPSAT. The next jeep was on the east side of the island, a red diamond slowly marching toward him. *Seven minutes*.

He kept climbing.

WITH two minutes to spare, he reached the foliage overhanging the edge. He groped around until his hand found a root and he pulled himself up. He snaked through the underbrush until he reached the edge of the road. A quick EM/NV check up and down the road revealed nothing. He checked the OPSAT: one minute.

The previous day's rain had left the road muddy—a perfect mold for footprints, so Fisher sidestepped along the grass verge until he found a spot where a pair of flat stones were half-buried in the dirt. He was leaping to first stone when he heard the grumbling of the jeep's engine. He hopped to the next stone, then to the edge, where he ducked down, slipped into the undergrowth, and dropped flat.

The jeep's headlights washed over the road. Half a foot away, a mud-encrusted tire rolled past Fisher's face. The jeep ground to a halt and a car door opened. A voice called something in Mandarin. The reply came from slightly farther away—the first voice from the passenger; the second from the guard who'd gotten out to scan the cliff face.

Half a minute later, the jeep was moving again.

Fisher maneuvered his arm up until he could see the OPSAT. He punched up the map. The outer ring of rain forest lay before him. Three miles of unbroken jungle, two escarpments, three gorges.

He had six hours before dawn.

41

FISHER came to a small stream gurgling its way through the undergrowth, and paused for a break.

On paper, three miles in six hours sounded like an easy stroll. He'd lived and fought and killed in jungles, sometimes for months at a time, and he knew there was nothing easy about it, especially at night. His every step, his every breath, his every hand placement was fraught with hazard.

His NV was virtually useless. With only the occasional game trail to follow, he had to force his way steadily through foliage so thick, all he saw in his trident goggles was a wall of leaves and branches that parted with his passing only to immediately close behind him. Every step involved either ducking or twisting or crab-walking around an obstacle. The canopy above blotted out all but fleeting glimpses of sky and moonlight. As it was, the ambient light was barely enough to feed the NV.

The heat, which hovered at ninety degrees, was coupled with ninety-percent humidty. In his peripheral vision, he could see bits of movement as the jungle's night creatures scurried away. Serrated vines and spiked leaves crisscrossed his path, scraping his exposed skin raw. Flying insects, some so small they were invisible, others as big around as a quarter, swirled around his ears and eyes and nose.

And while every facet of breaking a jungle trail was exhausting, Fisher knew the physical stresses were only the tip of the iceberg. No other environment on earth worked on the human psyche the way a jungle could. Facing a curtain of foliage left you with no points of reference. Everything you saw was homogenized. Where you were ten feet ago looked eerily similar to where you were now. Without a tight rein on your mind, hopelessness starts to creep in, followed by panic and mental paralysis.

For all its danger, though, Fisher loved the jungle. It was the great equalizer. Every hazard you face, your enemy faces; the same wall of foliage that hides him, hides you. The difference between killing your enemy or dying at his hands becomes a matter of patience and stamina and focus.

HE sat on the bank of the stream with his back against a trunk. He dipped his bandanna into the water. It was surprisingly cold. He wiped his face and neck; the coolness was invigorating. He pulled his canteen off his belt and drank it all down. The jungle sucks moisture from the body at an incredible rate—every breath and every drop of sweat is a step closer to heat stroke.

He laid the canteen on its side in the stream until it was full, then dropped in two chlorine dioxide tablets and recapped it. More often than not, jungle water carried enough bacteria, viruses, and cysts to either kill you or leave you hospitalized for months wishing you were dead.

All around him, the forest floor rustled with life, mostly of the insect variety, from ants to spiders to beetles. Something shook in the canopy, a monkey awakened by his passage. He felt something brush over the tops of his thighs. Moving very slow, he flipped his goggles into place and looked down. A line of leaf-cutter ants, each carrying a half-dollar-sized chunk of leaf, was marching across his legs.

He checked his OPSAT. He'd been going for an hour and had covered half a mile. He checked his coordinates to ensure he was on track, then stood up, stepped across the stream, and kept going.

THE hours passed steadily but slowly as he picked his way inland. At three A.M., he found a game trail barely ten inches wide and followed it as it meandered north. After an hour the trail started to descend. Fisher felt a change in the air, a drop in temperature that could mean only one thing: water.

He heard it before he saw it, a muffled roar some-where to his left and front. The trail became rockier, the stones slick underfoot. It veered right and kept descend-ing, and soon the roar changed into the unmistakable rush of water. The trail continued to descend for another two hundred yards before the trees thinned out and he found himself standing on a small granite shelf. Across from him was another shelf separated by a ten-foot-wide chasm. He walked to the edge and looked down.

The chasm was twenty feet deep. At the bottom, a river boiled through the confines of the granite walls. To his left, the chasm climbed steadily upward until it reached a small waterfall.

Fisher doubted be could get enough of a running start to jump the gorge, and he knew missing would kill him. The force of the river would grind him into hamburger against the rocks. Nor could he try farther up the trail; the jungle grew right to the edge of the chasm, making a leap impossible. Down, then.

He followed the trail another quarter mile until the ter-rain leveled out and the chasm widened to thirty feet. Here the water was slower, shallower, and dotted with boulders, but Fisher knew better than to underestimate the river. These were Class V rapids. Even at calf depth, the force of the water would be enough to knock him down.

He studied the boulders. The were wide enough for him and were separated only by a few feet, but they were also slick with algae. He checked his watch. He was be-hind schedule, and he had no idea what he'd find down-stream. This was the place, then.

He took a minute to plan his route, then walked to the edge, coiled his legs, and leapt. It was a frog-hop that landed him splayed, belly-first, across the rock. His tac-suit's reinforced Kevlar and RhinoPlate took most of the shock, but still, the impact knocked the wind out of him. He recovered, wiggled himself atop the rock, then hopped to the next one. He repeated the process five more times until he reached the opposite shore.

He found a cleft in the granite wall with natural built-in steps; the mud between the stones was indented with animal tracks. A game trail. He climbed up. At the top of the cleft he found another game trail.

BY five A.M., an hour before dawn, Fisher had closed to within a hundred yards of the cutback section of forest surrounding Shek's estate. He studied the tree line with his binoculars. Shek's people had done a decent job of keeping the jungle at bay, having cut back the under-growth in a nearly perfect curve, leaving only clumps of knee-high grass and small trees.

This was where things would get interesting. There was a full mile of this cutback zone between him and the compound. This was where the roving guards, sensors, and cameras began.

He started looking for a bolt hole in which he could spend the day. He found it half mile to the west: a dead tree that had fallen across some small boulders. He scooped out a hollow beneath the tree, then built a blind made of nearby foliage that he carefully uprooted, then replanted. Wilted leaves would be a telltale sign that no good security patrol would miss.

Once satisfied with the shelter, he crawled inside and pulled the foliage closed behind him. Piece by piece, he removed his harness and gear and laid everything within arm's reach. One more task before he could sleep.

He tapped out a message on his OPSAT:

IN PLACE, WAYPOINT ONE. ALL IS WELL. WHAT'S LATEST?

The message came back twenty seconds later.

IRANIAN KILO-CLASS SUBMARINE ATTEMPTED PENETRATION REAGAN BATTLE GROUP PERIMI- ETER, GULF OF OMAN. SUBMARINE DRIVEN OFF, RAN AGROUND NEAR JASK PENINSULA. EMERGENCY SESSION OF UN SECURITY COUN- CIL IN PROGRESS.

Escalation, Fisher thought.

42

THE day passed at a crawl as Fisher lay still inside his blind, alternately dozing and studying Shek's estate, which had with the light of day become partially visible through the trees. Over the roofs of the outbuildings he could see the pagoda's red-tiled roof, and here and there he caught glimpses of guards and grounds workers moving about. He saw only Chinese faces.

He was at roughly the nine o' clock position of the imaginary clock face that divided the cutback area. Each of the twelve zones was an acre, Fisher estimated. Since shortly after dawn, when an armed guard had passed within thirty feet of his blind, he'd seen no one outside the fence, which meant patrols were suspended during daylight hours.

According to his OPSAT map, there were four camouflaged cameras hidden in the trees along his front. On the screen, their ROD, or Range of Detection, was displayed as a rotating cone. Getting past them during the day would be impossible; The coverage was too complete, the timing too dicey.

At noon, with the heat and humidity at 90/90, three groundskeepers in a white tunics and straw hats exited the gate and strolled around the cutback zone for two hours, hacking at foliage with scythes and machetes, before returning to the compound.

Fisher spent the remainder of the afternoon lying as still as possible, conserving water and energy as he timed patrols, looked for blind spots, annotated his map, and waited for nightfall.

He thought about Bai Kang Shek.

The man's link to the *Trego,* and thereby the Slipstone attacks, seemed irrefutable, but neither did it make sense. Why would an eccentric billionaire recluse who'd retreated to his own private island fifteen years earlier orchestrate a radiological attack on the U.S.? Certainly, he had the money to pull it off, but what was the motivation? And why implicate Iran? What was to gain?

SHORTLY before dusk, Fisher watched through his binoculars as the compound's night shift came on duty. Singly and in pairs, guards began assembling near the main gate until he counted a dozen. Each man carried a Heckler & Koch MP-5 compact assault rifle. A supervisor called them together and gave them what Fisher took to be instructions and/or a pep talk. Weapons were checked, radios tested, and then the gate swung open and the guards filed out.

Time to go to work, Fisher thought. He donned his harness, replaced all his gear into his pouches and pockets, then checked his pistol and SC-20. He then buried the wrappers from his rations in pre-dug holes and filled them in.

Once through the gate, the guards parted company, each man heading toward his zone on the clock face. Fisher's guard, whom he named Stumpy because of his short legs and barrel chest, arrived five minutes later and began patrolling. He moved through the zone steadily, with purpose and precision, placing his feet flat on the ground, testing his weight before moving the next foot, eyes always moving, MP-5 held ready. This answered one of Fisher's lingering questions: the source of Shek's security force. If this guard was typical, Fisher was dealing with ex-soldiers, possibly special forces types. They weren't likely to make big mistakes or overlook small details.

Night fell quickly, fading from twilight to complete blackness in twenty minutes. Just as quickly, the trees around him went from the subtle insect drone of a daylight jungle, to a symphony of squawks and buzzes and croaks as the nocturnals came alive.

With the darkness came the urge to move, to get on with the job, but Fisher reined it in. He had eight hours of night ahead of him and he was prepared to use every minute of it, if necessary. Using infrared and NV, he

kept track of Stumpy as he meandered around the zone,
After forty minutes, Fisher's patience paid off. He began
to notice a redundancy to Stumpy's route: a Z-shaped
pattern, followed by an N-shaped pattern, and so on.

Having already timed the camera's movements, Fisher
waited for his moment, then slipped out of the blind and
ran, hunched over, to a patch of underbrush in a camera's
blind spot. Stumpy was to his left, moving along the
perimeter. Fisher checked the OPSAT. The cameras, one
to his left and one to his right, were rotating past him,
their ROD cones brushing against his hiding spot, but
not quite touching him.

He got up, sprinted forward twenty feet, ducked behind a tree, and checked Stumpy's position. He was now
thirty feet away, at Fisher's ten o' clock. *Wait,* he commanded himself. *Wait* . . . The next move was the tricki-
est. Once through the cutback, he had fifty feet of lawn to
deal with before reaching the fence. Separating the cutback zone and the lawn was a line of groomed hibiscus
hedges. Trimmed into a boxcar shape, they were lovely to
look at, but a security mistake he was only too happy to
take advantage of.

He waited until Stumpy passed by and disappeared
through the trees, then shimmied forward just in time
to miss an intersection of two camera cones, then stood
up and sprinted the remaining eighty feet to the hedges,
where he dropped on his belly, found an opening in the
branches, and crawled through to the grass verge. He
spread himself flat and went still.

The grass blades were topped in a layer of condensation

and the moisture felt cool on his skin. From the corner of his eye, he watched an errant nightbee land on a hibiscus bloom, gather some butter-yellow pollen on his legs, then buzz away. Beyond the hurricane fence, he could see the rear wall of one of the outbuildings. Along its eaves, spaced every ten feet or so, were floodlights. They were dark, which suggested they were motion-sensored. Mounted atop each fence post was a rotating camera. All but one of them—the middle one—faced outward. He switched his goggles to EM.

In the pulsing blue field, each camera was surrounded by a swirling halo—its own unique electromagnetic signature. Just as a radiologist learns to decipher seemingly obscure X-rays, Fisher had over time learned to read EM patterns. He could tell these cameras were night-vision-equipped.

This was going to be dicey. His timing would have to be perfect.

He watched and waited.

FOUR minutes later, a roving guard appeared around the corner of the outbuilding. He stopped, flipped open a small recessed panel, and punched a code into a keypad. This was the first Fisher had seen of a panel, but he immediately understood its purpose.

The guard shut the cover and strolled along the fence, moving right to left. None of the motion floodlights came on. Halfway along the fence, the guard stopped before the inward-facing camera for a count of three, then walked on and disappeared around the opposite corner of the building.

Watching the process told Fisher much: The guard's failure to stop at a second control panel meant the alarm override for the floodlights was on a delay; the inward-facing camera was a checkpoint; and the guard's lack of NV goggles meant his stroll along the fence was to check for breaches. The lawn, the hedges, and the edge of the cutback weren't his zone of responsibility.

The motion lights were the easiest to disable. Fisher pulled the SC-20 from his back holster, settled it into the crook of his arm, and took aim. He fingered the ZOOM toggle once, then twice, centering the reticle on the light. He fired. With a tinkle of glass, the light shattered. He adjusted aim, fired again, and killed the next light. He re-holstered the SC-20.

Next he pulled a scopelike object from his belt, attached it to the pistol, and flipped on the power switch. With a faint hum, the camera jammer powered up. Despite the jammer's obvious benefits, Fisher tried to avoid using it for two reasons: One, it consumed a lot of power, and he wasn't fond of carrying any more battery weight than necessary. And two, using it required precise and unwavering aim. One tremble of the hand or misstep of the foot and you risked dropping the interference. He checked his OPSAT, watching the fence cameras go through their rotation, watching their cones overlap and separate . . . overlap and separate. . . .

From behind the hedge came a twig snap as Stumpy passed by.

Overlap and separate . . . overlap and separate . . .

Now.

He rose into a crouch, took aim on the camera nearest him, pulled the jammer's trigger, and started walking forward. He kept his pace steady, his aim level. The camera made a rapid *tick-tick-tick* sound as the jammer scrambled the circuits.

When he was three feet from the camera, he released the jammer's trigger and flattened himself against the fence. *Safe. For now.* Surveillance cameras didn't cover close-in, horizontal surfaces very well; the mechanics of their motion usually left a blind spot along a wall or fence.

He waited for the cameras to complete a rotation, then mounted the fence and climbed to the top, where he flipped onto his back and shimmied over the razor wire until he was lying spread-eagle, back arched. He said a silent thank-you to Kevlar and RhinoPlate: handy against bullets and razor wire alike.

In one fluid motion, he pushed off with his feet and swung his arms up and over. The sudden momentum, combined with the spring of the wire, vaulted him backward. He did a full reverse somersault and landed on the grass in a crouch, then stepped to the fence and froze beneath the inward-facing camera. He waited until it panned away, then sprinted to the building, around the corner, and down the wall to the next corner, where he stopped and peeked around.

He was at the edge of a short dirt road. To his left, fifty feet away, was more hurricane fence; to his right, an open-fronted twelve-stall garage; the first six stalls were empty, the last six filled with jeeps like the ones he'd encountered on the beach road.

He felt the OPSAT vibrate on his wrist. He checked the screen:

INCOMING VOICE TRANSMISSION . . . RECEIVE ON ENCRYPED BUTTON FOUR.

Button Four was reserved for heavily scrambled and encrypted voice comms. What could be important enough to break radio silence? He keyed his subdermal. "Up on secure button four."

43

THERE was a five-second delay; then Lambert said, "Sam, we've picked up a stray radio signal from inside Shek's compound. It's coming from somewhere in the main house. Tell him, Grim."

"It's a burst transmission on a dedicated CIA operations carrier frequency. Don't ask me how or what—I'm working on it—but it looks like there's a good guy on the inside."

"The CIA is running an op on Bai Kang Shek? That doesn't make any sense."

"Maybe not," Lambert agreed, "but that's not our worry. Bottom line, if we've got an asset on the inside, let's see if we can use it."

"Langley may not like that."

"I'll worry about Langley. You worry about finding that agent. Grim's updating your OPSAT."

Fisher checked his screen. He waited for the rotating DATA UPDATING circle to stop, then scrolled and zoomed the island map until the pagoda filled the sreen. In the northeastern corner of the building was a a flashing yellow dot.

"I see it," Fisher said.

"Since we don't have interior blueprints, there's no way to tell where exactly that is—upstairs, downstairs. . . ."

"I'll figure it out. We don't know if this is an informant, a case officer, an agent—nothing?"

"Nope," said Lambert. "Use your discretion. Whoever it is, if they've got the inside scoop on Shek, get it. Whatever it takes."

Curveball, Fisher thought. He loved surprises as much as the next guy, but preferred his at Christmas and on birthdays, not in the middle of a mission. Then again, as the saying went, covert ops were about expecting—and handling—the unexpected.

HE ducked into the garage. The dirt floor smelled of oil and gas. He picked his way along the back wall and stopped behind the third jeep. He lay down on his back and squirmed under the chasis. From his pouch he pulled a quarter-sized plastic disk. Inside it was a six-gram wafer of WP, or white phosphorus, which when ignited burns at five thousand degrees Farenheit. If necessary, this would provide a spectacular diversion as the WP ignited the fuel tank and the rest of the jeeps exploded in domino fashion. He peeled back the adhesive and stuck the disk to the gas tank, then punched the correct screen on the OPSAT and checked the disk's signal.

He wriggled out and trotted to the garage wall and peeked around the corner. The road was bordered on both sides by outbuildings and ended at a circular driveway before the pagoda. All the outbuildings were dark, save for the third one on his left, where a light showed in a curtained window. From inside Fisher could hear strains of Chinese *guoyue* music and male laughter.

Off-duty guards or compound staff? he wondered. If the former, it would be good to know where reinforcements would be coming from in an emergency.

He creeped across the road until he could see through the curtain. He pulled out his binoculars and zoomed in on what looked like a card table. A hand moved into view and slapped down a mah-jongg tile. There was laughter and clapping. The owner of the hand stood up. Fisher saw a hip holster with the butt of a pistol jutting from it. That answered the question: guards.

Fisher considered his options, and quickly dismissed his impulse to plant wall mines. One on the door and one on the window would almost certainly wipe out everyone inside, but it would also draw down on him the remainder of the security force. As usual, less was more. No footprints.

He moved along the back of the guard quarters, paralleling the road until he reached another line of hibiscus hedges that bordered the turnaround. He dropped flat and peered through the hedge. Here he had a unobstructed view of the pagoda.

The overhead surveillance photos hadn't done it justice. Like a wedding cake with successively smaller layers, the pagoda's six stories formed a sixty-foot-tall truncated pyramid. Seeing it up close, Fisher now had a sense of its grand scale. The lower level measured hundred feet to a side, or ten thousand square feet; the next level was half that, and so on to the top level, the tip of the pyramid, which was no larger than an average-sized bedroom.

The pagoda's exterior was two-toned red and black, the paint so thick with lacquer it shone in the moonlight. The sloping roofs, each shorter than its predecessor by a few feet, were covered in terra-cotta tiles and supported by massive wooden crossbeams. Paper lanterns dotted the lower eaves, casting pale yellow light on the front steps and the wraparound porch.

Insane or not, Bai Kang Shek's taste in architecture was exquisite.

Fisher counted four guards, two on the front steps and two along the side closest to him. Unable to see the other two sides, he had to assume another four guards, for a total of eight.

His study of the surveillance package had revealed a chink in the pagoda's armor—and as with the hibiscus hedges all over the compound, it involved landscaping. The pagoda was enclosed on three sides by acacia trees. With thick, gnarled trunks and sturdy limbs, the acacia reminded Fisher of a slightly flattened broccoli floret.

These trees had been allowed to overgrow the third-floor roofline.

Twenty minutes later, having crawled inch by inch across the driveway and into the grove, Fisher stood up behind an acacia trunk and let out a relieved breath. He peeked around the tree to confirm the guards hadn't moved. He grabbed a branch above his head and chinned himself up.

The branch he'd scouted earlier extended horizontally from the trunk, over the heads of the guards, and ended a few feet over the roof. Here again, patience would be the key. If he hurried or panicked, he was finished. The guards would blast him out of the tree.

He started moving. The branch quickly tapered to the diameter of a fence post. With his every step it bowed slightly, forcing him to freeze and listen. A breeze had picked up, so the rest of the trees were moving, but he wasn't about to push his luck.

Step . . . freeze. Step . . . freeze. Step . . . freeze.

It took five minutes to cover the last ten feet, but finally he reached the end. He transferred one foot to the tiled roof, made sure he was balanced, then brought his other foot down.

He crouch-walked up the slope to the open-faced balcony, then snaked his flexi-cam up and over the railing and did a quick scan with NV, infrared, and EM. Nothing.

He grabbed the railing and pulled himself inside.

44

HE found himself in an empty room. Judging from the thick layer of dust and windblown silt on the teakwood floor, it had been empty for years. He padded to the door, pressed his ear to it. Hearing nothing, he slid the flexi-cam under the door. The lens revealed an empty hallway. Unsettled by the camera's passing, a dust bunny drifted past the lens like a fuzzy tumbleweed.

Fisher opened the door. Here, too, the floor was covered with an even layer of dust. There were no footprints, no marks. It was like freshly fallen snow. The rattan walls were bare, but he could see faint rectangular outlines where artwork had once hung.

What was going on here? Beyond the obvious lack of

furnishings and the layer of dust, there was an odd feeling to the place. Abandonment. Neglect.

He looked around and found three other rooms like the first, each of those also empty. The hallway was laid out like a plus sign, with one room on each of the four quadrants. At the end of the north hallway he found a spiral staircase. He climbed to the next level.

Though half the size of the floor below, it was identical in layout. He checked each of the rooms with the same result: empty. He climbed the stairs to the fifth level and found the same empty quad of rooms. He moved on. At the top of stairs, he found a locked door.

He picked the lock and eased open the door. Its movement stirred up a cloud of dust that swirled in his headlamp. The dust was where the similarity to the previous levels ended. Measuring roughly ten feet to a wall, the space was stacked high with dozens of cardboard boxes. The open-faced windows were covered with plywood that had been painted black.

Fisher opened the nearest box. Inside, he found empty picture frames, wadded-up clothing, a hairbrush. . . . Personal detritus. He checked another box: more of the same. He was turning to leave when something caught his eye. Behind one of the boxes, he saw the corner of a wooden footlocker.

Curious now, Fisher carefully moved boxes until he could reach the footlocker. He flipped the latches and lifted the lid. Inside was a thick, clear plastic bag, shrunken as though all the air had been sucked from it. Through the plastic he could see a gnarled brown . . . something. He leaned in for a closer look.

It took a few seconds for him to register what he was seeing.

Staring back at him was a human face.

He recoiled a few inches. Then leaned in again. Sealed in the bag's airless environment, the face and body had turned leathery with dessication, skin stretched taut over sharp edges of bone. Still, Fisher recognized the face.

Bai Kang Shek.

HE punched up the OPSAT's comm screen, set the encryption buffers, and keyed his subdermal.

"Good news, bad news," Fisher told Lambert.

"Good news first."

"I found Shek."

"Outstanding. Bad news?"

"He's a shrunken apple." He explained, then said, "I've got the first and second floors to check, but so far there's nothing here. My guess: This place hasn't been lived in for five years or more."

"Well, someone or something's there. Otherwise, why the security? Why the guards?"

"Both good questions. Are we still getting the CIA frequency?"

Grimsdottir answered. "No change. It looks like a beacon of some sort. Like an SOS."

* * *

FISHER went downstairs, passing the previous levels to the second floor. It was a mirror image of those above it, though on a much larger scale. At twelve hundred square feet, each of the four rooms had the square footage of a small house. He headed for the stairwell and started down.

The main floor was different from those above in only two ways. Instead of four rooms, there was only one, so vast it felt like a warehouse. And there was no dust. There were no signs of furniture or furnishings. On each of the four walls was a set of massive wooden double doors leading outside.

Fisher stood in the middle of the space, trying to make sense of what he was seeing.

He heard an echoing *click*.

He drew his pistol, spun around.

Behind him a rectangular outline of light appeared in the wall, and he immediately thought *door*. He sprinted to the staircase and up to the second floor, where he crouched down. He leaned forward until he could see the door.

It opened. A uniformed guard stepped out, shut the door behind him, and walked toward the nearest exit. Fisher made a snap decision. He drew the SC-20, flipped the selector to Cottonball, took aim, and fired. With a *thwump*, the projectile hit the guard in the thigh. He staggered sideways, swayed on his feet, and then fell over.

Time for some answers, Fisher thought.

To ensure their chat would be private, he lugged the guard's limp body up to the top level and laid him out on the floor beside Shek's footlocker/tomb. He bound the guard's hands and feet with flexi-cuffs, then sat down to wait.

He'd used a thigh shot to dilute the tranquilizer. After twenty minutes, the guard started to come around. Fisher flipped on his headlamp and aimed it into the guard's eyes.

The guard squinted, tried to turn his head away. He mumbled in Chinese, which Fisher guessed was something along the lines of, *What the hell's going on?*

"Do you speak English?" Fisher asked.

After a couple seconds, the guard said, "Yes, I speak English." It was heavily accented, but clear enough.

"If you make a sound or lie to me, I'll shoot you. Do you understand?"

All remnants of grogginess cleared from the guard's face. "What is happening? Who are you?"

Fisher ignored the question. "What's your name?"

"Lok."

"Who do you work for?"

"I do not know."

Truth. "How did you get here?"

"I left the Army last year. A friend of mine was hired by a security company. They pay well. I joined. I was sent here."

Truth. "How long ago?"

"Six months."

Truth. "Not counting guards, who's here with you?"

"No one."

Lie. Fisher moved the pistol in front of the headlamp so Lok could see it. "That was your one free lie. Let's try again: Who is here with you?"

Lok swallowed hard. "Six. They are down there, in the subbasement. I do not know who they are. They work in a room . . . we are not allowed in."

"And you don't recognize any of them?"

"No."

Fisher believed him. Private security firms were a dime a dozen and the quality of their work and personnel ranged from back-alley leg-breakers to professional soldiers protecting high-profile clients. Lok was one of the latter. Lok and his compatriots didn't need to know anything but where to patrol and what to guard.

Fisher asked. "Do you know the name Bai Kang Shek?"

Lok nodded. "As I boy I heard stories. He disappeared, I believe."

"Disappeared to here."

"That was one of the stories, but I have never seen him here."

Yeah, well, you're leaning against him, son, Fisher thought.

Fisher could think of only one reason why anyone would freeze-dry Shek and take over his island: anonymity. Conversely, there were several good reasons to maintain this level of security: one, to nurture the legend that Shek the Recluse was alive and kicking on his island haven; two, because there was in fact something worth guarding here. Whatever that might be, Fisher had no doubt it was somewhere in the subbasement.

45

HE questioned Lok for another twenty minutes, then darted him in the neck, left him sleeping in Shek's funerary tower, and headed back down to the recessed door. Per Lok's instructions, he found the latch embedded in the baseboard molding and gave it a soft kick. The door opened. Light seeped around the edges. He stood to one side, swung it the rest of the way open, and waited for the count of ten, then peeked around the corner. Clear.

He stepped inside, shut the door behind him. He was in a short corridor that ended at another door, this one with a small reinforced window set at chin height. Stenciled on the door was a cluster of yellow triangles on a black circular background—the classic symbol for a fallout shelter. Judging from the faded paint, this was a Shek-era addition, probably part of the pagoda's original design. Yet another eccentricity in an already-full quiver of oddities.

Fisher reached up and unscrewed the lightbulb above his head, then flipped his trident goggles into place, switched to NV, and peeked through the window. There was no one.

He went through the door and found himself in a concrete room. A giant yellow arrow on the left-hand wall pointed downward. A single-strip fluorescent light flickered on the wall of the landing. He started down. He stayed close to the far wall, careful to keep his shadow from slipping over the railing. At the first landing he turned down the next flight, and continued down six flights. At the bottom was another windowed door through which he could see the back of a man's head.

The guard was too close to the door to risk the flexicam, and without knowing whether the man had company, a snatch from behind was out of the question. Plan B, then.

From his belt he drew the sidearm he'd taken from Lok, placed it on the third step, then retreated beneath the stairwell. He drew his pistol and toggled the selector to DART, then fired at the door. The dart ticked against the steel, then skittered away. In the window the guard's head turned. Fisher drew back under the steps, lay down on his back, and flicked the pistol back to single-shot.

The door creaked open. There were three seconds of silence, then a Chinese voice—frustrated, disgusted. Fisher assumed the words amounted to, *Okay, which idiot dropped his gun?*

Boots clicked on concrete. Fisher pictured the man

walking and counted steps: four . . . five . . . six . . . Foot on the first step . . .

Fisher pushed off the wall and slid out, gun coming up. The man sensed movement and started to turn, but too late. Fisher fired. The bullet penetrated beneath his left earlobe. The Glaser Safety Slug had devastating effect, instantly pulverizing the man's brain stem. The man tipped sideways, but even as he started sliding down the wall, Fisher was up and moving. He caught the body as it fell, then dragged it beneath the stairwell. He checked the steps and wall for blood, wiped up two spots, picked up Lok's gun.

A quick peek revealed the corridor was empty and thankfully short, with two rooms on each side and a vaultlike door at the end—which led to what Lok had called "the room." The floor was covered with two black rubber tiles Fisher guessed were vibration dampeners. Shek had spared no expense on his doomsday bunker.

Fisher punched up OPSAT's comm screen: The mysterious CIA signal was still there, and unless he'd missed finding something above or there was yet another level below this one, the beacon was coming from the first room on his right.

Time to solve a mystery.

HE slid the flexi-cam beneath the door. In the fish-eye lens he saw what looked like a college dorm room. Two single beds, one each on the left and right walls, separated by a desk, a clothes bureau at the foot of each bed. On the left-hand bed, a man reclined. He suddenly sat up and dropped his feet to the floor. He was Chinese. He rubbed his face in his hands, looked around.

Agitated, Fisher thought.

He withdrew the flexi-cam, briefly considered his options, then decided simple was easier. He drew his pistol then lightly tapped his index finger on the door three times. From inside, the bed creaked, footsteps approached. The door swung open.

Fisher didn't give the man a chance to react. He barreled through the door, palm against the man's chest, shoving him, gun in his face. The man's legs bumped into the bed rail and he fell backward onto the bed.

"Not a sound," Fisher warned.

Mouth agape, arms raised, the man nodded. "Okay, okay . . ."

English. Well modulated, very little accent. "Shut up," Fisher snapped. "Interlace your hands across your chest."

The man complied and Fisher checked the room. Only one of the bureaus contained clothes. No roommate. Fisher stood over the man. "We're going to make this quick. I'm going to talk, you're going to listen. For the past few hours you've been transmitting a beacon signal on a CIA carrier frequency."

"No, I—"

"Yes, you have. Tell me why."

The man hesitated.

Fisher said, "If I had a problem with your beacon,

you'd be dead right now. The fact that you're not should tell you something. The fact that I'm not Chinese should also tell you something. You can either believe me, or not, but I don't have the time to waste on you." He leveled the pistol with the man's forehead.

"Okay, okay, wait. It's in the desk drawer."

"Open it. Slowly."

The man did so. He pulled out a white 30GB iPod Video, unplugged a wire, and handed it over. "There's a phone conduit behind the desk; I tapped into it."

"Clever," Fisher said. "Yours?"

"No. My handler gave it to me."

This would be a CIA case officer from the Near East Division. The modified iPod would have come from Langley's wizards in the Science & Technical Directorate. Fisher handed the iPod back.

"I'm going to put my gun away." The man nodded and Fisher sat down on the opposite bed. "What's your name?"

"Heng."

His face was chalky and his eyes were red-rimmed and underlined with bags. He was clearly exhausted, and Fisher knew lack of sleep had nothing to do with it. Whoever Heng was—agent, informant, or something else altogether—he'd been under tremendous stress for a long time.

"What's your job?" Fisher asked.

"You mean, what do I do here, or what am I doing for the agency?"

"The latter."

"For the past year, I've been feeding them information about Kuan-Yin Zhao."

Fisher felt like he'd swallowed a ball of ice. "Say that name again."

"Kuan-Yin Zhao."

And suddenly a big piece of the puzzle Fisher had been racing to assemble snapped into place.

46

IF the now-mummified Bai Shek was China's version of a Howard Hughes-ian cliche, then Kuan-Yin Zhao was its version of The Godfather, only more violent.

After a ten-year meteoric rise up the bloody ladder of Chinese tongs and triads, Zhao had for the last twenty years reigned as the undisputed kingpin of the Chinese underworld. Labor, transportation, gambling, prostitution, drugs—every vice or necessity of Chinese daily life was in some way, large or small, controlled by Zhao. It was the latter category, drugs, that had for the last eight years solidified his position, and he owed it all to something called Jagged.

A synthetic derivative drug developed by Zhao's own chemical engineers, Jagged was both an addict's nightmare and his fantasy. A dozen times more addictive than methamphetamine, Jagged provided the user with a mixed high—the smooth dreamscape of heroin combined with the energy rush of cocaine—all with an easy comedown that lasted less and less time with each dose, until the user couldn't go for more than an hour or two without a fix. Withdrawl symptoms could last a month or more and were similar to those of hemorrhagic disease: fever, migraine headache, cramping, vomiting, diarrhea, bleeding from the eyes, and ecchymosis, or the pooling of blood beneath the skin.

From a manufacturing perspective, Jagged was a dream come true. Its component chemicals were found in everything from food additives and pesticides to over-the-counter allergy medicines and household cleaning products—all cheap, legal, and nearly impossible to regulate. In the eight years it had been in circulation, Jagged's chemical makeup had resisted all replication, which left Kuan-Yin Zhao not only its sole producer, but also one of the wealthiest men on the face of the earth.

In the first three years of its existence, Jagged had spread like the plague it was from China to Vietnam, Thailand, Cambodia, and India, before finally leaving Asia and jumping into Russia and the former Soviet Republics, Eastern and Western Europe, and finally America. Everywhere Jagged went, rates of addiction and crime skyrocketed. It spread through high schools and colleges and into suburbia, addicting both the curious and recreational users as well as hard-core users.

The justice systems of affected countries were overwhelmed. State and federal legislators couldn't allocate money fast enough to find a place to house those convicted not only of possesion of Jagged, but also of the crimes that inevitably trailed in its wake: prostitution, theft, murder, assault, rape.

Fisher had read the stats and he'd seen the results on city streets. In the five years since it hit the United States, Jagged's rate of use—and thereby addiction—had outstripped its every competitior, having risen to 9.2 percent of the population, or almost 27 million people. For every ten people in the United States, one of them was a hardcore Jagged addict who would slit your throat for the spare change in your pocket.

THAT answered the *who* part of Fisher's puzzle. Kuan-Yin Zhao had enough wealth to buy anything and anyone he needed, but the question of why he'd launched the *Trego* and Slipstone attacks and why he seemed to be trying to orchestrate a war between Iran and the U.S. was still a mystery. Fisher hoped Heng might answer that question.

"What do you do for Zhao?" Fisher asked.

"Intelligence," Heng answered. "I was Second Bureau, Guoanbu."

"Foreign Directorate," Fisher said.

"Yes. One of Zhao's people recruited me. I lost a sister and a cousin to Jagged. I thought I'd get inside Zhao's organization and . . ." Heng stopped, threw up his hands.

"I don't know what I was thinking. I knew could not go to my superiors; Zhao's influence is everywhere. He has so much money. . . ."

"So you offered yourself up to the CIA."

Heng nodded. "I knew there was an undeclared station in Taipei, so I arranged to go on vacation there and I made contact."

"What have you given them?"

"Not much, I'm afraid. I don't think I'm Zhao's only recruit. He's got an operation going, but it's compartmentalized. I handle a piece of it, someone else handles another piece. . . . I'm sure you know how it works."

Fisher decided Heng deserved to know what was at stake here. "You know about Slipstone?"

"I saw it on news, yes."

"We think Zhao's behind that. He got his hands on some nuclear waste from Chernobyl."

Heng closed his eyes and sighed. "I had a chance to kill him once, you know. I should have."

"Maybe you'll get another shot," Fisher said. "But for now, I need your eyes and ears here. When did you last make contact with your handler?"

"A month, month and a half ago. About that time Zhao cracked down on security and we started moving. Communication was impossible."

Four to six weeks, Fisher thought. About the time Zhao would have put the *Trego* and Slipstone operations into motion. The fact that Heng was still incognito here suggested there was more of Zhao's plan yet to unfold.

"What's the last thing you did for him?"

"Two weeks ago, I went with two of his bodyguards to Ashgabat, Turkmenistan, to meet a man—an Iranian."

The two men the FBI had in custody from Slipstone had been ultimately bound for Ashgabat.

Connecting dots.

"And? Did you know him? Did you get a name?"

Heng shook his head. "I gave him a package and went over an operation with him—a raid of some kind. All I had was a map. No legend. It's somewhere along a coastline, but nothing looked familiar to me. I could tell it was some kind of military installation, but that's it. My guess is that someone else had already given the man the other parts of the operation. As I said—"

"Compartmentilization, I know. Draw it for me."

Heng drew the map from memory, but with no peripheral features it meant nothing to Fisher.

He continued questioning Heng, going backward and forward through his time with Zhao, but there was little else to glean. Heng's role had largely been that of a courier.

"I do have something that might be useful," he said. "In Ashgabat, I met the Iranian at a private home. I know where it is, and I remember a name: Marjani. Ailar Marjani."

"I'll look into it. What's in the room, the one with the vault door?"

"Zhao's nerve center. Communications, computers, satellite uplinks—he's got it all."

"How many in there?"

"Three or four."

"Is Zhao here?"

"No, but I think he's coming. I don't know when."

Fisher considered his options. Hunker down, wait for Zhao, and either snatch him or kill him? Or take what he had and get out? He chose the latter. Whatever was left to play out in Zhao's scheme, Fisher knew there was no guarantee the man's death or disappearance would stop it. Besides, while getting his hands on Zhao might be easy enough, getting off the island alive—with or without him—would be another matter altogether. "You know I can't take you out," Fisher said to Heng.

"I know."

"Lay low and keep you eyes open. Make contact if you can."

Heng nodded.

"One last question: How do I get into Zhao's nerve center?"

HENG'S answer was to take Fisher down the hall to the first door on the left. Fisher picked the lock and they slipped inside. It was a utility room with an air-conditioning unit, a few supply closets filled with sundry items, and an open circular pit in the floor surrounded by a fringe of steel plates secured to the floor by a padlocked chain.

Fisher sent Heng back to his room, then picked the padlock and pried up one of the plates, revealing a two-foot-deep crawl space. Cool air rushed up to meet him; it smelled of earth. Years ago, Heng had explained, when Shek had ordered his pagoda built, the foundation had struck a seasonal water table, so the fallout shelter's pilings had been raised to compensate for moonsoon flooding. Two months earlier, had Fisher pried back the well's plates, he would have found a small lake instead of dirt. The pit was a runoff sump for excess water.

Fisher shut off the overhead light, then dropped through the opening and pulled the plate closed behind him.

WITH a hum, his NV goggles powered up, revealing an expanse of dirt and concrete pilings. To his right, a pair of eyes flashed red; with a screech, the rat scurried away and disappeared.

He started crawling, angling to his left and counting feet until he was centered under the hallway. He adjusted course and kept crawling. He reached a horizontal steel plate that extended from the floor above to the dirt below. This would be the outer vault door. He crawled around the plate. After another ten feet, he came to a second one, the inner vault door. On the other side of this he saw a dozen squares of blue light cast on the dirt floor.

These lattice floor tiles were backups to the air conditioners, Heng had explained. Zhao's nerve center ran a lot of electrical equipment, all of which had to be kept cool.

Fisher slowed down now, moving a few inches, then stopping and listening before moving again. After ten feet, he heard a low-level buzz of electricity and hushed voices speaking in Chinese. He powered down his goggles and kept crawling until he could see through a tile.

He found himself looking at the back of a chair and a pair of feet resting on the floor. A computer workstation. He inched to his right until he could see through the next opening. Here he could see the corner of a plasma TV screen. He craned his neck until a station logo came into view: CNN. He moved to the next tile. Mounted on the wall above was what looked like backlighted sheet of Plexiglas. Fisher couldn't tell its width, but it seemed to extend from the floor to the ceiling.

It was a HUD, or Heads-Up Display, he realized, similar to the one in his own scuba faceplate or in fighter cockpit screens. On it was displayed a lighted map annoted with grease-pencil markings. The area displayed looked familiar, but it took a moment for him to place it:

Persian Gulf, western coastline of Iran.

47

THE upper rim of the sun was just edging over the horizon when *Houston*'s sail rose from the water fifty yards to his right. A seaman was waiting on deck, ready with a hand up. "Welcome back," the kid said.

"Good to be back," Fisher said. He meant it.

It had taken him the remainder of the night to extract himself first from the pagoda, then back through the security cordon surrounding the compound, across the island to the cliff road, and down to the beach, where he'd hidden his scuba gear among the rocks. He was bone tired, but buzzing with excess adrenaline. His mind was spinning, trying to fit together what he'd uncovered on the island.

After a quick towel-off and a change of clothes, he

found Collins and Marty Smith in the Control Center. "Was it everything you'd hoped?" Smith said with a grin.

"And so much more," Fisher replied. "Max, I need you to send the immediate extract signal, then clear the area at best speed."

"Bad news?" Collins asked.

"I think so. I just don't know what it is yet."

COLLINS guided the *Houston* north, then east, skirting the patrol areas of the 093s they'd passed on the way in, then ordered the the OOD to take her deep and increase speed to twenty knots. Two hours later, Collins called Fisher to the Control Center, wished him luck, and sent him topside. A hundred yards off the port beam, the Osprey was hovering over the ocean's surface. The rear ramp was down, and leaning from it, one hand hooked on a cargo strap, was Redding. He gave Fisher a wave.

Two minutes later, he was sitting at the Osprey's console staring at Lambert's face on the monitor. He quickly brought his boss up to speed.

"Kuan-Yin Zhao," Lambert murmured. "That's a twist I wasn't expecting."

"You and me both. But I know who can make sense of it."

"Tom Richards. I'll get him over here. Unless your new friend Heng is lying, the CIA's been running an op against Zhao. Now: About Ashgabat—give me that name again."

"Ailar Marjani."

The monitor went to split screen; Lambert on the right, Grimsdottir left. "Checking," she said. "Okay, got him. Ailar Marjani is the former head of the KNB—Turkmenistan's version of the CIA. He's got a thick file. Bad guy, this one. Human rights abuses, bribery, weapons trafficking, ties to Hezbollah . . ."

"Another Iranian link," Fisher said.

Lambert was silent for a few seconds, thinking. "Okay, I'm going to put Richards's feet to the fire on Zhao."

"And tell him he needs to get Heng out; the man's burnt out. He's going to slip up."

"I will. So: You feel up to a little jaunt to Ashgabat?"

"I always feel like a little jaunt to Ashgabat. You get me there, I'll get Marjani."

IN truth, Fisher had never been to Ashgabat, and so he had the same stereotypes in mind that most westerners did about the Central Asian republics—that they were backward, remote, dusty, and harsh. And while this was true for the rural areas, Ashgabat was, Fisher realized as his plane banked over the city, a stunning exception.

Nestled in a bowl between the southern edge of the Garagum Desert, which covers ninety percent of the country, and the Köpetdag Mountain Range, a belt of ten-thousand-foot peaks along the Iranian border, Ashgabat is a modern city of five million souls, with clean cobblestone sidewalks and plazas, fountains and monuments, a mix of traditional Islamic architecture and modern building design, and a network of small irrigation canals that feed the city's lush gardens and parks.

And memorials. Lots and lots of memorials, most of them dedicated to one man: Turkemenistan's President for Life Atayevich Niyazov, or Serdar Saparmurat Turkmenbashi—the Great Leader of the Turkmens. A former Soviet bureaucrat, Niyazov ruled his country with absolute authority. His visage was everywhere—in murals, on the sides of buses, on coffee mugs and T-shirts, in classrooms and museums, and on statues: Niyazov riding a stallion; Niyazov holding a baby; Niyazov sternly staring at accused criminals; Niyazov attending museum galas and government balls. He had changed the Turkmen alphabet, renamed the months and days of the year, and written the *Ruhnama,* or Book of the Soul, a practical and spiritual guidebook every Turkmen citizen is required to own.

Along with all the trappings of what was clearly a dictatorship, Fisher knew Niyazov's iron hand was backed up by a vast network of secret police and intelligence agencies. The sooner he could get to Ailar Marjani and get out of Ashgabat, the better.

This was the kind of place where a man could disappear and never be heard from again.

GETTING here so quickly had taken a lot of time in the air and Lambert's significant pull.

Ninety minutes after leaving the Zhoushan Archipelago, the Osprey touched down at Kadena Air Force Base, where Fisher was met by a tech sergeant, who drove him to a waiting F-15D Eagle. He was suited up, helped into the rear seat, and given a two-word briefing by the pilot: "Touch nothing." Five minutes later, the Eagle was airborne and heading southwest.

Exhausted, Fisher was quickly asleep, only waking for the Eagle's midair refueling with a KC-135 Stratotanker, then again for the landing in Kabul, Afghanistan, where he was met by another sergeant, this one of the Army variety, who drove him to a waiting Gulfstream V that Fisher assumed was part of the small fleet of executive jets the CIA maintained.

The flight from Kabul lasted a bare two hours, and now, eight hours after he swam away from Cezi Maji, the Gulfstream's tires touched down with a squeal on Ashgabat Airport's runway.

FISHER didn't leave the plane, but waited, sprawled in one of the cabin's reclining seats, as the simulated engine warning light that had put them down here was checked. Night was just falling when the airport's maintenance supervisor popped his head through the side door and told the pilot no problem had been found. They were cleared to leave.

Once airborne, the pilot radioed the Ashgabat tower and requested permission to circle a few times to ensure the warning light didn't reappear, then proceeded in a low southeasterly arc away from the airport.

"Eight hundred feet," the pilot called over the intercom. "Drop in three minutes."

Fisher was already strapping on his parafoil pack.

A thousand feet above and four miles from Ashgabat, Fisher jumped out the Gulfstream's side door. He waited for two beats, then pulled the toggle, heard the *whoosh-whump* of the parafoil deploying, and was jerked upward.

Ailar Marjani's retirement was without financial worry, Grimsdottir had reported. The former Turkmen spymaster had built an arabesque mansion eight miles from Ashgabat in the foothills of the Köpetdag.

Fisher followed the flashing waypoint marker on his OPSAT, and touched down in the rolling, grassy hills that lay between the city and the mountains. Even in the darkness, Fisher was struck by the landscape; had he not known better, he might have mistaken it for the western Dakotas or eastern Montana. The night was warm, hovering around seventy degrees, the sky clear and cloudless. A slight breeze swished the grass around his knees.

He donned his gear, took a bearing on the OPSAT, and started jogging.

AFTER a mile, he topped a hill and stopped. He lay down on his belly and pulled out his binoculars.

Even from a mile away, Marjani's home was impossible to miss, a sprawling structure of whitewashed rectangles and arches stacked atop one another and nestled at the base of an escarpment. Every window in Marjani's home blazed with light. Fisher scanned each one but saw no one. Clusters of palms rose from various points on the grounds, each one lit from beneath by an spotlight. Fisher counted two fountains that he could see, each a glistening plume of water.

He kept moving, using the troughs of the hills to make his way to within a quarter mile. He crawled up a hillock and through the grass. At this range, he could see a lone guard standing to the left of the arched driveway entrance. Through the entrance he could see a courtyard of hedges, and at the center, a glowing kidney-shaped pool. The guard wasn't so much standing as he was vertically reclined against the arch, his AK-47 propped against the wall a few feet away. Fisher wasn't even sure the man was awake.

He maneuvered to the left, crawling through the grass until he was at an angle, fifty yards from the arch. He pulled the SC-20 from its back holster, zoomed in on the guard, then panned through the arch, looking for more guards. There were none. Same on the infrared side. He refocused on the guard and laid the recticle over the man's chest.

He squeezed the trigger. The guard spasmed once, then slumped back against the wall and slid down into a pile. Fisher shifted his aim, shot out the ground spotlight, then shifted again and waited for another guard to come investigate the outage. Five minutes passed. No one came.

He holstered the SC-20, then crawled ahead until the

entrance arch blocked the mansion's upper windows, then got up and sprinted the remaining distance. He snatched up the AK-47, tossed it into the high grass, then grabbed the man's collar and dragged him through the arch. He turned left and stopped behind a shrub.

He heard the crunch of gravel to his right. He turned. A man walked down the driveway and stopped at the arch. An AK was slung over his shoulder. The man looked left, then right, then called, "Ashiq?"

Damnit.

48

FISHER took off his headpiece, laid it aside, then lowered himself onto his haunches, leaned against the wall, and dropped his chin to his chest. He drew his pistol and held it out of sight against his thigh.

"Ashiq?" the man called again.

Fisher let out a pained groan. In the corner of his eye, he saw the man turn. Fisher feebly raised his arm and let it fall.

"Ashiq!"

The man rushed across the driveway. As he drew even with shrubs, Fisher raised the pistol and shot him in the forehead. The man made an *umph*, then sprawled face-first in the dirt beside Fisher. Fisher grabbed him by the wrist and dragged him deeper into the shadows and laid him next to the first guard.

Two down.

HE took his time with the rest of the grounds, using the shadows and the landscaping to pick his way around the inner wall, eyes and ears alert for more guards as he periodically scanned the windows for signs of movment.

He found only one other guard, strolling along a topiary-lined gravel path on the east side of the house. Fisher waited for him to pass, then stepped out, clamped a hand over his mouth, and plunged the Sykes into the hollow beside his collarbone. The man stiffened, jerked once, went limp. Fisher dragged him out of sight.

He made his way to the rear of the house and to the glassed-in patio overlooking a second swimming pool. Unlike the floors above, the patio was dark. Save for the gurgling of the pool's aerators and the distant hum of the air conditioners, all was quiet.

The patio door was made of flimsy aluminum, with a push-button latch that took him fifteen seconds to pick. He slipped inside. A wave of cool air washed over him. He took a moment to breath it in, let it cool his face.

Marjani clearly had a fondness for the color white and shades of white. The walls, leather couches, and carpet were cream, with a few Turkmen art and sculpture pieces scattered around the room. On the far side, a stairway led upward.

Crouched over, he took the steps one at time, until he could see through the black wrought-iron balustrade. Predictably, the room was done mostly in white, with a rough-hewn tile floor inlaid with robin's-egg-blue mosaics. There was a seating area beneath the windows, through which he could see the driveway arch.

Fisher climbed the rest of steps, then searched the level, finding a gourmet kitchen in stainless steel, a formal dining room, and a bookcase-lined den. He moved to the second floor: a home gym, three guest bedrooms, and a bathroom with a steam shower, sauna, and whirlpool tub.

He was halfway up the steps to the third floor when he heard voices. He froze. It was a television.

"Welcome back to *American Idol*. Our next contestant is performing—" Then static, followed by, "But Ricky—" Then more static, and then the theme to *Gilligan's Island*.

Fisher smiled ruefully. Marjani was putting his golden years to good use.

He found the former Turkmen minister in a small room overlooking the rear pool. The man was sprawled in a white leather recliner, a bag of potato chips in his lap, the remote aimed at the TV. Fisher backed through the arch, searched the remainder of the floor, then returned. On the TV screen, Gilligan and a chimp were playing catch with a coconut.

Fisher flipped off the lights, dropped his NV goggles into place, and stepped behind Marjani's chair just as the man was sitting up. Fisher laid the Sykes across Marjani's neck and said, "Not a sound. Your guards are dead. If you don't want to the join them, you'll do as I say."

Grimsdottir's brief had said Marjani had a fair grasp of English, and his rapid nodding confirmed it. "Who are you, what do you want?"

The two classic questions, Fisher thought. Over the years he'd found that noncombatants usually said, "Please don't kill me," when someone put a knife to their throat. With bad guys, it was always a variation of what Marjani had just asked, with a slight edge of indignation to their voice.

Fisher whispered in his ear, "To answer your first question, none of your business. To answer your second question, I want to kill you, but I'm going to give you a chance to talk me out of it."

HE dragged Marjani down the hall, flipping off lights as he went, until they were in the master bedroom. He grabbed a pillow off the bed, then marched Marjani into the bathroom and shoved him into the whirlpool tub. He shut the door and sat down on the toilet next to the tub. Marjani was a fat man with slicked-back black hair and a lopsided mustache. He reminded Fisher of a stock villain in a Western.

Fisher hadn't turned on the bathroom lights; it was pitch black. In the glow of his NV goggles, he could see Marnaji's eyes darting around, his hands clamped on the edge of the rub. His face glistened with sweat. Fisher let him sit in the dark, letting it the silence stretch on until finally Marjani blurted, "Is anyone there? Hey, is—"

"I'm here."

"What do you want?"

"We've been through that. I'm going to ask you some questions. If I don't like the answers, you're going to die in that tub. No more *Gilligan's Island,* no more *I Love Lucy,* understand?"

"Do you know who I am? You can't do this!"

Fisher drew the Sykes and lightly jabbed Marjani in the thigh. He yelped and curled up, trying to make himself small.

Fisher said, "How about that? Can I do that?"

"You're crazy!"

"Sit up, straighten your legs, remove your shoes and socks, and rest your arms on the sides of the tub."

"What?"

"You have three seconds."

Marjani complied.

"Two weeks ago you had houseguests," Fisher began. "A Chinese man with two bodyguards, and an Iranian with his own bodyguards. What did they talk about?"

"I don't know."

That was true. Heng had said he'd met with the Iranian alone.

"How long were they here?"

"Two, maybe three hours."

That was also true. Using what he already knew, Fisher was establishing a baseline, gauging Marjani's tone, facial expressions, inflection.

"Who was in the room during this meeting?"

"Just the Chinese and the other one," Marjani replied. He'd hesitated slightly at "other one."

"Did they arrive separately or together?"

"Separately. Why are you—"

"Who is the Iranian?"

Fisher reached out and jabbed Marjani in the foot. Not so gently this time. Marjani screamed, reached for his foot. "Don't move," Fisher said, "or I'll take you toe off."

Reluctantly, Marjani leaned back. His lower lip was trembling.

Almost there, Fisher thought. The stress of being blind and not knowing when or where the next jab was coming was quickly breaking Marjani down.

Fisher hooked Marjani's pinky toe with the tip of the Sykes and stretched it backward. Marjani flinched, drew back his lips until his teeth showed. "Don't . . . please don't. . . ."

"Give me the Iranian's name."

Marjani hesitated, squeezed his eyes shut. "I don't know, please. . . ."

Fisher let the blade rest between his toes for five more seconds, then removed it. "Do you want to reconsider your answer?"

"I don't know who he is, I swear. He showed up and—"

Fisher picked up the pillow and tossed it into Marjani's lap. "What . . . what is this?"

"It's a pillow," Fisher said. "Put it over your face."

"What? Why?"

"The gunshot is going to be loud in here."

All the color drained from Marjani's face. "Please, I can't. . . ."

Fisher let him sob for a half a minute, then said, "Do you want to change your answer? Do you want to tell me who the Iranian is?"

Marjani nodded and started talking.

49

WHEN Marjani finished talking, Fisher had some answers and a lot more questions.

He darted Marjani, bound his hands and feet with flexi-cuffs, then fireman-carried him down to the garage, where he found a gleaming-white H1 Alpha Hummer. He shoved Marjani in the back, bound his feet to one of the tie-down eyelets, then climbed into the front seat. The keys were in the ignition.

Thirty seconds later, he was rolling the down the driveway, the air conditioner blowing at full blast. He turned left at the arch and headed northwest, headlights off as he kept to the depressions and used the moonlight to guide him. He drove for fifteen minutes until the hills began to smooth out into the fringe of the Garagum

Desert. He coasted to a stop and shut off the engine. He keyed his subdermal.

"Pike, this is Sickle, over."

"Go ahead, Sickle," Bird replied. After refueling at Kabul, Redding and the Osprey had followed an hour behind the Gulfstream, slipping across the Turkmenistan border and setting down sixty miles from Ashgabat in the desert.

"Request extraction, break; two passengers, break; map coordinates one-two-two-point-five by three-two-point-three; beacon is transmitting, over."

"Roger, Sickle, en route."

THE Osprey appeared twelve minutes later, skimming low over the ground, its rotor blades glinting in the moonlight.

"I have visual on you, Pike," Fisher said. "Confirm same." He flipped the Hummer's fog lights on and off.

"Confirm, Sickle, we have you."

The Osprey put down a hundred yards away atop a small hillock, and Redding came down the ramp to help Fisher with Marjani. "Friend of yours?" Redding asked.

"He doesn't think so, but he's going to come in handy."

While Redding took care of their passenger, Fisher walked forward to the cockpit. "Bird, how're we looking on radar?"

"Fine. Hell, Turkmenistan hasn't got a military radar station for a thousand miles. We could sit here for days." He glanced at Fisher. "We're not going to sit here for days, are we?"

"No. Just keep an eye out."

Fisher walked aft and sat down at the comm console. Lambert came on the monitor and said, "What's your status?"

"Out and safe. Marjani was paid by Zhao through Heng, but he doesn't know who was behind the money. He's never heard of Zhao. I don't know if I believe that, but there wasn't time to press him further. He says Heng's meeting was with an Iranian named Kavad Abelzada. He's from a village called Sarani, right across the border. He was born and raised there."

Before Lambert could ask her, Grimsdottir said, "I'm looking. . . ."

Lambert said, "I've got Tom Richards here. I've filled him in on the Zhao angle. I think he's got the piece we're missing."

"Let's hear it."

The screen split and Richards's face appeared. "You already know this, of course, but yes, we're running an op against Zhao—us, the Brits, and the Russians."

"Let me guess: Jagged."

Richards nodded. "Three years ago, the President signed a top-secret executive order declaring the spread of Jagged was a clear and imminent threat to national security. Moscow and London were seeing the effects in their countries as well, so it didn't take much convincing to get them to sign onto the operation. We code-named it Jupiter.

"For the past twenty-eight months, we've been waging war against Zhao along with the Russian SVR and British MI6. We started with his peripheral operations, cutting off the money, attacking the transportation, snatching low-level operators—that kind of thing."

"Does Beijing know about this?"

"Hell, no. Zhao has so many politicians and generals in his pockets we've lost count."

"Go on."

"Once we'd made a dent in his side businesses, we took the fight straight to him," Richards said. "Starting with his key personnel."

"How key?" Fisher asked.

"Very. Most of Zhao's empire is run by family members—brothers, cousins, uncles. We began eliminating them, one by one."

"Say again?"

"Each country put specially trained teams on the ground. There was no choice; we're at war as surely as if bombs were exploding."

Fisher wasn't shocked by Richards's admission that the CIA had fielded assassination teams, but rather that the President had made such a bold move. Right or wrong, if Jupiter ever became public knowledge, the resulting scandal would end his career and the careers of everyone attached to the operation.

"How many so far?" Fisher asked.

"Sixty-two. Twenty-three family members and thirty-nine non-family subordinates."

"And his empire?"

"It's running on fumes. Another six months and he'll topple. The flow of Jagged will slow to a trickle and then stop."

And there was Zhao's motive, Fisher realized. Revenge and self-preservation. Twenty-three members of his own family murdered; tens of billions of dollars at stake. Zhao had answered the U.S./Russian/U.K. declaration of war with his own, but knowing he couldn't win a head-to-head fight, he'd devised a strategy straight out of Sun Tzu's *Art of War*.

Launch the most devastating attack on U.S. soil in history and implicate Iran, which is already the world's new boogeyman; the U.S. responds in kind and begins marching toward war; then drag Russia into the fiasco using nuclear material stolen or sold from its own backyard. From there, momentum, world outrage, and Iran's own defiance would do the rest. The U.S., the U.K., and whatever coalition they managed to gather would be sucked into a protracted and possibly unwinnable third war in the Middle East; Russia would be a pariah on the world stage, having caused the deaths of five thousand or more innocent civilians through neglect and/or corruption. Lives would be lost on all sides, and for years to come the last thing on the minds of U.S., Russian, and U.K. politicians would be Kuan-Yin Zhao.

At worst, Zhao has his revenge; at best, revenge and a chance to rebuild his empire.

FISHER said, "Colonel, this is it. This is Zhao's game."

"Agreed," Lambert said. "But do we have enough evidence to prove it?"

"With Kavad Abelzada, we might," said Richards.

"He's the missing link. He had to have supplied Zhao with the crew for the *Trego* and the men at Slipstone."

Grimsdottir came back on the line. "And I think I know why. Up until eighteen months ago, Abelzada had spent the last nine years in a Tehran political prison. He was tried and convicted of 'inciting radical insurrection' and 'plotting to overthrow the government of the Islamic Republic of Iran.' When he was sent to prison, he had a rabid following that numbered in the thousands. The day he was convicted, there were seventeen suicide bombings throughout Tehran."

"Given its own track record, for Tehran to label Abelzada as a dangerous radical is saying something," Fisher said. "Grim, do we know what his problem was with the government?"

"I'm looking. . . . Okay, here: He was demanding they declare open war on the U.S., Israel, and all their allies. And I quote: 'We must burn the civilizations of the West out of existence and scatter the bones of the infidels to every corner of the globe. Anything less is an insult in Allah's eyes.'"

"Very nice," Lambert said. "So, Zhao somehow becomes aware of Abelzada's leanings; he makes contact and offers him a chance to not only bring down his own government, but also drag the U.S. into a bloodbath—all for providing a few loyal fanatics."

"The blue-light special of wars," Fisher said. "I can see why he couldn't resist the deal."

"So how do we get him?" Richards asked. "I can put together a team, but that'll take—"

Fisher cut him off. "I'll tell you how we get him. We're

twenty miles from the border. Another five miles beyond that is Sarani. We fly in, land on his damned house, and snatch him."

"That easy, huh?" Richards said.

"Not easy at all," Fisher replied. "But it's the best chance we've got. Colonel?"

On the screen, Fisher watched his boss squeeze the bridge of his nose and close his eyes for a few moments. He looked up. "Go get him, Sam."

50

BIRD powered down the engines and they sat quiet and dark as Lambert smoothed the way for their mission. Where Turkmenistan's airspace was a sieve, Iran's was a wall, with a constellation of overlapping early-warning radar stations and antiaircraft missile batteries along the borders that were in constant touch with Iranian Air Interceptor Command. Being spotted in Turkmenistan would draw curiosity. In Iran, it would bring down a rain of missile fire and fighters flying at Mach 2.

Right now Lambert was on the phone with the NRO, or National Reconnaissance Office, requesting an emergency retasking of a satellite, in this case one of the two radar satellites that kept Iraq under constant surveillance. With names such as Lacrosse, Onyx, Indigo, these RAD-

SATs orbited four hundred miles above the earth, weighed fifteen tons, and were as big as school buses—and they could see an object as small as a hardcover book through rain, fog, and the black of night.

"We got a map update downloading," Bird called from the cockpit. "On your screen."

Sitting at the comm console, Redding switched to the Osprey's navigation net. Fisher leaned in for a closer look. The new image looked like a standard topographical map showing the terrain between their landing site and the village of Sarani, but it had been enhanced with data from the RADSAT, adding three-dimensional depth to the geographic features.

Overlaying the map was a dotted yellow line that started at the Osprey's current position, arced around Ashgabat, then zigzagged through the Köpetdag Mountains, and finally ended at the collection of structures and crisscrossing roads that made up the village of Sarani.

Redding used the console's trackball to rotate and zoom the image, changing it from a high overhead view to the first-person view. He scrolled the wheel and the image glided forward, like a hawk flying through a steeply walled canyon. He touched the wheel again, and the view returned to overhead.

"We clip a wing on one of those walls and we're a fireball."

"I'm not worried about that," Fisher said. "Bird can fly this thing through a set of goal posts at four hundred knots. What I'm worried about are those." He tapped the screen.

Scattered along their course through the mountains were pulsing red squares, each one a radar station linked to a nearby missile site.

FISHER walked forward to the cockpit. Bird and Sandy were leaning over the console screen, studying the RAD-SAT image. "What do you think?" Fisher asked.

"I think I want a raise," Bird muttered, eyes on the screen.

"You get us in and out of there in one piece and I'll pay it out of my own pocket."

"From you, Sam, I'll take a steak dinner."

"Done. Can you do it?"

"Yeah, I can do it, but I can't guarantee I won't rattle the dishes a bit."

"LAMBERT for you," Redding called. He gave up his seat for Fisher. "Go ahead, Colonel."

"Update, Sam. The President has authorized strike operations for the *Reagan*'s air group. They'll be starting with the surface-to-surface missile sites along the coast, from Jask to Khark Island."

This made sense. The Iranian Navy maintained hundreds of shore-based missile sites, most of which were focused on the Strait of Hormuz, the natural chokepoint between the Gulf of Oman and the Persian Gulf. A variety of missiles, from Silkworms to C-801s, covered every square inch of water. The fact that *Reagan*'s strike aircraft were going for the missile sites first could mean only one thing: The 5th Fleet was preparing to enter the Strait and take up station along Iran's interior coast. If the Iranians were inclined to hit first, it would be as the battle group moved into the strait.

"How soon?" Fisher asked.

"Tomorrow morning, before dawn. DESRON 9 will be going in first. Once they're on station, you can expect a multiple Tomahawk strike in conjunction with *Reagan's* aircraft."

DESRON 9 was the group's destroyer SAG, or Surface Action Group. The ship-launched Tomahawks would be assigned Iranian command and control targets and radar sites further inland. Fisher checked his watch: nine hours. They had that long to deliver proof that Iran's role in all this was of Kuan-Yin Zhao's manufacture.

"We're lifting off in ten minutes," Fisher said. "With luck, we'll be back across the border with Abelzada in a few hours. Colonel, I've been thinking about Heng's meeting at Marjani's house. He briefed Abelzada on raid on a military installation—somewhere along a coast."

"I put out the word. Every base on our West and East Coast is on alert."

"Good," Fisher said. "If Zhao's got an ace up his sleeve, that's it. The question is, what exactly is it and when will he play it?"

THE Osprey lifted off and they banked northwest, picking up speed as they skimmed thirty feet over the hills and grasslands. They were flying dark, with no navigation lights and all emission sources powered down: no IFF transponder, radio, or FLIR (Forward-Looking Infrared Radar).

Within minutes, they'd skirted Ashgabat, which lay fifteen miles out the side window. Fisher could see headlights moving along the highways and surface streets.

They passed over the black oval of a lake and a rail line, and then the terrain began to change, hillocks turning into the rolling foothills of the Köpetdag. Redding sat at the console, watching the same map Bird and Sandy were using to navigate. One by one, villages disappeared behind them. Fisher read their names on the screen—Bagir, Chuli, Firyuza—until they were all gone and there was nothing but empty land.

"Five miles from the border," Bird called.

Fisher went to the cockpit and knelt between the seats. Through the windscreen he could see the Köpetdag Range, an expanse of jagged peaks and ridgelines stacked against the even darker night sky.

A red light started flashing on Bird's console, followed by a beeping. A robotic female said, "Warning, radar source at—" Bird punched a button, shutting off the voice. "Redding?" he called.

"I see it. We're at the edge of its range. Turn coming up in thirty seconds."

Bird turned to Fisher. "Better go get strapped in. The ride is about to get wild."

51

"**STAND** by!" Redding called. "Border in five ... four ... three ... two ... one!"

Fisher clutched the armrests as Bird put the Osprey into a sharp bank.

In the cockpit, the radar warning alarm was beeping. Across the aisle, Fisher watched the monitor over Redding's shoulder. Redding had changed the view to split sreen: overhead view on the left, first-person on the right. On overhead, a pair of peaks to their left and right front were topped with pulsing red squares. On the first-person view, the Osprey was nosing over a ridgeline into a gorge. The granite walls flashed past, jagged outcroppings reaching for the wingtips.

"Course change in twenty seconds," Redding said.

"New course, two-two-one, sharp descent to thirty feet."

Now the radar alarms were overlapping one another as the twin radar stations drew nearer. Fisher leaned over in his seat and looked forward. The view through the cockpit window was dizzying. The black line of the horizon twisted and rolled as Bird negotiated the terrain.

"SAM site two miles off our starboard bow," Redding called.

"Spare me the nautical crap," Bird yelled back. "Just tell me where!"

"Two miles, front right! Course change in three . . . two . . . one . . . now!"

Fisher was thrown against his seat back, then shoved sideways as the Osprey heeled over. On Redding's monitor he'd switched to full-screen first-person. They were flying through a notch between two peaks. The Osprey's wingtips were perpendicular to the ground.

"Break out the barf bags," Sandy yelled, then whooped.

The radar alarm suddenly went silent.

"What's next?" Bird called.

"Three miles to Sarani." Redding answered. "Ridgeline coming up fast. Gonna have to pop up five hundred feet, then bank hard and hit the deck."

They flew in silence for twenty seconds, and then the radar alarm started beeping again.

"Hard left!" Redding called.

The Osprey flipped over. Strapped to the bulkhead by cargo webbing, his hands, feet, and mouth covered in duct tape, Marjani had regained consciousness. He let out a muffled scream. His eyes bulged. Fisher gave him a wink and a wave.

"Whoa!" Redding shouted. "Right turn! *Now!*"

Fisher was thrown in the opposite direction. His ribs slammed against the armrest. A duffel bag came loose from the rack and tumbled across the deck, bounced off Marjani, and slammed into the ramp.

"What the hell happened?" Bird called.

"Fire-control radar," Redding said. "A SAM site. Wasn't on the map!"

"Did they paint us?"

"Doubt it. Not enough time to lock on."

Fisher called, "That's what I like to hear: optimism."

From the cockpit, Sandy said, "I see the ridgeline. . . . Hey, Redding, that looks a lot taller than five hundred feet."

"Nope, four-ninety-one. Trust me, you'll have nine feet to spare."

Bird replied, "Oh, well . . . nine feet. Plenty."

"Start climbing in three . . . two . . . one . . ."

Fisher kept his eyes locked on Redding's monitor. The ridge, a jagged line of rock and scrub trees, seemed to rise up to meet them. Then it was gone. Beneath his feet he heard something scrape the underbelly of the fuselage, like a giant snare brush trailing over a drumhead.

"Picked up some leaves on that one!" Bird called.

"Dive, dive, dive!"

Bird pushed the stick forward. The Osprey nosed over. In the cockpit, the robotic voice said, "Warning, warning. Collision imminent. Pull up, pull up, pull up. . . ."

"Shut her up, Sandy."

The voice went silent and was immediately replaced by another radar alarm.

"We're at its outer range," Redding said. "Ten seconds to turn. A quick jink to the right, then pull up and bank left."

Jink? Fisher thought. Jink didn't sound like a technical flying term.

"How many radar sites left?" Bird called.

"This one, and one more, then we're at the LZ. Turn now!"

This time Fisher was ready for it. He braced his legs against the deck, pressing his back into the seat. He clutched the armrests until his knuckles were bloodless. The Osprey seemed to turn nearly upside down. Fisher felt his stomach rise into his throat. A Styrofoam coffee cup floated past his face, then dropped straight to the deck and skittered away.

"So, Bird, is that what you call a jink?" Fisher called.

"No, son, that's a super jink. Walk in the park."

"Last radar station dead ahead, one mile," Redding called.

Fisher glanced at the monitor. The Osprey was flying low and level over a boulder-strewn valley floor. The altitude gauge read eighteen feet. The radar alarm chirped, then went silent for a few seconds, then chirped again.

"We're skimming below the detection nadir," Redding announced. "The waves are skipping along the fuselage."

"Nadir?" Sandy repeated. "Been reading the dictionary again, Will?"

"It means—"

"I know what it means, you dummy."

"Gimme steering," Bird called. "The ground is sloping up. They're gonna paint us."

"Hard right turn in seven seconds," Redding replied. "Course zero-nine-eight."

"I don't see anything!" Sandy called.

"It's a gorge. Trust me, it's there."

"How wide?"

"Wide enough. Stand by. . . . Three . . . two . . . one, now!"

REDDING was right: The gorge was wide enough, but barely, and Fisher could hear Bird in the cockpit muttering, "Missed me . . . missed me . . . missed me . . ." as he made tiny course corrections to avoid rock outcrops. After thirty seconds of this, the walls begin to widen as the gorge smoothed into another valley.

"Landing zone coming up," Redding called. "A gentle dogleg left, then you should see a narrow river. The north bank is your spot."

A few seconds later, Bird called, "I see it, I see it. . . . Hot damn! If that ain't the sweetest piece of dirt on the planet. . . ."

HE set the Osprey down and Fisher unbuckled and began donning his gear. Redding handed him the OPSAT. "It's updated with the new map. There's an Army outpost about four miles away in Qoppoz. They send out regular patrols, but with this terrain you should hear them coming a mile away."

Fisher nodded and walked to the cockpit. Bird was leaning back in his seat, a bottle of Gatorade halfway to his mouth. His hair was wet with sweat. "Good flying, you two," Fisher said.

"We aim to please," Sandy replied.

"Keep the engines warm. If I need you . . ."

"Ninety seconds from your call I'll have a rope dangling over your head."

FISHER trotted down the ramp, then turned and started jogging. He had a mile to cover before the valley opened into the bowl in which Sarani sat, and at this time of night he doubted anyone would be about. Still, he varied his course, zigzagging between boulders and stopping every hundred yards or so to look for signs of movement or heat.

In the moonlight the terrain had an otherworldly feel: sharp spires or rock rising into the dark sky, sheer walls, and clumps of boulders, some as large as houses. The dirt was so fine it felt like flour; his every footfall kicked up a puff of dust that hung in the air.

After twelve minutes of running, OPSAT told him he was getting close, so he slowed down and began picking his way forward, moving from boulder to boulder until the ground sloped up to a ridgeline. He dropped flat and crawled to the edge.

Down the opposite slope, a quarter mile away, was Sarani. All was quiet and dark save for a few lighted windows. In the distance a dog barked twice, then went silent. The sound echoed off the rocks before fading away.

Sarani was a collection of a few dozen mud brick buildings in shades of ochre and cream. In the middle of the village was a central square and a small mosque. Some of the homes were perched in tiers on the far slope with the uppermost tier backed up against a bluff. Each house was fronted by an arched walkway.

Fisher checked the OPSAT map, rotating and zooming until he found Kavad Abelzada's home. It was one of the homes sitting against the bluff. He zoomed in and scanned first with NV, which revealed nothing, then in infrared. Again, nothing. He was about to look away when a flicker of red caught his eye. Down the walkway beside Abelzada's home, he saw a man's arm move into view. Someone was there, sitting in the dark. Leaning next to him was an object. Fisher immediately recognized the shape: AK-47.

Where there was one bodyguard there would be more—especially given who Abelzada was. With thousands of fanatical followers, there was no telling how many people in this village—his own birthplace—would lay down their lives to protect him. Almost all, Fisher suspected, which was probably why Abelzada had fled here after being released from prison. If Tehran wanted him again, they'd have to fight their way in.

Fisher scanned the slope for weaknesses, and wasn't

pleased. The way to reach Abelzada's home was through the village and up a narrow switchback path. If even one person looked out their window and saw him, he'd find himself trapped with no retreat.

That left him only one option.

52

HIS option would add an hour to his time on the ground, but there was no helping it. Going through the village would be suicide.

He back-crawled away from the ridge, then turned and slid butt-first down the loose rock until he reached the bottom. He called up his map screen on the OPSAT and spent five minutes scrolling and zooming until he found what he was looking for.

He started jogging.

HIS path took him on a wide arc around Sarani, starting with the notch in the canyon wall he'd seen on his way in. The cleft was no wider than ten feet and the walls five times that high. After a few hundred yards the notch forked, one branch heading east, the other west. Fisher chose the eastern one, and followed it until it was bisected by a dry creek bed, which he followed north for another mile until the walls widened into a dry gulch. The rock walls were smoother here, water-worn by millennia of seasonal rivers. Fisher stopped to catch his breath and check the OPSAT. He was dead west of Sarani.

Now to see if he'd paid attention in high school geography class.

During the rainy season, this gulch would be coursing with runoff from the Köpetdag's higher elevations, and the RADSAT's pictures of the area had revealed the rims of the plateau's above were crenellated from thousands of years of overspill. In the monsoon season, overspill meant waterfalls; in the dry season, natural stairways.

It took fifteen minutes to find what he was looking for: a deep, vertical fissure in the rock with a gentle grade and plenty of handholds. He started climbing.

Five feet from the top, he froze. He closed his eyes and listened. The wind had shifted, whistling down the fissure and bringing with it the scent of burning tobacco. He adjusted his feet so he was braced in the fissure, then drew the SC-20 and thumbed the selector to ASE. He gauged the wind and then fired.

He holstered the SC-20, then changed screens on the OPSAT and adjusted the ASE to infrared. The plateau showed as a cool blue oval. To Fisher's left, over the edge of the plateau, he could see tiny blooms of dull orange;

these would be the dying fires of cookstoves in the houses in Sarani.

Fifty hundred yards to his front were two prone figures cast in yellow, red, and green. They were hidden behind rocks along the northern and western edges. Snipers, one for each canyon leading into Sarani.

Tricky, gentlemen, Fisher thought. *But not tricky enough.*

The ASE was drifting away, gliding over Sarani and down the canyon. He let it go a half mile, then transmitted the self-destruct signal.

He climbed the last few feet to the top, then eased himself over the edge and crawled a few feet to a nearby boulder. He braced the SC-20 against it and peered through the scope. Since he now knew where to look and what to look for, each sniper stood out clearly in the green of the NV. Fisher wasn't worried about the distance, but the wind over the plateau was moving at a good clip.

He zoomed in until the scope's crosshairs were centered on the back of first man's head, then adjusted his aim eighteen inches to the right. He fired. In a blossom of dark mist, the bullet struck the man behind the right ear. Fisher zoomed out, refocused on the next man, zoomed back in and adjusted for windage, then fired.

With the wind—and therefore sound—at his back, Fisher took his time crossing the plateau, using his OP-SAT to adjust his position until he was directly above his target. He stopped a few feet from the edge, then crawled the rest of the way and peered down.

Gotta love GPS, he thought.

He was looking down into the rear courtyard of Abelzeda's home.

The courtyard was done in rough-hewn brick and hemmed in by a six-foot-tall mud wall. At the base of the bluff, in the corner of the courtyard, was a pomegranate tree. To Fisher's right, sitting on a bench in the side walkway, was the AK-47-armed man he'd seen earlier. Now the man had the rifle laying across his lap and appeared to be polishing it with a rag.

Fisher backed away and creeped to his right until he was over the pomegranate tree, then shimmied back to the edge. He pulled a chemlite from his waist pouch and tossed it over. It landed behind the tree. The impact activated the phosphorescence. The glow immediately caught the attention of the man, who stood up and started walking toward it. He came around the tree and stooped to pick up the chemlite. Fisher shot him in the back of the head.

FISHER inserted a rock screw into a crack, clipped his rope into the D ring, then rappelled down the face. Ten feet from the bottom, as he drew even with the house's roofline, he slowly leaned backward until he was upside down.

The rear double doors were open. Through them Fisher saw what looked like a dining nook and next to it, a kitchen. Down a hallway, he could see the shadow of flickering flames dancing on a wall.

He righted himself, dropped the last few feet, then un-clipped and sidestepped behind the pomegranate. He waited for a full minute, watching and listening. Nothing.

He moved to the rear doors.

From the side walkway, the gate creaked open, then clanged shut. Footfalls crunched on gravel. Fisher drew his pistol, stepped to the wall, pressed himself against it. A second later, the tip of an AK-47 appeared on the walkway, followed by a man.

"Samad?" the man whispered. "Samad—"

Fisher shot him in the side of the head, then rushed forward to catch the falling body. As he did so, the man's left foot slid out from under him, kicking a shower of gravel against the wall. Fisher lowered him the rest of the way to the ground, holstered the pistol, and drew the SC-20. He stepped back to the doors, peeked through.

A figure darted across the nook and down the hall.

Fisher stepped through the doors, cleared the nook and kitchen, started down the hall. There were doorways to his left and right, both dark. He checked them: empty bedrooms. From the end of the hall came the sound of steel banging on stone and and image flashed through Fisher's mind: *a steel lid banging open against the stone floor*. He heard fluttering papers and the whoosh of flame.

Fisher rushed down the hall. At the end, he peeked right, saw nothing. Left, a small living room with a tattered Oriental rug, floor cushions, and an open-hearth fireplace. A man was crouched before it, tossing papers into the flames.

"Stop right there!" Fisher called.

The man froze. He turned. His profile was lit by the flames. It was Abelzada.

He studied Fisher for a moment, then narrowed his eyes.

"Don't do it!" Fisher warned.

Even as the words left his mouth, Abelzada's hand was moving. From beside his foot, he snatched up an object, started swinging it around. The gun glinted in the firelight. Abelzada yelled something, a cry for help.

He needed Abelzada alive, had to have him alive. But crouched as he was, there was no guarantee of a wounding shot and there was no time to change the SC-20's setting. Fisher fired a round into the hearth beside Abelzada's head. The man didn't flinch, kept moving, bringing the gun around. . . .

Fisher adjusted his aim and fired.

ABELZADA rocked back on his heels, then crumpled over into the fetal position. His gun clattered to the stone floor. Fisher rushed forward and checked him. Dead. The bullet had missed Abelzada's bicep by a half inch and entered under his armpit. It was a heart shot.

Fisher looked around, thinking, thinking. . . . The box at Abelzada's feet was still mostly full of papers He spotted a leather satchel lying on a nearby chair. He snatched it up, stuffed the papers inside.

In the distance, he heard alarmed voices shouting in Farsi.

He keyed his subdermal. "Pike, this is Sickle, over."

"Go ahead, Sickle."

"Pike, I am Skyfall; I say again, Skyfall." Translation: now operating in Escape and Evasion mode. "Home on my beacon, LZ is hot."

"Roger, hold tight, Sickle. We are en route."

SHANGHAI

"**MESSAGE** from Sarani, Uncle."

Zhao looked up. "Yes."

"There was an attack. Gunfire in the village."

"How big a force?"

"Small. They estimate less than a dozen soldiers."

"Not the Iranians, then. Abelzada?"

"Dead. He was in the process of burning material when he was shot. But if he talked—"

"He didn't," Zhao said, then went silent. He folded his hands on his desk and closed his eyes for a few moments. The board had changed; a piece had fallen. Zhao imagined the breach suddenly opening in his line, saw his opponent, now confident, moving ahead. *Would Abelzada's involvement be enough to unravel the strategy?* he wondered. No, the Iranian government had no credibility with the rest of world. Any denial would ring hollow.

"What about Abelzada's team?" Zhao asked.

"In place and ready."

"Then it doesn't matter. He's served his purpose. In fact, this is a lucky coincidence. Do you know why?"

Xun thought for a moment. "Abelzada's a zealot. He might have been tempted to speak out—to claim credit."

Zhao smiled at his nephew. "Very good. I'm impressed."

Xun smiled back. "Synchronicity, yes?"

"Perfect synchronicity." *One more move left.*

53

TWO hours later, they were out of Iranian airspace and 110 miles southeast of Ashgabat, crossing the Garagum Desert on their way to Afghanistan.

Bird had been true to his promise. Eighty seconds after Fisher's call, the Osprey had come roaring through the canyon and swept over Sarani's rooftops, then popped up, did a tidy hover-turn over the plateau, and dropped the ramp twenty feet from Fisher.

After scooping the papers into the satchel, he'd locked the front door, planted a wall mine opposite it, then gone out the back and planted two more mines along the side walkway before scaling the bluff to await the Osprey. As he mounted the ramp, he'd heard an explosion from inside Abelzada's house, followed by screaming, then by two more explosions from the walk-way.

The Osprey lifted off and Bird went to full power, leaving the same way he came in. A half-dozen desultory rifle shots trailed after them, but Osprey had turned down the canyon and was lost in the darkness.

The trip out of Iran went smoothly. Having had a couple hours to study and refine his flight plan, Bird took them past the radar stations along the border without incident and with a minimum of beeping from the warning alarm.

Now Redding and Fisher sat in the cabin, sorting through Abelzada's papers.

"Yeah, it's all in Farsi," Redding said.

"Got some Mandarin here," Fisher replied.

He checked his watch: six hours until the *Reagan*'s destroyers moved into the Strait of Hormuz.

There had to be something coming, Fisher thought. Zhao had meticulously planned his game—had probably spent two or more years laying the groundwork. He wouldn't be satisfied to simply let momentum and chance finish it for him. So what was his final move? Every base on the U.S.'s East and West Coasts were on full alert.

What was the last task Abelzada had sent his followers on?

TWO hours later they entered Afghanistan airspace. Fisher sat down at the com console and waited for his call to be patched through to Third Echelon's Situation

Room. Lambert's face appeared on the screen. Fisher said without preamble, "Abelzada's dead," and then explained. "When I found him he was making a bonfire. I got most of it—a few dozen pages in Farsi; some in Mandarin. And we've got Marjani. I suspect with the right incentives, he'll have more to say."

"Stand by." Lambert was back ten seconds later. "Our best bet for translators and interrogators is CENTAF." This would be the U.S. Central Command's Air Force Headquarters at Al Udeid Air Base in Doha, Qatar. "Give me your ETA; I'll get you cleared through *Reagan*'s airspace."

Fisher changed channels, got an answer from Bird, then switched back. "We have to refuel at the Marine base in Herat. From there, it'll be five hours."

"I'll make it happen," Lambert said. "Tell Bird to find a tailwind."

THEY didn't catch a tailwind, but a headwind, and five hours later they were just crossing Pakistan's Makran Coast into the Arabian Sea. Their escorts, a pair of Pakastani Air Force Mirage III's, waggled their wings and peeled off, their navigation strobes disappearing into the night. Dawn was still an hour away, but Fisher could see a fringe of orange on the horizon, toward India and the Himalayas.

Bird banked the Osprey west and headed into the Gulf of Oman. As they settled on the new course, Fisher walked to the opposite window and looked out. It took him a moment to find what he was looking for on the ocean's surface: a rough concentric circle of lighted dots— the *Reagan* Battle Group, steaming toward the mouth of the Strait of Hormuz. Farther still, out of sight from here, the warships of DESRON 9 would already be moving through the Strait, ready to meet the Iranian Navy should Tehran decided to contest the shipping lanes. It would be a mismatch, Fisher knew, but any exchange of shots would signal the end of the parrying and jockeying and the start of war.

From the cockpit, an American voice came over the intercom, "Pike, this is CoalDust Zero-Six, come in, over."

"Roger, CoalDust, we read you."

"Here to escort you to Doha. Stay on current heading and switch to button five for ATAC control from *Port Royal.*"

"Roger," Bird replied.

Fisher saw the wing strobes of an F-14 Tomcat slide into view out the window.

Behind him, Redding groaned. He was still sitting on the cabin floor with Abelzada's papers spread all around him.

"Problem?" Fisher asked.

"I've got some Farsi and some Mandarin, but I'm not fluent enough to make any sense of this."

"Another hour and we'll be at Al Udeid. Let them worry about it."

"Yeah, yeah . . . I mean, look at this here," Redding grumbled, and held up a sheaf of papers. "Clearly, Abelzada or someone was translating this, but we've only got bits and pieces. For example, this character here . . ."

Fisher walked over. As he passed Marjani, who was still strapped to the bulkhead, he glared at Fisher and tried to yell through his gag. Fisher leveled a finger at him. "Mind your manners." He squatted next to Redding. "Show me."

Redding pointed to one of the Mandarin characters. "This means snake or worm, I think. And this one here . . . I think that means cloth. Now, what kind of sense does that make?"

"Take a break. You'll drive yourself nuts." He stood up and walked back to the window.

"I guess so. . . . And this one . . . cat. So what's it mean: The early cat catches the cloth worm?"

Fisher turned. "What was that? What did you just say?"

"The early cat catches the cloth—"

Fisher held up his hand, silencing Redding. *Cat. Snake Cloth.*

"What is it, Sam?"

"You said that character could be a worm or a snake."

"Right. And cat, and cloth."

"Could it be silk?"

Redding thought about it and shrugged. "Yeah, I guess so. What—"

"Silkworm," Fisher murmured.

54

FISHER hurried to the console and got Lambert and Grimsdottir on the screen. "It's not a U.S. base, Colonel. It's here—it's somewhere out here." He explained about Redding's study of the Mandarin documents. "One character means worm; cloth could be silk; the other one, cat."

"Silkworm missiles," Lambert finished.

"Right. And Cat could be Cat-14."

For decades the Chinese government had been exporting surface-to-surface/antiship HY-2/3/4 "Silkworm" missiles to Iran, and had in the last five years begun selling them Cat-14 Fast Patrol Boats, mostly for special Pasdaran units. Each Cat was capable of fifty-plus knots—almost sixty miles per hour—and carried twelve Silkworm missiles, each of which had a range of sixty miles and carried a twelve-hundred-pound ship-buster warhead.

"Good God," Lambert murmured.

"Okay, let's think it through: Silkworm shore batteries are heavily defended, especially right now. Abelzada's men wouldn't have a chance of sneaking onto an Iranian Naval base, stealing a Cat-14, *and* getting away with it clean. What does that leave?"

"Given Zhao's influence, we have to assume he could, for the right price, get his hands on some Silkworms. Suppose Abelzada's men have their own supply. How would they deliver them? What would be the best way to strike the *Reagan* Group?"

Fisher thought for a moment, then said, "Shipyards."

"Explain," Lambert said.

"The *Reagan*'s recon aircraft have taken shots of every military facility on the coast. We're looking for a ship-yard that does repairs on Cat-14s. Find one's that's being refitted . . . some minor repairs. . . . Shipyard security isn't as tight as a Naval base's."

Lambert caught on. "A Cat that's operational, but stripped of missiles."

"Right."

GRIMSDOTTIR went to work, and came back ten minutes later. "The Iranian Navy has twenty-six Cat-14s in service. Twenty-two of them are operational and the Navy's tracking all of them. None are within eighty miles of the Group. Four are docked—one for crew rotation and three for repairs or refit."

"Put the shipyards on my screen."

The monitor resolved into an overhead view of the Iranian coastline. Two spots were marked by red circles: one at Halileh, south of the Bushehr naval base deep inside the Persian Gulf; and one near Kordap, just outside the mouth of the Strait of Hormuz.

"We just flew over Kordap," Fisher said to Lambert. "Get a hold of the *Port Royal* and tell them to cut us loose. We'll circle back and check it."

Redding said, "The Tomcats—"

"They're BARCAPs," Fisher said. "They're not loaded for surface targets. They'll have to divert some Hornets."

"How sure are you about this, Sam?" asked Lambert.

"Fifty-fifty. If we're wrong, fine. If we're right . . ."

"Okay, hold on, I'll get back to you."

Fisher got up and jogged to the cockpit. "Bird, slow us down and get ready for a U-turn."

Lambert was back. Fisher took the call in the cockpit. "You're cut loose," Lambert said. "Just don't make any sudden turns back toward the Group."

Fisher nodded to Bird, who eased the Osprey into a gentle turn.

"Are they sending planes to Kordap?" Fisher asked.

"Negative. I got the polite brush-off from NAV-CENT's operations officer. He says they haven't got time for a wild-goose chase. They know where each and every Cat-14 is."

"As of how long ago?"

"Don't know. What's your ETA to Kordap?"

Sandy mouthed, *Thirty.*

"Half hour, Colonel."

"Don't get shot down. The Iranians have F-16s up; they've been playing tag with the *Reagan*'s BARCAPs. They're getting pretty aggressive."

Bird interrupted. "Colonel, get me clearance into Dubai."

"What? Why?"

"Trust me. I'll explain later."

"Okay . . ."

Off the air, Fisher asked Bird, "What's that about?"

"A little sleight-of-hand. The Iranians have been tracking us since we left Pakistan. I'm lining up with Dubai's final approach lane. I'll drop some altitude to simulate a landing, then once we're below the radar, we'll swing back around. It'll add some time, but it'll save us a missile up the heinie."

Fisher smiled. "I like the way you think."

Bird descended steadily, crossing first into UAE airspace and then over coastline. When their altitude reached one hundred feet, he banked hard and swung around on a reciprocal course, heading back into the Gulf of Oman. Twenty minutes later, he called, "Iranian coast coming up. Kordap Shipyard dead on our nose, three miles. Powering up the FLIR."

"Give me a picture back here," Fisher called, and sat down at the console.

The FLIR image came on the monitor; it looked like an X-ray. As Fisher watched, the image slowly glided over the ocean.

"Shipyard in one mile," Bird called. The cockpit radar

warning alarm started beeping. "They're just tickling us," Bird called. "They haven't got us yet." Ten seconds later: "Should be seeing something at the edge of the FLIR."

Fisher did. Enclosed by twin pincers of land, Kordap Shipyard came into view. Fisher could clearly make out four piers, some cranes jutting up into the sky, and a cluster of manufacturing and refit buildings. He counted four ships at dock.

"Swing right," Fisher called. "I need a better look at the piers."

Bird banked the Osprey slightly and realigned the nose with the piers.

Fisher studied each vessel. The Cat-14 had a unique outline, mainly from its twin Silkworm launchers jutting at an angle from the port and starboard decks.

"It's not there," Fisher said.

"You're sure?" Redding asked.

"I'm sure. Bird, bring us about. Get us out of here."

The Osprey banked, swinging over the shipyard and back over the water. A minute and half later, they were out of Iranian territorial waters. Bird started climbing.

Trouble, Fisher thought.

In normal circumstances he wouldn't be worried about a lone patrol boat getting anywhere near the *Reagan*. Her picket ships, most of which were Aegis cruisers, would lock onto and destroy the Cat long before it came within Silkworm range. But these weren't normal circumstances. The *Reagan's* Group was split, with DESRON 9 moving through the Strait of Hormuz and the remaining picket ships restationing to give the huge carrier room to manuever. The mouth of the strait was a mere sixty miles wide—a tight fit for an entire battle group. Under those conditions, a fast boat might be able to get close enough to strike. And with as many as twelve Silkworms, at least one had a good chance of hitting something.

"Get Lambert on the line," Fisher called. "Have him contact NAVCENT—"

"Hold your horses!" Bird called. "Check your screen, Sam."

Fisher looked at the monitor. Dead ahead, cast in the FLIR's negative image, was the missing Cat-14. It was sitting still in the water beside a cargo ship. As they drew nearer, Fisher could see figures on the decks of both vessels scrambling for cover.

From the cockpit came the radar warning alarm.

"We're being painted!" Bird called.

The alarm went to a steady beep.

"Missile lock!"

On the monitor, Fisher saw a bloom of white appear on the Cat's aftderdeck. "Got a launch!" he yelled. "Shoulder-fired missile. Left side!"

The Osprey banked hard. Fisher was tossed from his seat. He and Redding collided and tumbled across the deck together. Fisher snagged a cargo strap and dragged Redding to it.

"Active homing!" Bird said. "It's got us!"

The Osprey heeled over again.

"Launch chaff!" Bird called.

There was a series of rapid pops outside the Osprey.

"Chaff away!" Sandy replied.

A long three seconds passed. Fisher heard a *whump* on the Osprey's right side. A dozen jagged, quarter-sized holes appeared in the fuselage.

"Hit!" Sandy called.

Through the cockpit door Fisher could see Bird's and Sandy's hands moving from control to control, their voices overlapping as they checked the aircraft's vital readouts: oil pressure, hydraulics, temperature, fuel. . . .

"We're okay, we're okay," Bird called.

"Where's the Cat?" Fisher said.

"Right side, two miles. They're thirty miles from the outer ring of the battle group."

Already within missile range, Fisher thought. He ran to the cockpit. "Can you get ahead of them—line up right on their bow?"

"Yeah . . . Whatchya got in mind?"

Fisher told him.

Bird looked sideways at him. "Jesus, Sam. . . . That's gonna get us another missile. We were just plain lucky this time. Next time, maybe not."

Fisher knew this, but if Abelzada's men managed to put even a single Silkworm into a U.S. warship, there would be no pulling back from war. An Iranian patrol boat armed with Iranian missiles, laying in wait in an Iranian shipyard. . . .

Within hours, U.S. warplanes and cruise missiles would begin raining down on Iran.

"Do it," Fisher ordered.

55

AS Bird came about and aligned the Osprey's tail with the oncoming Cat, now one mile back, Sandy got on the radio and started broadcasting in the blind on the battle group's emergency ops channel.

"*Reagan* Group, this is Pike. Be advised, Iranian fast patrol boat approaching your outer ring at bearing one-zero-nine. *Reagan* Group, this is Pike. . . ."

Sitting at the comm console, Redding called to Sam, "The Cat's up to forty-five knots and increasing. Distance to battle group, twenty-five miles."

At this range, traveling at Mach .9, the Silkworm would reach the outer picket ships in less than two minutes.

"Where are we?"

"A half mile ahead of them, dead on their bow."

Fisher called, "Bird, give me the ramp!"

"Ramp coming down."

Sandy yelled, "Okay, we got the *Reagan*'s attention. A cruiser and a frigate are peeling away. They're coming about, heading toward us."

The ramp groaned down and locked into position. In the predawn gloom, Fisher could see the Osprey's prop wash kicking up twin rooster tails on the surface. Farther back, he could just make out the Cat's bow plowing through the waves.

"Start decreasing speed, Bird," Fisher ordered. "How far, Will?"

"Quarter mile."

Fisher knelt down. He flipped open the front right ratchet holding the Skipjack to the deck. He moved to the next one, repeated the process.

In the cockpit, the missile alarm starting wailing.

"They've got us again!" Bird yelled.

Fisher scrambled for the rear tie-downs, flipped one, then moved to the next. He glanced out the ramp and could see, silhouetted by the rising sun, a man standing on the Cat's port bridge wing. A long, bulky object was resting on his shoulder. Even as Fisher thought *missile*, a gout of flame erupted from the rear of the launcher.

"Missile launch," he yelled, and flipped the last tie-down.

He put his shoulder to the Skipjack and shoved.

* * *

IN his mind, time seemed to slow. The wail of the missile alarm faded, along with the voices of Bird and Sandy talking to one another in the cockpit.

The Skipjack slid off the ramp, bounced once on the surface, then nosed over and started tumbling end over end. In the final second, the Cat's helsman must have seen the collision coming. He tried to turn, but too late. The Skipjack slammed broadside into the Cat's bridge. Fisher had a fleeting glimpse of the bridge disintegrating in an eruption of debris before Bird banked hard right.

". . . hold on . . . Active homing!" Bird was yelling. "Get that ramp up, get it up! Fire chaff!"

"Chaff away!"

Fisher felt a hand on his shoulder dragging him away from the rising ramp.

"Brace for shock!" Bird called. "It's got us. . . ."

The Osprey lurched to the right as though struck by a giant hammer. A jagged hole the size of a basketball appeared in the fuselage.

Bird's voice: "Engine hit, engine hit!"

". . . shut it down!"

". . . fire suppression!"

IT took two minutes, but working together, Bird and Sandy managed to get the damaged engine shut down and the fire extinguished. With only one engine, the Osprey yawed to the right.

Fisher turned to Redding. "Rig the fast-rope."

He made his way to the cockpit. Sandy was sending out the Mayday: "*Reagan* Group, this is Pike. Mayday, Mayday, Mayday. We have taken a missile strike. . . ."

"Where is it?" Fisher asked. "Where's the Cat?"

"Hell, I don't know—"

"Find it. Put me over the deck."

"What?"

"We need to be sure, Bird. Get me there."

Bird rotated the undamaged engine to three-quarters vertical and coaxed the Osprey around until they spotted the Cat out the side window. It was sitting dead in the water. Bird slowed to a hover over the afterdeck. Fisher clipped into the fast-rope, jumped out the door, and zipped to the deck. He unclipped, drew the SC-20, and flipped the selector to Sticky Shocker.

The boat was a wreck. The Skipjack had exploded on impact, oblitering the upper half of the Cat's lightweight superstructure. Chunks of fiberglass and aluminum littered the deck. Glass crunched under Fisher's feet.

He saw movement to his right. He spun. A crewman was stumbling up the ladder from belowdecks. His face was bloody. He held a pistol in one hand. Fisher fired. The shocker hit him in the chest. He stiffened, quivered for a few seconds, then fell back down the ladder.

Fisher heard a moan. He cocked his head, trying to pinpoint it. The moan came again. Fisher turned and saw a man lying on the bridge wing. He was feebly reaching for the railing as he tried to stand. Fisher left him whre he was and kept moving, heading aft. As he ducked under the starboard Silkworm launcher, he heard a steady beeping coming from his left. He crouched down and peered around the launcher's mount.

A man was kneeling beside before an access hatch on the port-side launcher. A red light flashed inside the panel. The man punched more buttons. Fisher rose up and creeped up behind him.

"Hey," he called.

The man froze for a moment, then glanced over his shoulder.

"What did I tell you about playing with missiles?" Fisher said.

The man spun back to the panel, fingers flying over the buttons. Fisher shot him in the back.

HE found an an interior ladder and followed it belowdecks. He found three more crewman, one dead, two alive and in various states of consciousness. He entered the engine room and located the last man hiding in a corner behind a steam conduit.

Fisher leveled the SC-20 at him.

"Kill me," the man muttered. "Kill me. . . ."

Fisher shook his head. "Sorry, pal, can't help you. You've got a date with an interrogator."

56

THE Air Force captain opened the conference room door and waved Fisher through. Fisher had changed out of his tac-suit and had been given a spare pilot's jumpsuit. It was too tight in the crotch. It felt funny when he walked.

The conference room was empty save for a dozen chairs and some prints on the walls depicting various events in Air Force history. On the far wall above was a plasma screen. Lambert was there. "Hello, Sam."

"Colonel."

"Nice duds."

"When do we get out of here?"

The Cat's aborted attack on the battle group had caused a dramatic reaction. Led by her Aegis cruisers, the

Reagan had reversed course and moved out into the Gulf of Oman with DESRON 9 following in rear guard.

The cruiser and frigate that had peeled away from the group to intercept the Cat arrived forty minutes after Fisher dropped onto the boat. The frigate's boarding party found Fisher sitting on the afterdeck, surrounded by five of Abelzeda's men, each one bound and gagged.

Now, twelve hours later, he, Redding, Bird, and Sandy were still being kept incognito. Clearly, they had been vouched for and labeled off limits, which was fine with Fisher—except that no one could or would tell them what was happening in the outside world. Of course, given how they'd arrived on scene and what they'd brought with them—a stolen Iranian fast-patrol boat loaded with two Silkworm missiles; a handful of Iranian radicals; and an indignant former Turkmen Minister of Defense—Fisher couldn't blame them.

"You certainly know how to make an entrance," Lambert said.

"It's not how I would've preferred it, Colonel."

"I know. You got the job done, though. That's what counts."

Fisher nodded. "So, what's new in the world? How's the stock market? Read any good books lately? Are we at war with Iran?"

Lambert smiled. "No, we're not at war. The documents from Abelzada's house combined with his men from the Cat did the trick. In fact, the irony is something to behold: They were so anxious to take credit for the 'glorious attack on the Great Satan' that they haven't

TOM CLANCY'S SPLINTER CELL

stopped talking since they landed. Their own zealotry is their own worst enemy.

"The connections we put together between Zhao, the *Trego*, Slipstone, and Abelzada were enough for the President. As we speak, the Saudis are delivering a back-channel message from the President to Tehran. How they'll react is anyone's guess, but since Abelzada is a problem they failed to solve, I think they'll jump at the chance for mutual stand-down. Over the next few days the *Reagan* will slowly withdraw into the Arabian Sea and Iran will recall the bulk of its Naval forces to their bases."

"And how does all this get explained to the world?" Fisher asked.

"That's a good question."

"And it's not our worry."

"Right."

"What about Zhao?" said Fisher.

"In about an hour, the Chinese ambassador will be sitting in the Oval Office. The message will be similar to the one to Tehran: Zhao was your problem; you let him run loose and did nothing about him. Give him up quietly or the world learns how a Chinese mafia kingpin who's got half of Beijing in his pocket killed five thousand Americans, turned a town in New Mexico into a radioactive wasteland, and almost started Gulf War Three."

"And if they refuse to cooperate or Zhao goes to ground?"

"He can't hide forever," Lambert replied.

57

THE pilot's voice came through Fisher's subdermal: "Sir, we're crossing the border."

"How're we doing?"

The electronic warfare officer, or EWO, answered: "Not a peep. As far as anybody on the ground cares, we're a KAL flight en route to Moscow."

They were in fact an MC-130E Combat Talon. Courtesy of the CIA, the transponder code they were squawking was genuine, a match for a Korean Airlines commerical flight out of Seoul with an equally genuine official flight plan.

"Distance to drop?" Fisher asked.

"We'll be feet-dry in twenty minutes. Providing the North Koreans don't change their minds or send up interceptors to put eyeballs on us, we'll be in the zone in seventy minutes."

"Wake me in a half hour," Fisher said.

TWO days earlier, as both Iran and U.S. started to draw down their forces and the region eased back from the brink of war, the President's ultimatum to the Chinese ambassador sent Beijing into a tailspin.

Eight hours after the message was delivered, simultaneous raids were conducted on Zhao's homes in Shanghai, Nanjing, and Changsha, as well as on his retreat on Cezi Maji. Zhao was at none of them; he had disappeared. Every border crossing, port, and airport was put on alert, but so far there had been no sign of him.

Thirty hours later, as Fisher, Redding, Bird, and Sandy were touching down stateside, a familiar signal on a CIA carrier frequency was intercepted by a NSA monitoring station in Japan and routed to Third Echelon's Situation Room.

"That's Heng's beacon," Fisher said. "His modified iPod."

"Confirmed," Grimsdottir said. "Same frequency, same pattern."

"Can you triangulate it?" Lambert asked.

"Working on it. . . ." She had an answer two minutes later. She put a satellite image to the plasma screen. "Liaoning Province, northeastern China. Assuming Heng is still with Zhao and they're on the move, it looks like he's heading for probably the only place in the world that would have him."

"North Korea," Fisher said.

THE Talon's loadmaster finished checking Fisher's equipment and straps, then patted him on the shoulder and walked him to the open door. At 35,000 feet, the air rushing through was bitterly cold. Beside him, the loadmasters were wearing parkas and face masks. Fisher could feel the cold around the cuffs of his tac-suit and the rubber-sealed edges of his oxygen mask and goggles.

He spread his legs wide and braced his arms on either side of the door. Outside, he saw nothing but blackness and the faint shadow of the Talon's wing and the rhythmic pulse of the nav strobe.

He took a breath, closed his eyes, pictured Sarah's face in his mind.

He felt a pat on his shoulder.

Above his head, the bulkhead light went from red to yellow.

Green.

He jumped.

AS it had with his *Trego* jump, with a *whump* the Goshawk deployed into its compact wedge shape and lifted Fisher straight up. He glanced to his right in time to see the Talon's strobes disappear into the darkness.

The engine noise faded and Fisher was floating in a void, with only the rush of wind to suggest he was moving.

Having exited the Talon six and a half miles above the earth and 110 miles from his target, he was using the only insertion method that had a chance of slipping past the radar stations along the Chinese-North Korean border: HAHO, or High-Altitude, High-Opening.

He tested the toggles, veering first right, then left before locking them into position. He lifted his OPSAT to his face mask and punched up the navigation screen. Grimsdottir had overlaid his satellite map of the area with seven waypoints. He would break through the cloud layer at roughly twelve thousand feet, at which point he would, if he'd stayed on course, find himself aligned with the Yalu River, which formed the natural border between China and North Korea. The river would lead him straight to his destination.

According to a high-resolution pass by a KH-12 Crystal, Zhao had chosen to hole up in an abandoned Buddhist monastery on the banks of the Yalu, thirty miles northeast of Dandong. How long Zhao would remain there Fisher couldn't tell. He suspected it depended on when the powers-that-be in Pyongyang arranged to send a special forces team to collect him. Fisher prayed he got there first. If Zhao managed to reach North Korea, he'd be beyond U.S. reach.

AT 11,500 feet, Fisher broke through the cloud cover. Far below him, the Yalu was a ribbon of dull silver winding its way across the terrain. On either bank for as far as he could see were clusters of lights, each one a village or city along the border.

He took another bearing on the OPSAT and pulled his right toggle, sending the Goshawk into a gentle spiral that brought him in line with his next waypoint, eight miles upstream from the monastery.

Fisher pulled on the toggles and started bleeding off altitude.

AT three thousand feet, the ribbon that had been the Yalu changed into a mile-wide expanse of water. Four miles away he could see the monastery's crenellated walls and spired towers rising from the forest along the northern bank. He angled that way.

HE made a perfect stand-up landing in a clearing a mile from the monastery. He gathered the Goshawk, took five minutes stuffing it back into his pack, then checked his bearings and slipped into the forest, heading southeast.

When he'd covered half the distance, he angled back toward the Yalu and sat in the trees, watching and listening until certain he was alone, then crawled down the bank and into the water. The current caught him immediately and drew him downstream. Alternately watching for boats on the river and checking his position on the OPSAT, he floated for ten minutes, then breaststroked to the shore and crawled onto the bank. Though he couldn't yet see it, he was directly south of the monastery, some three hundred yards up the forested slope before him.

He began picking his way up the slope, stepping from tree to tree until he found a break in the canopy. He pointed the SC-20 skyward, launched an ASE, holstered the rifle. On the OPSAT, he studied the monastery in the faded green/black of the ASE's camera.

Abandoned at the turn of the ninteenth century, the monastery was laid out more like a medieval fortress than a religious retreat. Fisher took that as a clue as to why it had been abandoned. Had the natives or local government been unfriendly? The monastery's eight-foot stone walls seemed to suggest so, as did the watchtowers that rose from every corner. The interior courtyard contained the remains of three pagodas—a larger one in the center and two smaller ones to each side.

A series of cobblestoned pathways linked each building. Several arched footbridges rose from the landscape, covering what Fisher assumed were once streams and ponds. The outer walls showed massive cracks in several places, as did the the pathways and pagodas. The roof of the larger structure looked as though it had been shoved to one side by a giant hand; it leaned, mostly intact, against the side of the pagoda. The other two structures had partially collapsed into a jumble of stone blocks; each one had remanants of its roof left, but the walls lay open in places, exposing the interior.

He switched to infrared. He saw nothing. If Zhao and his bodyguards were in there, they were laying low, waiting for his Korean benefactors to come get him. There would be lookouts, Fisher knew, and he had an idea where he'd find them.

He shut down the ASE and sent the self-destruct signal.

He checked the OPSAT map. What he was looking for should be to his left. . . .

HE found it ten yards away, an old drainage canal, about three feet wide and four feet deep. Though now choked with weeds and partially filled with silt, the canal had continued doing its job over the years, diverting rainwater runoff from the courtyard and down to the river.

Fisher dangled his legs over the side and dropped down. He flipped his goggles to EM, checked for emission points that might indicate sensors, but saw nothing. Zhao had probably gone to ground as soon as he realized his plan had fallen apart, and had been running hard ever since. For him, this monastery was to be a last stop before reaching safety.

Fisher was determined to make sure that never happened.

He began moving up the canal.

58

ABOUT fifty yards from the monastery, the trees thinned out and ahead he could see the outer wall. To his left and right were the watchtowers. He pulled out his binoculars and focused on the tower to the right.

A man was standing in the tower's rectangular window, gun lying on the sill before him. Fisher checked the other tower: a second lookout. They were watching for the North Korean escorts, which probably meant they were were in touch with Zhao by radio.

He drew the SC-20, mentally tossed a coin, them zoomed in on the loser—the lookout in the left tower—and shot him in the forehead.

* * *

HE picked his way up the canal to the wall, and was about to slip under when that little voice in the back of his head, the voice of instinct, whispered to him. He stopped. He switched his trident goggles to EM.

Twelve inches away, mounted at waist height on either side of the wall, was a paperback-sized emission point. Wall mines.

Fisher dropped flat and crawled beneath the mines. Once clear, he poked his head up and scanned the grounds. He saw no movement, no heat sources, no EM signatures. The moon had broken through the cloud cover, casting the courtyard in milky gray light. To his right, where the the walls met, there was a dark doorway at the base of the tower. He boosted himself out of the canal and sprinted to it.

Inside he found a spiral stairwell. He took the cracked steps slowly, pausing to listen each time he placed his foot. Halfway up he heard the scuff of a shoe on stone. He crouched down, drew his pistol, and continued climbing.

Three steps from the top he crouched down again. Ahead was a doorway and through it he could see the lookout standing at the window, silhouetted by moonlight. Fisher holstered the pistol and drew the Sykes. He creeped through the door, then clamped a hand over the guard's mouth with one hand, pressed the edge of the Sykes to the his throat with the other.

"Good evening," Fisher said in serviceable Mandarin. "Do you speak English?"

Fisher moved his hand and the man whispered, "Yes, I speak English."

"Where is Zhao?"

"I do not know."

Fisher pressed the Sykes into the flesh beneath his chin. "I don't believe you. Tell me where Zhao is and you live to see another sunrise."

"Please . . . I do not know. Someone came earlier this evening, but I do not know who it was or where they went."

"You work for Zhao, correct?"

"Yes."

"But you have no idea where he is?"

"Yes, please. . . ."

Fisher's gut told him the man was telling the truth. He pulled back the Sykes, struck the man behind the ear with the haft, then let him fall.

HENG'S iPod beacon was still transmitting. The signal seemed to be coming from the remains of the smallest pagoda, near the north wall. Fisher made his way across the courtyard, then circled around the ruins of each pagoda. He wanted to hurry, to find Heng, but he forced himself to go slow. If Zhao had laid a trap, these ruins were rife with ambush points.

He returned to the smaller pagoda and slipped through a hole in the wall. The interior was partially blocked with chunks of stone from the upper floors, which lay exposed above him. A staircase, neatly cleaved in two, wound up the side of the wall and ended at the top floor.

Fisher picked his way through the rubble, following

the signal until he reached a square hole in the floor. A set of steps disappeared into the darkness below. He descended. At the bottom he found a corridor; it was mostly undamaged, with only a few chunks of stone blocking the way. Doorways on each side stretched into the distance; at the far end he could see a square of faint light. He was momentarily puzzled until he oriented himself. This corridor stretched underground to a similar entrance in the central pagoda. He was seeing moonlight streaming in from the opposite entrance.

He checked his OPSAT. Heng's beacon was twenty feet down the corridor on his right. He moved forward, pistol drawn, checking rooms as he went. Inside each was what looked like the remnants of a wooden bunk. *Personal quarters*.

As he drew even with the sixth doorway, the beacon symbol on his OPSAT started blinking rapidly. He pressed himself against the wall and peeked around the corner.

Inside, a figure lay curled on the floor. Fisher stepped closer. Next to the body was a white iPod. He flipped his goggles first to infrared, then to EM, checking for patterns that might suggest a booby trap. There was nothing. He reached out with his foot and rolled the figure over. It was Heng.

FISHER stood still for a moment. His first thought was *trap*. He backed out of the room, glanced up and down the corridor. It was empty and quiet. He planted a pair of wall mines, one on each wall beside the door, then went back to Heng. He clicked on his headlamp and felt for a pulse. It was weak, but there.

The back of Heng's head was encrusted in blood. Fisher probed with his fingers until he found a serrated hole in his scalp. He'd been shot in the head. The skull bones beneath were shattered and partially pushed inward. Fisher kept probing until he found a hard lump—a .22-caliber bullet, he guessed—beneath the skin above the forehead.

Fisher felt his stomach boil with anger. They'd shot him execution-style, but botched it and then left him for dead. The bullet had entered the back of his scalp at an angle rather than straight on, then flattened itself on the bone, and followed the curve of the skull to its resting place.

Careful to keep Heng's head immobile, Fisher rolled him onto his back. He opened each eyelid, checked his eyes. The left one was fixed, the pupil blown. Brain damage. The impact of the bullet had caused bleeding and swelling in his brain. It was a miracle he'd survived this long. Fisher checked his ears; both were leaking blood.

He checked Heng's body for other wounds but found none. He broke open a smelling-salts capsule beneath Heng's nose. Heng sputtered and his eyes popped open. Fisher held him down, held his head still. "Don't move," he whispered.

Heng blinked a few times, then focused his one good eye on Fisher. "You. . . . What are you. . . ."

"I couldn't find an iPod like yours, so I came to borrow it from you."

This elicited a weak smile, but only one side of his mouth turned up. "They shot me. . . ." he murmured. "They put me on my knees. I heard the gun's hammer being cocked. . . . I don't understand. What's going on?"

You're dying, Fisher thought. *You're dying and there's nothing I can do about it.* Heng wouldn't survive the trip to the extraction point. It didn't seem fair. To survive a bullet to the head at point-blank range only to slowly slip into death as your brain bleeds into itself.

"You're alive, that's what's going on," Fisher said. "The doctors are going to call you a miracle."

Heng let out a half chuckle. His left pupil rolled back in his head and stayed there.

"Heng, I need to find Zhao. Where is he?"

"Not here."

"What?"

Heng blinked a few times as though trying to gather his thoughts. "We came here yesterday—no, the day before yesterday. The North Koreans were supposed to, uhm. . . ."

"I know about the North Koreans. What happened next?"

"They found my iPod . . . figured it out. Zhao took three or four men with him and left the others here with me."

"How long ago?"

"A few hours after we got here."

Damnit. Zhao had a two-day head start.

"Sam, he's got more."

"What? He's got more what?"

"More material . . . from Chernobyl. I saw it."

OSPREY

FISHER wasn't two steps up the ramp before he said to Redding, "Get Lambert on the line."

"Problem?"

"You could say that." Fisher made his way to the cockpit. "Bird, how long to Kunsan?"

"Gotta stay under the radar until we're clear of Korea Bay. Past that, figure an hour or so."

"Fast as you can without getting us shot down."

"You're the boss."

Redding called, "Sam, I've got Lambert."

Fisher sat down at the console. On screen, Lambert said, "Well?"

"Zhao's gone—been gone for two days or more. The monastery was a diversion."

"What about Heng?"

Fisher sighed. *Heng.*

KNEELING next to the man watching him die, Fisher considered his options, then made his decision. Given what Heng had had been through—what he'd done for the U.S.—he deserved a chance to live, even if that chance was too slim to calculate.

Using remnants from the wooden bunks and some para-chord he kept in one of his pouches, he cobbled together a cage he hoped would keep Heng's head as stable as possible. In the back of his mind he knew it probably wouldn't make any difference, but the less Heng moved his head, the longer he might last.

Once done, he left Heng lying still and made one more ciruit of the monastery, both inside and out to make sure there would be no surprises, then went back inside, picked up Heng, and carried him down the slope and into the river. He draped Heng's arms over a bundle of planks he'd tied together, then pushed them off into the current.

TEN miles and two hours later they reached the village of Gulouzi. On Fisher's OPSAT map, a waypoint was flashing; next to it was set or longitude and latitude coordinates. He pushed Heng to the bank and then, following the coordinates, picked his way down an inlet until he came to a small pier.

As promised, the river sampan was waiting. How the CIA had arranged the transportation Fisher didn't know, nor did he care. With luck and guile, the single-masted fishing boat would take them the rest of the way to the extraction point.

Fisher donned the local clothes he found stuffed beneath the stern seat, then pushed off and poled back to where he'd left Heng.

* * *

IT took the rest of the night, but with only a few hours of darkness left, Fisher reached the Yalu Estuary, where he hoisted the sail and pointed the bow into Korea Bay. An hour after that the Osprey appeared out of the gloom, skimming ten feet off the ocean's surface, and slowed to a hover beside the sampan.

"HE didn't make it," Fisher told Lambert. "He died on the way down the river."

"I'm sorry, Sam. We'll get Zhao. The world's not big enough for him to hide in anymore."

"And the material? Heng claims he had a couple hundred pounds of the stuff."

"Zhao's running for his life. Even if he's still got it, he'll get tired of lugging it around. We'll find him *and* we'll find the material. Come on home, Sam. You've done your part."

59

LAMBERT had offered to send a Gulfstream to Kunsan so Fisher could fly home in much-deserved comfort, but he declined, opting to fly back with Redding, Bird, and Sandy. They'd been through a lot together and it seemed only right they come home together. Besides, Fisher told himself, he was so exhausted he didn't need comfort—just a horizontal surface on which to recline.

Also, he needed time to decompress. Time to think about everything and about nothing. When he got back to Fort Meade, there would be days of debriefing as the powers-that-be tried to piece together what had happened in the Gulf and what role Third Echelon had played.

Whether it was simply exhaustion or something

more, Fisher didn't know, but Heng's death haunted him. The man had sacrificed everything to help the CIA wage its war on Kuan-Yin Zhao when his own government had refused to lift a hand. According to Richards, Heng had never asked for money or recognition or a way out, and in Fisher's book that was the definition of courage. And what did he get for it? A bullet in the head and slow death aboard a rickety sampan in the middle of the Yalu River. Though Fisher knew better, a part of him wondered if he could have, or should have, done more.

DRIFTING in a deep sleep, he became aware of a hand shaking his shoulder. He snapped open his eyes and reached for the leg holster he'd taken off hours ago.

"Relax, Sam," Redding said. "Relax."

Fisher rubbed his eyes. "Sorry. What time is it?"

"Just after midnight. We're fifty miles west of Eugene, Orgeon. You slept through our refueling stop."

"And why am I awake now?"

"Lambert's on the bat phone."

FISHER sat down at the console. On the screen, Lambert's expression was dour. Fisher was immediately awake. "What's happened?"

"Since you left Kunsan, Grim's been trying to put together some of the missing pieces. She found something. Go ahead, Grim."

"Sam, you remember the *Duroc*—the yacht that picked up the *Trego*'s—"

"I remember."

"I tracked down the registration. It belongs to a man named Feng Jintao, a Chinese mobster out of San Francisco. The FBI claims Jintao is one of Zhao's underbosses."

"Okay, so he loaned out the *Duroc* and its crew to handle the *Trego*'s crew. Tell the FBI to arrest the bastard."

"Here's the problem: Jintao's got two other yachts, one in Monterey and one in Los Angeles. Both of them left port about eight hours ago without notifying harbor control. We've found the one from Los Angeles; it's headed back into port. The Navy's dispatched a destroyer to meet it and a helo is en route with a SEAL team."

"And the other one?"

"It was found run aground and abandoned near Eureka, California. Take a look at the satellite."

Fisher's screen changed to a gray-scale overhead image of a coastline. In the lower right quadrant he could clearly make out what he assumed was Jintao's yacht resting on the beach, its deck canted to one side.

"Here's the thermal," Grimsdottir said.

The image changed, zoomed in. On the yacht's afterdeck there was a dot of yellow-red.

"Look familiar?" Grimsdottir asked.

"Same signature as the *Trego*," Fisher replied.

"Yes, but not nearly as hot. It's a residual signature. Whatever was aboard, it's gone now."

* * *

LAMBERT said, "The FBI has agents from its field offices in Sacramento and San Francisco heading for Eureka, but they won't get there for a couple hours. The Eureka PD and Humboldt County Sheriff's been alerted, but they're not equipped to—"

"I know," Fisher said, then to Bird: "You've been listening?"

"Sure have. At best speed, we can be there in fifty minutes."

Lambert said, "Do it. We'll keep you unpdated en route."

TWENTY minutes later, Lambert was back: "The Eureka PD found a man shot at a place called Spruce Point Rail Adventures. He's the night security guard there. They run one of those novelty lines—old-style trains that travel up and down the coast . . . see the giant redwoods, that kind of thing."

"And they're missing a train?"

"'Fraid so. A locomotive, three cars, and a caboose. Eureka PD's not sure how long the guard's been dead, so there's no telling what kind of head start the train's got. Grim's putting an overlay of the track on your map. It runs north to south only and ends at Olema, just north of San Fransisco."

Zhao's roundabout method of reaching San Francisco made sense, Fisher decided. After 9/11, dozens of port cities, including San Francisco, had installed a network of radiation detectors. Slipping Jintao's yacht past them would be impossible.

"Detonate a couple hundred pounds of radioactive waste in San Francisco, and it'll make Slipstone look like nothing," Fisher said. "It'd be a wasteland for centuries. Are there controls on the line? Shunts or spurs they can divert it to?"

"Fifty years ago, yes, but not now. It's a straight run down the coast. We're retasking a Keyhole to look for her, but we're talking about a three-hundred-mile stretch of track, most of it running through heavy forest and mountain passes. It's going to be hard to spot—plus, this isn't your run-of-the-mill locomotive. According to Grim, it's been converted to run faster so it can make more round trips. Top speed: sixty miles an hour."

There was only one way to stop it, Fisher realized. An F-16 or an F-15 could be overhead in minutes with a laser-guided Paveway missile, but the resulting wreck would spread radioactive material for miles. Better than it happening in San Francisco, but still unacceptable as far as he was concerned.

"Then we do it the hard way," Fisher said. "We fly down the track until we overtake her."

"And then?"

"And then we improvise."

60

OSPREY

"**WE** got her, Sam," Lambert said. "She's eighty miles south of Eureka between the towns of Cedar Creek and Blue Flats. Satellite image is on your monitor; we're streaming it real-time."

The screen showed a stretch of heavily forested moutainous terrain. At first Fisher saw nothing, and then, breaking from a line of trees, a locomotive appeared, followed by three passenger cars and a caboose. A plume of black smoke trailed from the locomotive's stack. The train rounded a bend in the track and disappeared into forest again.

"Grim, do you have infrared?"

"Yep, here."

The train reappeared. In the center of the third car, just ahead of the caboose, was a reddish-yellow oval.

"How far away are we, Bird?" Fisher asked.

"Twenty minutes."

Lambert said, "Humboldt County Sheriff's has a SWAT team. They're airborne and a few minutes ahead of you. They're going to try and put men onto the train's roof."

FIFTEEN minutes later, Bird called, "Got a visual. Descending to five hundred feet."

Fisher trotted to the cockpit and peered through the windscreen. Ahead and below, the Humboldt SWAT helicopter was trailing behind the train's caboose as the train chugged up a hill. The helo's spotlight was focused on the locomotive, but Fisher could see no one moving in the cab. On either side of the track, redwoods and pines crowded the embankments, so close their branched seemed to almost scrape the sides of the cars.

"Humboldt SWAT, this is Federal zero-nine," Bird radioed. "Taking station on your six o' clock high. Ready to assist."

"Roger, Federal, stand by. We're going to make a pass, see if we get an officer onto the roof."

The Osprey's console monitor was in FLIR mode, showing an X-raylike image of the scene below. Fisher reached out and tapped a spot on the screen. Bird nodded and keyed his microphone. "Humboldt, be advised, you've got a narrow gorge ahead. Two miles."

"Roger, Federal."

The helicopter picked up speed and descended until it was ten feet off the roof of the second car A rope uncoiled from the helicopter's open door and an officer climbed out, clipped onto the rope, and began descending. Fisher saw a figure appear on the coupler platform between the locomotive and the first car. There was a pinprick of light, then another, then four more in rapid sucession.

Over the radio, the helo pilot's voice: ". . . taking fire . . . taking fire. Get him back in!"

The officer jerked as though hit with a current of electricity, then went limp, dangling sideways.

". . . hit. . . . Christ almighty, he's hit." In the background Fisher could hear bullets hitting the helo's windscreen. "I'm pulling up . . . !"

The helicopter angled upward and banked over the trees, falling back until it was even with the Osprey. Fisher looked out the side window. In the door of the helo two men were struggling to reel in the dangling officer.

"Federal, this is Humboldt SWAT. Be advised, I have one casualty and a heat warning on my cooling pump. I'm going to have to find a place to set down."

"Roger, Humboldt, understood. Luck. Federal out."

The helicopter dropped farther back, then came around and headed west over the trees.

Bird turned to Fisher. "It's your call, Sam."

"We're going to take some fire."

Bird grinned. "It'll take more than a little popgun to ground us."

"That's what I thought. Give me two seconds over the roof and then get out of here."

AS the train entered the gorge, Bird climbed to a thousand feet and eased back on the throttle, letting the train get ahead. It burst from the far mouth of the gorge, chugging black smoke. Bird nosed over and dropped in behind the caboose, twenty feet off the track.

"How tall you think that thing is, Sandy?" Bird asked.

"Twelve feet—no thirteen. Why?"

"I'm not giving any more of a target than I have to. Sam, you and Will get ready. Grab ahold of something. Gonna get a bumpy."

Fisher hurried back into the cabin, where Redding was checking the SC-20 and pistol. He handed them over. "Both loaded. Harness."

Fisher took it, slipped it on, adjusted the fit over his shoulders, then slid the SC-20 into its back holster and the pistol into its leg holster.

Bird called, "Sixty seconds, Sam. Ramp coming down."

The ramp door groaned open. Wind whipped through the cabin. Over the drone of the Osprey's engines, Fisher could hear the syncopated chug of the locomotive, could smell coal smoke. He walked down the edge of the ramp and crouched down. Twenty feet below, the track whipped past, a blur of steel rails and wooden cross-ties.

"Stand by," Bird called. "I'm moving ahead."

The caboose's coupler slid into view, followed by the roof, and then the windowed cupola. Fisher kept his eyes fixed on it and tried to ignore the trees flashing past on either side.

Fisher glanced back at Redding, who stood at the ramp's control panel, and gave him the signal. Fisher braced himself. The ramp lurched down and crashed against the roof. The jolt was harder than Fisher had anticipated and it rocked him backward onto his butt. His left foot slipped over the edge. He jerked it back.

Bird called, "Taking a little gunfire up here, Sam."

Wait . . . wait. . . .

He somersaulted down the ramp onto the caboose roof and spread himself flat. Redding gave him wave and then the ramp started closing. The Osprey nosed up, dropped back, then banked over the trees and out of sight.

DOWN the length of the train he could see two figures standing atop the locomotive's coupler. Muzzles winked at him through the coal smoke. He couldn't tell if the shots were accurate or wildly off, but it didn't matter. He started crawling.

The train lurched forward, picking up speed. Fisher felt his stomach drop and he realized they were going down a grade. He crawled to the edge of the roof, braced himself, then flipped his trident goggles into place, switched to NV, and ducked his head over the side.

He was looking through a window. On the other side was a man holding a radio to his ear. He spun, saw Fisher, then raised a pistol and fired. The window shattered. Fisher jerked back, but not quickly enough. He felt warm blood trickling down his chin and neck. He plucked a frag grenade off his harness, pulled the pin, counted *one-one thousand,* tossed it through the window. There was a muffled boom. He peeked back over the edge. The man lay sprawled on the floor.

Beside Fisher's head, a bullet punched into the roof. He looked up in time to see a man running toward him down the second car's roof. He rolled to the right, drew the pistol, and snapped off two shots. The first one went wide, but the second one hit center-mass. The man doubled over, dropped to his knees, then tipped over the side and tumbled down the embankment.

Fisher crawled forward the last few feet, then turned and dangled his legs over the edge and dropped to the coupler below. As he landed, the door to the third car slid open. A man stood in the opening, a .357 Magnum leveled with Fisher's chest. They stood staring at one another for a few seconds. And then, from behind the man, a face appeared. It was Zhao. "Shoot him, you idiot! Shoot . . . !"

Fisher knew there was nothing he could do; he was going to take a bullet. He was about to give his tac-suit's RhinoPlate a true-life test. Not wanting to give the man a chance to adjust his aim and go for a head shot, Fisher went for his pistol.

The man fired. Fisher saw the muzzle flash, heard the

blast, and felt a hammer-blow in the middle of his sternum. Even as he crashed backward into the door, he drew his pistol and shot the man in the throat. Behind him, Zhao dove to one side. Fisher adjusted aim and fired twice, but Zhao was gone.

Fisher reached back, groped for the door handle, turned it. The door crashed inward. His pistol slipped from his hand and disappeared under the train. He sprawled onto the floor. He rolled over, crawled to the door, slammed it shut.

The pain in his chest was crushing. He couldn't catch his breath; it felt as though an anvil was sitting on his chest. Still alive, though. RhinoHide had done its job.

He felt the floor tilt beneath him as the train started up a grade. He climbed to his feet and looked around. The hot spot had been here, somewhere in this car. . . . The car was divided by a center aisle, with long, tourist-friendly benches on either side facing the windows. Ten feet away he saw the corner of a steel box beneath the bench. He rushed forward, dropped to his knees.

Made of brushed stainless steel, it was no bigger than an average suitcase with a latching footlocker lid. He laid his hand on the steel. It was warm to the touch.

Gotchya. . . .

The box shifted, sliding farther under the bench as the train chugged up the grade.

And then a thought: What had Zhao been planning to do with the box? He would have worked that through, would have had a plan—and it would have been something more than simply dump the material into San Francisco Bay. Something to maximize the spread. . . .

He pressed his ear to the lid and plugged his other ear with his finger. It took a few seconds to tune out the chugging of the locomotive and the wind whistling through the shattered window, but as those sounds faded, he heard something else. A faint mechanical whirring.

Like a flywheel.

And then another thought: Humiliated and hunted, his empire in ruins and his family dead, Zhao wouldn't be satisfied by letting his revenge *happen*. His ego would demand that he do it. . . .

That he be the one to push the button.

Fisher pushed himself to his feet. Pain shot through his chest, doubling him over. He straightened up and stumbled down the aisle, fighting the incline of the floor. He reached the door, threw it open.

Across the coupler platform, he saw Zhao sitting in the doorway to the second car, legs splayed out before him. At least one of Fisher's bullets had found its mark. The side of Zhao's neck and face were bloody and his right arm hung limb at his side. With his eyes locked on Fisher's, Zhao reached his left arm across his body and into his jacket.

Fisher lurched forward, but he lost traction on the sloped platform and fell to his knees. He got up, tried again. He grasped the hand railing and dragged himself forward.

Zhao's hand came out holding a cell phone. He flipped it open, starting working the keypad with his thumb. Fisher drew the Sykes from its sheath and plunged it into Zhao's thigh. Fisher felt the blade hit bone. Zhao screamed and dropped the phone, which slid toward the edge of the platform. Fisher reached out, snagged it with his fingertips, drew it back. On the screen was a nine-digit number. Underneath it, the words "Send? Y/N?"

He punched "No" and flipped the phone closed.

Zhao lay curled into a ball, his face twisted with pain. With his good arm he was reaching feebly for the knife jutting from his thigh. Fisher knocked his hand away. He grabbed the haft and gave it a twist. Zhao screamed again and arched his back. Fisher jerked the knife free and resheathed it. He stood up and looked down at Zhao.

"I think it's time you and I say good-bye," Fisher said.

Zhao didn't respond, but turned his head and glared up at him.

"No arguments," Fisher said. "Better we part company while we're still friends."

He grabbed Zhao by the foot and dragged him farther out onto the platform. Using a pair of flexi-cuffs, he first secured Zhao's left arm to the railing, and then his right, which made a sickening grating sound as Fisher manipulated it. Zhao set his jaw and said through gritted teeth, "Go to hell."

"Maybe someday," Fisher replied, "but not today."

He leaned out over the railing and looked forward. Ahead he could see the locomotive was almost at the top of the grade. Fisher knelt down, reached between the platform joint, and grabbed the release lever. He jerked it upward. There was a steel *clank-clank*.

"What are you doing?" Zhao said.

Fisher didn't answer. He stepped to the other side of the platform and knelt down. He grabbed the second release lever.

"Tell me what you're doing!" Zhao screamed.

"To tell you the truth," said Fisher, "I don't know what they call it in China." He felt the locomotive lose momentum ever so slightly as it topped the grade, then lurch forward as it started down the opposite slope. "But in this country, it's called checkmate."

He pulled the lever.

— *EPILOGUE* —

FISHER stopped before the seven-foot-tall figure. Above a hawkish nose and long bushy beard, his narrowed eyes gazed implacably over what Fisher imagined were the barren Russian steppes. In his left hand the giant carried a ruby-encrusted war club, twice as big around as a baseball bat and topped by a spiked steel globe the size of a miniature soccer ball.

Beside the wax figure a plaque displayed a lengthy description in Cyrillic, but in English at the bottom, it simply said, "18th Century Slavic Warrior." Behind him was a mural depicting a village in flames with women and children fleeing before horse-mounted soldiers.

Another day in the life of your typical eighteenth-century Slavic Warrior, Fisher thought.

The Kiev Museum of Wax Figures was a far cry from Madame Tussaud's of London. There were no figures of Prince William or Brad Pitt or Richard Nixon, but plenty of Ukrainian and Russian historical figures, most of which the owners had classified as either a "Slavic Warrior" or a "Saint." Whatever their avocation or history, Fisher had yet to see a smile, either from a wax figure or a patron—most of whom looked like locals. Apprently, the museum did not cater to many tourists.

For all that, though, he was enjoying the downtime. It had been hard won.

AFTER Fisher had lifted the second release lever, the coupler had given another metallic *clank-clank*. Then the caboose and the third car had begun sliding away from Zhao's car. Fisher had timed it well. Now free of the third car and the caboose, and without a brakeman to control its descent, the locomotive rapidly picked up speed, hurtling down the slope. Spread-eagle on the platform of the second car, with his legs dangling in space and his wrists bound to the railing, Zhao never took his eyes off Fisher, even as Fisher's car slowed at the top of the slope, paused, then began rolling backward.

Fisher rushed down the length of his car, across the next platform, and into the caboose, where he found the brake controls. He leaned on the lever with his full body weight. The caboose continued rolling down the slope, but slowly the brake started to work, slowing the descent.

The caboose filled with smoke and the lever grew hot in Fisher's hand, but finally, two minutes later, the caboose slowed and came to a rest at the bottom of the slope.

THIRTY minutes later, he heard the chopping of helicopter rotors echoing down the pass. A pair of Blackhawks swooped in and stopped in a hover above the track. Men in standard-issue blue FBI windbreakers jumped down and rushed toward Fisher, guns drawn.

An hour after that, a fourth Blackhawk arrived and disgorged a NEST team, which cordoned off the car and the caboose and took charge of Zhao's container.

When it was opened two days later at a secure facility, they found 245 pounds of nuclear debris.

A Blackhawk was dispatched down the track to look for Zhao's locomotive and the first two cars. They had jumped the track at the bottom of the slope and tumbled down the mountainside. Zhao's arms were found still bound to the platform's railing. The rest of him lay two hundred feet away, crushed under one of the locomotive's wheels.

IN the Persian Gulf, the fragile truce between U.S. and Iranian forces continued to hold as the *Reagan* Battle Group withdrew farther into the Arabian Sea and the Iranian Air Force and Navy continued to stand down units. A week after the Saudis had delivered the President's message to Tehran, alert levels on sides were back to normal.

As analysts and anchors for round-the-clock news channels pondered and speculated how and why the two countries had pulled back from the brink of war, both governments continued talking through the Saudis. The U.S. was not anxious to admit it had been duped into nearly starting a third war in the Middle East, and Iran wasn't anxious for the world to know that one of its own zealots had not only been instrumental in the scheme, but had also been directly responsible for the deaths of the 5,289 Americans at Slipstone. More importantly, for both Presidents the near-war had been a preview of sorts, and neither man had liked what he saw.

According to Lambert, an argument was raging in the Oval Office about when and how the details of the near war would be revealed to the world. There was no one left alive to blame, which, Fisher knew, would not sit well with the American public. Predictably, the Iranians and Chinese had moved quickly to paint Abelzada and Zhao as rogue criminals, who had acted with neither the support nor the knowledge of their respective governments. Fisher suspected in the end the crisis would be portrayed as a "fine example of a multi-national, cross-culture cooperative effort that defeated a massive terrorist plot." From there, the media would do the rest, filling in the gaps and assuaging the public's curiosity with a slew of books, movies, and documentaries.

Fisher couldn't care less. He'd done his job and come out the other side. The rest was trivia.

* * *

FISHER glanced to his left and saw a man enter through an arch and stop beside the dwarfish figure dressed in Eastern Orthodox garb, one hand carrying a giant Bible, the other a bronze censer. Fisher had already read the figure's biography. He was an "18th Century Saint."

The man who had just entered stopped before the saint, studied him for a few seconds, then sat down on the bench before it. After a few minutes he got up and walked away, leaving behind his brochure. Fisher walked over and took the bench. The man's brochure had been folded in half, with the upper left-hand corner turned down twice. If it had been folded any differently, it would have been the "wave off" signal for Fisher. Not safe; leave.

Whether the man was an agent or a CIA case officer Fisher didn't know, but he'd done his job, which was all that mattered. Their target had been tailed and found clean of surveillance. Fisher unfolded the brochure. Written on the inside cover in block letters were two words: **COSSACK ROOM**.

FISHER saw her seated on a bench before what he assumed was a Cossack: knee-high leather boots, handlebar mustache, mouth frozen in mid-scream as he charged toward nothing.

Fisher walked up behind her and stopped. "If you ask me, he looks angry at being fed substandard *borshch*," he whispered.

Elena turned in her seat. Her eyes went wide and her

mouth worked several times, but nothing came out for a few seconds. "What . . . ? What are you doing here?"

"Taking in the wax figures, what's it look like?" He sat down next to her.

"I was told to meet my . . . friend here."

"He couldn't make it. Asked me to fill in for him."

Elena's brow furrowed with worry. "What's happening? I don't understand what's happening."

Fisher pulled an envelope from his pocket on the bench between them. "Open it."

She did, and stared at the contents for a few moments, then said, "It's a passport."

"Not just any passport," Fisher corrected. "*Your* passport. You did say you wouldn't mind coming to the U.S., didn't you?"

"Of course, but—"

"Our plane leaves in two hours."

Elena frowned, then sighed. She laid the envelope back on the bench, hesitated for two beats, then snatched it up again. "I can't just leave."

"Why not?"

"I just . . . just . . . I don't know."

"It's your choice, Elena. I have a few connections; I'm sure there's a job somewhere in the government for a biologist slash *borshch* connoisseur."

They sat in silence for five minutes, during most of which Elena seemed to be having a whispered argument with herself. Abruptly she turned to him and said, "Okay."

"Yeah?"

She nodded firmly. "Okay."

Fisher smiled. He extended his hand. "I'm Sam, by the way."

"Not Fred."

"No."

Elena clasped his hand. "Nice to meet you, Sam."

The *New York Times* Bestselling Series

Tom Clancy's
SPLINTER CELL®

Created by #1 *New York Times* bestselling author

Tom Clancy
written by David Michaels

**Sam Fisher works alone.
But he fights for us all.**

SPLINTER CELL   0-425-20168-6

SPLINTER CELL: OPERATION BARRACUDA

                                       0-425-20422-7

**AVAILABLE WHEREVER BOOKS ARE SOLD
OR AT PENGUIN.COM**

From the #1 *New York Times*
Bestselling Phenomenon

Tom Clancy's
NET FORCE®

Created by Tom Clancy and Steve Pieczenik
written by Steve Perry and Larry Segriff

Virtual crime.
Real punishment.